Praise for the novels of *New York Times*
bestselling author HEATHER GRAHAM

"Mystery, sex, paranormal events.
What's not to love?"
—*Kirkus Reviews* on *The Death Dealer*

"Captivating...a sinister tale sure to
appeal to fans across multiple genre lines."
—*Publishers Weekly* on *The Death Dealer*

"An incredible storyteller."
—*Los Angeles Daily News*

"Graham's latest is nerve-racking
in the extreme, solidly plotted and peppered
with welcome hints of black humor.
And the ending's all readers could hope for."
—*Romantic Times BOOKreviews*
on *The Last Noel*

"The intense, unexpected conclusion
will leave readers well satisfied."
—*Publishers Weekly* on *The Dead Room*

"A writer of incredible talent."
—*Affaire de Coeur*

"Graham's rich, balanced thriller sizzles with
equal parts suspense, romance and the
paranormal—all of it nail-biting."
—*Publishers Weekly* on *The Vision*

"There are good reasons for Graham's steady
standing as a best-selling author. Here her
perfect pacing keeps readers riveted as they
learn fascinating tidbits of New Orleans history."
—*Booklist* on *Ghost Walk*

HEATHER GRAHAM

DEADLY NIGHT

MIRA®

MIRA®

ISBN-13: 978-0-7783-2585-7
ISBN-10:   0-7783-2585-7

DEADLY NIGHT

www.MIRABooks.com

Printed in U.S.A.

As always, to the incredible city of New Orleans, especially to Mary LaCoste, aka Scary Mary, who gives the most delightful tour, and to Betty Titman, who gives real credence to "Southern Hospitality."

To Mac, sexy, funny, dynamite voice and an all around great guy.

Prologue

It was there....

Home.

Everything he knew and loved, so close.

Sloan Flynn sat atop Pegasus, the tall roan that had taken him from the battlefields at Sharpsburg, Williamsburg, Shiloh and beyond, and looked to the south.

Farmland. Rich and fertile, as far as the eye could see.

When he turned to the north, though...

Tents. Arranged in perfect military order. Campfires burned; weapons were being cleaned. One view was of beauty, peace and perfection. The other promised a land drenched in the blood of its sons, a land laid to waste.

He had no more illusions about war. It was ugly and brutal. It wasn't just death. It was maimed and broken men screaming on the battlefield. It was a man walking blindly, crying out for help, because cannon fire had burned away his vision. It was the earth strewn with severed limbs, with the bodies of the dismembered, the dead and the dying. And, in the worst of times, it was their loved ones, as well, weeping over them.

Any man who still saw war as a way to solve differences had not been at Sharpsburg, Maryland, had not seen Antietam Creek running as crimson as the Red Sea, so choked with blood that it looked like a garish ribbon across the landscape.

Sloan had begun the war as a cavalry captain in a Louisiana unit. But that had been then. And this was now. Now he was militia, assigned to Jeb Stuart and the Army of Northern Virginia. They'd been sent south to scout out areas of the Mississippi, but this morning they had been recalled north.

It would be so easy to just go home....

But a man didn't quit a war. He didn't wake up and tell his commanders or his men that he knew war was wretched and created nothing but misery, so he was leaving. He fought, and he fought to win, because winning, too, was war. The indignant rallying cry to support the great cause of states' right, which had once rung as clear as a bugle's call in his heart, was now a silent sob. If they could go back—if they could *all* go back—and drag the politicians and the congressmen out to the battlefield and force them to look at the mangled and crimson-soaked bodies of their sons, they would not have come to this.

But they had. And now they were gearing up for another confrontation. They weren't going to try to take back New Orleans. Not now. They were gathering to head north. General Robert E. Lee was ordering troops from all over the South to head north. He wanted to take the war to the cities, farms and pastures of the Union. His beloved Virginia was in tatters, stripped again and again of its riches, marked by carnage.

Sloan looked longingly once again in the direction of home.

The Flynn plantation wasn't one of the biggest, wasn't one of the grandest. But it was home. And it was *his*.

She would be there. Fiona MacFarlane. Fiona Fair, as they liked to tease her. In truth, though—and secretly, because of the war—she was Fiona MacFarlane Flynn.

It had been so long....

Her own home, Oakwood, had fallen into ruin soon after the war had begun, so Fiona had come to stay at Flynn Plantation, his family's home. It wasn't grand—his family hadn't come to Louisiana with money; they had come with a desire to work—but there was room for Fiona. There would always be room for Fiona.

The plantation was barely hanging on now, he knew. Despite the war, he had exchanged letters with his cousin Brendan, a lieutenant with the Union army, and he knew the property wasn't doing well. Since New Orleans had fallen under Yankee control, Brendan had spent time out at the plantation, and his letters had been honest. The two men might be mortal enemies on the battlefield, but they were still cousins, which made the correspondence dangerous for them both. Brendan had written about "Beast" Butler, Union military commander in the parish, and how he had warned the family to avoid contact with the Union forces at all costs.

And if that warning had come from a Union officer...well, Sloan didn't like to think about what that meant.

Sloan hesitated for a moment, knowing he should be riding north; his reconnaissance mission had yielded a promise of heavy skirmishing if the troops were to approach too near to the heart of the parish.

But he was so close...

To home.

To Fiona.

He could steal an hour. Just an hour. A host of soldiers riding in would bring instant reprisal, but he could slip in alone.

No. This was war, and he'd been given his orders.

He kneed his horse and started south, despite the warnings in his head.

Soon the long drive shaded by the oaks stretched ahead of him. From this vantage point, the house was still beautiful. Graceful, built in the classic style, with a hall that ran front to back to facilitate the breeze wafted up from the river, bringing the cooler air. The wraparound porches on the first and second floors were still covered in ivy, and a hint of flowers could be seen. As a child, he had helped build this house. It was home, and the mere sight of it sent a river of bittersweet nostalgia sweeping through his system.

He didn't ride up the front drive; he detoured through the surrounding grove, passing fields that were overgrown and neglected. There, Sloan left Pegasus tied to a tree, then made his way to the stables directly behind the house. Henry, their caretaker, was there, a lean man of mixed Choctaw, Haitian and probably German blood, a free man of color, and the real boss of the place for as long as Sloan could remember.

"Henry?" His voice was soft but urgent.

Henry, busy repairing a saddle, looked up with a smile, his features ageless and strong. "Sloan?"

Sloan slipped from behind a bale of hay.

Henry dropped his leather needle and rose, and the two men embraced. But Henry withdrew quickly, his features grim.

"There's a couple of soldiers up to the house," he warned Sloan quietly. "They just got here this morning."

Sloan frowned. "Soldiers? Why?"

"Why?" Henry echoed bitterly. "Because they own the place now that New Orleans surrendered."

Sloan frowned, refusing to let himself think about Beast Butler's warning for the moment. "What about everyone else? Is anyone left in there? I heard the news about Ma. Brendan wrote me last summer, when she died." Even if he'd known in time, he wouldn't have been able to attend her funeral. He had been watching the soon-to-be-dead massing at Sharpsburg. "But what about Fiona and Missy and George? Are they still here?" Missy and George had been with the family as long as Henry had.

"Yeah. They're all still there," Henry said, looking uncomfortable. "But Miss Fiona, she told me to come out here and stay out of the way, 'less she calls for me."

Sloan looked at Henry, and he knew, because he knew Fiona, why she had given the order. She was afraid it might not be the cream of the Federal troops who had come to the house. She didn't know what they wanted, and she didn't want Henry getting killed if she needed to defend herself.

Sloan looked off into the distance. Henry still seemed distinctly uncomfortable. What the hell was going on here?

"Henry, what is it? What the hell is it?" he demanded.

"Nothing. Nothing. It's just…Well, it's been a long time since you've been home. A year, almost."

Sloan stared at him. "What does that have to do with anything?" he demanded.

"Brendan…he ain't around right now, neither. He's been away. When he's here…well, this place belongs to his kin, so the troops, they leave it alone."

"And?"

"I just said, 'he ain't been here for a while now.'" Henry drew a deep breath. "It ain't good. It just ain't good. The Yankees is one thing. They be good men, and they be bad men. But there's bad men from right here, too. Bad men who don't care for no cause, just for making money. I go into town when I can, and I try to listen, see what's up." Henry looked away for a minute. "There's one local fella…he finds girls. Finds them for this officer. Then…they ain't seen again. I try to trip him up. Sometimes I can. I hear things, like where folks is gonna be. And I try to keep us clear of it, since I can't stop it. But there's folks what like to let other folks know what's going on, like when women are alone…. Miss Fiona, she don't like to believe it, but she be gettin' in trouble if she not careful."

Sloan felt his heart trip. Good old Henry, trying to keep Fiona out of harm's way. But she was apparently convinced she could deal with the enemy soldiers on her own. Fear cascaded in icy rivulets through his blood.

He turned and headed out of the stables, but Henry tried to stop him.

And Henry was one big son of a gun, so Sloan turned and landed a hard punch to the other man's jaw. He felt bad when Henry went down with an audible groan, but this was one battle he had to fight on his own. He wasn't about to drag Henry into it.

Sloan drew his gun, a repeating rifle taken off a dead man at Sharpsburg, and headed for the house. As he did, he heard the scream. And then, there she was, racing out to the upper level balcony from the master bedroom.

Fiona.

Her beautiful deep red hair was streaming out behind her,

her features contorted into a mask of fear, her slim body tense with desperation.

Hard on her heels, a man was chasing her. Laughing at her obvious distress.

Raising his gun to his shoulder, Sloan started to run.

The Flynn Plantation
Present Day

It was high excitement. It was subterfuge. It was the biggest adventure of her life.

Sheila Anderson slipped through the darkness, armed with her flashlight. She could feel the note burning in her pocket. *Meet me at the Flynn place. Midnight. I figured out the truth behind the legend.*

She didn't know who had sent the note, but she assumed it had to be a fellow member of the historical society—maybe even a secret admirer. With Amelia Flynn dead and the new owners of the Flynn plantation coming to town to claim their inheritance, the society had to find a way to purchase and preserve the house. Neither the state nor the federal government was proving helpful. There were a lot of old places in the New Orleans area, and money talked loudly. The area was coming back in a big way, and there were too many corporations trying to buy up land along the river. The historical society needed a break, some piece of information about the house's past important enough to make sure that *they,* who loved history and all it stood for, could keep the place from going on the block before they had enough time to raise the money to buy it themselves.

So here she was, slipping through the darkness. Making her way through the old family cemetery, shielding the narrow beam of her flashlight so no one would spot her, looking for the truth behind the legends surrounding the plantation in the hope that it would be enough to ensure the house's historical standing.

It was frightening, but it was also fabulous. Better than a movie, better than a roller coaster. The old Flynn plantation had always been surrounded by ghostly tales. The locals all claimed it was haunted. The Flynn family had all but exterminated itself here, and that was just the beginning of the story.

The truth behind the legend.

It was such a great legend, too. There had been one woman and two men. Cousins, fighting on opposite sides in the War of Northern Aggression, as they called it down here. The men had met back at the estate and killed one another over her. She had died, too, and it was said that her screams could still be heard, while a figure made of white light raced along the upstairs porch.

Sheila paused, letting the atmosphere of the place seep into her. Anxious, she was almost afraid to look through the trees toward the house, where it sat in lonely darkness. With Amelia Flynn dead, her friend Kendall Montgomery was no longer staying there as a companion to the woman who had lived through decade after decade in that house, then died in the very room where she had been born.

The heat of the day had faded, merging with the dampness off the river, and now the land was rolling in fog. The gravestones and the mausoleums rose against the mist and the darkness, and a sliver of moonlight danced across the marble.

There was no ghost to be seen that night, but even so, Sheila could feel her heart beating rapidly.

"Sheila, over here!"

She jumped, startled. But the voice—a man's voice—was real, and she smiled, aware she was about to find out the identity of the person who had decided that she should be in on such a valuable discovery, historically speaking.

A rush swept through her. *This was it!* She was about to help make history.

"Where?" she called out, then started hurrying through the overgrown brush, dodging sarcophagi as she went. She tripped over a broken gravestone, and her flashlight went flying. She heard the lens break, and now all that was left to guide her was that sliver of moon, doing its best to pierce the rippling fog. Her heart thundered as she lay on the ground and thought of the woman in white who raced across the upper wraparound porch.

She got quickly to her feet, fear outweighing excitement for a moment.

"Sheila!"

She could hardly see her way, what with the fog and the darkness, but she knew the cemetery well, having walked it often enough in daylight. But now she was disoriented. She moved carefully in the direction from which she thought she had heard the voice. She stumbled again, but this time she caught herself against a crumbling mausoleum before she fell.

A cloud moved across the moon, and she was left in total darkness.

"Sheila?" It was a whisper this time, but close.

"Come on, help me out here," she called. "I lost my flashlight." She was surprised at how tremulous her voice sounded, and realized that she actually was afraid. In seconds, what had been minor trepidation rose to the level of sheer panic. Coming here had been stupid, she realized, and she had been an idiot. Running around a cemetery in the middle of nowhere in the middle of the night after getting an unsigned note. What had she been thinking?

She was going to find her way back to her car, drive home, have a huge glass of wine and chastise herself severely for being such an idiot.

"I'm right here," the voice said impatiently.

"Screw this," she muttered.

When she started to turn away from the voice, it seemed as if a huge black shadow rushed up behind her, pushing her. She stretched her hands out instinctively, trying to keep from falling, and touched something that felt like rusting metal. She heard a screeching sound as the metal gave against the pressure of her hands, and she stumbled.

Then...

Another push.

And then she screamed, because she was falling....

The Flynn Plantation
1863

Brendan Flynn had returned from the delivery of a prisoner of war to Beast Butler's headquarters in New Orleans, though he had never actually seen the infamous general.

Bill Harvey, a no-account drifter who had fit well into the army—if being mean, vicious and even sadistic added up to being a good soldier—had been lounging outside when he arrived.

"Hey, Flynn."

"Bill," Brendan had muttered, reaching to open the door to the plantation house where Butler had made his headquarters.

"You know the rule, right?"

Bill Harvey was grinning ear to ear with licentious pleasure, which was always a bad sign.

"What are you talking about, Bill?"

Bill's grin deepened, if that were possible. "Why, you know what General Butler said about these women, spitting at us soldiers and all. If they spit, if they're nasty, well, then, they're just whores, and we can treat 'em like the whores they are. And that gal living up in the Flynn place…she's the nastiest bitch of all."

"Fiona?" He was honestly puzzled at first. Fiona's upbringing had ensured that she would never be anything but polite on any occasion. And he'd warned her never to go near the Union soldiers. The property hadn't been confiscated, because he would inherit it, should Sloan be killed in the war. He had made it clear—precisely to avoid anyone trying to confiscate the house, at least—that he had staked his claim.

"Uh-huh. A few of us fellows were out along the river last week, looking for food. And she was nasty as hell," Bill said.

Brendan took a step closer, then struck, his fingers closing like a vise around Bill's throat, pinning him against the column where he'd been lounging just seconds before. Bill squawked and wriggled, but he was no match for Brendan, and he knew it. "What the hell? You'll face a court-martial for this!" he gasped.

"What did you do to her?" Brendan demanded.

"Nothing! Nothing, I swear!" Bill's face was turning red. Other soldiers had gathered around, but they just stared. Bill was an ass, not well liked. And most of the men were sickened by the cruelty that had been shown to their conquered brothers—and sisters.

"It's Victor Grebbe.... He took off this afternoon with... Art Binion."

Brendan released the other man. "How long ago?" he demanded.

Bill started rubbing his throat. His face was still red. "Fuck you, Flynn—" he began.

Brendan had him pressed against the column again in seconds.

"Thirty minutes," Bill gasped.

Brendan swore. He could do something about the situation through the proper channels. But proper channels wouldn't save Fiona.

Or his cousin's infant son.

Brendan forgot all about the prisoner waiting to be handed over, turned on his heel and headed straight back for his horse. Mercury had been bred on the family plantation, just like Sloan's faithful Pegasus. Poor damned horse. He had to be exhausted. But Brendan kneed him hard, racing down the street and out to where the roads turned bad and rutted, where they'd been worn down by too many horses and too many men.

Worn down by too much war.

Damn the war, damn the death. Damn the circumstance that allowed men to forget right and wrong, mercy and humanity.

The skin at his nape prickled. He'd heard things about Victor Grebbe. Heard that he had a sick thing for women, and that some who'd gone with him hadn't been seen since.

It was a long, hard ride out to the plantation. He urged his horse on, hoping he could overtake the men bent on abusing their power, men bent on rape and maybe even murder, but they had too much of a head start, and no doubt fresh horses, besides.

And then, finally, it was there, ahead of him. From a distance the house looked as quiet and gentle as his family had once been. Until the war.

War was about causes, about territory.

But this? This was personal.

As he raced along the oak-lined drive, there was but one thought in his mind.

Fiona.

He arrived just in time to see her plummeting from the balcony. He heard her scream, and he saw the enemy, a Confederate soldier, in the yard. The Reb fired at the balcony, screaming in raw fury, a Rebel yell like nothing Brendan had ever heard. The shot exploded in the beautiful stillness of the spring day, and Brendan did what any man would do.

He drew his weapon.

And he fired on the enemy.

It was only when the enemy turned, mortally wounded, to shoot in return, that he saw who was wearing the butternut and gray.

Sloan.

As the bullet hit his chest, he knew he had killed his own cousin. But not on purpose, God forgive him. Not with intent, and never with malice. Oh, dear God, what an end for all of them, damned in the eyes of those who would come after…

How ironic that Sloan had managed to kill him, as well. For he was dying, he knew.

It was then that he saw Victor Grebbe, swearing where

he stood on the balcony, holding his injured shoulder, blood seeping out between his fingers from where Sloan's bullet had taken him.

His own arm was cold, and he knew he was nearly dead. He had no strength. Still, with one final effort, he lifted his weapon and strained to pull the trigger.

He fired. Fired at Grebbe, a man who shamed any uniform, who shamed humanity.

Grebbe, who had damned them all.

As he died, he heard the terrified wails of the infant inside the house. Sloan's son. Sloan had never even known he had a son, because that was news Brendan had never shared, thinking it Fiona's place. He prayed to God that the child would live, would somehow make up for the cursed fate of his family.

For they were damned to memory, damned in the eyes of men.

What about the eyes of God?

All too soon he would know.

He could only hope that God—and time—would forgive them all.

The Flynn Plantation
Present Day

Sheila came to. She felt a keen sense of confusion. She could hear...water. And she could smell an awful dampness and decay that seemed entrenched in the walls...wherever it was that she lay. She blinked several times, but it wasn't foggy now; it was pitch-dark.

She sat up, trying to fathom where she might be.

Suddenly there was a light. Just a pinprick, but it didn't help. It was too bright, boring painfully into her eyes. She raised a hand to try to protect herself against the blinding brilliance of it.

Hand raised to her eyes, she looked to the side and sucked in a huge gulp of air in stunned horror.

There was a face in the darkness. Hollow eyes, sunken cheeks, rotting flesh. It was floating in the water that was rising around her, and it looked as if it were staring at her.

Halloween, she reminded herself. Halloween was coming. This was undoubtedly just someone's macabre idea of a prank.

But deep inside, she knew it wasn't. This was real. This was a human head, no longer attached to a body.

She opened her mouth to scream, her heart and soul filled with terror, but before she was able to make a sound, the voice stopped her.

"Sheila…" it whispered gently, even affectionately.

And then…she knew she would never scream again.

1

"It's a bone," Dr. Jon Abel announced.

"Obviously," Aidan Flynn noted dryly.

The doctor shot him a glance. "A thighbone."

"And it's human," Aidan said.

"Yes, it's a human thighbone," Dr. Abel agreed. He stood on the muddy bank at the side of the Mississippi and shrugged, looking at the faces around him. It was heading toward evening, but it had been a hot, sultry day, and only the breeze coming off the river hinted that a cooling-down was coming. Beyond the muddy shore where Aidan had found the bone, the churning water was an ugly shade of brown. A mosquito buzzed nearby, and the doctor slapped at his arm and shook his head in disgust. He'd never been much for working out in the field.

Aidan was the one who had asked that he be called out, but since Aidan was just a P.I. out of Florida who, along with his two brothers, had just inherited the old family plantation, it was Hal Vincent, parish homicide, who had actually placed the call. Jonas Burningham, local FBI, had attached himself to the "case," such as it was, too, in case they were looking at a serial murderer taking advantage of the disorder—and all too often violence—left in the wake of Hurricane Katrina.

"You know," Abel said, "we're still finding all kinds of…remnants stirred up by the storm. That's going to go on for years. We didn't always bury aboveground here, and there are plenty of old family plots along the river. Down in Slidell, there was a woman who had three coffins in her yard for months after the storm. No one knew where they belonged, and she couldn't get any agency to come get them, so she just called them Tom, Dick and Harry, and said hello to them every time she came and went." Jon Abel was a tall, thin man of about forty-five who looked more like a mad scientist than what he really was: one of the most respected medical examiners in the state. He looked out at the brown water. And sighed. "Hell, that river has seen more bodies than you and I could ever begin to guess, and it would take a dozen lifetimes to sort them all out."

"That's it?" Aidan asked him. "No investigation? You're just going to dismiss it out of hand?" As he spoke, the sky darkened. Storm clouds, only hinted at earlier in the day, were boiling into great menacing shadows across the heavens. He pointed at the bone. "Looks to me like there's still some tissue on it, which means it's fresh and there might be more body parts somewhere nearby to go with it. If I thought I'd stumbled on something old, I'd have called in an anthropologist."

Jon Abel sighed again. "Right. I don't get enough people with bullet holes in them. Slashed to ribbons. Mangled in car accidents. Dead under a bridge somewhere. Sure. I'll just take this thighbone that *might* have a bit of tissue on it and get right on it."

"Jon," Hal Vincent said quietly. "There might be something to this. I know your office is busy and you've got a lot of pressing cases, but do what you can, huh?"

"Male or female?" Aidan asked.

"It's just a bone right now."

"Male or female?—your best guess," Aidan insisted.

The medical examiner shot him an aggravated look.

"Female," he said. The man had been at it a long time. Unwilling participant in today's proceedings or not, he was tops in his field. He adjusted his glasses and shook his head. "Offhand, I'd say she stood about five-six." He looked closer. "Probably between twenty and thirty. I can't tell you anything else. Not even guessing."

"I'm guessing she's dead," Hal said dryly.

Jonas stepped in, trying to keep things civil. Jonas was a definite "suit." At forty, he was tall and hard-bodied, with slick tawny hair and attractive features. Even in the muck, he looked impeccable and unflappable. "We'd deeply appreciate it, Dr. Abel, if you can tell us more as soon as your schedule will allow. Look, Jon, we know you're busy. We also know you're the best."

Jon Abel grunted in acknowledgment of the compliment, but he cast Aidan a look of irritation. As far as he was concerned, Flynn was an outsider. He came to New Orleans often to see friends here, but he was still an outsider—at least to Jon Abel.

Aidan had been in the area this time because of a missing persons case. Runaway teens had taken to camping out in the swampy bayou area off the river here. He'd found the subject of his search, and she'd been dirty enough, wet enough, hungry enough and miserable enough to be grateful that her parents wanted her home.

And Aidan had been grateful that he'd found her alive. That wasn't always the case with runaways. And maybe not for the woman whose bone he'd found nearby, either.

Jonas and Flynn went back a long way. They'd gone through the FBI Academy together. Jonas had stayed with the Bureau.

After a few years, Aidan hadn't.

It was mainly Jon's friendship with Jonas that had brought him out here today.

"I'll do what I can," Jon said. He lifted a hand to his assistant, Lee Wong, who had been listening attentively to everything going on. He meant to go places, and working with Jon Abel was the way to do it.

The thighbone was duly tagged and bagged; then, grumbling to himself, Jon headed for his car, Lee trailing behind. Jon waved goodbye and spoke without turning back to them. "I'll get back to you when I know something."

When he was gone, Hal Vincent spoke again. "I'll get a few men out here to search the area." He was a tall man, a good six-four or five, and thin, but every inch of him was muscled. His skin was copper and his eyes were green; his hair had gone white, and he wore it cropped close to his head. His age was indeterminate, and Aidan thought that when he was a hundred years old, he wouldn't look much different. Born in Algiers, Louisiana—right across the river—he knew the area like the back of his hand. He was a good man, solid, no bullshit.

"Thanks, Hal," Jonas told him. He looked at Aidan and shrugged. "You know…that might actually be…an old bone."

"Yeah, it might be," Aidan agreed. "But then again," he pointed out, "it might not." He tried to keep any hint of sarcasm out of his voice.

"We'll search, and let you know." Hal looked at his watch. "I'm off duty as of now, and I could use a beer. Anyone want to join me?"

"Sounds good to me," Jonas said. He'd wanted to be assigned out west, but he'd drawn New Orleans instead, then surprised himself by falling in love with the place. He'd ended up marrying a local girl and moving to the French Quarter. "Aidan?"

Aidan shook his head. "Sorry. I'm late already. I have to meet my brothers downriver."

"I heard you boys inherited the old place out on the Mississippi," Hal asked.

Aidan grimaced. "Yeah, it's quite an inheritance."

"You never know," Hal told him. "The place has one hell of a history. Comes with a legend, ghosts, the whole bit. It's decaying, but does have the original stables, smokehouse—even the slave quarters. If you want to do something with it, do it fast. The local preservationists will be all over you any day now."

"Yeah, well…I don't know what we're doing. That's part of what we're meeting up to decide," Aidan said.

"I heard the three of you went into the private investigation business together," Jonas said. "How's that working out?"

"Well," Aidan said briefly.

"Floridians. Taking on that old house," Hal said. How he meant it, Aidan wasn't sure. "Let's get that beer, Jonas. Aidan, we'll be in touch if we hear anything about that bone of yours."

Aidan nodded, and they all trekked back through the

muck. When they reached their cars, they waved. The other two men headed toward the city.

Aidan started down the river road.

Twenty minutes later, he was with his brothers.

And they stood, the three of them, staring at the house on the rise that wasn't exactly a hill.

Then again, the building wasn't exactly a house. Not anymore. Decades of neglect had left dangling shingles, broken columns, and paint that was flaking and peeling. The effect was of something from a horror movie set.

The promise of a storm wasn't helping, either. In the distance, thunder was rumbling, and the sky had turned a strange color. But at least the coming weather had alleviated the heat. A cool breeze was blowing. It actually had a slight chill to it. And the darkness seemed to have taken on a life of its own, sweeping across the sky and down over the trees, crawling like a fog along the ground, a shadow-mist that smelled of violence and decay.

Aidan was the oldest of the three and, at six-three, the tallest by half an inch. His features were weathered, and he was the most physically imposing of them. A stint in the military had left him fit and wary; his reflexes were quick, and he had retained a suspicious perception of the world around him and an invisible Keep Away sign. Once, he supposed, he had been decent-looking. He had blue eyes, referred to as "icy" these days, and pitch-dark hair. Serena had found him compelling enough. It was his manner rather than his appearance, he figured, that tended to keep people at a distance. Then again, he probably hadn't been as remote and chilly when he had been with Serena. There had been

promise in the world when she was alive. Now…well, it was
a good thing he had work to do. Lots of it. Keeping himself
from falling into the emptiness.

His brothers, his family…them, he trusted, but others…
He'd gone through Quantico, but when life had convinced
him he was no longer a team player, he'd left the FBI. Given
his background, he had opted for private investigation.

Maybe he should have investigated the house.

"Hmm," Jeremy, the second in age, said. Jeremy had been
the first to suggest they form a business. When Aidan had
left the Bureau, Jeremy had been ready to leave his position
with the Jacksonville police divers. Unlike Aidan, his hell
hadn't been a personal one; he had simply been the first to
come upon a van full of abused foster children, drowned
when their vehicle leapt a median and drove straight into the
St. Johns River. He'd been at it a long time; he'd seen horrific
sights. But that one had haunted him. Jeremy loved playing
his guitar, though, and music brought him through. He'd
quietly begun a charity to find homes for abused, abandoned
and orphaned children, and discovered a talent for broadcast-
ing along the way. He had come to New Orleans to work
with a popular DJ on a dinner-dance to be held at the aquarium to raise funds for Children's House, his charity, which
was involved in finding homes for area children who had
been orphaned by Katrina.

Jeremy liked people, and had always loved New Orleans
and the Gulf region, but even he was speechless now that they
were seeing their unexpected inheritance for the first time.

Plantation, Aidan thought.

The word summoned up visions of long, oak-shaded
drives, rich and verdant fields, pastures—and a Greek Re-

vival house painted pristine white, with beautiful women in long flowing dresses sitting on the porch sipping mint juleps.

If anyone were caught imbibing anything here, it would be derelicts chugging beer out of bottles hidden in brown paper bags.

Oh yeah. He definitely should have investigated.

Zachary, the youngest of the trio, who was a mixture of his eldest brother's hard stoicism and his other's open-mindedness, let out a breath.

"Well, I guess you could call it a fixer-upper," he mused dryly.

Aidan turned to stare at him. Zachary stood a half inch over six-two, just like Jeremy. It was as if the three brothers had been cast in the same mold, then painted in different shades. Aidan's own eyes were a blue that varied from icy to almost as black as his hair. Jeremy's eyes were cloud-gray, his hair a dark brown with a touch of auburn. As a kid, Zachary had fought to toughen up, because he'd been born with strawberry-blond curls. The color had deepened as he aged, but that red tint remained. His eyes were almost aqua. Aidan and Jeremy had teased him mercilessly when they were young, but the truth was, he was as striking as a Greek god. He had grown up fighting—but then, as their mother had mourned frequently, there was a reason for the expression "fighting Irish." Regardless, the years had been good for Zach. He could hold his own in any fight, but his first love had always been music, and, like Jeremy, he turned to it often. *The soul's solace,* he called it.

He had been equally ready to opt into the family business. After years in the Miami forensics unit, he had hit his limit when he was called in after a crack addict dad had micro-waved his infant son. He had already acquired a part own-ership of a number of small recording studios around the country, but when he had heard the plan to open an investi-gations office, the idea had intrigued him, and he immedi-ately quit the force.

Aidan was thirty-six now, Jeremy thirty-five, and Zachary thirty-three. They'd done a hell of a lot of fighting as kids, but as adults, they had grown into being friends.

"We should just sell it," Aidan said.

"I'm not real sure what we'd get for it, in its present con-dition," Zach pointed out.

"Sell it?" Jeremy protested. "It's our...well, it's our heritage."

The other brothers turned to stare at him, frowning. "Our heritage? We didn't even know the placed existed until that lawyer called," Aidan reminded him.

Jeremy shrugged. "Maybe so, but hey, a whole lot of Flynns lived in that house, and now it's come to us. I think that's cool. How many people wake up one morning and discover that they've inherited an antebellum plantation?"

Aidan and Zach stared at the house, then back at their brother.

"Come on," Jeremy protested. "The land alone has to be worth something."

"Right," Aidan said. "So I say we should sell it for its land value."

"No, we should do something with it," Jeremy said, shaking his head. He stared intently at the house, rather than at his brothers. Then he turned to them at last. "What's to keep us from moving to the area, huh?"

Aidan started to object, but he crossed his arms over his chest, instead.

It was true.

He'd come to New Orleans to hunt down a runaway teen. Now that he'd done that, he'd been intending to return to the place he'd called home for some time now, Orlando, Florida. But why? They could relocate the business anywhere they wanted, and without Serena, there was really nothing to tie him to Orlando.

And all three of them liked New Orleans and could find plenty to do on the side here. Jeremy could keep working with Children's House, and Zach often came here anyway, to play in a band with some old friends. And now, after the recent death of Amelia Flynn, they were the only family left to inherit her falling-down plantation.

Maybe it shouldn't have been as much of a shock as it was. They knew their father's family went way back in the South, but he'd been an only child, and *his* father had been an only child, and before him...well, people lost track of people, and that's the way it was.

Not that their branch of the Flynn family had gotten far, Aidan thought wryly.

"We can all chip in to fix it up, then sell it," Jeremy said. "If we get it into decent shape, we'll probably make a pretty good profit. Once it stops looking like a haunted house, people will be all over us to buy it."

"Haunted house?" Zach said.

"It really is supposed to be haunted, isn't it?" Jeremy asked.

"Yeah," Zach said. "Something about cousins who fought on opposite sides during the Civil War and ended up killing each other on the front lawn. Creepy."

"That's tragic, not creepy," Aidan said impatiently.

"It *is* sad, but it's a little creepy, too. I mean, they were our ancestors. Our family," Zach said.

The wind whistled softly, as if in agreement.

"I'm with Jeremy. I say we restore the place," Zach announced firmly.

"Absolutely. Turn her back into a grande dame," Jeremy agreed.

Aidan stared at the two of them. "Are you two nuts?" he demanded.

Zach grinned as he looked at him. "What's the matter? Scared of ghosts? I doubt it's really haunted," he teased.

"We're investigators, not builders. And all old houses are supposed to have ghosts," Aidan said, surprised that he felt so irritable about it. "And if it has a reputation for being haunted, that means we'll have all kinds of idiots coming out of the woodwork wanting to research or whatever."

Jeremy was still grinning at Zach. "I have to admit, I think it's exciting, owning a piece of history. And we belong to the house as much as it belongs to us. I mean, this is Flynn Plantation, and we're all that's left of the Flynns."

Aidan groaned aloud. He was already outvoted. And he didn't know why, but when he looked at the house, he didn't want anything to do with it.

It was nothing but a white elephant, he decided. No, not white. A peeling gray elephant.

"We don't even know if it's structurally sound," he said.

As he stared up at the house, the sun blinded him for a moment. And then…

Then he saw a woman on the balcony. She was tall, with flowing dark auburn hair, and she was wearing something long and white that seemed to float out behind her, just like her hair. She was oddly beautiful—and she looked very real.

He blinked, and she was gone.

"Hey, did you just see someone?" he asked his brothers.

"No, but the woman who was helping Amelia might be here. The lawyer said something about her coming by to pick up her things."

"I thought I saw someone in a...never mind," Aidan said.

He searched the balcony, then the windows. There was no one there.

If his brothers had noticed his intense survey of the house, they weren't saying anything. They were too busy arguing about their carpentry skills.

He left them behind and started walking toward the house.

"Aidan!" Zach yelled. "What are you doing?"

"Taking a closer look," he called back.

They caught up with him a minute later, and they all walked together up the graveled drive, under parallel rows of mature oaks that offered a welcome respite from the sun. As they neared the house, Aidan saw that the paint was in even worse shape than he'd realized. The place would need some real work, he thought with an inward groan.

"We can't possibly have any zoning problems out here," Zach said.

"If it's a historic landmark, we'll still have to deal with someone," Aidan pointed out.

Zach shook his head. "I'm sure it must have some kind of historic designation. But...historic properties are important. Aidan, I don't know about you, but sometimes...hell, sometimes I feel like we've got to at least try to make a difference somehow."

Aidan's features tightened as he stopped walking and stared at his brother. "What are you talking about?"

Zach shrugged. "I've seen so much bad shit out there—hell, we all have—and I can't help it, but I just feel that this is something important, something we're meant to do."

"What if the historical society wanted to buy the place?" Aidan demanded.

Zach stared at him. "I know it's been years since the storm, but you and I both know it's going to take a decade for real money to start flowing into the region again. I'm sure the historical society has done all they can do to fix up the properties they already own. But *we* could do something important by putting this place back the way it was. There could be lectures and concerts here, maybe even reenactors to remind visitors of everything it took to make a country." Zach flushed, probably a little surprised by his own speech, but he didn't back down.

When Jeremy added his own "Count me in," Aidan lifted his hands in surrender. "In fact, I have an idea," Jeremy went on.

"Oh?" Aidan said.

"Why don't we give ourselves a real goal? Like Halloween. We could host an event to benefit Children's House."

Aidan looked at Jeremy. His brother was serious. And why shouldn't he be? When his job had thrown him the worst he could imagine, he hadn't turned bitter or given up. He'd taken up a cause, so more kids wouldn't end up dead at the bottom of a river.

Sure, Jeremy could be a little obsessive, but so what? Maybe it was in the blood. Hadn't he himself stood on a riverbank less than an hour ago, insisting that a single bone, which everyone else seemed happy to assume was just an aftereffect of nature's wrath, had to be taken seriously and fully investigated?

Zachary had supported Jeremy's cause wholeheartedly from the beginning, but what the hell had he, the oldest, done?

Nothing, that's what. He'd let his soul die.

Well, enough of that. He owed his brother.

"An event?" he said, still careful to be the voice of logic.

"A Halloween party." Jeremy smiled as the idea grew. "We can decorate the place, hire people to dress up and be scary."

Aidan groaned aloud.

"Think about it, Aidan. This place was like a gift to us, so why not use it to help other people?" Zach asked, siding with Jeremy.

They didn't need his blessing, Aidan knew. He was outvoted.

But they wanted his support.

"Let's spend today worrying about whether the house will stand up if it rains, huh?" Aidan said. "I'm open to anything later."

"He's open to anything. Did you hear that?" Zach asked Jeremy.

"Yeah. He must've been out in the sun too long," Jeremy replied with a grin.

Aidan started walking again. They followed, giving him space. They knew him so well, he thought.

He could remember how, growing up, they'd fought constantly, driving his parents insane. He had been expected to behave the best because he was the oldest. Most of the time, he had stopped things before they got too bad. They'd been brothers, though. Whenever anyone went up against one of them, they'd shown a united front. They were the Flynn brothers, as close-knit as a clan could be when the chips were down.

But then he'd gone into the military, trading his service for money to help with his education. Even when he was gone overseas, he'd gotten family visits, of course—at least when he was stationed in Germany. But it hadn't been the same as being here. He'd moved on first. The other two had been, if not at home, at least in the state and near the family home. And Jeremy and Zach shared their love of music—not that he wasn't fond of it—which further bonded them. Then, when he came home for good, he'd gone into the FBI. The classes had been fascinating, even if rigorous, but somehow, the structure of it all—maybe because of his years in the military—had felt uncomfortable and constraining. He'd left, hopefully with no hard feelings. He was pretty sure he was in the clear; he'd gotten discreet help a few times when he'd come up against dead ends through civilian channels.

Then, of course, there had been Serena.

It all came down to Serena. She'd been the real beginning of his world.

And the end.

She'd been through it all with him, going back to high school. She'd helped him work through his doubts over all his major decisions. College or the military? Graphics or criminology? Stay with the military or go for a job with the FBI?

Then life changed in an instant, and he was sorry they hadn't put aside his work and her political career. A doped-up drag racer had jumped the median, and Serena had been killed. And after that, nothing mattered at all.

But that had been five years ago. And despite doing work

he was proud of, in spite of the good things he'd accomplished for other people, he still had no real purpose in life. Days came, and days went.

"I don't think the two of you can begin to imagine how much work you're talking about here," he said. "And the licenses and the permits and insurance and—"

"Don't sweat it. We're the brothers Flynn," Zachary said, stepping between Aidan and Jeremy and setting an arm around each of their shoulders. "How can we go wrong?"

Aidan looked up at the house. He felt an odd sense of dread again, which wasn't like him at all. He was the logical, pragmatic brother. He didn't get strange sensations like this.

He gave himself a mental shake. Well, what the hell?

"The brothers Flynn," he agreed.

2

Damn.

They were here already.

The heirs hadn't been around when Amelia was sick, and they hadn't been around when she died. According to the lawyer, they hadn't even known she existed until he contacted them with news of their inheritance, an excuse that sounded pretty damn suspect to her.

Kendall Montgomery receded from the balcony, where she had so often sat with Amelia, back into the master bedroom, hoping she hadn't been seen. She knew that the attorney had met with the Flynns and given them title to the place.

She just hadn't expected them to show up here. Not yet.

She had come to pick up the last of her things. Books and CDs she had loaned Amelia, some clothing she had left out here for the nights when she stayed over to keep the old woman company. She had done all she could to help Amelia, offering her love and loyalty, because the elderly woman had been there for her when she had needed someone so badly. Amelia had been a sweetheart, pleased to pass on fascinating bits and pieces of local history and the legend surrounding the house. Amelia had lived through a lot, and she had managed to hang on to the plantation—even if she'd been unable to keep it from falling into decay—which said a lot about the kind of woman she'd been.

Kendall looked down and realized she was holding something. The marvelous old diary she had discovered in the attic one day when Amelia had asked her to bring down an envelope of papers. She had set the diary by Amelia's bed, thinking she would read it later, but somehow she'd never gotten around to it. Until today.

Today, when all she had intended to do was get in, get her things and get out, she had found herself picking it up.

And it was fascinating. It had been written by a woman living in the house during the Civil War, and once she had gotten into it, Kendall had found herself deeply involved. She had marveled that she was holding a book that went back over a hundred and fifty years, that she was reading words written that long ago. Words describing the thoughts of someone living in the midst of a horrible war that tore families apart. Words about survival. There were little tidbits of day-to-day life in the diary, and there were also hopes and dreams for the future.

The diary was what had kept her out here long after she should have gone home, and now the heirs were arriving.

She quickly stuck the diary into her backpack.

It didn't belong to her. It belonged to the men who were Amelia's only living relatives.

But she had to finish reading it. She wouldn't keep it, only borrow it until she'd read all the way to the end. She would give it back as soon as she was done. For now, she had to figure out how she was going to deal with the plantation's new owners.

Kendall thought about hiding. About slipping out the back. But they would probably notice her car, parked around by the stables, before she could get to it. No. Better just to face the music of being here, where she supposed she shouldn't be, not without their permission.

She would apologize for trespassing, explain that she'd only come to get her things, then get the hell out.

She'd heard Jeremy Flynn on the radio the other day, talking about raising money to help the children who'd lost their families in the hurricane. He was clearly a mover and a shaker, and he talked sense. She had to admit that she had liked him on the radio.

The lawyer had told her that there were three brothers, and that they ran a private investigation agency. Snapping pictures of married men having affairs and spying on baby-sitters, no doubt.

The French Quarter was a pretty close-knit group, and she'd heard that another one of the brothers was a nice guy and a hell of a guitarist.

The third brother, though…

A real hard-ass, she'd heard. Military, then FBI.

He'd probably have her arrested for trespassing.

The truth was, *they* owed *her* some genuine gratitude. She was the one who had been there for Amelia. And not for any personal gain. She had taken to spending almost all her time out here, because Amelia had been *afraid.* Amelia had spent her life in the old place, but in the last few months she'd become convinced that strange things were going on around her, that long-gone spirits from centuries past were present day and night—in the house *and* in her dreams. Once upon a time, a violent tragedy had played itself out on the grounds of the old plantation. As death neared for Amelia, she seemed to think her ancestors were creeping up on her, reaching for her with bony fingers from their graves.

And yet, in the hours before her death, she had seemed so peaceful. Glad to see the ghosts, as if they were family members who loved her and had come to take her home.

I was creeped-out and scared silly half the time I was here, Kendall thought, *but I stayed because I cared about Amelia.* Where were these guys when she could have used some real family around her? How could they have been totally unaware of the existence of a member of their own family?

That was a question that would have to wait for another day. The most important thing right now was that she still had to get the hell out of here.

But how?

Walk out the front door and screw those assholes, she decided.

She tossed her hair back and walked down the stairs, setting her backpack down by the door so she could use both hands to undo the dead bolt. By the time she opened the door, they were on the porch.

"Hello," she said, as if she had every right in the world to be there. Which she did, she reminded herself.

A tough-looking, raw-edged man with cobalt eyes and dark hair stared at her coldly. Luckily the other two brothers looked decidedly friendlier, and one even offered her a curious smile.

"I'm sorry. I'm Kendall Montgomery. I was staying out here with Amelia—your...aunt?—during her last days," she explained. "I...left some things out here, so I came by to get them. I assume you're the Flynn brothers?"

"We are," the one who'd smiled said. "Oldest brother, Aidan, to my left, and Zach, the youngest, to my right. I'm Jeremy."

"Well," she said uncomfortably. "I'll just—"

"I thought Amelia died three months ago," Aidan said.

She looked at him. He was tall, all muscle and striking, and his features were clean-cut and rugged. But it wasn't the warrior edge about his face that chilled her; it was the tone of his voice and something about the dark ice in his eyes when he looked at her.

"I work for a living. I put together her funeral, took care of her last bills and had everything set up for you three to come in," she said, aware that her own voice had taken on a biting tension.

"Have you been living here since then?" he asked curtly.

"Aidan…" Zach murmured.

"I took care of Amelia. *You* didn't even know she existed," she said flatly.

"That's right, we *didn't* know she existed. We didn't know anything about this place. We should have, I suppose, but… we just…didn't," Jeremy said quietly.

"Honestly," Zachary added. "We always loved this area, but we had no idea we had family here. Clearly, you cared about Amelia, and now that we know, we're grateful."

"She was a very fine lady," Kendall said, looking away for a moment. A knot had risen to her throat. "Very sweet." She stared at the eldest brother. At five-ten, she wasn't exactly short, but she had to look up to meet his eyes, and she resented it.

What the hell? None of it made any difference. If he was too much of a jerk to be grateful, what did it matter? Amelia was dead and gone, and she had her own life; she hadn't given it all up to care for Amelia. She would just go back to it and let these idiots have the place to themselves.

No, that wasn't fair.

They didn't all seem to be idiots, just the one.

"Well, as I said, I do work for a living," she said. "You're here, and I need to get going, so…"

"Just what kind of work do you do?" Aidan asked.

She was furious with herself for hesitating, but she knew all too well that he would only make fun of her and would probably decide she was nothing more than a leech, preying on people's weaknesses, if she admitted the complete truth.

"I own a café and gift shop," she said. "Now, if you'll excuse me…"

"Miss Montgomery," Jeremy said, a wry smile curling his lips, "we don't know a thing about this place. If you know anything and can spare a few minutes, we'd be eternally grateful if you'd show us around."

"Please," Zach added.

She let out a long breath. The eldest brother was still just staring at her. "…All right. Come on in. We're, uh, in the foyer." She stepped back, pointing in the appropriate directions as she spoke. "Grand staircase, ballroom to the left, parlor, dining room—you'll find a wall of family paintings in there, if you're interested—and kitchen to the right. The kitchen was added after the turn of the century and last updated in the fifties, I'm afraid. As bad as it looks, the place is structurally sound. There's a huge basement beneath us, four bedrooms upstairs, and an attic with storage and a little garret room. It's really a beautiful home. Some of the pillars need work in front. And there are over a dozen outbuildings, some in better shape than others. You've got the original kitchen, original stables, a smokehouse, and ten little buildings that were slave quarters. Actually—" She broke off. There was no need to share any more with them. She'd given them the basics, and now it was time for her to get out of here and leave the house to them.

They owned it, after all.

And they would almost certainly be looking to sell. With luck, one of the historical foundations would be able to buy it.

"Actually what?" Aidan asked sharply.

"Oh…nothing to do with the house," she said. "I'm sure you'll be fine."

"Seriously, what were you about to say?" Zach asked. He had a killer smile, she noticed. He was extremely good-looking, but seemed confident without being conceited.

She shrugged. "Amelia was afraid. At the end. Terrible things happened here during the Civil War, and she…well, she heard things at night, and she was…afraid. That's why I stayed with her."

"She thought the place was haunted?" Aidan demanded. He didn't snort out loud, but she felt that, inwardly, he *was* snorting with derision. Big, tough he-man. He wouldn't understand fear.

"Every good plantation is haunted," Jeremy said with a grin. "Right?"

The two younger brothers definitely seemed decent enough, she thought. She wasn't surprised, though. Her employee and friend, Vinnie, had met them both, even asked them to sit in with his band, and he said they both had talent and were nice guys, besides.

She shrugged, feeling uneasy. "This house has a lot of history. Your family was almost wiped out during the Civil War."

She paused for a moment, thoughtful. "And it wasn't just the war. There were other events, too. Other deaths. In the 1890s, the owner had an affair with one of his housekeepers. She was stunningly beautiful, they say, with eyes as green as emeralds and skin the color of chocolate."

She saw a slight smile on Aidan's lips as he said, "So the wife killed the gorgeous housekeeper—or the housekeeper killed the wife—and now she's haunting the place, right? Better yet—they killed each other and now they're both haunting the place."

Kendall looked at him and finished the story. "The wife demanded that the housekeeper be hanged. The Klan had a lot of influence in the area then, so they took care of it. Her head…she was decapitated when she was hanged. They say she haunts the property, looking for it. Oh, and she cursed the wife as she was being dragged over to that oak—" she pointed to a huge tree on the left side of the house "—to meet her death. The curse apparently worked. The wife died, falling down the grand stairway, one year to the day after the maid was executed."

"Great story," Jeremy said, smiling. "Is it for real?"

"I'm not sure. You'd have to check with the historical society. To be honest, several of the plantations claim that or a similar legend. I grew up here and heard all the stories about the local plantations. I can't guarantee the truth of any of the tales about this place—except the one about the cousins and the Civil War. That story's in the history books."

Aidan turned his hawklike stare from her face and directed it at the house, shaking his head. "I'm back to thinking we should sell it and get the hell out," he said to his brothers.

"Just look at it," Jeremy said, opening his arms to the house, as if in greeting. "It's beautiful. It's our heritage. Hey, we're related to those ghosts."

"Maybe not," Aidan said.

"Maybe not?" Jeremy echoed questioningly.

He shrugged. "Who knows if one of the mistresses of the house was fooling around on the side?" Was that a sense of humor he was demonstrating? Kendall wondered. "The men were known to fool around with the servants, so maybe their wives were fooling around with the grooms. Who knows what could have happened?"

Jeremy laughed. "My brother is a cynic, in case you hadn't noticed," he said.

"So it seems," she agreed pleasantly.

"He's different on the inside," Jeremy assured her.

"Really? I was actually thinking that he's just plain old nasty on the inside."

She couldn't believe that the words she had been thinking escaped her lips. Not that she expected to see any of these men again, but still, she was usually civil.

Her words had clearly startled Aidan. His eyebrow hiked up, and she would have sworn that he almost smiled.

"That's calling a spade a spade," he said. "I'm sorry, Miss Montgomery, that I seem to have made such a poor impression on you. Anyway, thank you for the tour, and now we'll let you go."

"Thanks."

"Wait. Did *you* ever see anything happen here?" Aidan

asked, his eyes hard again and his voice flat and emotionless, as if he were grilling her in an interrogation room.

She stared back at him. "No," she said.

She was lying. And judging from the way he was assessing her, she had a feeling that he knew it.

She *had* seen something. She just didn't know what. She wasn't even sure that Amelia's words and fears hadn't crept into her mind, and made her *think* that there were…

That there were strange lights in the darkness, and that the noises that had awakened her in the middle of the night had no earthly cause. As if something—or someone—was being dragged across the lawn below her window. That there were whispers of sound in the middle of the night, eerie and unfathomable, as if some mad scientist were at work on the property.

"No, of course not," she said with more certainty, tossing her hair back with feigned impatience.

Because all those things were imaginary, she insisted to herself.

She knew the explanation. Hadn't she managed to graduate with a three-point-nine average, and degrees in both psychology and drama? She understood the depths of the human mind. She had simply been sharing Amelia's nightmares, which were themselves a very understandable manifestation of her fear of death.

Kendall couldn't allow herself to believe—*ever*—that any of it had been true.

Because Kendall was a fraud. She was an excellent performer, and she was a total fraud.

Although there had been a few times when…

The psychologist in her kicked in and insisted that there

had been nothing inexplicable about those few times, either. She had been trained as an actress, pure and simple, and now she made both psychology and theater pay by playing psychic for a living. And "playing" was the operative word, she reminded herself. She wasn't a real psychic, if such a thing even existed. Everything she had experienced could be explained. The mind was an amazing combination of logic and imagination, and it was the logical part's job to kick in when the imagination became too fanciful.

"Guess what we want to do with the place?" Jeremy asked her.

"It's not what *we* want to do," Aidan corrected before she could answer him.

"I have no idea," she said to Jeremy, ignoring Aidan.

"Restore the house and find a way to use it to benefit the community," Zachary answered for Jeremy.

"Oh?" she said politely. Looking at the two younger Flynns, she could believe they were sincere, but she suspected things would go quite differently if Aidan had anything to say about it.

"I thought," Jeremy explained, "that we'd give ourselves the goal of getting it up and running by Halloween, then open it to the public and use the profits to benefit Children's House."

"You mean open it as a haunted house?" she asked.

Aidan gave a disgusted snort.

Zachary said, "Well, we'll have a party, anyway, though a haunted house would be great. We'll have to give that some thought."

"I'm sure it *would* be great," she said, but a chill seemed to sweep through her.

She wanted to tell him not to do it, and she didn't know why. All she knew was that the idea of creating a haunted house here was a bad one. A *very* bad one.

Why? she mocked herself. Did she really think they could wake the dead?

"It could really benefit the kids," Jeremy told her. "I can take this to a whole new level. And I can use the radio spots I've already taped to promote it."

"It—it sounds good," she had to admit.

"The party would just be a grand opening," Zachary said. "I'd like to see this place brought back to its original grandeur, and then we can use it for all kinds of functions to benefit the community."

Could they really do it? she wondered. She felt the sun on her face at that moment, shining through the odd storm clouds that had gathered earlier, and the breeze suddenly gentled. A good omen? She did love this old house, and it would be nice to see it restored and being used for something important.

She knew this place backwards and forwards. She'd been young when Amelia had entered her life, young enough to fall under the spell of the plantation's legends and ready to have fun with its spooky history.

"Let's not get so far ahead of ourselves," Aidan said firmly, looking at his brothers.

Not just an idiot, a killjoy, too, she decided.

Then he turned to look at her, and for a moment there was a genuine smile on his face.

It changed him. It made him look approachable, human. Sexy. Now where the hell had that thought come from?

"I'm sorry if I was rude earlier, Miss Montgomery. Could

you possibly give us the grand tour?" he asked her, and
added politely, "If you have the time."

"I…"

"Please," he said.

One word didn't change the fact that he was an idiot, she
told herself, even if he *was* still smiling. Suckering her in.
Well, too bad for him, because she was no fool.

On the other hand, she had just been thinking about how well
she knew and loved the house—their house now—so what
would it hurt to go through it one last time, only with them?

"Sure. Come on."

She walked past him. Her backpack with her belongings—and the diary—was resting against the entry wall.
For a moment she felt a twinge of guilt about the diary, but
she told herself to quit worrying about it and kept going. She
could hear them following behind her. "As you can see, this
is the shotgun hall. It got the name because—"

"A shot fired from the front door would just go straight
through and out the back," Jeremy said. "And will you look
at that stairway?"

"Don't forget to look at the wood rot," Aidan said.

"Easily fixed," Zachary assured him. "Honestly, Aidan. I
bought a studio that had wood rot. All it took was a decent
carpenter to get it fixed."

The house really was beautiful, Kendall thought as she
always did whenever she was there. Its grandeur was decaying, sure, but the elegance was still there behind the peeling
paint and the rotting wood. There were floor to ceiling windows in the ballroom. The parlor was still furnished with a
Duncan Phyfe love seat and nineteenth-century needlepoint
chairs. There was even a grand piano—badly in need of

tuning, Kendall warned them—along with elegant occa-sional tables, a secretary and more. They paused to study the wall of family portraits, some beautifully painted works of art, others less accurate and attractive records of the past.

"Amelia?" Aidan asked, looking at the photo on the far right.

Amelia hadn't been painted as a young and beautiful girl. She'd had the painting done only a few years ago, and it showed her as Kendall knew her, with a cap of snow-white hair, fine features worn with time, bright eyes and the kindly smile she had always offered.

"She looks like a nice woman," Zachary said.

"She was," Kendall assured them.

Upstairs, Aidan tested walls and stomped on the floors. He gave a cursory glance up the stairs into the attic, which was filled with trunks.

"Family history," Zach assured him.

But even that drew nothing more than a noncommittal "hmm" from Aidan as they headed back downstairs.

Despite its age, Kendall had always found the kitchen quite charming, with its *Leave It to Beaver* wholesomeness.

All three brothers looked at it skeptically, clearly not sharing her enthusiasm.

"It's wonderful. See, there's a dumbwaiter," she said, and showed them the small pulley-drawn elevator that had once brought hot food upstairs and returned dirty plates, laundry—and probably a small child or two, upon occasion.

At last they went outside. She showed them the original kitchen, now a caretaker's cottage, should there ever again be a caretaker, and the smokehouse, which still smelled of smoke. Even the stables, which were in the best condition of any place on the property, still smelled of hay and horses, though Amelia hadn't had a horse in over twenty years. They walked on to the neat row of old slave quarters, all of them two-roomed, most of them in serious need of repair. As they walked toward the last in line, Aidan said, "Someone has been living out here."

"Really?" she said, surprised. He looked at her, and she realized he had been studying her reaction. She could tell that he believed her, but she resented the fact that he had doubted her at all.

"How do you know?" Zach asked, frowning.

Aidan kicked at a pile of broken two-by-fours. "The soup cans," he said dryly.

"Great. And we're detectives," Jeremy muttered ruefully. "We would have seen them—eventually," he added.

"Soup cans and beer bottles." Aidan looked at Kendall. "You really didn't know."

It was a statement, not a question.

She shook her head. "But…Amelia said she saw lights. Maybe she wasn't imagining things."

"And you never checked that out?"

"Hey," she said firmly, "I came out to be with her when she was alone and sick and afraid. I wasn't employed by the estate. She…saw lots of things at the end."

"Well, if she saw lights, she was right," Aidan said, and kicked the pile again.

Then he frowned, his features tense. He bent down and started digging through the rubbish.

"Aidan, what the hell…?" Jeremy asked, as Aidan pulled something out from under the rest of the garbage.

"What is it?" Kendall asked curiously.

He held it up then, and she felt a churning in her stomach, thinking it couldn't possibly be what it looked like.

But it was.

"A thighbone," he said. "A human thighbone."

3

At least they hadn't made her stay while they called the police, Kendall thought, although they'd told her the police would certainly want to talk to her at some point.

And, she thought dryly, not even Aidan Flynn seemed to think *she* was responsible for the bone being there.

A human thighbone.

She felt a chill sweep through her.

She tried to convince herself that it wasn't really shocking. Even now, so long after the storm, terrible things were still turning up. This was, no doubt, just another sad relic washed from a flooded grave. She *had* to dismiss her fear and unease.

Most of the time, she could make it from the Flynn plantation back to the French Quarter in thirty minutes, but that day the traffic was so bad that it was four o'clock by the time she finally made it back to her shop. She rushed in feeling guilty, since she had told Vinnie she would be back by three. His band was playing on Bourbon Street that night and needed to start setting up at five.

She let out a sigh of relief when he called out a hello to her and didn't sound angry.

He was standing behind the counter where they brewed coffee and tea for their customers, and offered pastries from the bakery down the street. He was absentmindedly twirling a lock of his long dark hair—necessary for his job as guitarist and vocalist—and reading the newspaper. He looked up at her, his dark eyes and half-smile filled with curiosity.

"So you didn't get in and out before the long-lost heirs appeared, huh?" he asked.

"No."

"Details, please."

She shrugged. "There are three of them."

"Right, like the whole parish doesn't know that. I've already met two of them, remember? Tell me something new."

"I don't know what to tell you."

"What did you think they were like?"

"The two you've met are nice—the third one's a jerk."

"The youngest one, Zach, has given a lot of struggling musicians a break. He owns a few studios. Small places, but he lets new talent use 'em for free sometimes, and they've been able to get their music out there and make a little money."

"You know more than I do, then," she told him.

"Well, of course I do," Vinnie said. "I—unlike some other people—have a life. I actually get out there and talk to people."

"I'm so happy for you," she assured him dryly.

"So the oldest brother is the dickhead?"

"He's…"

"A dickhead," Vinnie repeated.

"Hey, they came, I left, it's over. It doesn't matter."

She pretended to busy herself, arranging a local artist's hand-painted greeting cards more neatly in their display slots.

"Then what's wrong?" he demanded, then answered his

own question. "Why am I asking? That place should have gone to you."

"I didn't stay with Amelia because I hoped she would leave me the house," she said firmly. "I figured it would go to back taxes, to tell you the truth. I don't know a thing about construction, but even I know it needs big money put into it just so it stays standing."

"Maybe you can buy it," Vinnie suggested. "When it's fixed."

"Oh, yeah. Right."

She stared at the cards. "There aren't enough tarot cards for me to read in all of New Orleans to make enough money to buy that house." She paused, and looked at Vinnie. "I wouldn't even have this shop if it weren't for Amelia, although I did pay her back. Every penny."

"I know you did. And you did a lot more for her than that."

"She was like my honorary grandmother," Kendall reminded him.

"It's probably because of his wife," he said. "The brother, I mean."

It took her a minute to change gears. "Um, the oldest brother is probably a jerk because of his wife?" she asked. "What, is she a bitch or…something?"

Vinnie looked at her, frowning, and shook his head. "She's dead."

"Oh, sorry." She paused. "How on earth do you know all this? The attorneys told me they were in business together, and then the lawyer called this morning and said they'd be taking possession today. And I'd heard the middle brother on the radio, but…"

Vinnie walked over to her and affectionately brushed her jaw with his knuckles. "I've played with two of them," he reminded her.

"Then you know them—and anything about them—better than I do, and I don't know why you're asking me questions," she told him impatiently.

He laughed and shook his head. "I can't say that I *know* them, not really. And I've never met the oldest one, but apparently he can't play guitar. Hey, maybe that's why he's a dickhead."

"Back up, bozo," she commanded. "What about the wife?"

"I told you, she's dead."

"But…how?"

Vinnie brought a finger to his lips. They heard voices coming from the back. Mason Adler appeared in the hallway, escorting a small woman with a T-shirt printed with a New Orleans Saints logo. She was carrying a map of the French Quarter, sporting a sunburn and wearing sunglass with alligators encircling the lenses. If she had worn a sign that proclaimed her a tourist, it couldn't have been more obvious.

But she was laughing, and she looked flushed and happy. "Mason, you are just too good," she cooed.

Mason looked at Kendall over the woman's head and shrugged. He was a good tarot, tea-leaf and palm reader. Like her, he had majored in psychology, and he could home in on people and make his predictions believable, instead of telling them that they would find love in a month, receive a huge sum of money in a year or have two children within the next decade. He was also a striking-looking man, over six feet in height and bald as a buzzard, with black eyebrows and a gym-hardened body.

He wore one gold hoop earring, and it was seldom that people forgot him once they met him.

"Well, you know, Miss Grissom, you give off very strong vibes," he told the cooing woman. "And look, here she is. Kendall, this is Fawn Grissom. She wanted to see *you*, but I did my best."

"Oh, really?" Kendall smiled at their customer and offered the woman a hand. "Nice to meet you."

"How do you do?" The other woman shook her hand firmly. "My friend Ellen—do you remember her? She said you were wonderful. That's why I came here. And I'm sure you *are* wonderful. But Mason was...well, he just *sees*."

"He really is terrific, and I think this means you were meant to see him," Kendall assured the woman.

The woman's eyes widened as if Kendall had just said the wisest thing in the world. "Of course. I think it was meant to be."

Kendall kept her smile in place. "Absolutely."

"If you'll all excuse me, I've got to get going. I've got a gig tonight," Vinnie said. He waved and started toward the door.

"Vinnie, wait!" Kendall called.

He paused in the doorway, with its tinkling bell. "What's up? I gotta get going," he reminded her.

"Never mind. It's nothing." She waved him on, and chastised herself inwardly. She didn't know why she was so curious, but she was. She wanted to know how Aidan Flynn's wife had died, not that it was any of her business. She would never see the man again.

"This is such a wonderful shop," Fawn Grissom told her. "You have the most delicious tea, the best reader and lovely merchandise."

"We like to feature the work of local artists—and thank you very much," Kendall said.

"I love those voodoo dolls," Fawn told her, pointing to a display of elaborately dressed cotton dolls that sat on a high ledge behind the counter.

"They *are* clever, aren't they?" Kendall asked, wishing the woman would shut up. She usually enjoyed talking with the customers, but today…

Today she felt off. She just wanted the woman to leave.

"Those are one of a kind," Mason said with enthusiasm. "They're made by a lady we call Gramma Mom, and they say her dolls make everyone feel good."

What a crock! Kendall thought. They were voodoo dolls. But they *were* one of a kind. And she was always happy to help support the old woman who lived out in the bayou.

"I'll take two," Fawn said. "No, what am I thinking? I need three of them. One for me, and one for each of my sisters."

"They're a bit expensive," Mason warned, telling her the price. "She spends a week, at least, on each doll."

"Oh, that's fine. They're worth it. They're unique. That's what I love about this city. You can buy so many unique things in so many different shops."

She produced a credit card and held it out to Kendall, who was thinking about Aidan Flynn again and didn't even notice. Mason gave a little cough to catch her attention. "Do you, uh, need me to help Miss Grissom at the register?" he said.

"Oh, sorry," she said. What was wrong with her today?

It was great for them—and Gramma Mom—to sell three dolls at once.

Fawn delightedly studied the dolls she'd chosen as Kendall rang up the sale and Mason produced boxes to hold the purchases.

"Voodoo dolls," Fawn said thoughtfully, then looked at Kendall and grinned. "My sister's husband is a real bastard. Think she can fix him with a few needle pricks?"

Startled, Kendall said the first thing that came into her head.

"I think she should fix him with a divorce, if he really hurts her."

Fawn nodded gravely. "Still, a little prick…" Then she was all happiness again, bidding them goodbye and promising to return.

As soon as the door closed behind her, Mason turned to Kendall. "What's up with you?" he asked. "She could have changed her mind while you just stood there, staring at her credit card. Have we decided we don't want to make money here?"

"No, no, I'm sorry. I guess I'm a little tired," Kendall said, apologizing quickly and realizing how lucky she was to have employees who were also friends. She had known Vinnie practically forever; they had gone to grade school together. Mason had appeared the first day she opened the shop. He'd been working in a place closer to Jackson Square, and he'd admitted he had come to check her out. She had been fumbling around awkwardly the next day, trying to figure out how to watch the front while doing a private reading, when he had returned. With a wink, he told her that he had seen it in the cards—she was going to need help. He'd worked for her ever since, and with some part-time help from Vinnie, they ran the place themselves and did very nicely. Katrina might have done them in—not that they had lost much merchandise, but because the city had all but gone into a coma—except for the fact that they had so many loyal customers, so they had been able to re-open quickly and maintain enough business to support themselves until the tourists started coming back.

Amelia had even let them do readings at the plantation for the brief period before they could reopen the store itself.

She felt another pang for the woman who had done so much for her and closed her eyes tightly for a moment. Amelia had lived a long life. She had seen so much, war and peace, people both good and bad. Given her age, her death had been sad, but not tragic; it had been inevitable.

Kendall suddenly realized Mason was staring at her again. "I gather it didn't go well with the princes come to take over the castle."

"Don't be so dramatic."

He pointed a finger at her. "You resent them."

"I don't. Really."

"Liar."

"I'm just sad that Amelia never got to meet them and be surrounded by love at the end."

"Kendall, she never knew them. She *did* know you. And she *was* loved. Heck, we all loved her. You, though…you were special to her. It was as if you lost a grandmother. Then, to have these usurpers come in, well, it has to be a bit traumatic."

"I had to go and hire a psychology major." She sighed.

He laughed. "I imagine they'll sell immediately."

"No."

"No?"

"They say—at least the two younger brothers say—they want to fix the place up."

"And live in it?"

"I guess." It occurred to her then that they'd never actually mentioned anything about that part of it.

He looked thoughtful for a moment, then said, "That won't work."

"What do you mean?"

"The princes have arrived—but there can only be one king of the castle. Everybody knows that."

"Well, who knows, maybe they won't live there after all. They said they want to preserve the house, use it for some kind of benefit and then make it into a place where they can do community events."

"You're kidding," Mason said skeptically.

"I'm just telling you what they said. How should I know what they'll *really* do?"

"You're growling," he warned her.

"I am *not* growling. My tenure at Flynn Plantation is over. Done. *Finis.* I have to move on. I have a life."

Mason started to laugh. It was truly irritating.

"I have a life," she repeated more firmly.

"Let's see…you work. You have a few drinks with Vinnie and me occasionally. You occasionally see a few friends. Female friends. You have a cat. A *cat,* Kendall."

"A great cat, if you don't mind," she told him. "Hey, it's not easy, keeping this place open. And I like my life. I don't need to go out all the time or have a million friends."

He shook his head. "The problem is, you spent too much time caring for Amelia. It was your whole purpose for being for far too long."

"Mason, stop being so negative. I owed her and I loved her."

"And what you did was good. But now you have to shake ll that off and start over again."

She lifted her hands in surrender. "I know. That's what I lan on doing."

"You should go out on a date."

"Really? And where am I meeting this date? Want me to ick up a drunk college kid on Bourbon Street?"

He gave her a stern look. Then a smile crept over his lips. You could start that way. I mean, how long do you intend live without sex?"

"How do you know how much sex I have?"

"I don't. I just know how much sex you *don't* have."

"You're really aggravating, you know that?" she said.

"Maybe you don't know how to date anymore." He re- ected, ignoring her insult, then shrugged. "So start with x."

"I'll keep your extremely helpful suggestions in mind," he assured him.

"You could always have sex with me," he teased.

"Though at the moment I can't think why, I treasure our iendship far too much for that," she teased back.

"There are 'friends with benefits' these days."

"Mason, go pick up a college hottie if you're that desper- te. Okay?"

"It's just about closing time." He moved to the counter nd tossed her a dishcloth. "You clean up the kitchen area. ll count out."

"Hey! I'm supposedly the boss here."

"Right. But as a good employee, I'm not letting you any-

where near the cash register. You're too spacey. It's qui
today, so let's just close up. I don't think we're going to hav
any emergency readings," he said lightly. "And I'm read
for a drink."

"You go. I can finish up here. You and Vinnie covered fo
me this afternoon, so go on, get out of here."

"Not without you," he said.

"Why not?"

"You need a drink more than I do. Come on. We'll go ou
and you can tell Uncle Mason all about what's really buggir
you."

"Nothing's bugging me."

"Bullshit. You want to visit massive vengeance upo
those wretched plantation thieves. I know you do."

She laughed. "Honest to God, no, I don't."

"Then what *is* bothering you?"

"Nothing," Kendall insisted. To change the subject, an
also because it actually seemed like a good idea, she sug
gested, "Hey, maybe I should call Sheila and see if she wan
to meet us for a drink. I haven't seen her in a bit." Sheila wa
another old friend. She had always been a bookworm, an
now she worked for the historical society. Kendall felt
little guilty about her, actually. Sheila had always wanted t
explore the Flynn place, but Amelia hadn't wanted othe
company.

"You can call her, but it won't do any good," Mason sai

"Why?"

He sighed. Mason liked Sheila, Kendall knew. No, mor
than that, he had a crush on her. He just wouldn't speak u

"She's on vacation, remember?"

"Oh, right." How could she have forgotten?

Sheila had planned a three-week trip to Ireland. She wouldn't be back until the weekend, and this was only Monday.

"But," Mason said firmly, "*we* are going out. We. You and me. And you're going to tell me what's bugging you."

It wasn't until the clock struck five, until the place was cleaned and closed and they were sitting at a corner table at the Hideaway, the bar where Vinnie was playing, that she finally told him what was upsetting her.

"I think it's the bone."

"The bone?" Mason repeated. "What the hell are you talking about?"

She looked at him. "Apparently some bum—or maybe more than one—was living out in the slave quarters. There was a lot of trash there. And a bone."

He was still staring at her, frowning. "Chicken bone? Sparerib?"

"Human," she told him, and took a long swallow of her beer.

Aidan didn't mind having a drink with his brothers. But, after the day they'd just had, he would have preferred a few quiet beers in the hotel bar. However, both his brothers were intent on catching every group that played, not just in the French Quarter but in the whole parish. They had chosen this place tonight because they had not only met the band, they'd jammed with them.

He sat back in his chair, appreciating the quality of the music. He wasn't sure he could say the same for the band's appearance, though. They weren't exactly Goth, but they were all wearing long black cotton jackets over black jeans.

He wasn't quite sure what look they were going for. Vampire? Voodoo? They did call themselves the Stakes.

Still, the music was good.

And music and alcohol might ease some of the tension he was feeling.

Right now, most of that had to do with Dr. Jon Abel, Detective Hal Vincent and even Jonas Burningham.

He could understand their attitude up to a point, but only to a point.

Yes, New Orleans and the entire Gulf region had been devastated. Yes, hundreds of bodies that hadn't been interred in aboveground "cities of the dead" had been washed out of their graves and their corpses and coffins washed up, along with the fresher corpses of those who'd died in the storm.

But that didn't deny the fact that the discovery of a human bone needed to be handled with respect and a certain urgency. And it was just too bizarre to find two human thighbones in one day, even if they had been miles apart.

Aidan had expected Jon Abel to complain about being called back out. But he was a medical examiner, and he was best qualified to determine whether there was some connection between the two bones. And in fact he had immediately made the observation that the bones had come from different people—unless there had been a woman walking around at some point with two right legs. He'd been curt and clearly annoyed at being there, though.

Hal Vincent had seemed equally unhappy, pointing out that they were actually outside his jurisdiction. He was at least polite, though, agreeing that the discovery of any human remains had to be taken seriously. Even Jonas had acted as if he thought Aidan was making a mountain out of a molehill and suggested that maybe he was suffering some kind of delayed reaction to Serena's death.

Even his brothers had been somewhat perplexed by the strength of his reaction, especially when a thorough search failed to produce any more body parts.

That fact actually disturbed Aidan more than anything else.

The others—including Jeremy and Zach—believed that the most plausible explanation was that the bone had washed up from the old family graveyard just behind the house and slightly to the east of the slave quarters.

The graveyard was an impressive place. It had a number of vaults—the largest one, where most of the Flynns had been interred, being the most impressive. Others had apparently been erected for the families of married daughters, distant relatives, servants, even friends. There were both in- and aboveground graves. And he supposed that it wasn't actually illogical to think that the bone might have come from there, though there wasn't any actual evidence that the river had topped its banks and washed anyone away.

What bothered him, he supposed, was everyone's easy assumption and acceptance that the bone must be old. What the hell was the matter with them? Were they too jaded not to wonder or care if someone had met with foul play?

Or was he himself so determined to find evil intent, even where there was none, that he was creating a crime scene out of nothing? After all, the second bone, at least, had shown no trace of tissue and had been found not far from a graveyard.

"What do you think?" Zach asked, talking loudly to be heard above the music.

"What?" Aidan turned his attention back to the present moment.

"Of the band?" Zach clarified.

Aidan leaned forward. "They're good. They're dressed a little morbidly for my taste, but the singer's got a great voice."

Zach nodded, still looking intently at Aidan.

"What?"

"You okay?" Zach's voice was concerned.

"Yeah, why?"

"You're scowling."

"No, I'm not."

"Yeah, you are," Zach said.

"Hey," Jeremy said, joining the conversation. "Don't let the fact that you dealt with a pack of hyenas today stay with you. Whether that bone washed up or not, it would have taken an idiot not to look into it."

Aidan nodded, then lowered his head, smiling. One for all and all for one. His brothers. Hell, not everyone had that. He was lucky.

"Yeah."

Jeremy and Zach were both studying him. "I'll get on the computer first thing in the morning," Zach said. "Start looking into missing persons."

Aidan shook his head in self-deprecation. "Hey, this might just be me being neurotic, you know," he said. "And it's not like we have a client."

"I'll go by the police station," Jeremy offered. "I've gotten to know some of the officers through the Children's House campaign. I can see if they've got anything to suggest. There are still hundreds of people listed as missing from the hurricane, but I'll concentrate on the more recent cases."

Aidan nodded. "Thanks," he said quietly. "I'll keep on pestering Jon Abel for the time being."

"As for the house, Aidan," Jeremy said quietly, "I know you think we're biting off more than we can handle, but there's something about the place… Anyway, you don't have to deal with it if you don't want to. Zach and I can talk to the carpenters and whoever."

Aidan shook his head. "It's my responsibility, too—if we decide we're keeping it… Oh hell, one way or the other, we know we're going to do some restoration. First things first. We need a structural engineer. I'm not taking anyone's word for the soundness of the place, not until we've had a pro out," Aidan said.

"First things first," Zach agreed.

Aidan leaned back, watching the band again. After a few minutes, he found himself studying an old man who was watching the musicians—and the room—instead. He had a complexion that was more golden than black or brown, and features that indicated a heritage made up of some combination of white, black and Cherokee. There was strength in that face. And sorrow. He was leaning against a pillar to the right of the stage, and something about his relaxed pose suggested that he came here often.

"Know how you can tell these guys are better than most of the bands in town? Because the locals come out to see them," Jeremy commented, drawing Aidan's attention away from the stranger. Then he frowned and tensed suddenly.

"What?" Aidan demanded.

"Your medical examiner's over there, sitting with a bunch cops, including that Hal Vincent guy. He cleans up well. He's looking a little less like some mad scientist."

"Jon Abel? Here?" Aidan asked, definitely surprised.

He'd figured the guy for a loner, the kind who went home at the end of the day and played in his basement lab.

But Abel was indeed sitting at a table with a group of cops. He was in jeans and a T-shirt, and looked younger than he had earlier in the day. He was wearing contact lenses, apparently, and had actually drawn a comb through his hair. He seemed to be enjoying his time off. No wonder he didn't want more work than was already pouring in from a city that was still in the process of making a precarious comeback.

"Don't look now," Jeremy said, nodding to indicate the side door, "but here comes another one of your pals."

"My pals?" Aidan asked, confused, then turned to look, despite his brother's warning.

Jonas was walking in with Matty, his wife of many years.

Sure, the band was good and the locals hung out here. But it was also downright strange, Aidan thought, that they had all ended up in the same place on the same night.

And he began to wonder what the hell was really going on.

4

Jonas was in jeans, too, but they fit as if custom-made and probably bore a designer label. His polo shirt appeared to have been ironed, and his hair was still perfect. Matty was a beauty in matching designer jeans topped by a silk blouse that hugged a body that had probably been good to begin with and then had been nipped and tucked into perfection. Not a platinum-blond hair on her head was out of order.

"Yeah, it's Jonas, and that's Matty, his wife," Aidan said. As he spoke, they saw him. Jonas lifted a hand in greeting and then looked away, obviously tired of his company for the day, and headed over to join the cops. Matty, however, walked over to them. "Hey, if it's not Aidan Flynn, and these must be your brothers. Jonas told me you guys inherited a house down here. How are you?"

Her body might be largely composed of silicone held together by stitches, but her greeting was sweet and sincere. Aidan rose to give her a hug and a kiss on the cheek; his brothers rose, as well, and he made the introductions.

"So, Jonas says you're going to keep the place!" she said, as Jeremy drew up a chair for her.

"We're hoping to," Jeremy said.

"I'm so glad you're going to live here," Matty said. "This area needs people who want to be here, who want to work, to make it a community again. And there's plenty of private security work and stuff here," she added, her eyes a little troubled as she looked at Aidan. He realized that she felt awkward about Serena. They'd been a foursome often enough during his FBI days, and she knew it was Serena's death that had been behind his decision to leave the Bureau.

Live here?

He hadn't actually thought of living here. But then, he hadn't hung around any one place for long, not even the place he called home, in years. He'd kept moving. Grabbing all the cases that gave him the opportunity to be in a different city.

Running.

Well, he was free and over twenty-one. Running was fine, if that was what he chose to do.

Strange. Despite all that was enhanced about her physical appearance, inside, where it counted, Matty was the real deal. She cared.

He smiled. "Hey, who knows? We'll see."

"Look. Isn't that the girl from the house?" Zach asked suddenly, and indicated the bandstand with his beer bottle.

Aidan glanced toward the stage. The bass player was announcing an original number; the guitarist—dressed in boots and a sweeping black cape à la every hot movie vampire—was leaning down, accepting a drink from Kendall Montgomery.

Aidan had just begun to settle down, maybe due to Matty's warm welcome. Now every muscle in his body clenched all over again. With all the bars and the music available along the length of Bourbon Street, why had Kendall Montgomery ended up here tonight, too?

The guitarist grinned, accepting the plastic cup of whatever, then took a long swig and handed it back. Before he got ready to play again, he nudged the drummer, who looked at Kendall, and offered her a grin and a salute.

After that, she returned to the table where she'd apparently been sitting. She was with a tall, well-built bald man with thick black brows, who lifted his own beer bottle toward the stage, as if toasting to their success.

"What a pretty woman," Matty announced, making Aidan like her all the more. She wasn't the type who was always putting other women down.

"She's got beautiful hair," Zachary noted.

"Are you sure you're only looking at her hair?" Jeremy asked lightly.

"I might be looking at the whole package," Zachary replied, grinning at Matty. "She really is stunning—right? One beauty assessing another, of course."

Matty laughed. "The compliment is both charming and appreciated. And, yes, that young woman is absolutely stunning. You know her?"

"We met her today. At the house," Jeremy explained.

Aidan found himself studying Kendall more closely. She was indisputably stunning, but had her dignity and pride earlier today been for real? Or had she been a leech, using Amelia Flynn until the very end?

Truthfully, he didn't think so. He had learned to read people fairly well over the years. He usually knew if someone was lying. There were little physical tics and twitches he'd learned to pick up on when someone was telling an outright lie or even coloring the truth. Lashes fluttered too quickly; pulses raced. People had a hard time looking you right in the eye when they were lying. Some liars were better than others, of course, and had learned to stare back—they were the seasoned liars. But even then...palms grew a little sweatier, and the veins in the throat were a giveaway. On top of that, just taking into consideration the way she dressed and the car she drove, she looked as if she were doing all right, but she wasn't clad as if she was rolling in money. There were no diamonds dripping from her fingers, for instance. She just didn't look as if she'd been milking Amelia to increase her own income.

She had only veered away from his direct approach once, and that had been regarding Amelia and the things she claimed went on at night. Even then, her anger with them—no, with *him*—over any implied insult to Amelia had been real.

She did have beautiful hair, he realized now, examining her more closely. It was long and rich and luxurious, a color like fire, even in the muted light of the bar. Her features were perfect: clear, large eyes, well-set; sculpted jawline; high cheekbones; perfectly formed, generous mouth; straight nose, not small, not large, just right for her face. She was like a poster child for symmetry. But the fact that she truly was stunning had even more to do with her demeanor than with her looks. She was tall, and she carried herself well. Elegantly. She moved gracefully, easily, her shoulders straight. She was the type of woman who could not only draw every eye in a room but keep it.

It interested him that he could make such observations so clinically—then he wondered if he was really so clinical after all. She seemed to be a large factor in his tension. Well, they could try all they wanted to be contemporary males, but nature didn't change. The woman was perfectly built, and it was just about impossible not to look at her and think that she would be great to touch—hell, that she would be great in bed.

He turned away, annoyed at his own thoughts. It wasn't as if he'd become a monk after Serena's death. He had gone out with women since then. A lot of women. The game had changed since the last time he'd been dating on a regular basis. Some women were looking for a relationship, but plenty of others were only looking for a one-night stand, and those were the ones he liked. He didn't want to see another face on the pillow next to his when he woke up in the morning. He didn't want to be friends. He sure as hell didn't want to fuck a friend.

The women he went out with definitely weren't friends. They were barely acquaintances.

He turned to see that the bald man was staring at their table. Staring at *him*.

"Will you excuse me?" he said politely to Matty and his brothers.

"Absolutely," Matty said with a knowing smile and a tilt of her head in Kendall's direction.

He didn't bother to explain that her hopes were in vain. He wasn't sure himself why he was going over, but it certainly wasn't because he wanted to ask Kendall out to dinner.

He headed straight for her table. "Hello," he said, and introduced himself to the man, then offered his hand. The guy was a good-looking son of a bitch, probably her boyfriend. "Miss Montgomery, nice to see you again."

The bald guy smiled. "So you're Aidan Flynn. I'm Mason Adler. I work for Kendall. Nice to meet you. Join us?"

Aidan drew out a chair for himself. It was still early by Bourbon Street standards, so the bar wasn't overly crowded and there was plenty of room.

No, it wasn't overly crowded. It was just bizarrely full of people with whom he'd had contact during the day.

Kendall was staring at him with her deep green eyes. She appeared neither pleased nor displeased.

"What are you doing in here?" she asked him finally.

He hiked both brows. "Having a beer, listening to the music."

"But...*here?*" He almost laughed aloud. Kendall, too, seemed suspicious. Or wary.

"Zach suggested this place, said he likes the band, especially the guitarist."

"Vinnie *is* good," she said, then asked, "How did it go with the bone?"

He shrugged and grimaced. "They think I'm an alarmist."

"I'm sorry?"

"I found another bone earlier," Aidan said.

She frowned at that. Mason didn't hesitate to jump in.

"Wait, you found another bone the same day?" He glanced over at Kendall with reproach, as if she hadn't shared everything she new. "On the property?"

Aidan shook his head. "By the river."

"Another...human bone?" Mason asked.

Aidan nodded, leaned back and decided to explain. "I'm a private detective. I was hired to find a runaway. She and a group of kids were living in an old cottage by the river. I saw the bone when I was with the kids, so I went back with the cops and an M.E."

"And the girl went home?" Kendall asked.

He nodded again. "It all ended well."

"But it doesn't always," Kendall said. It wasn't a question. "So what did the M.E. say?"

"That it was an old bone. That it washed up from a grave somewhere. That there are lots of old bones popping up these days."

"That's sadly true, you know," Mason said.

The guy looked like a bouncer, Aidan thought, but he seemed decent enough.

"I'm sure it is," he agreed.

"You spend a lot of time here?" Mason asked him.

"On and off, over the years," Aidan said.

Mason shook his head. "It's amazing. All that time…and you never had any idea you had family here? That you were heir to a plantation?"

"Absolutely none," Aidan assured him.

A waitress came by and set down three beers. Aidan looked up at her quizzically. "Vinnie sent them over," she explained, and walked away.

"So Vinnie the great guitarist is a good friend of yours?" Aidan asked Kendall, as if he hadn't noticed her with the guy a little while ago.

"Since grade school," she said.

"I'm not sure I get the outfits," Aidan said. "They're a little weird."

Kendall laughed then. "Weird? Come on, this is New Orleans."

"You never even knew that there was a *Flynn* plantation?" Mason pressed, ignoring the turn the conversation had taken.

"Mason…" Kendall said softly.

Aidan shook his head. "Never knew a thing about it. And even if I had, Flynn is a pretty common name."

"I hear your brothers are both good musicians," Kendall said, clearly trying to get off a difficult topic.

Aidan nodded.

"How did you escape it?" Mason asked.

"Sorry?"

"The music thing?" Mason persisted.

"The United States Navy," Aidan told him.

"You know, you should come by for a reading," Mason told him.

"Mason!" That time Kendall didn't speak softly at all, and the blood actually seemed to drain from her face.

"Come by for a *what?*" Aidan asked, frowning.

Kendall stood abruptly. "I'm going to ask your brothers if they want to join us. Or maybe I should just go. It's getting late."

"Kendall," Mason protested, "it's eight o'clock."

"I know, but I have to open the shop tomorrow." She seemed agitated, as if she had chosen the wrong excuse.

"Where is your shop?" Aidan asked her. *A reading?* Just what kind of shop did she run?

"We're on Royal. It's called Tea and Tarot," Mason answered for her.

"I see," Aidan said slowly. Again, that strange clenching of his muscles. Tarot. Psychic readings. She was clearly some kind of a quack. He felt strangely disappointed, a feeling he chose not to examine too closely.

"We handle the work of a lot of local artists," she said coldly, obviously reading him quite clearly.

"I'm sure you do," he said politely.

"Listen, forgive me, I'm really going to call it a night," Kendall said determinedly.

"Vinnie will be heartbroken. He was going to sing a new song he wrote," Mason warned her. "He wanted you to be here for it."

"I'll hear it next time. I have to go. Good night."

She turned and strode toward the door. Aidan was surprised to find himself on his feet.

"Does she live far?" he asked Mason.

"No, she lives down on Royal, too, toward Esplanade. It's safe," Mason assured him. The man was definitely curious, but there didn't seem to be anything going on between him and Kendall other than friendship. No man acted that nonchalantly about a woman with whom he had something going.

"I think I'll just make sure she gets past the drunks out there okay," Aidan said.

Mason nodded. "Sounds like a plan. I think I'll go introduce myself to your brothers."

Whether Mason did or didn't go over to the table, Aidan didn't know, because he hurried out of the bar in Kendall's wake.

Bourbon Street. Early on a Monday night, it was fairly quiet. Shills were out in the street, trying to entice passersby into their establishments. Good old country music was pouring from one place, while across the street, neon legs kicked up and down on a sign advertising a strip club. A group of fraternity boys, arms entwined, plastic cups sloshing, was walking past singing an unfathomable song. Two women with balloon hats on their heads giggled as they passed the frat boys.

He didn't see Kendall anywhere on Bourbon, so he took the side street over to Royal.

Royal was almost dead quiet. An elderly couple was walking a small terrier. Aidan could see someone just beyond them, moving quickly. Kendall.

He hurried to catch up with her. He wasn't trying to be

quiet, but she must have been deep in thought, because when he touched her shoulder, she started, spinning around quickly with a little gasp.

"Oh!" she said, when she recognized him.

"Sorry. I didn't mean to scare you."

"You didn't *scare* me, you *startled* me. It's not the same thing."

She was indignant again. Defenses all in place. Well, it was true. He didn't think much of palm readers, tarot readers, whatever readers. He didn't believe in any of it. And he was pretty sure *she* didn't believe in any of it, either, though he couldn't have explained why. Maybe she just seemed too levelheaded, too real-world.

"Sorry. I didn't mean to *startle* you."

She inhaled. He could tell from the visible pulse in her throat that her heart was beating too quickly. He *had* scared her, no matter what she said.

"So. What do you want?"

"I just thought you… I wasn't sure…hell. I thought I should walk you home."

She stared at him hard. "You thought I needed someone to walk me home?" Indignation and disbelief were fighting for dominance in her tone.

"It's night. It's dark," he said lamely.

She looked up at him. Her tone was dry when she said, "I read tarot cards. And palms. I'm supposed to be some kind of psychic. Don't you think I would *see* danger?"

"I don't know. The Psychic Network went bankrupt. You would have thought one of them would have seen it coming."

"I live here. I have lived here all my life. I know where I can walk without being in danger. And this really isn't a bad city, no matter what people think. We have problems, sure. All cities have problems. I can see myself safely down the next two blocks to my home. And I thank you for your concern, but I'm not really sure that's the reason you followed me."

"No?"

"No," she said flatly. She sighed, as if genuinely weary. "So I'll ask you again. What do you really want from me?"

He didn't hesitate. He didn't lie. It would be foolish.

"I want to know more about you."

"Me?"

"You—and the time you spent with Amelia. And what went on at night. What she saw, what she dreamed, what she said, and just what it was that scared her—and you."

She stared back at him.

"Ghosts?" she suggested softly, almost as if she were mocking herself.

"You believe in ghosts?" he asked her.

It seemed like a genuine question, she thought. He wasn't mocking her; he just seemed curious.

"No, of course not," she told him.

And that was the truth, wasn't it?

They started walking, and he mentioned that one of the reasons he had always loved the city so much was its architecture. She started telling him stories about some of the buildings they passed, and ten minutes later, they were still talking.

In her apartment.

Kendall couldn't figure out how she'd managed to invite him in when she didn't even like him, but he was definitely there.

She lived on the first floor of a beautiful old house built

in 1816, a large shotgun that provided the current owners with four rental units, two on each side of the hallway. Her door opened into the formal parlor, and the parlor opened onto a hall that passed both bedrooms, one of which she used as an office, and then ended in the kitchen and family room, both of which had been tastefully modernized. A long counter stretched across the back of the kitchen, separating it from the family room, which opened onto the courtyard. Rather than sliding glass doors, double French doors led out to a patio and yard, which had originally been the front of the house. An alley ran behind the picket fence that marked the property line, and there was still a gate; people had once come visiting by way of what was now the rear.

"Nice," Aidan commented.

Since he was there, she had felt obliged to offer him a drink. Now he absently swirled Scotch in his glass as he stared out the back.

"It's home," she said.

"You own it?"

"I rent."

"Your shop does well?"

"Yes."

"I guess people really do come here to dabble in voodoo and the occult," he said.

"Most people only do it for fun," she told him.

He turned and walked back into the kitchen, where he perched on one of the bar stools.

"What about the people who don't do it just for fun?"

She took a long sip of her own drink, vodka and cranberry. "Voodoo is a recognized religious practice."

He lifted a hand, dismissing her comment. "I can go online

and become a minister of half a dozen different religions. Doesn't make them real."

"Voodoo was the religion of Haiti. It's a mix of old African religions and Catholicism. Its practitioners pray to, or through, the saints. They believe in a supreme being, in God."

"And that they can injure a man by sticking a pin in a doll, and that a priest can bring people back from the dead as zombies."

"Do you have a secret communication going with the Supreme Being, God, Allah, Jehovah, or whatever you want to call him—or her?" she asked.

He had the grace to smile at that. "It's not people's beliefs that worry me. It's people who play off others' beliefs."

She shrugged. "I…don't mean to insult you here—honestly—but I'm not sure why you're so convinced there's something terrible going on. Not just bones, but whole rotting bodies were floating in the Mississippi not so long ago."

"I know. And it was a horrible tragedy."

"We're still picking up the pieces on a daily basis. It just takes time. Not a day or a week, or even a month or a year. It's going to take years—plural. And a lot of commitment."

"I know."

"But you're still convinced that something's going on." She flushed. "Besides bums living on the plantation and me not even being aware of it."

He shrugged, and a rueful smile played across his lips as he lifted his glass to her. "I'm sorry if I made you feel bad about that. You were just two people, one of them old and dying, in a huge old house on a big piece of property. Hell, you didn't have to be a caregiver, though I'm grateful that you were, and you sure as hell couldn't have been a groundskeeper, as well. So why does all this bother me? Call it a hunch. Or maybe the bone I found at the house only seemed suspicious because of the one I found earlier, by the river."

"Bones can turn up anywhere in this area."

"Yes, they can."

"But…?"

"Tell me about Amelia," he said, surprising her with the change of subject.

Kendall's giant black Persian cat, Jezebel, chose that moment to walk in and rub against his legs, purring so loudly that Kendall could hear her from ten feet away.

She found herself almost leaping across the room to pick up the cat, silently chastising her. *I guess I didn't name you Jezebel for nothing,* she thought, shooing the animal toward the front of the house as she set her down.

"That's a beautiful animal," Aidan commented.

"Thanks," Kendall said curtly.

He didn't comment on the fact that it seemed to bother her that her cat had been affectionate to him.

"Amelia?" he said.

"She was exceptionally kind to me—always. We had a bond, I guess. She was intelligent, sweet, a really fine woman. She died of cancer, though I guess the lawyer told you that."

"She took a lot of morphine for the pain, I take it?" he asked.

Kendall nodded. "Yes," she said warily, knowing exactly what he was implying.

"And she saw things?"

"Yes." More wariness.

"And you did—or you didn't?" he asked. So much for pleasantry. Those eyes of his were on her again, deep blue touched by frost, and his tone had changed.

"I really don't know what you want me to say. For about two weeks before her death, she seemed to be afraid all the time. I had dragged a cot into her room, to be with her at night. Sometimes she woke up screaming about the lights. I was always still half asleep, so I honestly don't know if I saw the lights or not. We're not talking huge, the-aliens-are-landing lights, just pinpricks of lights out back and from the area of the cemetery. Or sometimes she would hear things, and again, I'd be half asleep. Did I hear anything out of the ordinary? I'm not certain."

"What *did* you hear?"

"Wind, sometimes. It can sound like a cry when it moves through the old oak trees. Rustling sounds—again, possibly the wind, or maybe squirrels. Everything can be explained, I'm certain. Except, then, at the end…"

"At the end…what?"

He was a good interrogator, she thought. His voice had softened in a gentle and encouraging way.

She took another sip of her drink. "I was only afraid at the end, I guess." She hesitated for a long moment. "You can make fun of me, if you like. But most of the time…I felt completely safe at the plantation. As if it were…protected by the past, by a benign spirit or something. Maybe it's just the beauty of the area, I don't know. But at the end, Amelia did unnerve me a few times. I mean, at night, it really feels like the plantation is in the middle of nowhere. And despite the feeling of being safe in the house, I kind of grew uneasy about there being something…evil, I guess, going on around it, but if I kept quiet and stayed in bed, I'd be safe. Maybe I did hear things, maybe I didn't, but I did sleep with a base-ball bat at my side."

"You needed a gun."

"That would be just great. I don't know how to shoot. I'd have blown a hole in myself or Amelia."

He smiled at that. "You should learn how to shoot—especially if you plan on spending any more time at derelict plantations in the middle of nowhere. You know, there's a lot worse out there than ghosts. Real live monsters."

"Well, I don't plan on sleeping in the wilderness anymore, so I guess I'm okay without being a sharpshooter," she said.

"Go on. Tell me more about the end."

Inadvertently, Kendall shivered. She hated herself for it, knowing he was watching her every move. "Nothing happened at the end. She just started talking to people I didn't see."

"Saying what?"

"Different things at different times."

"Go on."

"It sounded as if she was teaching a history class. She talked about Reconstruction—after the Civil War—and World War I, World War II, Martin Luther King...all kinds of things. She talked about being proud of the old house. She seemed happy. She seemed to be talking to..."

"Ghosts?"

"Yes, exactly."

"But she was on a lot of morphine."

"Of course.... I wasn't alone with her at the end, you know. She didn't want to die in a hospital. She'd been born in that house, and she wanted to die there. But I'm not a nurse, so I hired an RN to stay with Amelia when it was clear she was getting near the end. Still..."

"What?"

"She had been unconscious, in a coma, when she suddenly opened her eyes and sat up. She looked right at me and said goodbye, and that she loved me. Then she reached out, as if she were taking someone's hand—you'll never convince me she didn't see something, some*one*—and she said, 'It's time. I'm ready now.' And then she died."

"Morphine," he said softly. He actually said it as if he were trying to reassure her.

She looked directly back at him. "Sure."

And then she suddenly felt uncomfortable. He was standing some distance from her, and he wasn't threatening in any way. In fact, he was being extremely decent, almost kind. Humoring her? Maybe not. He seemed sincere, and when he smiled, or even when he just looked thoughtful, he was astonishingly appealing. It might have been his self-confidence, the fact that he didn't just pretend not to care what others thought; he really didn't give a damn. His height and the breadth of his shoulders made him naturally imposing, and the hardness of his features somehow made the sculpted strength of them more intriguing. There was a leashed energy about him that seemed to emit a heat, even a sexual charisma.

She wondered once again what had happened to his wife.

But she sure as hell wasn't going to ask him.

She told herself that her sudden unease was ridiculous. Just because he was an unattached man and she was an unattached woman, that didn't mean they were about to jump one another. Oh, God. What a bizarre thought to have pop into her head. She had disliked him the moment she met him, and she still didn't like him. It was just that she'd stopped believing his horns and tail popped out when he was alone.

And she was aware that as a man...

As a man what? she asked herself irritably. He thought she was a fraud.

Well, weren't there times when she thought so herself?

She needed him out of her house. She was weary. She felt a strange weakness, and she didn't like it. She needed the logical portion of her mind to come leaping forward, and she felt just too tired to manage it.

She cleared her throat. "I really need to get some sleep."

"Sure." He seemed to recover a bit himself. He had been staring at her, just as she had been staring at him. How long? Something seemed to pass across his eyes. A flicker. As if he had seen something inside her that he actually liked.

"Of course."

He set his glass on the counter, and avoided touching her as he walked by.

"Thanks for the drink." The words were polite. Distant. And she didn't follow him as he walked away down the hall.

When she heard her front door close, she walked slowly to the front of the house and locked it.

To her surprise, the expected pleasure in being by herself in the apartment, with time to relax and sleep, didn't come. Instead...

She felt uneasy.

And ridiculously, she wished that he were still with her. Her apartment usually seemed so welcoming.

Now...

It just seemed empty.

And she felt alone, as she hadn't in years.

Jezebel let out a meow. Kendall picked up the cat and rubbed her chin against the Persian's soft fur. She loved all animals, but with her work schedule, a cat was definitely the best choice for a pet.

"Why am I suddenly wishing you were a dog?" she asked. "Like a huge mastiff, or a pit bull?"

Jezebel just meowed again.

"You're a big help," Kendall told her sarcastically.

But it wasn't the cat's fault. Even holding Jezebel, Kendall still felt that same sensation of being alone.

And afraid.

5

Death.

It could be violent or peaceful, on a battlefield or in the streets, at home or in a hospital. It could leave a person looking as calm as if they were asleep, or torn to shreds, ravished, decayed.

In the modern world, it was quickly sanitized whenever possible. Disasters, though, meant field hospitals, temporary morgues, sometimes even mass graves and burning.

But the storm was behind them. New Orleans was getting back up to speed.

Katrina had wreaked havoc all over the city, including at the morgue. A lot here was new. Visitors entered a quietly tasteful reception area that could have belonged to any business or doctor's office. There was music softly playing, and a young woman with a gentle voice was on duty to offer assistance.

Every effort had been made to hide the presence of death there, where so often the bereaved came for a last glimpse of those they loved. Not only that, this often ended up being the place where the police talked to the living as they tried to solve the mystery of the dead, and a calm husband did a better job of recalling what his wife had done before her death, for example.

Aidan was familiar with the morgue, having been here several times before when he was in New Orleans on a case. And like all morgues, despite every attempt to mask it, there…was still something that seemed to permeate the very walls. No music system could really drown out the tears of a mother who had lost her child. And no amount of bleach could ever fully wipe out the smell of death.

But the girl at the front was pleasant, perhaps genuinely compassionate, perhaps just a good actress after days of greeting cops, parents, siblings and friends, those who came in fear of finding out a loved one was dead, and those who were relieved that the days of caring for a loved one were over.

"Hello, Mr. Flynn," she said.

Apparently he had met her before. Great P.I. he was, not to remember her. Good thing her name tag identified her as Ruby Beaudreaux, so he could fake it.

"Hi, Ruby." He smiled. "I'm hoping to see Dr. Abel. Is he in?"

"I'll see."

She smiled and put through a call, then began to frown at the response she received from the other end. Aidan could hear Jon Abel yelling.

Ruby hung up and looked at him apologetically. "He's really busy. Sorry."

"That's okay. I can wait."

Ruby was young. She blushed easily, and she did so then. "Um, I don't think that will help."

"I have all day," Aidan said pleasantly, and sat. "Just tell him that. I'll be here—whenever he comes out." The place was bound to have a back door, and Abel would no doubt use it. He just wanted the man to know he didn't intend to let go.

"You want me to…call him again?" Ruby said. She looked as if he had just asked her to walk into the lion's cage.

"Sure, if you don't mind."

She hesitated, then came out from around her desk. "Mr. Flynn, you have to understand. We were overwhelmed for… months after Katrina. You can't believe how bad it was. Dr. Abel isn't a bad guy. He's just been through a lot, just like everyone here."

"I do understand," he said gravely.

"Oh." It wasn't a question, but she didn't move, just stood there waiting for him to leave.

Praying for him to leave, he thought. He was sorry for Miss Beaudreaux, but that wasn't going to happen.

"Look, no matter what's happened in the past, people are still dying now," he told her. "There are still killers out there, and Dr. Abel is aware of that fact."

"Oh, God! Are you investigating a murder?" she asked.

"A possible murder," he said.

She nodded, straightened purposefully and walked back to the phone. She spoke quietly into the receiver, and when she hung up, she said, "I'll lead you back."

When she stopped outside an autopsy room, she pointed to a rack of white jackets. "You may want to suit up," she told him.

He entered the room, slipping into a coat and mask. It looked as if Jon Abel had just started his current autopsy.

Aidan was sure that this body had been awaiting a break in the M.E.'s schedule, when the man had made time for it in order to avoid seeing him.

"I told you, Flynn, I'm busy," the doctor said, without

looking up. He made his first incision, and something green and putrid streamed from the body. One of his assistants muttered something and jumped back.

Abel looked up, clearly hoping that Aidan was also disturbed.

It *was* disturbing, Aidan thought. Death was frequently disturbing. It could be the natural end to a life long lived, but too often it was ravaged flesh and shattered bone, and horror in the open eyes of someone who had died violently. He had seen the bodies of those who had been killed in war, murdered, assassinated, even tortured. It was never easy. But he had learned not to react. Not usually.

He had reacted when he had seen Serena.

He pushed the thought from his mind. "I imagine this guy sat around in the heat a while before being discovered?" he asked.

Abel grunted—maybe granting him a modicum of respect? "Leroy Farbourg. I'm guessing he spent about a week up in a hot attic. The cops say his wife claimed she shot him by accident—shot him by accident four times. Now that ain't easy."

"What did she have, an Uzi?"

"Just old Leroy's shotgun," Abel said. He had backed away to let his assistant wash away some of the putrid fluid.

"Anything on those thighbones?" Aidan asked him.

Abel tensed with irritation. "As you can see, I'm busy."

"You could give them to a coworker or an assistant," Aidan suggested.

That drew a venomous stare. "Mr. Flynn, do you know how many unclaimed bodies we've dealt with? Wait—how many body *parts* we've dealt with?"

"Too many to count, I imagine," Aidan said evenly. "But…please. When you can, look into those bones for me."

Abel stared at Aidan. "Are you after a missing person, Mr. Flynn? Do you have a client breathing down your neck? If so, that client will have to wait until I am able to make a thorough forensic investigation. Am I clear?"

"I don't have a client," Aidan told him.

Abel's silence was deadly.

"I would deeply appreciate your help," Aidan said.

Abel rolled his eyes, but then he said gruffly, "I'll get to those bones within the next few days. And when I do, I'll call you."

"All right, thanks. If I don't hear anything, I'll call you," Aidan assured him pleasantly.

Abel's scalpel cut deeply into the dead man. Aidan wondered if there was any law against the use of excessive force on the dead. But for the moment, there was nothing more he could do here. He thanked Jon Abel politely again and departed.

Kendall had heard all the stories about Marie Laveau, the famous voodoo queen of New Orleans. The woman had clearly been talented, but had she been truly psychic or only a superior practitioner of the art of listening, then drawing conclusions? Kendall's mental jury was still out on that one. Actually, reading the tarot cards was easy. They all had several meanings. The Death card didn't always—or even often—mean death. It frequently indicated change, the end of one thing and the beginning of something else. It was the same for all the cards. Reading tarot cards really meant appearing to be in deep concentration, asking a few carefully targeted questions and then giving answers general enough that they could never be proven wrong.

The tea leaves were a little trickier—and also a little easier. They were tea leaves, for God's sake. No one could predict exactly how they would appear when a client had finished her cup of tea, and a clever reader could see anything she wanted in them.

Ady Murphy had been coming to see Kendall for years. She was a seventy-year-old widow, small and spry, and as sweet as could be, and she loved to have her tea leaves read. Luckily Kendall loved making up stories to tell her. Ady had six children, nineteen grandchildren and eleven great-grandchildren. Almost anything Kendall said would connect to one of them. Mostly, however, Kendall—just like Marie Laveau—listened. And then she carefully crafted what to say.

They were chatting now as they went back to the little room with the pretty cloth-covered table, crystal ball and stack of cards. Ady carried her teacup with her. She always had the same tea: Irish cream.

"So that rascal Amelia *did* have relatives!" Ady said. She and Amelia had met and gotten to know each other at the tea shop. They always wore similar cotton dresses, pillbox hats and little white gloves, and they had gotten on famously from day one. When Amelia was born, the family had been rich. She had died with only her house and a few trinkets. Ady had been born on a plantation, too—in a shack where her father had worked the cotton fields. There had been no running water or electricity. Amelia had never had a child; Ady had produced a football team, with all her descendants. But the women shared something special: a love of the same manners and morals. One had been white, one was black, and each one had counted herself lucky to have the other as a friend.

Actually, Ady wasn't all black. Her skin was a lovely

copper color, and she had bright amber eyes. She liked to say she knew white because she had some in her, and she was always telling Amelia and Kendall that they should have had a little black in them, that it would have made them stronger. "Nothing strong as a black woman, honey. Not even the biggest he-man out there," Ady would say.

"I met the Flynns. They seem decent enough," Kendall said now.

"Hmph. What decent boys wouldn't visit a lonely great-aunt?"

"They didn't know she existed," Kendall explained.

"Now that's just strange." Ady hmphed again. "Now let's see what the tea leaves say. Maybe they'll tell me I'm about to win the lottery. I don't play the lottery, of course. But maybe I will. What do you think? Should I?"

Kendall laughed. "Now, you know I won't give that kind of advice, Miss Ady." Though a widow, Ady was always "Miss" Ady.

"And you know I don't gamble, child," Ady said, and laughed. "Come on, tell me what's in my leaves."

Kendall rolled the cup and studied it. The leaves did seem to be forming into a very definite swirl. It was just the way they had landed on the bottom of the cup, she told herself.

She stared at them. As she did, the room seemed to…go out of focus. Of course it did, she chided herself. She was staring so hard into the bottom of the cup that her vision was blurring.

But she couldn't look away. Her vision kept on blurring, and then it was as if she were seeing a picture at the bottom of the cup. No, she *was* seeing a picture. A whole scene. She was back at the plantation on the day Amelia died. And there was Amelia, so frail, comatose in her bed. The nurse had said that she probably wouldn't regain consciousness.

But she did. She sat up, and Kendall started forward, taking her hand. Amelia looked at her, told her that she loved her…then looked toward the foot of the bed and smiled, and said she was ready. She reached out, and…

In the teacup picture, in the vision swimming before her mind's eye, Kendall saw something there. Some*one*. Someone wrapped in a sheen of light was reaching out to Amelia.

Kendall almost dropped the cup as she heard a voice—Amelia's voice—whisper in her ear.

Help Ady. Please help her.

Ady suddenly jumped to her feet, and the movement broke the spell—no, *memory,* Kendall told herself.

"Miss Ady, what is it?"

"I will *not* go to the doctor," Ady said.

"What?"

"You just said, 'Get to the doctor, Ady. Go right away, and they'll be able to stop it.'"

"No, I—no. I didn't say anything," Kendall protested. She reached for Ady's hand.

As she took it, she felt as if a shaft of lightning shot through her. It was knowledge. Deep, certain knowledge. Ady had cancer.

The older woman was looking at her in horror, and she herself was shaking inwardly. She'd had no idea she had spoken. And the way Ady was staring at her was frightening.

But she *knew.*

"Miss Ady, I'll take you myself. You have to get to the doctor right away."

"I don't like the doctor. He pokes and prods me."

"Miss Ady, I think you're sick, but the sickness can be stopped if we just get you help fast."

Miss Ady looked around, clutching her little handbag to her chest. Then she stared at Kendall and frowned. "Is Luther Jr. going to win that football game Saturday night?"

Kendall told her, "I don't know. I do know you have to go to the doctor. I'll go with you, I promise. But you *have* to go."

"Maybe."

"I'll call your daughter Rebecca," Kendall threatened.

Ady's oldest girl was fifty-two, a lab technician at the morgue, and a no-nonsense woman who loved her mother dearly. She sometimes came in for a tarot reading herself. "Just for fun," she always said, and it *was* fun; she and Kendall always ended up talking about all the different things the cards could mean.

Miss Ady stared at her stubbornly, frowning. "The tea leaves say I can get better?" she asked. "'Cause if not, I am not going to be poked and probed and have needles stuck in my arms. Folks like me, we've had a good time of it, we've been blessed. We don't mind dying. We just want it to be in our own homes."

"You're not going to die, not if you go to the doctor," Kendall insisted.

"Well, all right, then."

"Come on. We'll make an appointment for you right now," Kendall said.

When they reentered the front of the shop, Mason, who had been showing a customer a spectacularly pretty crystal, looked up in surprise as Kendall and Ady went straight to the phone. As they called the doctor and arranged for an appointment, Mason made the sale. The gentleman who bought the crystal held the door open for Ady to leave.

"What was that all about?" Mason demanded.

"I think she has cancer," Kendall said.

"What?" Mason looked at her as if she had lost her mind. "Since when did you start believing your own PR? Why on earth would you scare an old woman like that?"

Just what the hell had happened in there? Kendall wondered. She wanted to shake it off; she wanted to tell herself it was nothing more than the fact that she cared about Ady, and it wouldn't hurt to have her make a trip to the doctor, just to check things out. But no matter how hard she tried to explain things to herself, she still felt uncomfortable. Something about this was genuinely frightening.

As frightening as it had been the first two times. But she had been doing tarot readings then, and it was easy to get tired when she was concentrating on the cards and her customer, easy to see things that weren't really there.

"I...I think it must be because I spent so much time with Amelia," she said quickly, because Mason was staring at her.

"So now everyone who is older has cancer?"

"No, of course not. Maybe it just gave me an instinct. Or maybe I'm wrong. You know I would never do anything to hurt her. But it can't hurt for her to go to the doctor, so I'll be a bit late on Thursday. I'm going to take her to her appointment." Kendall walked toward the counter, then added, "If anyone else wants their tea leaves read today, you do it, okay?"

Mason looked at her quizzically, then shrugged. "Sure. If that's what you want."

"Thanks. It is."

When he arrived at the plantation, Aidan found that the structural engineer they'd booked had arrived early. Luckily

Jeremy had been early, too. They were already walking through the house. Aidan met the man and shook hands with him, saw that Jeremy had the inspection under control and left them to their own devices.

Aidan walked back out front and stared up at the house, though he didn't know what he was looking for. Yesterday he had been certain he had seen a woman in white on the balcony. Had it been Kendall? It must have been. What other possibility could there be?

But when he had met Kendall at the door, she hadn't looked like the woman he'd seen. That woman had been paler, and dressed in white. *The woman in white.* Clearly he'd read too many old ghost stories in his day. There had been no woman in white. It had been a trick of the light, of the strange weather, with its wind and roiling dark clouds, followed by sun and clear skies.

He closed one eye, staring at the house almost defiantly. What bothered him most, he knew, wasn't the woman he'd seen, who really might have been a trick of the eye. What bothered him was his gut feeling about the house. There was something disturbing about the place, something dark and forbidding.

He gave himself a mental shake. Houses didn't have personalities. They were wood and brick and stone, nails and plaster.

He walked back toward the house, but didn't go inside. Instead, he found himself tracing his steps past the house and back to the last slave cabin, where he had found the soup cans and the bone. The place looked as if it had been invaded by moles, the police had dug so many holes, looking for other bones or anything else suspicious. He hunched down, looking at what the search had turned up. There *had* been other bones at the site: chicken bones. They went nicely with the discarded container from a fast-food restaurant.

Nothing very intriguing in that. Some homeless person had been using the area as a base. With the number of people still displaced by the storm, that shouldn't be surprising.

It would be good to find out who, though.

Lights. Amelia had seen lights. She'd been convinced her ancestors were haunting the house, that they were coming for her. Those lights could be explained now, as could the noises. Someone sneaking around back here would undoubtedly have made noise.

But then there was the bone.

This was actually pretty high ground—on the river, yes, but above sea level. How high had the water come? High enough to shift bones from old coffins?

He rose and surveyed the domain that was now the Flynn brothers' legacy. It was in sad shape, at least cosmetically, but comparatively speaking, it had survived the centuries well. The house and stables were intact; the slave quarters decaying and in need of repair, but they were still standing.

Just as they had stood for nearly two hundred years.

Maybe his brothers were right; maybe this place really was important and represented their chance to do something good, to make a difference.

He looked across the overgrown lawn and untended brush to the family burial ground, its white mausoleums and stone monuments just visible through the trees. There was a line of bent and twisted old oaks, dripping with moss, that more or less defined the edge of the cemetery.

He walked toward it.

A low wall of stone, covered with lichen and crumbling with age, ran alongside the trees, a truer demarcation of where the cemetery began and ended.

An angel sat atop a sarcophagus that stood at least five feet high. Only one name was listed on it: Fiona MacFarlane. Below her name, the etching grown faint with time: *Beloved in this house.*

Nice sentiment. He wondered what her connection to the family had been. He really should get hold of some of the old family records and trace the connections.

There was a row of in-ground graves with simple plaques to mark them, each one etched only with a first name, making Aidan think they might have been graves for the family slaves, as well as those who had chosen to stay on to work for the plantation as free men after the war, since several were from the 1870s and '80s.

None of them seemed to be disturbed.

His attention was drawn next to the large family vault he'd noticed the day before. It was an imposing stone structure with a marble facade. Clearly, it had been built long ago, when the family had been flush with money. Before the War Between the States. He walked up the broken stone path to the heavy iron door. He assumed it would be locked, but it wasn't.

He pushed open the door and stepped inside. It was cool—and dark, so he drew his keys from his pocket and switched on the little flashlight attached to them, then shone it around.

He had expected more cobwebs. And there were dying

flowers here and there, so apparently someone still came now and then to honor the dead.

Amelia had been dying of cancer. In the end, she had almost certainly been bedridden. So who had it been? Kendall?

He didn't think it possible that any of his ancestors' bones had escaped from the tombs that lined the walls, or from the two sarcophagi that sat in the middle of the mausoleum, facing a small marble altar backed by a tall golden cross. Behind that, a stained-glass window depicted St. George slaying the dragon. The window faced the trees, rendering its purpose moot, since the heavy branches of the oaks prevented the sun from showing off the beauty of it.

He walked back out of the mausoleum, wondering what he was looking for, what he was expecting to find. There was a simple and reasonable explanation for everything that was bothering him. Shifting earth and rising water had resulted in bones showing up in all kinds of odd places. Amelia had been sedated, so was it any wonder she had seen and heard things, that she had talked to ghosts? Some down-on-his-luck guy had been living on the property, eating chicken and making soup.

Whatever was bugging him, it was something he had to shake, and he should start by getting the hell out of the cemetery. He and his brothers weren't rolling in cash, but they could afford this project. He was between cases and had time to plunge into the restoration of the house. It might be good for all of them.

He started back toward the house and almost tripped over a broken gravestone.

Swearing softly, he regained his balance, looking down to see what had nearly made him fall.

He frowned, noticing a suspiciously familiar stain on the stone.

He hunched down and studied it more closely. It looked as if something had splattered or…dripped onto the stone. It was brownish and, up close, completely recognizable.

Dried blood.

6

Kendall groaned. "Mason, no. I can't go out tonight."

"You have to."

"No, I don't. What's that old saying? Only two things are certain in life—death and taxes. And we don't even have to pay taxes if we don't want to. We can just go to jail and then die. I do not have to go out tonight." She was tired, and she didn't know why. And she was afraid that she would run into Aidan Flynn again, which she definitely didn't want to do, and she didn't know exactly why she felt so strongly about *that,* either. If the guy was going to be living near the city, she could end up running into him a lot, so she was going to have to learn to deal with him, because she wasn't about to let anyone change her life, her friends or her habits.

Not that she always hung out on Bourbon Street. The locals all said that Bourbon Street was for the tourists; anyone who still wanted real blues or a genuinely Southern-style bar usually headed to Frenchman Street.

But Vinnie played on Bourbon. And lots of her friends went there to see him. The truth was, any musician looking for a full-time gig that actually provided a living wage was lucky to get a job on Bourbon Street.

Mason pointed a finger at her. "Fine. If you want to break Vinnie's heart, be a no-show. He was crushed last night when you weren't there to hear his new song."

"Oh, come on. He knows I'm his biggest fan," Kendall protested.

Silently, though, she admitted that Mason was probably right. Vinnie was sensitive when it came to his music. Artists! She knew enough of them. Once upon a time, she had intended to be one. But making a living had superseded certain dreams, and she did love her shop. She even loved the opportunity to use her "powers" to help people when they were hurt, anxious or just in need of a friendly hand to hold.

She knew the disappointment of rejection all too well. That was another reason why she had loved Amelia so much.

"Young lady," Amelia had told her, "don't you ever let anyone put you down. You are strong and talented, and don't you forget that, no matter what anyone else says or does. Life is a fight. You need to know when to retreat, when to go forward. You need to know yourself, and know your own value."

In short, Amelia had told her to never let 'em see her cry.

Amelia had given her so much.

"Mason, Vinnie is my best friend. But…"

Her voice trailed away. Why would she want to hurt a friend's feelings, adding to the pain life was always so ready to dish out?

Mason gave her a look. *The* look. He was good at it. The look made her feel as if she were worth about two cents, as if she were cruelly betraying her best friend, as if she were nothing but a sniveling coward.

She threw up her hands in resignation. "All right."

* * *

Bourbon Street was still struggling during the week. Only on weekends could any place guarantee a crowd. Things were getting better, but better hadn't yet brought them back up to their pre-storm par. That would still take years, most residents realized. Even so, the shills were working hard to entice them as they headed down Iberville and moved on to Bourbon.

"Three drinks for the price of one!" A guy wearing a sandwich board tried to hand them a flyer. "Oh, hell, it's you, Mason," he said.

Mason laughed. "Sorry, Brad. We're on our way to hear Vinnie."

Kendall recognized Brad Humphries. He managed a place that had been forced to downgrade to canned music during the week. He was doing his best to survive: managing, bartending, being a DJ—and wearing a sandwich board in the street.

She set her hand on Mason's arm and smiled at Brad. "We'll come in for a minute."

Mason looked at her, hiking up a brow. "Yeah?"

She nodded. "Thanks," Brad said, clearly meaning it.

Inside, a few people were hanging out at the bar. The place offered live country music on the weekends and had a mechanical bull, but even the bull looked forlorn that night.

"I guess Brad's been hitting up a lot of the locals," Mason said, as they collected their drinks from the bar and took chairs at a high table.

"What do you mean?" Kendall asked, looking around at the mostly empty place.

"Cops," Mason said. "Off-duty cops."

Kendall turned in the direction he'd indicated and saw a couple of the cops who worked the French Quarter during the day. Sam Stuart was there, a nice guy of about thirty, with a little paunch, and Tim Yates, the same age, but dark-haired, fit, and something of a local Lothario. She had always steered clear of him; he had a slick line, and she didn't need to read the tarot cards to know he thought of himself as a player and only wanted to add more notches to his belt. He was a good cop, though. He had stood fast during the terrible ordeal of Katrina and the lawless chaos that followed.

A third man joined them at the table, a man there was no mistaking. Hal Vincent was tall, and his close-cropped hair was shockingly white. He was lean and straight as a ramrod. He'd taken down some of the city's toughest criminals and gained the respect of his fellow officers, as well as the public. She'd heard he was working homicide these days.

He sat down with his fellows, a tall beer in his hand. He joked as he sat, then looked up and saw Kendall and Mason.

He frowned, as if he were seeing a picture he shouldn't be seeing, then said something to the other two cops and came over to say hello.

"Hey, you two. Kendall, haven't seen you in a while. How are you doing?"

"Fine, Hal, thanks. And you?"

He nodded. "Doing all right."

"I haven't seen you around for a while," Mason said.

"Thank God. We don't need murder in the French Quarter. We're getting a bad enough rap for the violence in certain areas as it is."

"You here just trying to help Brad build his business back up, too?" Mason asked.

"Yeah, I guess. Didn't really have anything else to do. My wife is away for a while, taking care of her mother over in

Crowley. Broken hip. I'm kind of lost without her giving me chores at night."

"We're going down the street in a few minutes to catch Vinnie's band," Kendall offered.

"Yeah. Kendall just decided we needed three beers for the price of one first," Mason explained.

Kendall looked at the glasses on the table in front of her. She'd told the bartender she didn't really need three beers, that she wouldn't be able to drink them in the time they had.

But she had downed one quickly, and now she was in the middle of the second.

"Never knew you to be a drinker before," Hal said with a laugh.

"I guess I was thirsty."

"Probably just wanted to drown out the voices in her head, now that she's decided she's a real psychic," Mason said in a teasing whisper.

"Oh?" Hal asked.

"Pay no attention to Mason," Kendall cautioned. "He just likes to torment me."

"She's taking old Ady Murphy to the doctor on Thursday. She's convinced the woman she has cancer."

"You get a feel for these things when you spend time taking care of someone who's ill," Kendall said, trying to sound perfectly calm and logical—and just slightly aggravated.

Hal looked at her and nodded. "Guess you were spending most of your time up at the old Flynn place, huh?"

"A lot of my time, yes," she agreed.

To Kendall's surprise, Hal said thoughtfully, "Maybe that place really does have some kind of weird vibe."

"What?" Kendall asked, startled.

"Met the guy taking over," Hal said.

"There are three guys taking over," she pointed out.

"I'm talking about the oldest brother," Hal said. "I got a call to meet him at the river, and then at the house. The guy seems to have a knack for finding human bones. No, not just finding them—getting obsessed with them."

"Well," Kendall said, surprised to hear herself defending Aidan Flynn, "you've got to admit, most people would get concerned if they found even one human bone, much less two."

Hal took a long swig of his beer. "Not around here," he said sadly. "Not around here. Hell, we had bodies everywhere...." He lowered his head, shaking it. "Everybody failed us...city, parish, state, country."

Kendall set a gentle hand on his arm. "I know, but that doesn't mean we can just give up fighting crime now."

Hal straightened. "Of course not. I'm a good cop, and you know it."

"Of course you are," Kendall agreed. "Hal, you're one of the best."

"Yeah, well, I hope this guy realizes I've got too much on my plate right now to go crazy over a couple of old bones."

"He *is* persistent," Kendall admitted.

She swallowed the last of the second beer and, to her surprise, started on the third.

"So, Hal," Mason said, "want to come see Vinnie with us?"

"I'll come by in a bit," Hal said, then winked at Kendall. "I don't want to make it look like an exodus. Might hurt Brad's feelings."

"Good thinking," she told him.

She was surprised to find she had already finished the last of her three-for-ones. The alcohol seemed soothing tonight.

She slid off her stool and discovered that the world was teetering just a bit. Damn, she was actually tipsy.

She immediately sought to cover up her inebriated state. She stood very straight, perfectly balanced. "Okay, Mason. Let's go claim a table while it's early, just in case the place starts to get crowded later. Hal, we'll see you over there."

She wasn't so sure Hal would really come, though, because Brad had wisely decided to keep the level of his canned music down. It might be one of the only places on Bourbon where people could actually hear each other talk.

There was more of a crowd listening to Vinnie tonight, but even so, Mason spotted an empty table toward the front. As she started to weave her way through the dancers and the other tables, she looked up to see Vinnie staring at her. He offered her a huge smile, and she was glad that Mason had guilted her into coming, despite the strangeness of her day.

Besides, she was probably just imagining things. She was overtired, and her mind was playing tricks.

That was absolutely it, she decided.

She smiled back at Vinnie and waved, then sat down and leaned back to enjoy the band. Mason arrived a minute later—carrying another three beers. All the bars seemed to be using the same early evening come-on.

"I can't drink three more beers," she told Mason.

He raised his voice to be heard above the music.

"You said you couldn't drink the first three, either."

True. She lifted one of the bottles to him in a toast. "Thanks for making me come out tonight."

"My pleasure. I like hanging out here. I do it a lot."

"Too much alcohol," she said sternly.

"Yes, Miss Prim. Although I've been known to have three sodas for the price of one, you know," he said in mock indignation.

"Not tonight."

"Hell, no, not tonight. Tonight I'm trying to keep pace with *you.*"

She made a face at him. Just then a waitress came by, and Mason took it into his head to order a large plate of chicken wings and a large order of fries. The food seemed to help some with the tipsiness, she decided, once it arrived.

As she nibbled on a chicken wing, she noticed an older black man who was one of the place's regulars. He noticed her, too, and smiled and lifted a hand, then turned his attention back to the band.

One day, she decided, when she hadn't been drinking so much, she was going to introduce herself to the guy, seeing as she saw him so often. She loved New Orleans because it was home to such a mix of people, and he was a part of that mix. Black, white and maybe something else. Asian? Indian? She wasn't certain.

The group took a break then, and Vinnie came over and sat down at their table. "Hey, you—you ran out on me last night," he told Kendall, but he was smiling to take the sting out of the accusation.

"I'm sorry, Vinnie. But I'm here now." She grinned at him.

Vinnie looked at Mason. "She's tipsy," he said, amazed.

"I know," Mason said, laughing.

"'She' is *not* tipsy," Kendall protested.

"The place seems to be doing a pretty good business," Mason said, "especially for this early in the week."

"Yeah," Vinnie agreed. "We lucked out and got some free PR. This guy Jeremy Flynn—one of those guys who inherited that plantation of yours, Kendall—has been talking us up when he pushes that charity bash he's planning."

"It was never *my* plantation, Vinnie," Kendall objected.

"Whatever." He waved away her objection. "He's sitting in when we come back from our break."

"If he's playing, how am I going to hear the new song?" Kendall asked. Her good mood was evaporating. She didn't know why. Jeremy Flynn hadn't done anything to her. His older brother was the one she didn't like. Didn't *want* to like, a small voice whispered inside her.

All of a sudden, she felt uncomfortable. She looked around, trying to figure out what could be upsetting her, but the clientele hadn't changed all that much from the night before. There was a group of businessmen, their ties loosened, to the far right. She was pretty sure she had actually seen one or two of them the night before. Hal had come in, as he had promised, and was hanging out in the back with the other two cops he'd been with earlier. There was a man she vaguely recognized sitting alone at a table to her left.

And then the brothers Flynn arrived.

Vinnie saw them, too. "There they are," he said cheerfully and waved at them.

"We've only got one extra seat," Kendall quickly pointed out, shocked by how strongly she wanted Aidan Flynn to stay away.

"That's okay," Vinnie said. "I'm getting up, and Jeremy is playing with us."

He rose and walked through the crowd to greet them, then

led Jeremy with him toward the stage after pointing to the table where Mason and Kendall were sitting.

"Oh," she moaned, sinking into her chair.

"What's the matter with you?" Mason asked, perplexed.

"Nothing."

Zachary and Aidan came and sat down, and their waitress—a pretty girl in a skimpy outfit that showed off her ample cleavage—came hurrying over. The newcomers ordered beers, six of them, which quickly materialized.

Her first beer gone, Kendall reached for a second.

Aidan Flynn, deep eyes as probing as ever, leaned toward her. "I hear we're here tonight because of you," he told her.

"Me?"

"Your friend Vinnie asked Jeremy to sit in so he could concentrate on his vocals. Some new song he wants you to hear, I gather."

Was that a hint of jealousy she heard in his voice? she wondered. No, it couldn't be.

The band was chatting onstage, picking up their instruments. Vinnie seemed unfazed to be handing his precious Fender to Jeremy Flynn. He barely let her touch it. Then again, she wasn't a guitarist.

"Vinnie is a very good friend," she told him.

"I hear you're quite a musician, too," Mason told Zachary.

Zachary shrugged off the compliment. "I like to play. But Jeremy is the one with the real talent."

Mason asked Zachary something about guitars, which unfortunately left Aidan free to lean even closer and converse with her. "I'd like to take you out to eat sometime," he said. "You can tell me more about Amelia."

"Really?" She was still sober enough to be skeptical, she

realized. "I've told you what I know." To her own surprise, she leaned closer. "And you should be careful. You're ticking off the locals."

"I'm sorry. But I have to do what I feel is right," he said flatly, his eyes unwavering.

"You have to understand where you are. We have problems right now. No one has time to be looking into the past."

"I know you can help me. When you just start talking, you help me a lot."

"Help you *what?*" she asked in exasperation.

"Put it all together."

She took another long swallow of her beer. He was like a dog with a bone.

Bone.

She almost laughed.

"You're creating a mystery where there isn't one," she told him. "You found a bone. Two bones. And that's sad, but seriously, it's not a huge surprise."

"The bones? Maybe not. But the blood may prove to mean something."

She started, suddenly feeling very cold. But she didn't get a chance to ask him what he was talking about, because just then the drummer pounded out a rhythm to get the crowd's attention, and then Vinnie took the microphone.

"We want to do a brand-new number for you tonight, one I wrote myself. Well, not entirely by myself. I had a little help from a friend. We started it together about ten years ago, and my cowriter is sitting right in front of me. I think we've got to get her up here to do this with me, don't you?"

There was a roar of approval from the crowd as Vinnie

stared straight at Kendall, one hand stretched out to urge her to the stage.

She wanted to crawl under the table. No, she wanted to fall through the floor. She felt her face flush, the breath rush from her chest.

He *couldn't* be doing this to her!

She glared at Mason, who merely offered her a knowing grin. Damn him. He'd known all about this, she realized.

Oh, God, she'd had a few drinks, but not nearly enough for this. She glared at Vinnie, who just smiled and gestured for her to get moving.

The drunks in the room had started pounding on the tables.

"It will only get worse the longer you delay," Aidan offered in amusement.

She stood, silently cursing Vinnie. The room—especially the drunks—seemed to appreciate the fact that she had just stood up. It was going to be okay. No, it wasn't. If only Aidan hadn't been there...

Maybe she wouldn't care so much about making a fool of herself then.

She closed her eyes for a minute. The room was spinning.

"Never let the world get you down," Amelia had said.

Kendall walked to the front of the room. Maybe she was just drunk enough to see this through.

Vinnie clasped her hand to help her up on the stage. She turned to look out at the room, then realized she shouldn't have. The lights seemed much too bright. She tried to imagine that the room was empty, that no one was there to see her fail as spectacularly as she was sure she was about to.

But then someone got up from a table and left the bar,

ruining her self-delusion. She dimly thought that it might have been the man she'd thought she recognized.

"Ready?" Vinnie whispered excitedly. He was so proud of himself.

"I don't know what you've done with this," she whispered back, trying to maintain a smile. "I haven't thought about it in years."

"Just follow my lead."

The years seemed to fall away. She remembered a time when her parents had still been alive, when she'd assured Vinnie that he was going to grow up to be a great musician. And she had promised she would be right there behind him. So they had sat down and worked out the lyrics, and then Vinnie had penned the chords to go with them.

The drummer counted off, the guitar kicked in and the keyboard carried the melody. To her amazement, she remembered both the lyrics and the tune. She'd always just been the backup, and the changes he had made were easy to follow. She reminded herself that she'd promised to stand behind him, and that this was something he had worked on to honor their friendship. Didn't matter. She still could have killed him. If only he'd let her in on it, if he'd let her practice or…

She hadn't even sung karaoke in years, for heaven's sake.

Somehow she made it through the song. She couldn't decide whether she wished she hadn't had anything to drink or that she'd gotten totally bombed. But eventually it was over, and she gave thanks for drunks, because they made for the least discerning audience she'd ever seen.

Only as Vinnie hugged her and gave her a kiss on the cheek and introduced her to the crowd, explaining how they had grown up together, did she feel that familiar sense of unease settle over her again.

She didn't want to be pointed out to the crowd.

Mason helped her down from the stage. But when she reached their table, she realized that at least part of her fear had been for nothing.

Neither Aidan nor Zachary was still at the table.

She felt strangely deflated. She ought to feel relieved, but instead she was inexplicably…

Disappointed.

"I thought you quit," Aidan commented, watching as Jonas lit up another cigarette.

Jonas gave him a glare. "I did. But being bugged by people like you wore away at my resolve and I started again," Jonas said.

"Jonas, I found dried blood out at the plantation, and I collected a sample. It needs to be analyzed."

"I'll make sure the lab sees what they can do with it. But we both know, if it's compromised enough, nothing will come from it."

"I know that, but I'm hoping you'll take this matter a little more seriously now," Aidan said impatiently.

Jonas laid a hand on Aidan's shoulder. "Look, we're old friends. You were one of the best the Academy ever turned out. But…" He paused, shook his head and continued. "When Serena died, something happened to you. You have to get a grip, buddy."

"Serena died three years ago. And now you tell me to get a grip on myself?"

"Just take it from me—we will do our best to analyze that

blood. And while we're waiting, cool down… In the meantime, you can't go barging into the medical examiner's office or calling the local homicide guy and just generally driving everyone crazy. Due process, okay?"

Aidan looked at him and nodded.

Jonas had asked him to come out back with him just after Aidan had noticed that Hal Vincent—who had been hanging in the back of the room—had made a sudden departure. He wondered if there was a connection. Maybe he really was making himself a local pariah.

He had headed straight for Jonas's office after finding the blood, certain that he didn't want to go back to Jon Abel and not at all sure Hal Vincent was in a mood to pay him any attention.

But he hadn't done a damned thing tonight to make Hal walk out. He'd just taken a seat with his brother to hear the music.

"So," Jonas said, looking at him, "stop following us around."

"What?"

"You came here because…we hang out here, right?"

Aidan laughed. "Get over yourself, Jonas. I came here because my brother was asked to sit in with the band."

"Oh." Jonas stared at him. Then *he* laughed, too. "Oh."

"You didn't realize that was Jeremy up there?" Aidan asked.

Jonas shook his head sheepishly. "Sorry. I just saw you sitting there, like you were going to start interrogating the Montgomery girl who took care of Amelia."

"No, the Montgomery girl, as you call her, is friends with Vinnie, the guy she just went up to sing with," Aidan explained, realizing that because of this conversation, he'd missed hearing Kendall sing.

She'd definitely been a little drunk tonight, he thought.

Maybe enough to make her say more of what she might be thinking.

"I'm not following you around. So chill."

"I think I'll head home anyway."

"Your wife didn't join you tonight."

"She doesn't join me every night," Jonas said, sounding defensive. "I like to hang out with the guys sometimes."

Aidan didn't think he'd spoken with any reproach; maybe Jonas was suffering from a guilty conscience.

Jonas waved and started off down the alley toward Bourbon. If he'd been asked to walk a straight line, Aidan knew he wouldn't have made it.

Aidan started back into the bar alone.

He should have expected it, he thought, when he saw Zach still at the table with Mason and no sign of Kendall Montgomery.

Aidan hesitated, but he knew where Kendall lived.

With a shrug, he headed back outside and started in that direction.

A headache had started knocking against her skull the minute Kendall had left the stage. She had quickly kissed Mason on the cheek and made a hasty departure.

Bourbon Street was no problem to traverse, despite several groups who were three sheets to the wind. But she cut over to Royal more quickly than she had intended. With her head pounding, she just wanted to get away from the crowds. To her amazement, she wound up disoriented and ended up close to Canal before realizing she was going in the wrong direction. She must have been even drunker than she realized, because she should have been able to walk home in her sleep.

She silently cursed Vinnie as she finally headed in the right direction. He had gotten her all upset with that surprise of his. On top of that, she couldn't help but feel a little hurt. With the man plaguing her for assistance, she would have thought he could sit through her song, just to be polite. Then she cursed her own insecurity and forced Aidan Flynn out of her mind.

No going out tomorrow night. She was going straight home after work.

She was about a block from her house when she thought she heard someone calling her name.

She paused and looked back. Nothing. She looked around; she was already on a mostly residential block of Royal. Windows were closed; the streetlights flickered. She felt alone, chilled. A mule-drawn carriage full of tourists went by on the cross street, and she taunted herself for being an idiot. She had walked this way hundreds of times in her life. She'd never seen so much as a fistfight in this neighborhood.

She turned for home again, then became convinced that she heard footsteps following her.

She turned again, and again there was nothing. But the chill had returned, and this time there was no carriage passing by to provide the illusion that she wasn't alone.

She quickened her pace, then thought she saw a shadow emerging from a narrow alleyway.

Instinct—and fear—took over.

She started to run.

7

Kendall heard someone call her name—loudly.

Loudly enough to carry down the street.

She stopped and turned, panting slightly, relieved to see that she wasn't being hailed by a shadow but by a flesh-and-blood man. She saw him coming down the street and recognized him immediately, though from this distance, it was only his tall, broad-shouldered form she knew.

Was she crazy? Or had the shadow she thought she'd seen by the alley disappeared?

When Aidan Flynn reached her a moment later, she knew her heart was still pounding too quickly. "Were you calling my name before?" she asked him.

"No, just now. Why?" he asked, looking at her curiously.

"Must have been someone else," she said. Her head was throbbing, and she didn't want to accept the fact that he had hurt her feelings by ducking out earlier.

"What do you want?" she demanded.

"You never answered me," he said.

"About what?"

"Dinner."

"What?"

"Dinner. Whatever you'd like, wherever you'd like to go."

"Out of the Quarter," she said without thinking.

What the hell would have been wrong with, "Thanks, but no thanks?" she thought immediately.

"Sure. Out of the city entirely, if you like."

"I can't tell you anything helpful, you know," she said, and was alarmed that she sounded almost as if she were pleading with him.

"Maybe. Maybe not."

"You could at least try being polite to me, you know."

He drew in a breath, looking away. "I guess I'm not known for my charm," he said ruefully. "But, I swear, I *can* be courteous."

"You know, I can afford to feed myself. I make a good living, even if you consider me to be a quack."

"Do you think you can read the future?" he asked her.

"No," she said flatly.

Then he smiled. She hated the smile. It didn't just make him human. It made him ruggedly striking. Sexy and even charming.

She took a step back. She wasn't about to be charmed by him.

He was ex-FBI, she reminded herself. He had, no doubt, been taught to be charming when necessary as an interrogation technique.

"You're crazy, and you're driving everyone else crazy," she told him.

His smile deepened suddenly. "Let me see you the rest of the way home."

"I live on the next block."

"I know."

They started walking, and Kendall remembered his earlier claim.

"You said you found blood?" she asked.

"On one of the gravestones," he agreed. "Old blood," he added, when she stopped and stared at him.

"How old?"

"I don't know. I took some scrapings and brought the samples to Jonas."

"Jonas the FBI guy who was there tonight?"

"Right. We're old friends," he told her.

They reached her front door. She hesitated, then slipped her key into the lock and looked up at him, praying he would go away.

He laughed. "Don't worry. I'll see you all the way in."

"I've lived here a long time," she told him. "I have nice neighbors."

"I'm sure you do. But I'll still see you in."

She stepped into the hallway and unlocked the door to her apartment, relieved when he didn't try to follow her in.

He did catch her arm before she could enter, though.

"Dinner? Tomorrow night?" he asked her.

"Yes, yes, I suppose. Just go away now, all right?"

"Sure," he said and, smiling, released her arm and turned away.

She watched him go out the main door, heard the lock click automatically in his wake.

The world was still spinning and her headache was getting worse, but only one thought was plaguing her as she leaned against the door.

Damn, but she hated it when he smiled.

Impatient with herself, she noted that though the evening

had begun early, it had gotten late. Well, *later*, since New Orleans's standards of late had little to do with the rest of the world. It was ten o'clock, so at least she hadn't gone through as much beer as quickly as she'd feared.

In the bathroom medicine cabinet, she found some aspirin. Swallowing a few, she remembered that she hadn't eaten, either, and decided that a sandwich now might help avert a painful morning, so she quickly prepared a grilled cheese on rye, poured herself a mammoth iced tea and sat down to watch the television in her family room.

She shared bits of the grilled cheese with Jezebel, after which the cat slept lazily at her side, completely happy.

The drapes to the courtyard were open. As Kendall watched TV, she felt as if her peripheral vision was catching shadows. She gave up her attempt to watch the show and looked out toward the back. Unnerved, she stood up and pulled the drapes across the double French doors.

She was making herself crazy, she thought. Maybe she had started going crazy along with Amelia.

No. She had taken enough psychology classes to understand that emotions could easily cause the mind to play tricks. Fear fed on fear. A bit of uncertainty could undermine all logic.

She was going to bed, she decided firmly.

In her bedroom, she turned on the television to keep her company and fell asleep watching reruns.

She didn't know if she started to dream because she'd been thinking so much about Amelia, or because she'd fallen asleep watching *The Addams Family*.

At first, it was a whimsical and fun dream. She was outside at the Flynn plantation, and she was so light that she almost floated as she moved. She glided up to the front door, where the knocker smiled, then giggled and said, "Ouch!" when she reached for it.

She realized she was dreaming and groaned, mocking herself. It was *Through the Looking Glass* all over again! She couldn't even come up with an original dream.

The door opened on its own, beckoning her in, and she headed for the staircase. From the ballroom, she could hear singing, so she stopped to look in. Vinnie and the Stakes were playing, floating in mid-air. Vinnie waved and tried to get her to come sing with him. She shook her head and moved into the next room. The dream grew darker then. The room looked like a mad scientist's lair. Someone in a lab coat was hanging bone pieces on a wire frame in the shape of a skeleton. The head was in place, and it was talking, empty eye sockets turned in Kendall's direction.

She quickly slammed the door. Somehow she knew that she was supposed to go upstairs, so she forced herself to move on to the stairway.

When she looked up, there was a woman at the top of the stairway. *A woman in white.* And she was beckoning Kendall to follow.

Kendall didn't want to, but she couldn't stop herself from gliding upward. She couldn't really see the woman's face, but she heard her words.

"You have the diary!" The tone was accusing.

Kendall tried to jolt herself awake.

Yes, she had the diary, but she was planning to give it back. She just hadn't finished reading it yet.

She wanted to scream. She wanted to wake up. Even though nothing overtly threatening had happened, she was terrified that something would happen to her if she didn't—and didn't they say that if you died in your dreams, you would die for real?

She felt a gentle touch. The woman in white was gone and now Amelia was there.

"They just need help," she said. "We have to help them, Kendall. Don't you see?"

There was a sudden scream in the night. A loud, horrified scream.

"If I'd only had the strength to help them," Amelia said, shaking her head slowly.

Her touch on Kendall's cheek felt so very real….

I have to wake up, Kendall told herself. *I have to wake up!*

The awful scream came again.

Amelia's image faded away, and the scream faded with her.

Kendall found herself falling, falling because the stairway had disintegrated to dust and there was nothing but a giant black abyss beneath her.

She woke with a start, covered in a sheen of sweat. For long moments she gasped, the dream still terrifyingly vivid in her mind.

The sound of the television pulled her back to reality. An infomercial had come on. Couples were expounding on the joys of an erectile dysfunction pill.

She leaned back, almost smiling at herself. She knew she should never drink more than one or two beers, at the most. She just couldn't hold her liquor. She was all right; she was just combining thoughts of her recent life with visions from some of the more inventive authors she loved.

Everything made sense when she thought about it that way.

She started to go to sleep again, but she still wanted the TV on, so she flicked it to a channel that was showing old cartoons.

When she straightened her legs, getting comfortable, she felt something at the foot of the bed.

"Jezebel, you little rat. You're scaring me," she said, half laughing and half angry.

But even as she spoke, she saw Jezebel across the room, sleeping on one of the throw pillows Kendall had tossed onto the floor when she got into bed.

She frowned, then felt around under the comforter to find out what was in the bed with her.

She looked at what she'd found, then gasped and jumped back so fast that she slammed against the headboard.

It was the diary.

The diary she had taken from the Flynn house.

The diary that should still have been in her backpack.

Jonas was hiding something, Aidan thought.

An affair? Maybe.

But there was no reason why he should have been as defensive as he had been. Of course, he'd been drinking, and if he'd been drinking a lot, that alone might have made him feel paranoid.

Aidan didn't know what kind of reaction he was going to get when he paid a visit to Jonas the following morning, but he knew he couldn't sit idle.

He'd never worked in the office here, but he'd gotten help from the Bureau staff before. He knew that in a country full of various and competing law enforcement agencies, there were bound to be a few bad eggs. But in general, people who went into law enforcement did so because they wanted to uphold the law, because they believed in their country and its legal system, and wanted to be helpful. Still, due to the kinds of cases they worked, the FBI tended to be more guarded than most other agencies, other than Homeland Security, and they saw a threat in everything. That was what they were paid to do.

Aidan arrived at the office early on Wednesday morning. He asked to see Jonas Burningham, half expecting Jonas to try to evade him, just as Jon Abel had done. He'd brought in the vial of dried blood yesterday, and Jonas had sighed wearily, but he had taken it. Aidan was certain, however, that it hadn't been given priority.

Jonas came out to the main reception area to shake his hand and ask him back to his office. Once there, he closed the door, took his seat behind the desk and rested his forehead on his palm. "What now? More blood? More bones? Did you dig up a whole body?"

"No."

Jonas looked up suspiciously. "What are you here for, then? I hope you're not about to give me a lecture on the pitfalls of Bourbon Street."

"Why would I do that?"

"Because you've gotten strange."

"I haven't gotten strange."

"You used to be thorough. But now you're a pit bull."

"Can't help it. It's my nature. And I didn't come to torture you. I just wanted to see if you had any open missing-persons cases."

Jonas stared at him. "Are you kidding me?"

"No."

"Do you know how many people are still missing after the storm?"

Aidan shook his head. "I want recent cases. Women who might have been in this area or headed for this area when they disappeared."

Jonas sighed.

"Come on, Jonas. Humor me."

Jonas nodded slowly. Aidan had the feeling that he was going to help, not because Aidan was a good investigator, but because he wanted him to go away.

"I'll call Hirshfield, my assistant, and ask him to get you the relevant files from the last year. Will that do?"

"That'll be great. Thanks."

Jonas didn't use his phone to call his assistant; he left the room. Was he going to ask Hirshfield to filter the files he was going to let Aidan see? Why would he do that?

He was gone a long time. So long that Aidan began to suspect that he might have led him on just to ditch him somehow anyway. After all, he was under no obligation to give Aidan any help. Aidan's relationship with the Bureau remained good, but once you were gone, you were off any kind of priority list. Friendship was all he had left.

Just when Aidan was about to give up and leave, Jonas returned. He seemed nervous. He ran a finger beneath his collar and handed a stuffed manila envelope to Aidan. "This is everything that might be helpful in any way. Everything."

"Thanks, buddy."

"So, Bourbon Street is your new hangout, too, huh?"

"I don't really have a hangout." Aidan hesitated. "Seems like folks *are* drawn to that bar."

"One local frequents a place, others follow. Locals go

there because they know they'll find other locals there. That's the way it goes. Or are you saying there's something spooky going on? Shit, maybe you're right. Maybe people *are* drawn there. Who the hell knows?" He changed the subject. "Are you going to move out to the house?"

"I hadn't intended to. There's a lot of work going on there. We hired a contractor after the engineer gave us a thumbs-up," Aidan told him.

"Well, good luck with it."

"Yeah, thanks."

Aidan took the files with him back to his hotel, where he hesitated, then gave Jeremy a call. Odd, they were a close family, but they each had a different place in the city where they preferred to stay. He was at the Monteleone, which was family-owned and where the current boss had gone above and beyond for his employees after the storm. Jeremy preferred a small place on the other side of Jackson Square called the Provincial. Zach was especially fond of a certain bed-and-breakfast.

"Hey. How's it going?" he asked, when his brother answered his cell phone.

"Well, I visited my friends at the police station," Jeremy told him.

"Yeah?"

"I'm going through the information I got. You?"

"I got what I could from Jonas. I'm about to start going through the files now. Where's Zach?"

"At the house, with the contractor. He's been playing on the computer, says he has some facts and figures that might prove interesting. He said we should meet at the house tomorrow. He's convinced the place can be ready by the end

of the month, so we can host that benefit for displaced kids."
Jeremy's tone showed how grateful he was that at least one
of his brothers was embracing his cause.

Strange, Aidan thought. We all look so damned normal
and even strong. But every one of us gets obsessed, as if
somehow we can erase the horrors of our past.

"Good. We can talk more tomorrow."

Jeremy agreed. Aidan rang off and started on the files.

Jonas had been as good as his word. He hadn't held
anything back. He had in fact given Aidan far more than he'd
needed to. Most of the files were worthless; they were just
reports that had gone out, and the person might have been
anywhere. Many looked as if no foul play was involved; they
concerned people who had wanted to break with the past and
start over somewhere else. Some were of people who had
apparently disappeared, only to reappear.

But there were a few that seemed relevant, and one of
those caught his attention right away.

Jenny Trent.

She'd left Lafayette for New Orleans three months ago,
planning to spend one night before heading for the airport
early in the morning. Her disappearance hadn't been reported for over a month, because she was a teacher on
summer vacation and had only one living relative, her cousin's widow, Betty Trent. Betty, raising three children on her
own, hadn't reported that Jenny was missing until the school
had called her, as next of kin, to find out why Jenny hadn't
returned to work.

Jenny was described as standing five feet three inches tall
and weighing one hundred and ten pounds. At twenty-eight,
she'd worked hard and, after six years of teaching, saved up

for her dream trip to South America, where she had planned to remain for twenty-eight days. An investigation of her home computer had shown that she'd printed her boarding pass; checking with the airlines had shown that she'd never boarded the plane that was to take her to Caracas via Miami.

No one knew where she had stayed—or planned to—in New Orleans. Her credit card receipts hadn't led the police anywhere.

If she was dead, it had only been three months. Not time enough for her body to have decayed down to nothing but bone. Unless the process had been given some help. If she'd been cut into pieces, then left out in the intense, baking heat of New Orleans or hidden in a shallow grave, it might just be possible. He wasn't a forensic expert, but he'd been around enough crime scenes, and five-three would fit the length of the first bone he'd found.

He was grasping at straws, he knew, but he just had a feeling, and over the years, he'd learned to trust his gut. As he read the file, he felt a surge of indignation. Here was a young woman who had done all the right things: she'd studied, landed a good job. She'd worked; she'd saved. She'd planned a long-dreamed-of holiday—and she had disappeared. And with only an in-law—a woman trying to raise a family alone—to pursue what had happened, the trail had grown cold and the case had been shelved.

There were a few other files that appeared interesting, but Jenny Trent's seemed to be the most on the money.

He picked up the phone and called Jeremy.

"I thought we were meeting in a few hours," his brother said.

"We are. Do you have anything on a Jenny Trent?"

"Yeah, I have that file right on top, as a matter of fact."

"What I have says there are no credit card receipts for a hotel, motel or bed-and-breakfast. I don't have any of the other charge records. Do you have anything?" Aidan told him.

"I have a list of merchants. Most of them we'd have to track down, but…get this. She has a charge from a place we know and love," Jeremy said.

"Yeah?"

"The Lair of the Undead."

The name didn't mean anything to Aidan. "And that is…?"

"The corporate name for the Hideaway—the bar where I played last night."

"Ah," Aidan murmured. He wondered why the owners didn't just call the place The Lair of the Undead. It seemed a lot catchier. "What do you have for next of kin?" Aidan asked.

"Mrs. Betty Trent, cousin-in-law, Lafayette."

"Same as I have. I think I'll go talk to Mrs. Trent."

"It's a two-hour drive, Aidan."

"I know. I need you to do something for me."

"What?"

"Drop by Tea and Tarot, on Royal."

"To see the very impressive Miss Montgomery?"

"Impressive?" Aidan asked. Yes, she was impressive, he admitted. But why was Jeremy saying so?

"Oh, that's right. You missed her performance last night," Jeremy said. "She's quite a singer. I wonder why she's running a psychic place," Jeremy mused. "So…why am I going to see her?"

Aidan looked at his watch. He needed five hours.

"Tell her I'll pick her up at her place at seven-thirty."

"Okay." Jeremy didn't ask why, but the question was in his voice.

"I think she can tell me more about the Flynn plantation."

"Sure," Jeremy said.

"And…I'd like to find out more about her relationship with Vinnie."

"Vinnie from the Stakes?" Jeremy asked.

"Yeah. Your buddy. How well do you know the guy?"

"Not well at all, really, other than musically."

"Doesn't he seem a little weird to you?"

"The costume?" Jeremy asked, amused. "Hell, brother, it's Bourbon Street."

"Hang around for a while. See if you can find out more about Vinnie and Mason Adler."

"Because they know her and hang out at the bar? Aidan, you'll have to get to know half the people in the city if that strikes you as suspicious—the place is a local hangout."

"Might as well start with two out of the tons, huh?"

"Sure. No problem." Whatever Jeremy was thinking, he didn't say more. They rang off, and Aidan called down for his car.

Kendall felt like absolute hell. It wasn't a hangover; it was the lack of sleep, or rather, the unmercifully restless sleep she had endured after discovering the diary in her bed.

She couldn't escape the feeling that it wanted to be read.

Ridiculous. People wanted other people to read books; books themselves didn't ask to be read. But no one had been in her apartment in the last few days, except for Aidan Flynn, and he had never been alone in her room.

Besides, as much as she resented the man, she couldn't see

him sneaking into her bedroom to slip a book beneath her covers. People sometimes did things subconsciously, so she must have taken the book out of the backpack herself, and for some bizarre reason, put it in her bed, then forgotten what she'd done. Easy enough, a sensible answer. She must have been thinking about something else and remembering that she hadn't finished the diary, absentmindedly picked it up and tossed it on the bed. She should have been more careful with it. The diary was remarkably well-preserved, but it was still over a hundred and fifty years old and probably very valuable.

And it definitely needed to go back to the heirs.

But not until she finished reading it.

She thanked God that morning that she never opened until ten, that Mason was capable of taking care of things until she showed up, and that things would probably be slow, since it was a Wednesday. Weekenders might take off a Friday, or even a Thursday, to create a mini vacation. Or, they might stay over Monday, or even Tuesday, in the same vein. But Wednesday was usually the deadest day of the week. Once she pulled herself together and went in, she might even be able to make herself a cup of tea, munch on a pastry and chill out in the back, reading, all day. Not especially good for the bottom line, but today, it would work.

She wrapped the diary in a protective book cover stitched by a local artist, slipped it into her large carryall and headed out.

When she reached the shop, Mason was there and hard at work, dealing with boxes strewn all over the place.

"Halloween," he said happily, as she entered. Then he paused, looking at her. "Coffee is brewed. And you look like shit."

"Thanks so much."

"It's true."

"I couldn't sleep last night."

"Hangover?" he teased.

"If I had a hangover, it would be all your fault. But, honestly, I just didn't sleep."

"Coffee will help," he said. "We have to deal with all this. We're running late getting the decorations up."

So much for her dream of spending the day in reading and recovery.

They *were* running late. Even with Vinnie's help, Mason couldn't do everything, and she had been gone so much when Amelia was ill. Even though her friend had died several months ago now, Kendall still felt as if she were playing catch-up.

"Coffee," Mason said, handing her a cup.

Tea might be their specialty, but she carried flavored coffees, as well, and Mason had brewed a pot just the way she needed it: strong.

She sipped it as she watched him unwrap a lifelike skeleton wearing a pirate hat and carrying a realistic, albeit plastic, sword. "By the door," she told him.

"Absolutely," he agreed.

She finished her coffee and, with the renewed energy it brought, her desire to go through the boxes of decorations awoke. She sat on the floor and dove in, and between them they soon had the place looking ready for Halloween, boxing a few of the more ordinary items that had been on the shelves to make room for the holiday pieces.

In an hour, Vinnie made an appearance. He had a grin on

his face as he looked at Kendall, as if he had arranged for her to win the lottery.

"Well?" he demanded.

"Well, you took me by surprise, all right," she told him.

"Kendall, you were fabulous. Everyone was clamoring to hear you up there again."

"Vinnie, I could kill you. We wrote that a decade ago, at least. And don't you think you might have asked me if I wanted to join you?"

"If I'd asked, you'd have said no. You've got to start working with the band. And what about that dream you had in college of founding a community theater?" he demanded.

"I opened a shop, and I love my shop," she said.

"So keep the shop. It's a good backup plan. Come on, you have to start working with me again. You used to have dreams, remember?"

"And now I have bills. Vinnie, help Mason get that pumpkin hung up, huh?"

"You look beat," Mason commented, when Vinnie went over to help him.

Vinnie flushed. Kendall found herself studying her friend. He was still as slim now as he'd been in college, but the darkness of his hair and eyes gave him a compelling appeal; he would fit right into any vampire movie. He did look tired, though.

But he smiled. "I had a hot date."

"Oh?" Mason asked.

Vinnie grinned again. "A cute little coed out of Boston. Hot, hot, hot."

"You seeing her again?" Mason asked.

Vinnie laughed. "No, she's heading home today. But I

didn't mind being her New Orleans adventure. I mean she could—"

"Vinnie, we do not want details," Kendall protested.

"I do," Mason said.

Kendall groaned.

"Maybe you *need* the details," Mason teased her. "I'm worried you've forgotten how it's done."

Before Vinnie could answer, the little bell above the door jingled and Jeremy Flynn entered. "Hey," Kendall said, surprised to see him. She hadn't thought of him as a tea drinker.

"Place looks great," he said. "All ready for Halloween."

"We're getting there," she told him.

"You want to play with us again tonight?" Vinnie asked him.

"Probably not tonight," Jeremy said. "I've got some work to take care of."

"Are you interested in a tarot reading?" Mason asked.

"Not today," Jeremy said. "I just came by to tell Kendall that Aidan is going to pick her up at her apartment tonight at seven-thirty."

Kendall felt her face redden deeply. Both Vinnie and Mason stared at her.

"Oh," Mason said.

"Oh, indeed," Vinnie echoed.

"Thanks, Jeremy," she said. She was tempted to ask him to tell his brother that she couldn't go. After all, she had agreed merely to get him to go away. "He wants to talk about the house," she said, looking at Mason and Vinnie, then realized she had snapped out the words.

The bell rang again, and a pair of pretty young women

entered. One was wearing a Saints T-shirt; the other was in a halter top. "Oh, my God, this is the neatest place!" exclaimed the girl in the halter top.

"Thanks, may I help you?" Kendall asked, glad of the interruption.

The two girls started to giggle. "Sorry," said the shorter girl, "we're just a little nervous. We came for readings. Is it possible?"

Kendall didn't know why she hesitated before answering. Yes, she did. Jeremy Flynn was there. She was afraid he would tell his brother and Aidan Flynn would think she was even more of a nutcase.

"Absolutely." Mason stepped forward and said, "Vinnie, you gonna hang around a bit?"

"Sure," Vinnie said, "I can watch the place. Hey, Jeremy, you want some coffee? I see it's already made."

"I'd love some," Jeremy said.

"Perfect," Mason said, then turned to the girls. "Kendall and I will be glad to read for you."

Before Kendall had a chance to object, he had everything arranged.

Kendall told herself to calm down. So what if Jeremy Flynn went back and told Aidan what she'd been doing? This was her business. It was how she lived. She entered the little room where she did her readings, introduced herself and discovered that the girl she was reading for was named Ann, asked her if she was enjoying New Orleans, then handed her the tarot deck, instructing her to cut it.

Kendall turned over the first card. Death, personified by a skeleton, appeared, and suddenly the room seemed to fill with fog.

And the skeleton on the card seemed to come to life.

8

A dog barked from somewhere as Aidan pulled up at the suburban home of Betty Trent. The houses weren't large or expensive, but the lawns were manicured and the fences were painted. It seemed like a place where people didn't have much but worked hard with what they did have.

As he exited the car, he saw a gate to a backyard, where a woman of about thirty-five was hanging laundry. Near her, a child of four or five was playing on a tricycle.

He didn't want to startle the woman, so he called out as he approached, asking if she was Betty Trent. She frowned as she looked up, then studied him with curiosity. She looked wary but not frightened.

"Yes, I'm Betty Trent. Can I help you?"

She had probably been a beauty at a younger age, and she remained an attractive woman, but he saw her hands as she finished hanging a shirt, and they were worn. Deep creases lined her forehead.

He extended his hand. "Hi. My name is Aidan Flynn. I'm a private investigator, and I recently came across your cousin-in-law's file."

A look of hope appeared on her face and was quickly gone

as she met his eyes. He realized that she had hoped at first that he had come with good news and knew now that he hadn't.

"Beginnin' of October, and the days are still mighty hot. Would you like some iced tea, Mr. Flynn?" she asked.

"That would be nice," he said.

She called to the child, whose name was Billy, and explained that her twins were still at school, but that kindergarten ended earlier. She led him into a comfortable ranch-style home with threadbare furniture covered by handsome needlepoint throws.

They sat in the living room. "Well, at least there's interest in the case again," she said. She lifted her hands as if she understood an explanation that had never been given. "They've been busy, the police have. I know that. But it just seems to me that they investigated so far, came to a dead end…and didn't try any detours."

"So according to the records, Jenny's car was found in a public lot. And she checked in for her flight on the computer before she left home, and had something to eat and drink at a place called the Hideaway. Can you add anything to that?"

"That's what I've heard. I told them everything I knew, which wasn't much. It's as if Jenny just…vanished. She told me she was going to spend a night in New Orleans before she left, and that's really all I know."

Betty stood and walked across to an occasional table by the door. She picked up a picture and brought it back to Aidan. It was probably a few years old, but the woman in it had pretty brown eyes and soft brown hair, both glowing. Her smile was hopeful. Her energy and happiness had somehow come out in the picture. Aidan felt a twist in his gut and was glad.

Glad that he was feeling pain? Yeah, it was a good thing. It was better than being numb. And the girl in the picture deserved more than just his obsessive drive; she deserved someone on the case who cared.

"That's Jenny. My husband, Phil, didn't have any family left to speak about, just Jenny. She was eight years younger than he was, but they were pretty close. And I have to say, I grew to love her. She was wonderful with my kids. She had no-account parents who drank themselves to death. Well, Jenny's dad died in the oil fields, but that was because he went to work drunk. She worked so hard and came out on top of it all. She paid her own way through college, and the kids where she taught loved her. She tutored on the side, and in the summers she worked banquets for one of the local catering companies to earn the money for that trip." She paused, looked at him suddenly, and frowned again. "Did someone hire you, Mr. Flynn? You did say you're a *private* investigator, right?"

Even if he'd had some kind of smoke-and-mirrors explanation planned to account for his interest, he wouldn't have used any subterfuge. This woman deserved better.

"No. As it happens, I have just come into some property in the area, and I heard about Jenny in the course of something I was looking into and thought maybe I could do something."

He was startled when a tear suddenly slid down Betty's cheek.

"I don't have any money," she told him.

She looked as if she were going to collapse. Billy had been playing with a Lego set, but now he looked up, distressed.

"Mama?"

"Mama's fine, Billy," Betty said quickly, wiping her face.

"I don't want any money, Mrs. Trent," Aidan assured her firmly. "But if you don't mind, I *am* going to say that you're my client."

She looked at him, shaking her head. "I…don't mean to be looking for charity. Phil died so sudden, of a heart attack…and he was young, and we didn't have life insurance. I don't mean to be complaining—there were so many who lost everything, and I have my boys. But I haven't ever taken any kind of charity, and—"

"Mrs. Trent," he interrupted, "*you'd* be doing *me* the favor." He set the picture aside and took her hands. "Frankly," he said solemnly, "right now the police just think that I'm being a pain in the a—" He remembered Billy and amended what he'd been about to say. "In the butt. With a contract, I'll have a legitimate reason to be a huge pain in the behind and follow any lead I want to. We can draw up a contract in which you pay me a dollar. How's that?"

"But…why? Why would you do this for me? For Jenny?" she asked.

Why?

"I need to know," he told her honestly. "I'm…" He hesitated, but he couldn't think of a better word. "I'm *haunted* by all this. Now, please, sit down and tell me about Jenny. What she liked, what she didn't like. Did she have a boyfriend? Was she friendly, trusting…?" He hesitated for a moment. "Betty, did you ever get any of her things? They said her car was found, but what about her luggage?"

Betty shook her head slowly. "No. And to be honest, I never thought about it. I hadn't expected her to contact me. I prayed for a long time that maybe she had just decided for some reason to go off with someone, go somewhere else. But I knew it wasn't true."

"How?"

"Because I knew Jenny. Oh, the FBI got in on it and everything, thinking maybe she'd crossed state lines or something. But I know it's not true, because if she could have, Jenny *would* have called me. She loved me. And she loved the boys." She took a deep breath. "I know that Jenny is dead. I know it. But I still sure would love to know the truth. Have an ending to it, and see whoever killed her locked up or executed. You didn't know her. They say good Christians shouldn't support the death penalty. But I knew Jenny. I'd happily pull that lever myself if I knew who had hurt her. She deserved to live. Don't you see? She was everything good about the world. I'll do anything I can to help you find the truth."

"Pay me a dollar, Mrs. Trent. That will do it."

He looked at the picture of the lovely young woman with all the promise in her eyes.

And for some reason, just like Betty Trent, he *knew* that she was dead.

And he was almost certain he had touched a part of her earthly remains.

It was as if the card were staring up at Kendall. As if it were mocking her. She could have sworn she heard diabolical laughter, as if Death were being given a gift and she was privy to the knowledge of it, but there was nothing she could do to stop it. She was cold, icy cold, as if the skeleton's fingers were clutching her very bones.

"What? Oh my God, what is it?" Ann cried, alarmed.

Kendall blinked hard and fought the vision. She tore her eyes from the card and focused on the young woman in front of her. "Nothing." Her voice had a tremor. She forced herself to stare at the girl and not down at the card. "It's nothing. I'm so sorry if I frightened you."

"But that's…Death."

"No."

"Yes, look at it!" the girl said.

"No, no, honestly," Kendall insisted. "People see this card and they automatically think the worst, but I swear, that's not the case at all. What this signifies is change, the end of something and the beginning of something else," she went on, forcing her tone to be smooth, even and relaxed.

Even though inside she felt as if she were going crazy.

"An end and a beginning?" the girl asked blankly.

"Have you broken off a relationship lately?" Kendall asked Ann.

Ann's jaw fell. "Oh my God! How did you know?"

Relief swept through Kendall. She was going to be all right. *Ann* was going to be all right. The whole ridiculous thing was going to return to normal.

She started turning over the other cards. "Here, see. Are you planning a trip, maybe?"

"Yes," Ann said in amazement. "I'm heading out on a cruise ship from here."

"That's wonderful," Kendall said, adding silently, *You need to get out of here.*

Oh, God, what had made me think that?

Ann frowned then, totally unaware of Kendall's thoughts. "I'm not going to fall for the same lines and go back with Rodney, am I?"

"Not if you're strong," Kendall answered. That was an easy one.

"Rodney and I…he was a jerk. Such a jerk. He cheated on me, and I knew it. He even hit me once, and then he apologized all over the place, so I took him back, like an idiot. I am *not* going to do it again."

"What the cards really do is tell us what we need to look for in ourselves," Kendall said. "And the important thing— always—is to know that what happens in our lives depends on us."

"Right."

Kendall tried to move on to the other cards without looking at the skeleton again.

But it was still there, mocking her, grinning.

She tried to tell herself that she just needed more sleep. That Ann was not going to die, that she was going on a nice safe cruise. But her thoughts wouldn't stop racing.

What about yesterday, and Miss Ady and the cancer?

Things like this didn't happen to her, she told herself firmly.

But the evidence said they did.

Her hand suddenly jerked across the table.

Ann started again, and Kendall forced herself to laugh. "I'm sorry. Late night last night, I'm afraid."

"Wait, I recognize you," Ann said.

"You do?"

"I saw you sing last night—you and that guy out there, Vinnie. Hey, you two were great."

"Thanks."

Ann kept talking. Vinnie was really wonderful. Vinnie was so cute.

Kendall just nodded absently. Vinnie did have that effect

on women. Meanwhile, she couldn't seem to concentrate. All she could think about was the strange things that seemed to be happening.

Weird sensations. Cards…coming to life. Nothing like this had ever happened to her before, although once or twice she had felt unnerved, uneasy, and the cards had looked… off.

As if she needed an eye doctor.

More sleep. *That* was what she needed.

She heard her own voice. Somehow, despite the absurd panic that kept seizing her, she was speaking, even making sense. She was rising and wishing Ann a great trip and a good life, reminding her that her fate was in her own hands.

Ann left, and Kendall could hear her talking excitedly to her friend and the two men up front in the shop.

"What's with you? You look like you've seen a ghost," Mason asked from the doorway of the room where he'd been doing his reading.

"I'm tired. I told you that," Kendall said.

Mason looked past her into her room. "Hey, your cards are all over the floor," he told her, and swept in to pick them up. "Grab that one right under your feet."

She looked down. The skeleton was looking up at her. Doing nothing, nothing at all.

It was just a tarot card.

And yet, as she reached for it, she felt again as if ice-cold fingers of bone were somehow closing around her heart.

Somehow Aidan managed to get back to the city by six.

He'd made a couple of calls from the road, so after he returned his car to the hotel valet, he walked down the street to meet Jeremy at a quiet place near the old convent school. He filled his brother in on the information he had learned about Jenny Trent, and Jeremy showed him what he'd gotten on her credit card files.

All her charges in the city were from a single day. She had gotten gas at a station just off I-10; she had charged a café au lait and a beignet that morning at Café du Monde. She had purchased a T-shirt on Decatur Street, lunched at Bambu in Harrah's.

He knew already that she'd been to the Hideaway on Bourbon Street that night, and a charge to a business listed as Dreams, LLD, was the only other item.

Aidan looked up at Jeremy. "That address..."

"Yeah, it's Kendall's shop."

"Did you ask her about Jenny, by any chance?"

Jeremy shook his head. "The only picture I have is really grainy. Besides, I knew you were seeing her tonight."

"I have a better picture. Betty Trent provided it." Aidan frowned. "Kendall didn't object when you told her what time I'd be picking her up, did she?" He should have asked if she had protested his coming by for her, period.

"No. She didn't say anything. They had customers. Looked like a couple of Valley girls," Jeremy told him.

Aidan looked at his watch. Six-thirty. He had to be at Kendall's apartment at seven-thirty, but they could walk the few blocks to Bourbon and he could still get back to pick up his car again with time to spare.

"Let's go," he said. "I feel like stopping by the Hideaway."

"Hoping to catch the Stakes again?" Jeremy asked.

Aidan only nodded.

It was exceptionally early by Bourbon Street standards, but the Stakes managed to bring in the locals looking for a quick drink on their way home from work. Jeremy paused to say hello to a few of the cops in the place, probably those who had helped him. Aidan noted that there were a few single people sitting at tables in the shadowy far corners of the place. He chose a spot close to the band. When the waitress came with the beer he'd ordered, he drew out the picture of Jenny Trent.

"Thanks," he said, as she set down his beer. "Mind if I bother you for a minute?" He smiled and dropped a bill far larger than his tab on the tray.

"Sure. And it's three for one tonight. I just thought I'd keep your other two beers cold," she said pleasantly. She was no kid but an attractive woman of about thirty. She wasn't spilling out of her outfit, either. Some people just worked, and worked hard, on Bourbon Street, he thought.

"Do you remember seeing this girl in here?" he asked her.

"Sure," she said, after examining the picture closely for a minute. "A few months ago. She was a sweet kid."

"Was she alone?"

"Wow, that's hard to say. She was friendly. I think she talked to half the people in here that night, including the guys in the band. They might be able to help you."

"Do you remember if she left here with anyone?" Aidan asked.

"You might want to ask the guys about *that,* too," the waitress said, and laughed. "Especially Vinnie. He's always such a flirt. He was taking her requests all night, I remember."

"Thanks," Aidan said.

A minute later, his brother sat down across from him. He

indicated the departing waitress and asked, "She remember seeing Jenny?"

Aidan looked at his watch. Time to go. "Yeah. Hey, I'll be back in here about ten. Keep an eye on your buddy until then, huh? And I guess it wouldn't be a bad thing to take note of some of the other clientele, as well."

"You got it," Jeremy told him, and shrugged. "At least the music is good."

Aidan grinned. The work they had chosen was often deadly dull, watching someone or, worse, some *place* for hours on end. Good music was definitely a plus.

The Stakes's official hours at the bar seemed to be from six to one o'clock in the morning, Aidan noticed on the billboard out front. He had plenty of time.

He headed back to his hotel for his car.

Kendall had never intended to treat her dinner with Aidan Flynn like a date. She had planned to do a little light housekeeping, catch some news or just chill out while she waited for him to come by for her.

But she had been keyed up and nervous all day, though at least there'd been no repeat of the incident with Ann. Her psychology courses weren't helping a bit. Maybe she needed to see a shrink. Tarot cards did not come to life. She tried to tell herself that she was simply playing her role too well. Act like Marie Laveau long enough and it was natural that you would begin to imagine things.

It had been easy to explain away her intuition about Ady Murphy. The woman was old, and she herself was very wary of cancer now, after Amelia's death.

But today…

She poured herself a glass of wine and walked out to her courtyard. To her amazement and distress, she felt uneasy outside, almost exposed. She walked back into the apartment and locked the French doors.

She turned on the evening news. The screen blurred, and her thoughts took control again.

When had the tarot cards seemed…strange before?

The first time, it had been with a stranger. A young woman from Louisiana, but not New Orleans. She was getting ready to go on vacation.…

The second time, it had been with her friend Sheila Anderson, who was also planning a vacation. She'd freely admitted to Sheila that she was really a fraud, that reading cards was just learning which interpretations went with which card, what all the possibilities were. It was kind of like being a therapist or a bartender—listening to what people said—or didn't say. Skeptics were easy to spot, and it didn't pay to try to convince them that anything was possible. It was better to deal with them subtly and let them draw their own conclusions. It was amazing to see the biggest doubters begin to read what they wanted to see into the cards.

She felt her hands trembling and forced herself to keep a grip on her wineglass.

Sheila…

She found that she was suddenly afraid for Sheila.

She told herself that was ridiculous. Sheila was off having the time of her life, and she would be back soon. Safe and sound.

Kendall wished her friend were home already, though. She wished that she could just pick up the phone and call her.

She wished that she didn't feel such a dull sense of fear in her heart. A sense of…

Fatality?

Now that was *truly* absurd.

She looked at her wineglass and realized she had drained it. She was tempted to refill it, but she didn't want to start out an evening with Aidan Flynn half soused. But she needed to do something to distract herself, so she quickly hopped into the shower, then went through her wardrobe, even her jewelry. The clock seemed to crawl.

To her amazement, she couldn't wait for him to come to her door, even though he was the biggest skeptic in history and able to rouse her temper without even trying.

Something brushed against her ankle, and she almost shrieked out loud. She looked down, and managed to laugh, then stooped to pick up Jezebel. The massive Persian snuggled against her. "Sorry, baby. I forgot to feed you," she said.

More busy work. She fed the cat. And then she looked at the clock again, hoping Aidan would be on time.

Jeremy nursed his beer slowly, though he knew the waitress was anxious to bring him another. He would have to go through his brother's extra two and then his own before he needed to order again, and he knew as well that the woman was working for tips. He motioned to her and asked for one of the cold ones, so he could give her a few dollars, even though he was sure his brother had tipped her well. It wouldn't hurt to have the waitstaff on their side.

Without being obvious, he kept track of who was coming into the bar. An attractive black woman of an indeterminate age was there with an Asian woman of about thirty and a brunette Caucasian who looked to be about twenty-five, and the whole group greeted the cops when they arrived, then took a table on the opposite side of the room. He walked over on the pretext of inspecting a poster advertising the upcoming Halloween festivities to listen in. The women turned out to be lab techs from the coroner's office, so it was natural that they were buddies with the cops.

He walked back to his own table and took his seat again, aware that he was being followed. He turned and was surprised to see Jonas Burningham's wife, Matty. She smiled at him. "Mind if I join you?"

"Please do," he told her politely, rising to pull out a chair for her.

She joined him, looking around.

"You out by yourself?" he asked her.

"I…I thought I might find Jonas here," she admitted.

"I guess he comes here a lot after work," Jeremy said.

"I guess," she agreed. She flipped her hair back and looked over at the band. She waved. He wondered who would wave back.

He wasn't surprised to see that it was Vinnie. Good old Vinnie. He knew everyone.

"Do you come here a lot?" Jeremy asked her.

"Now and then," she said. The waitress came over and Matty ordered the house drink, which combined two kinds of rum and three kinds of fruit juice.

The place was filling up. There seemed to be a lot of young people tonight. He heard one girl asking anxiously if she had arrived in time for the three-for-one special. He turned slightly, glad of the table Aidan had chosen, and knowing exactly why he had chosen it. He could easily see the band, the room and the door from here. Someone came in just then to join the party from the coroner's office. None other than Jon Abel.

"Oh, there's Jonas!" Matty said, and smiled, when she saw her husband enter a moment later. She half rose, and her smile faded when she saw Jonas head straight for the bar and immediately start talking to several of the women congregated there.

Jeremy rose. "I'll let him know that you're here," he said. He strode to the bar, easily elbowing his way in next to Jonas.

"So what time does the ship leave in the morning?" Jonas was asking a blonde.

"Early." The girl laughed. "But we're partying it up tonight. You can sleep when you're dead, right?" she added.

"Your wife is here," Jeremy said flatly, without looking at Jonas.

He felt the other man stiffen. "Thanks," he said curtly.

When Jeremy turned to watch, he saw Jonas slick his hair back and smile. "Matty!" he called, as if thrilled beyond measure to see her there.

Jeremy stayed where he was for a moment. Then he looked around curiously, feeling a prickle at his nape telling him that he was being watched. He looked down the bar. The elderly black man with the dignified face was watching him. The other man gave Jeremy a nod of approval, then shook his head with a look of disgust—for men who cheated on their wives, Jeremy assumed. Jeremy smiled in return and decided to go meet the guy. He looked away for a moment to see Jonas sitting with Matty, and when he looked over again, the man was gone.

Jeremy headed back to the table. Not only was Jonas

there, but Jon Abel had also come over. He also noticed that during the few minutes when he'd been at the bar, more people he knew had arrived, as well.

Mason Adler, who saw him, grinned and waved.

And Hal Vincent, homicide cop, who was walking over to join the other cops in the room.

Jeremy caught Hal staring at him. The man didn't seem happy to see him there. Jeremy stared back, but the cop didn't wave at him or otherwise acknowledge that he was there. The guy was probably just tired and feeling harassed by the Flynns.

Mason, however, called out to him. "Hey, you going to go up and play something with the group tonight?"

"Not tonight, I'm just hanging out," Jeremy called back.

Vinnie was watching him from the stage. Jeremy felt it. When he turned to look toward the band, he found that he was right.

"You should join us, man," Vinnie called.

"Maybe later."

As he moved on toward his table, he saw that Matty was gazing lovingly at Jonas, who was still acting like the perfect husband.

Sorry, Matty, your husband is an ass, he thought.

But could he be something worse?

9

Aidan was outside Kendall's door at exactly seven-thirty. She answered the door in a light blue denim dress. Her hair was especially sleek—freshly washed, he thought—and shimmering down around her shoulders. He was actually pleasantly surprised that she had bothered to shower and change for his benefit. He might have told her that it wouldn't have mattered what she was wearing, that she could wear a garbage bag as an outfit and make it look good, that she had the kind of natural beauty that shone through with or without makeup, and that her hair looked good wound up on her head or flowing free. He refrained.

In her heeled sandals, she was only a few inches shorter than he was. She was regal, even in denim. Her scent was delicate, not the kind that slammed you in the face. It was merely a hint, the kind that lingered in memory, like a haunting refrain.

"I'm just going to grab a jacket," she told him. "It's finally beginning to cool down."

"Fall," he responded.

When she came out, he indicated his car, which was—miraculously—parked at a nearby meter.

"We're driving?"

"I thought you wanted out of the immediate area for the evening," he told her.

"Sounds good," she admitted.

She was beautiful, the perfect date. Except, of course, that this wasn't a date. She had simply agreed to go to dinner because he'd said he wanted information. She was polite, but he thought that might be due to the fact that she also seemed distracted.

So was he. He needed to take everything about this—about *her*—slowly and carefully.

"Any suggestions?" he asked her. "I didn't get a chance to make a reservation."

She looked at him, giving him both a frown and her full attention. "Do you eat sushi?" she asked doubtfully.

He smiled. She was probably imagining that he wanted nothing less than a full side of beef. "I eat anything," he told her.

She smiled at that. "Okay, sorry, do you *like* sushi? Or Japanese, I guess. The place I'm thinking of grills your food right at the table. Although, if you want to talk, it's a little difficult, since they seat eight to a table, if you want your food cooked in front of you."

"Sushi at a table for two will be fine," he assured her.

She directed him onto I-10 and down to an exit in Metairie. The restaurant parking lot was nearly full. He wondered if they should have called ahead, but since they just wanted a small table, they were quickly led to the left side of the restaurant, where the booths were private and a wall separated them from the area where chefs were busy showing off their knife skills: slicing vegetables, meat and fish at tables with built-in grills.

They politely asked one another's likes and dislikes, and found several rolls they would both enjoy but differed on their sashimi choices. Miso soup was followed by ginger-dressed salads, and they kept their conversation light until the rolls and sashimi came, and they'd had iced teas refilled, and it seemed as if they wouldn't be interrupted again for a while.

She looked at him, as if on cue, and told him, "I honestly don't know what you want me to say. I think I've told you everything."

He offered her a half-grin and admitted, "I'm not even sure myself. Maybe I'm just looking for the history of the area and the plantation." Which was true, as far as it went.

It was also true that he wanted to know how come a woman who had disappeared had been a customer at her shop *and* had spent the evening hanging out where Vinnie played.

Of course, her other employee, Mason, also hung out at the same bar.

As did half of Louisiana, he reminded himself. Or so it seemed.

But as far as he knew, cops and medical examiners and their lab techs didn't go into Kendall's shop for psychic readings.

"You know this area—and the plantation—well, so why don't we just start there?" he suggested.

Kendall paused, adding a touch of spicy mayonnaise to a piece of dragon roll. "I know about the Civil War, of course. Or the War of Northern Aggression, as people down here still like to call it." He noticed that she had a single dimple, in her left cheek when she smiled. "I actually had one teacher who refused to refer to it any other way. The heir to your property, a man named Sloan Flynn, wound up in Lee's army. He had been a captain in the Louisiana militia, but after the first year and a half of the war, more and more of the troops were called out to help Lee. The truth is, the North had more men. The South had some of the most talented generals, but when a man went down, he wasn't easy to replace, while the North was bringing in immigrants who landed on their shores daily, and then there was conscription and so on. Anyway, Sloan was off with the army when New Orleans and most of the surrounding area came under Union control in 1862. Supposedly Sloan's cousin— who had joined the Union army—was trying to keep an eye on the Flynn plantation, and his cousin's secret wife, Fiona, who he'd married on the sly because of the war and Sloan being a Reb. Anyway, Sloan made a detour down to the old homestead, and his cousin was there, along with several other Union soldiers. The cousins shot each other, and according to official reports, Fiona threw herself over the balcony in despair. So naturally a beautiful woman in a white gown can be seen screaming and running across the upstairs balcony, and both Union and Confederate soldiers can be seen on the grounds. By those looking for ghosts, of course."

"Of course," he said, staring at her.

He felt a strange trickle of unease. Hadn't he thought he'd seen a woman in white on the upper level?

But that had been Kendall Montgomery. It had to have been.

At least he hadn't seen any soldiers marching around.

"What else—historically?" he asked.

She was thoughtful for a moment. "Well, there's the story that came along later. I told you about it at the house. The one about the beautiful servant who supposedly had the affair with the master. She was hanged, and the wife fell down the stairway. You know, I have a friend who's with the historical society. She's on vacation right now, but she's due back this weekend. I can introduce you to her. She'd love to tell you all she knows."

"That would be great, thanks," he said. He picked up a piece of salmon roll, studying her as he did so. She looked more than gorgeous every minute, her perfume was a truly intoxicating scent, and she seemed completely focused on him.

She wasn't, though. He was sure of it. She was distracted. Something was bothering her.

Well, something was bothering *him*, too.

"May I ask you a personal question?" he said.

She stared at him, features betraying wry amusement. "Can I stop you?"

"You can refuse to answer me. I'm just trying to figure out how you came to be so close to Amelia."

"Really? I'm trying to figure out how you never knew she existed."

"That's easy enough. My father was an only child. His father was killed during World War II. I guess my great-grandfather was the first to settle in the Gainesville area, and that was pretty much all we knew about his family. My mother was first generation Irish, and her folks died when I was young. And that was that."

She reached over to try the salmon roll, but before she popped it into her mouth, she said casually, "I wonder how Amelia knew you all were out there, then. I mean, I could see it if the property had gone to your father. But all three of your names were listed in the will." She stared at him, and smiled. "You know, the lawyer said she wrote that will right before the end of her life."

"Your turn. Should she have left the property to you?"

"Probably not. I couldn't have kept up with the insurance and the taxes."

He was good at reading people, and she seemed to be speaking honestly and without rancor.

"Amelia might have thought she would just have been leaving a giant burden tied around my neck," she went on. "She might have thought I would try to carry it and fall down with the effort." She took a drink of tea. "I guess your business does fairly well."

He shrugged. "Well enough. Just when we were getting started, Zachary pulled in a gig from a certain rock star I can't mention. His daughter had disappeared in Brazil. We found her, managed to get her back. Her father wanted to pay us a fortune in gratitude, so we let him. It set the agency up well."

"Do you only work for rich people?" she asked him.

He felt himself tense. There was a definite edge to that question. *What the hell did it matter what she thought?* he asked himself. It wasn't as if she was some selfless do-gooder. In his opinion, any psychic reader was just playing off the hopes, dreams and pain of others.

"Actually, at the moment, I've taken on a case for a dollar," he told her. She looked up at him, clearly curious, so to get off that subject, he quickly asked, "So what was the story between you and Amelia?"

"She rescued me," Kendall told him.

"From what?"

"When I was sixteen, my folks were killed in an automobile accident," she said, her tone matter-of-fact. "They left nothing. I mean nothing. They were musicians, more in love with playing than making a living. I didn't blame them—

they did well enough, and we had a nice little house close to Rampart Street. I was put in foster care. I met Amelia when she hosted some of us kids out at the plantation for a field trip. She heard about what had happened. I actually ended up moving in with Vinnie's folks, but they had a hard enough time making ends meet without me there, so Amelia helped them feed another mouth. I started spending weekends with her, helping her with the house—she still had a caretaker and a maid back then, but she always found something interesting for me to do. I managed to get a scholarship to Loyola, and once I was out of school, I started working. Nothing exciting, just a job to pay the bills. When the shop on Royal came up for lease, Amelia and I took a plunge together, because she liked my idea for what to do with it. So she took out a small mortgage to give me some start-up capital, and thank God, I was able to pay it back quickly. I believed I could make a go of it, and Amelia believed in me. So you can understand why, when she got sick, I was determined to help her."

A simple enough story, he thought. Too simple, maybe, given that a lot more had certainly happened over the ten or twelve years since her parents had died.

"What about *your* family?" she asked, staring straight at him.

Her eyes were like emeralds, he thought. Emeralds glittering with amber lights. The flame of the candle on the table was reflected in them, constantly changing the color.

"Similar story, actually," he said. "My parents died my senior year of high school. My mother caught a flu they couldn't stop, and I think the pain of losing her made my dad's heart give out. They left enough for me to hang on to the house until we could all graduate. Zachary was just a sophomore at the time, and Jeremy was a junior. I figured the only chance we really had was for me to join the navy, so I did. I could go to college while my brothers finished high school, then do my basic training after. A legal aide attorney helped get me custody of Jeremy and Zach until they reached eighteen themselves."

"Very admirable," she told him.

He shook his head. "The two of them picked up the pieces. They learned to cook and clean, and they both got into local bands that made money playing for weddings, graduations, that kind of thing. When I got out of the service, I studied graphics first. I almost started into architecture. But I'd been on a few covert missions in the service, so when Jeremy went into criminology, and then Zach, I found myself following. The next thing I knew, there was an FBI guy trying to recruit me, and I was intrigued. Jeremy wound up becoming a police diver, and Zachary headed down to the Miami area to work forensics." He shrugged. "I guess you can only go so long in that line of work before you have to make a change. You just hit a breaking point."

She looked at him. "And yours was?" she asked softly.

"My breaking point wasn't professional," he said.

"Your wife?"

He never talked about Serena. Never. And he didn't want to start talking about her now.

Maybe not talking was worse.

"Car accident," he said briefly.

He was startled when he felt her hand on his. Warm. And her eyes startled him even more. There was an empathy in them that touched him as no other attempt to comfort him had done before.

He was tempted to jerk his hand away. The feeling of warmth was too gentle. Lulling. It was the kind of thing that could take him off guard.

"Well, we're a pair, aren't we?" he said abruptly.

"Not that bad," she told him, pulling her hand back and flushing slightly, telling him that she had never meant to touch him. "Vinnie is like a brother to me. Mason is the world's greatest employee as well as a friend. I'm from here, so I have a lot of good friends, really. But…"

"But now you've lost Amelia. Followed by a good kick in the face—my brothers and me."

She laughed. "I honestly don't dislike you for that."

"So why *do* you dislike me?"

"Well, you walk around like a thundercloud, and you're… you're rude."

"Ouch."

"It's all right. You're kind of like a neighbor's cranky dog. After a while you get accustomed to the growling."

"That makes me feel so much better," he assured her. They were both smiling. It was almost an awkward moment.

"Another personal question," he said.

"I'll answer if I choose."

"Vinnie has been your best friend forever, but you two were never romantically involved?"

"Vinnie and me? Good God, no!"

He wasn't sure she'd wanted to be quite so honest with him; his question had obviously taken her by surprise.

"Sorry." He laughed. "It just seems like the guy has more than his fair share of admirers."

"Oh, he does. No, it's just that…we were kids together. Like I said, he's as close to me as a brother, really. He was a geeky kid, small and thin. He's tall now, and he's found a way to make those dark eyes and the long hair pay, plus he's a respected guitarist. He's come into his own. I'm really happy for him. But as to ever having any kind of romantic feelings for him…" She trailed off, her smile broad. "He's a friend. A really good friend."

"But he had a tough time as a kid?" Aidan asked. Childhood rejection was something profilers always looked for. He was tempted to ask her if she'd ever seen Vinnie torturing small animals.

"Who doesn't have a tough time as a kid?" she asked, then eyed him knowingly. "Except, of course, the guys on the football team."

"I wouldn't know. I never played," Aidan told her.

"You didn't play sports?" she asked skeptically.

"Tennis and golf," he told her. "Someone once told my mother that you should buy your kids a tennis racket, golf clubs and a guitar. My mother took it to heart. Oh, I also have a decent bowling average."

She smiled. "Sorry. I was stereotyping you, I guess. The bruisers usually go out there and…inflict bruises."

"And it sounds as if you've gone through life acting like Vinnie's older sister, bolstering him up, looking out for him. A cheerleader, right?"

She laughed. "No. School newspaper—I wrote about the cheerleaders."

"Snide little digs?"

"Not at all. I have nothing against cheerleaders *or* football players."

"Vinnie must be grateful to you for looking out for him, though," he said.

"Friends don't have to be grateful to friends," she told him, frowning. "He's always been around when I've needed him, and I'm there when he needs me."

Her tone indicated that she knew Vinnie was under some kind of attack—and she wasn't going to have any of it.

"I guess it's nice that Mason and Vinnie seem to be such good friends."

"Of course it's nice." She looked at him, confused, but instinctively wary. "Vinnie's not an actual employee, but he still works at the shop when I need him and he's free. When I'm not around, it's often the two of them. Of course I'm glad they hit it off."

Aidan kept his features impassive. Inwardly, he couldn't help but think of the occasional serial killers who worked in pairs. It wasn't that he was suddenly convinced Mason and Vinnie were some kind of bloodthirsty symbiotic duo, but he couldn't ignore the possibility. Frankly, he had no real evidence that *anyone* was a killer, but had to start somewhere. And Jenny Trent's last credit card charges had been at Kendall's shop and the bar where Vinnie played and Mason hung out.

"What are you getting at?" she asked him.

He hesitated, then drew Jenny Trent's picture from the breast pocket of his jacket and laid it down in front of Kendall.

Her reaction was far worse than he had expected. She turned white. Pure white. Her eyes rose to his, stricken.

"Why are you asking me about her?" she demanded.

"She disappeared in New Orleans. She was supposed to be heading—"

"On a trip to South America, I know. What happened to her?" Kendall asked. She was staring at him with dread.

"No one knows what happened to her," he said. He leaned closer. "You tell me. I know she was in your shop. Obviously something happened there."

"Nothing happened in my shop," she protested.

"Then why are you whiter than Christmas snow?"

"She came in for a reading," Kendall said.

"And did she say a stranger had been following her? Was she nervous about anything?" he pressed.

"I remember her because she was full of life and very nice. That's all," Kendall said.

"You're lying, Kendall," he accused evenly, quietly.

"Is this why you asked me out to dinner?" she asked. "To accuse me?"

"No. I didn't know what I know about this woman until today."

"That's right. You wanted to know about the house, about Amelia. Well, I've told you what I know. And anyway, what does the past matter? The house is yours now."

She was nervous and defensive. He couldn't understand what about the photo of Jenny Trent could have thrown her so badly.

"What happened at your shop?" he asked again.

"She was like any tourist. She came in," Kendall told him, her voice hard. "She wanted a tarot card reading. I gave her one. She was pleasant. She told me she was a teacher and that she'd saved for years to pay for her vacation. She was excited to be going on such an adventure."

Everything she was saying was true, he knew; she just wasn't saying everything.

"That's it?" he asked.

"That's it," she told him firmly.

"Then why did you look as if you'd seen a ghost?" he demanded.

She shook her head, just staring at him. Then she said, "I know why the cops hate you."

"'Hate' might be too strong a word." Or was it?

"You're never going to make it here. You aren't an insider. You don't know the area. You come in here like you think you can save the day when we've all been picking up the pieces for a long time. Seriously, just who do you think you are?"

It was strange, he thought. She was genuinely indignant.

And just as genuinely afraid.

"I'm not that much of an outsider—I've been coming around here forever," he said curtly. "My brother is involved in a major benefit for the area kids. So you think I'm an intrusive ballbuster? Well, I'm pretty sure this girl is dead," he said. "And I think I found a piece of her remains."

Kendall stared at him. He was surprised she hadn't gotten up and walked out on him yet. But she was just staring at him, her eyes very wide and her skin ashen.

"What makes you so positive that you've found this girl?"

"I'm not positive about anything."

Almost unconsciously, she ran fingers over the picture as she stared down at it. For a moment he thought she was going to cry. She was definitely distressed. He reached across the table, setting a hand on hers. "Kendall, what the hell is it?"

"She was very sweet," she said.

She started to move her hand away; he held firm.

She shook her head. "If I told you, you wouldn't believe me."

"Try me."

"So that you can look down on me even more?" she asked bitterly.

"I don't look down on you." All right, so he was lying then, at least a little bit. But hell, it *had* looked as if she'd been living off a frail old woman. And he did have a problem with people who indulged in all that psychic claptrap, believers or not.

"All right, so I'm a skeptical man," he admitted.

"I think I should go," she said.

"Please, stay. Help me. I know I'm floundering in the dark."

She was searching his eyes, wondering if he was sincere. His hand was still on hers, and he sincerely hoped she wasn't going to bolt.

"Please," he said again.

"If you laugh at me, I swear, I will never speak to you again," she said. She meant it. He could tell.

"I don't find anything about Jenny Trent to be amusing," he said.

Her lashes fell; she looked toward the table. "There was something strange when I tried to give her a reading...." She looked up at him again. She seemed to sit taller; she was stiff and regal. "I don't actually believe in psychi*c* powers myself. Yes, I give readings. Good ones, I think. But I graduated with degrees in psychology and fine arts. I had a teacher who taught me once that entertainment has to do with knowing your audience, and psychology taught me how to do that. So then the shop came up, and I was positive I could make a go of it, but *I never thought I could read anyone's palm or* *look into a crystal ball and tell someone their future.* But I knew something—that presentation could make or break a show, and giving readings, giving people what they want, is a way of putting on a show."

As she spoke, he found himself wanting to reach out and stroke her cheek, wanting to tell her that it was all right, that she had done everything right. Except he still didn't know what she was getting at.

"I see," he said, but the truth was, he didn't see at all.

She took a deep breath. "There have been a few times when something really strange has happened. One of those times was with Jenny Trent."

"Kendall, what happened?"

"Tarot cards have more meanings than you can begin to imagine. A good reader should have instincts to help sort through those meanings as they relate to each client." She took a deep breath. "What I'm trying to explain is that they really are a perfect tool for…well, for a psychologist, for a way of listening and then trying to point out certain aspects of life that someone might want to be blind to. Every card can mean many things. The Death card doesn't mean death. Not usually. It means change."

He stared at her, pinning her with his eyes. "And you drew the Death card for Jenny Trent? You…you *saw* death for her?"

"Yes and no." She took a deep breath and went on. "I just explained that the cards have all kinds of meanings. That the Death card doesn't mean literal death. It indicates an ending for something. Depending on what other cards turn up, it can mean a major upheaval, the end of a relationship. But it's also associated with the concept that when one door closes, another opens."

"So why did it bother you when the card appeared for Jenny Trent?"

She looked at him across the table, and he could see her steeling herself to answer.

"It laughed at me," she told him.

"What?" He wasn't sure what he'd expected, but it certainly hadn't been that.

She jerked her hand back at last. "I knew I shouldn't have said anything. I knew you would just laugh at me and think that I must have been drunk or that I'm crazy, or I am just taking myself too seriously. Look, I've told you my history, Jenny's history, and I've even answered your ridiculous questions about Vinnie. What more do you want from me?"

"I wasn't laughing at you," he said.

"May we please leave?" she asked.

"I swear, I wasn't laughing at you. I just don't understand."

"No, and I don't think you're going to, so I want to go."

All right, maybe he did think she had just been seeing things. But even so, her reaction to Jenny Trent's picture had been real. Whatever was really going on, *she* clearly believed something strange had happened that day.

And didn't everything he himself was doing now come from something unexplained? A hunch?

"Kendall, I promise I wasn't laughing at you, and I'm sorry if you thought I was," he told her soberly. He glanced at his watch. He did want to get to the club, but he didn't want to end the evening with her feeling like this.

"May we leave?" she asked again, her voice cold. Clearly she wasn't buying his apology.

"Of course."

He motioned the waitress for the check. Kendall didn't

speak, wouldn't even look at him, while he waited for the return of his credit card.

As they rose, she spoke as if by rote. "Thank you for the lovely dinner."

"It was my pleasure," he told her, knowing he sounded equally wooden.

They drove in silence the whole way back.

He went around her block twice without being able to find on-street parking.

"You can let me out anywhere along here," she told him.

"No, I can't," he said.

"Then just double park and see me to the door."

"No."

Stubbornly, he drove around the block again and finally found parking. She waited impatiently while he put coins in the meter. She was clearly anxious to shake him, but even so, she was going to be polite and not take off without him.

She didn't protest when he took her arm to escort her down the street, but he could feel the tension in her. He walked her to the door of her building, and then to the door of her apartment.

When she turned to say good-night, he was ready.

"Kendall, you're fighting with yourself right now, not me. I didn't say a word to you. No, I don't understand. But I know that something happened, and that it upset you. I saw the way you reacted to Jenny Trent's picture. I know you're sincere, and that you're telling me the truth."

She stared at him blankly. Then she took a breath. "I hope you find her. But…you have to lay off Vinnie. He's a good guy. And I know it."

"Sure."

"Liar."

"If he's a good guy, I'll know it."

"But you won't take my word for it?"

"I wouldn't take my own mother's word for it. That's not the business I'm in."

She seemed agitated, and not just about Vinnie.

"Are you all right?" he asked her.

"Of course."

"No, you're not."

"I can't explain."

They just stood there for a moment, and it was very strange. It was as if he could feel waves of expectation emanating from them both. If they'd been on a date…

Hell, he could hardly remember dating, and it wasn't the same anymore, anyway. People seemed to meet one another casually—in a bar, mostly—size each other up and head for the bedroom, sometimes even before they made it to a first-name basis. He'd done it himself. He'd woken up once or twice not even knowing the name of the woman with whom he'd slept the night before.

And it hadn't mattered. They wouldn't meet again.

But Kendall…Kendall was different. He knew her name well. It often haunted his thoughts. He knew her eyes, and he was coming to know her moods, her smile, even her laughter. Her resentment, her sense of justice, her pride. He knew all those things, knew he was being charmed by them. And he knew, as well, that he was equally seduced by the softness of her skin, the curves of her body, the silken brush of her hair.

So what the hell was the matter? Yeah, he knew her name, and she knew his. But screw it. Why couldn't it be what it had been for him before, and a fast and casual physical fling for her? The attraction was there: chemical, carnal, whatever. Get it over with. Leave.

He had never been more tempted to simply step forward and take a woman in his arms. Explore every part of her in a mindless need to explore, and spend the night in a tangle of sheets and naked flesh.

No. He knew her name too well. And that changed everything.

He stepped back. "Good night. And thank you."

"Thank you."

She looked at him for a moment.

And in that moment, he thought that she was thinking the same thing he was.

But the moment passed.

She stepped inside and closed the door.

And he headed up to Bourbon Street.

Kendall's cheeks were flushed. She pressed her palms against them. If he'd stood there a moment more, she would have dragged him in.

Because she didn't want to be alone.

And even more, because she couldn't remember ever wanting someone so much.

She was an idiot. She'd been an idiot to tell him about the reading, and worse, she was an idiot to be anywhere near him. Her first impression was the one she needed to go by.

It didn't matter. What she liked about him, what she didn't

like, the good, the bad, it all combined to create an attraction that verged on embarrassing. She wanted to sleep with him.

Even though he undoubtedly thought she was crazy.

Not even that mattered. It was as if she could feel the remnants of his energy around her, as if she were still inhaling his scent, something woodsy and compelling that haunted her, made her want to run out to the street and try to be matter-of-fact and polite and invite him back for after-dinner sex, just as she might have invited him in for coffee.

Jezebel meowed, striding sinuously between her legs. She absently stooped to pick up the cat.

She couldn't believe she had told him about the tarot card.

Jenny Trent's tarot card.

Death, coming to life.

Just as it had today. For Ann. The pretty little thing who was heading out on a ship tomorrow. The girl who was, no doubt, out there right now, celebrating with her friend, unaware that danger could be stalking her.

Kendall had no idea what she would even say to her if she found her, and anyway, there were so many places where she might be.

No, there was only one place where tourists went looking to party in the decadence of the Big Easy.

Kendall set the cat back down on the floor, turned and left her apartment, heading straight for Bourbon Street.

10

It was just after ten when Aidan reached the bar. The early crowd had come and gone.

It was still busy, with the late crowd coming out in force. Several wore name tags that identified them as a group that would be leaving on one of the cruise ships in the morning. He was glad to see them there; he knew that the city's economy counted on the passengers to come and stay before sailing to the Caribbean, or after they returned.

Jeremy was at the bar when Aidan came in, standing at one end and resting his back against the wall, so he could see everything going on. When he saw Aidan, he indicated a nearby empty table that was also against the wall, affording a bird's-eye view of those who came and went.

The only other person Aidan recognized in the place at the moment was Vinnie, and he was playing his heart out on stage.

"How was dinner?" Jeremy asked once they sat down.

"Fine. Kendall remembered Jenny Trent." He didn't add that Kendall was convinced a tarot card had taken on a life of its own when she had done Jenny's reading.

"So we can more or less trace her steps until she arrived here," Jeremy said.

Aidan nodded. He was surprised when the waitress dropped by the table, planting a beer in front of him. "There you go. Still cold."

"Thanks," he told her.

"That's only beer number two. Your brother is a slow drinker."

"Sorry," Jeremy said.

"It's all right. You play the hell out of a guitar. Glad to see Vinnie talked you into joining him after all."

"Thanks."

Aidan watched the woman walk away, then said, "Kendall saw Jenny. And earlier the waitress said she was flirting with the band, or the band was flirting with her. They both said she was a nice woman."

"So what next?" Jeremy asked.

"You need to go sit in for Vinnie."

"Again?"

"I need to talk to him."

Jeremy looked at his brother. "Isn't this a long shot?"

"I've got to start somewhere."

"Well, just so you know, for what it's worth, your friend Jonas was in here. So was Matty. Thing is, I don't think he was expecting her. He was flirting with some girl at the bar when I let him know she was here."

Aidan shook his head. "That's sad. She had all that surgery to make him happy. And she was a pretty girl from the start."

"Your buddy Jon Abel was in, too, with a group from the coroner's office."

"Oh yeah?"

"Yeah. And Hal Vincent was in, too. Looking like a lost puppy dog."

So Jonas was on the prowl. Hal Vincent seemed to need a nightly beer. And Jon Abel happened to frequent the same place. Abel was a weird-looking little pissant, even cleaned up. He didn't want to believe that Hal could be a bad guy, and Jonas...no, it couldn't be Jonas. Maybe he was fooling around on Matty. That was sad, but it didn't make him a monster.

Vinnie was a womanizer who had been victimized as a child, teased for not being tough enough. He dressed like a vampire. He had a connection to Kendall's shop, so he had quite likely been both places where Jenny Trent had last used her credit card. Mason was connected to both places, too, but he had yet to see Mason come on to a woman.

"See if you can get Vinnie over to me," Aidan told his brother.

Jeremy rolled his eyes and walked toward the stage. He waved to Vinnie, who grinned and, never missing a note of the number they were playing, looked across the room, saw Aidan and nodded.

Aidan nodded back.

When the number was over, Vinnie reintroduced Jeremy to the crowd, then came over to Aidan's table.

Vinnie's smile appeared sincere. "This place is becoming a hangout for you guys, huh?" he said. The waitress was nearby, and he reached out, catching her by the arm. "Gretchen, be a darling, huh? Bring me a drink. Something sweet. The house special."

Gretchen noted Aidan and lowered her voice. "You gotta pay your bill tonight, Vinnie. Max says so."

"Sure," Vinnie said quickly.

"You need to stop buying drinks for every half-decent woman who walks in here, you know?" Gretchen said, then smiled. "It's all right. This one will be on me."

As she moved away, Vinnie's smile faded a bit. Then he caught Aidan watching him and forced the grin back into place. "Hey, I like people," he said. "Sometimes too much, I guess."

Aidan pulled out the picture of Jenny Trent and set it in front of the other man.

Vinnie looked at the picture, then up at him.

"What's up, man?"

"You know her?"

Vinnie shrugged. He was thoughtful for a moment. "You have no idea how many women come in here," he muttered, then frowned thoughtfully. "Yeah. I remember her. I mean, I can't say I know her. But she was in here. So? She was a nice girl."

"That's what I hear."

Vinnie straightened distrustfully in his chair. "What's going on?"

Gretchen put a drink in front of him just then. "Enjoy," she said, winking.

"Thanks, Gretchen," he said. Aidan imagined he had his appeal. He had the dark soulful eyes of the quintessential artist and aesthetic features. His long dark hair accentuated the look.

"Do you remember her name?"

"Let me think. June…Jessie…Jenny. That's it. Her name is Jenny. And what the hell is the problem, anyway? She said she's over twenty-one."

"No one said she wasn't," Aidan said, noticing Vinnie's use of the present tense.

Vinnie leaned back. "I don't have to answer any of your questions."

"No, but I'd appreciate it if you would."

Vinnie was frowning by then. "You tell me what the hell is going on first." He stared at Aidan. If he was acting, he was good.

Gretchen came back around. "Mr. Flynn, you doing okay?" She stopped, staring at the picture on the table.

"Hey, Vinnie, that's a great shot of that cutie you were trying to pick up, huh?" she teased, nudging him with her hip. Then she seemed to sense the tension at the table and stopped talking, looking embarrassed.

"We're good, Gretchen, thanks," Aidan said.

"Sorry, Vinnie," she said, and moved on.

Vinnie groaned. "What is it with this girl?" He stared at Aidan. "Oh, God, don't tell me something's happened to her."

"She's missing," Aidan said.

"Missing?" Vinnie looked puzzled.

"Missing. Never went to South America. Never went home. She's missing."

"Hey, I saw her back to her bed-and-breakfast, and that was it. We kissed on the doorstep and said good-night. I didn't even sleep with her. She was staying pretty far over toward the edge of the Quarter, near Rampart and Esplanade."

Aidan hid his surprise; there was no record of Jenny Trent having stayed anywhere.

"You walked her to her bed-and-breakfast?" he said.

"That was it. I swear," he said.

"Can you remember exactly where it was?" Aidan asked.

"Sure."

"Can you take me there?"

"Tomorrow, if you want," Vinnie agreed, still defensive. "And now you need to excuse me. I have a gig to finish."

Aidan reached out to catch hold of Vinnie's lapel. "Don't you pull a disappearing act on me, huh?" he said.

Vinnie looked as if he was about to say something, then smiled suddenly. "Hey!" he called loudly.

Aidan looked up. He'd been so intent on his conversation with Vinnie that he hadn't been watching the door. He saw now that Kendall Montgomery had come into the bar, and she was staring at him with an angry scowl as she walked straight over to his table.

"What the hell is going on here?" she demanded.

"Your friend thinks I did away with this girl," Vinnie said pleasantly, giving her a poor-me grin.

He was a rodent, Aidan thought. Or like a little kid, crawling behind his mother's skirts because he had done something wrong on the playground.

Except this was a grown-up and deadly playground.

He slowly eased his hold on Vinnie, who straightened his jacket. "I've gotta go back up on stage. You explain, huh, Flynn?"

He stood and walked away.

Aidan watched as Kendall took the chair Vinnie had just vacated, staring at him venomously. "You son of a bitch," she told him.

He didn't blink. "Jenny Trent was in your shop and at this bar. Vinnie is always in your shop and at this bar."

"What makes you think he was in the shop that day?"

"When isn't he?" He leaned toward her at last. "The waitress told me he'd been flirting with Jenny, and that makes him a natural person with whom to start. And he admits that he walked her back to her B and B."

"So go question everyone else who stayed in the same place," Kendall told him, seething with hostility.

"I don't know where she stayed. Vinnie does."

"And he told you that—so you're threatening him? How interesting."

He decided it was time to turn the conversation. "I'll tell you something else interesting. I thought you wanted out of this scene for a while. We went to dinner out of the Quarter— at your request." He lowered his voice but leaned even closer, so she could hear him clearly despite the music. "Then you about turned into a ghost when you saw Jenny Trent's picture and jumped to attention on behalf of Vinnie's reputation. So what are you doing out here now? Checking in with him?"

She gaped, then quickly recovered. "You are a jerk."

"Jenny Trent is missing, and probably dead. If I have to be a jerk to find out what happened to her, so be it."

She stood up, telling him what he ought to do with himself, then headed to the bar.

Jeremy returned to the table and took a seat across from him.

"Wow. You really know how to make friends and influence people, huh, partner?" he said dryly.

"Something is going on with her," Aidan said.

"I agree. She's ape-shit angry because she thinks you're persecuting her friend," Jeremy said.

"No. She was really unnerved by Jenny's picture. I thought it might be because she was worried about Vinnie. But that wasn't it. She wasn't angry, she was stunned."

He stood, and Jeremy looked up at him. "What are you doing?"

FREE Merchandise is 'in the Cards' for you!

Dear Reader,

We're giving away FREE MERCHANDISE!

Seriously, we'd like to reward you for reading this novel by giving you **FREE MERCHANDISE** worth over **$20.** And no purchase is necessary!

You see the Jack of Hearts sticker above? Paste that sticker in one of the boxes on the Free Merchandise Voucher inside. Return the Voucher promptly ... and we'll send you valuable Free Merchandise!

Thanks again for reading one of our novels – and enjoy your Free Merchandise with our compliments!

Pam Powers

Pam Powers

P.S. Look inside to see what Free Merchandise is **"in the cards"** for you!

What would you prefer…
Romance OR Suspense?

Do you prefer spine-tingling page turners or steal-your-heart stories about love and relationships? Tell us which type of books you'd enjoy – and you'll get **2 Free ROMANCE Books** or **2 Free SUSPENSE Books** with no obligation to buy anything.

OPTION 1
Romance

Get 2 FREE BOOKS that will capture your imagination with modern stories about life, love and relationships.

FREE!

FREE!

OPTION 2
Suspense

Get 2 FREE BOOKS that will thrill you with a fast-paced blend of suspense and mystery.

REMEMBER: Your Free Merchandise, consisting of **2 Free Books** and **2 Free Gifts**, is worth over $20.00! No purchase is necessary, so please send for your Free Merchandise today.

Plus TWO FREE GIFTS!
We'll also send you two wonderful FREE GIFTS (worth about $10), in addition to your 2 Free "Romance" or "Suspense" books!

YOUR FREE MERCHANDISE INCLUDES…

2 FREE Romance OR 2 FREE Suspense books

AND 2 FREE Mystery Gifts

The Reader Service - Here's how it works:

Accepting your 2 free books and 2 free mystery gifts places you under no obligation to buy anything. You may keep the books and gifts and return the shipping statement marked "cancel." If you do not cancel, about a month later we'll send you 3 additional books and bill you just $5.49 each in the U.S. or $5.99 each in Canada, plus 25¢ shipping & handling per book and applicable taxes if any.* That's the complete price and — at a savings of at least 15% off the cover price — it's quite a bargain! You may cancel at any time, but if you choose to continue, every month we'll send you 3 more books, which you may either purchase at the discount price or return to us and cancel your subscription.

*Terms and prices subject to change without notice. Sales tax applicable in N.Y. Canadian residents will be charged applicable provincial taxes and GST. Offer not valid in Quebec. All orders subject to approval. Books received may not be as shown. Credit or debit balances in a customer's account(s) may be offset by any other outstanding balance owed by or to the customer. Please allow 4 to 6 weeks for delivery. Offer available while quantities last.

If offer card is missing, write to The Reader Service, 3010 Walden Ave., P.O. Box 1867, Buffalo, NY 14240-1867

BUSINESS REPLY MAIL

FIRST-CLASS MAIL   PERMIT NO. 717   BUFFALO, NY

POSTAGE WILL BE PAID BY ADDRESSEE

The Reader Service

3010 WALDEN AVENUE
PO BOX 1341
BUFFALO NY 14240-8571

NO POSTAGE
NECESSARY
IF MAILED
IN THE
UNITED STATES

"I'm going to find out why she came back out tonight."

Jeremy shook his head. "More community relations. Great." Aidan looked at him. "Hey, good luck. Should I follow Vinnie out of here?"

"Not a bad idea," Aidan said, and strode for the bar.

Kendall didn't look his way, but she had known he was coming, because she spoke the minute he stopped beside her. "Don't you ever give up and go away? I don't have to talk to you. I'm out on the town—so what? You can investigate all you want, but you're not a cop, and the cops don't want to talk to you. Give up. Go away."

He slid onto the bar stool at her side anyway. She had ordered a sweet drink, too, and was playing with the fruit garnish that came on top.

"Look, Vinnie can take us further on Jenny's trail than we've been able to get before."

"So you decide to manhandle him?"

"I was just making sure he wasn't giving me a line."

She swiveled on her stool, eyes still flashing with anger. "You are a piece of work."

"I need to find the truth."

She shook her head. "Why?" she whispered. "You found a bone. Just a bone. If you had been here every day for the last couple of years, you wouldn't have thought anything of it."

"But now I know there was a real girl who disappeared and I *do* think something of it."

She looked tired suddenly.

"You've been in the service, you've been FBI. God in heaven, you must know that sometimes people disappear. Why the hell do you care?"

"Someone should," he said.

She lowered her eyes, then looked up at him again. "Then help me."

"What?"

"Help me now," she said.

"What are you talking about?"

She hesitated, took a deep breath, exhaled. "You want help. You crash into all our lives and think we should just help you because you have a hunch. Well, I need help, too, because…that thing with the card that I told you about? It happened again today."

"The card smiled at you?"

"Worse. It laughed."

He fought to keep his composure. Crazy as it seemed, it was clear that she believed what she was telling him.

And crazy as it seemed, he felt he had to try to understand. "Okay. So…?"

"I need you to help me find her, the girl I was giving the reading to. I want to make sure this girl, Ann, gets on that cruise ship tomorrow."

"What did she look like?"

"Blond. She was wearing a halter top and slim-fitting jeans. She had green eyes, she was young, and she was with a girl in a Saints shirt."

They were interrupted when the bartender stopped in front of them. "Last call."

"We're good, thanks," Aidan said.

The man went on; the band announced the last number. It was one o'clock. It seemed early for a place on what was known as *the* street in Sin City, U.S.A., to be closing.

But at least a few other places would still be open. The strip clubs often hung on the longest.

He glanced over at the table. Jeremy nodded to him, arched a brow, then stood and started walking toward them.

"This isn't a ploy to keep me off Vinnie's tail, is it?" he asked.

Her eyes remained even on his. "Your brother is following Vinnie, right?" she asked sweetly.

"My brother likes Vinnie," Aidan said. "They're friends."

"What's this about your brother?" Jeremy asked pleasantly.

Aidan kept his eyes on Kendall. "Describe the girl you're talking about to Jeremy."

Kendall did so.

"Yeah, she was in here. There were a lot of people in here from the ship," he said.

"They were all together?" Aidan asked.

"Yeah," Jeremy said. "Most of them left about an hour and a half ago. Excuse me. I'm going to go help the band pack it up."

As Jeremy walked away, Aidan felt a tap on his shoulder. He turned. The black man he'd noticed the night before was standing next to him. "Don't go lettin' that gal out on her own, you hear?" he said gravely.

"Don't worry, I won't," Aidan said. "I'm Aidan Flynn, by the way, and this—" he turned back to Kendall "—is Kendall Montgomery, though you two may know each other already." He turned back to the other side.

So much for introductions. The man was gone.

"Who are you talking to?" Kendall asked him, frowning.

"No one. He's gone," Aidan said, and set money on the bar.

"But—" Kendall began to protest.

"Forget it. Let's go find your girl," he said.

"Really?"

"Yes, really."

They started off on Bourbon at Canal; despite the hour, Kendall was determined to try as hard as she could to keep trying to find Ann, even though she'd struck out in all the places she'd tried on her way to the Hideaway. The streets had grown quieter, though plenty of places were still open, a number of them the strip clubs.

They were thorough. In one place, Aidan saw a number of the men wearing the badges that identified them as the cruise-ship crowd, but there were no women with them, and when he chatted with them, he discovered they were a group of CPAs out of Salem, Oregon, and they had been on their own all night.

As they continued on, he realized Kendall was deeply anxious. He didn't believe a tarot card meant anything, but she definitely did. Block by block, they made their way from bar to club to bar. At one point Kendall saw a friend, a tall, good-looking black man with a smile that was pure friendship. Kendall gave him a hug, introduced Aidan so quickly that he didn't catch the man's name, and then described Ann.

"Yeah, I saw her. Pretty, bouncy little thing. Couldn't sing worth a damn, but she and her friends had a good time doing karaoke anyway. They wanted to keep going, but we had to close. Someone suggested they check up the street."

"Thanks."

"How long ago?" Aidan asked.

"No more than half an hour."

The man waved. "Hope you find your friend!"

There was no crowd at all anymore as they walked along the street. Aidan felt a strange sensation creeping down his neck. He stopped and spun around.

Someone was just slipping into an alleyway that led to a strip club that was missing several of its blinking neon lights.

"What is it?" Kendall asked nervously.

"Nothing. Let's go."

One more block and they would be just about out of clubs. But there was an open one on the next corner. Again Aidan turned to look around. The street was empty. But there had been someone following them; he was certain. He wanted to double back.

"Aidan, come on, please," Kendall insisted.

They went into the bar. There were several pool tables, and a few people playing at one of them. At the bar, laughing and talking loudly, were the remnants of the cruise group.

"Is she here?" Aidan asked.

"Yes!" Kendall cried triumphantly. "Over there."

"Now what?" he demanded.

"I try to talk to her."

"Go right ahead."

Aidan perched on the edge of an unused pool table, watching as Kendall straightened her shoulders, then walked up to the group at the bar. The girl, Ann, recognized her immediately and started introducing her around.

The girl looked pretty drunk. Aidan had to wonder how much success Kendall was going to have getting her to agree to anything. And what was Kendall going to do, anyway? Try to talk her out of taking the cruise? Or just ask her to not fool around with any unknown men?

Once again, he had that feeling at the back of his neck.

He turned quickly toward the door. Nothing. But he was convinced someone had just been there, looking in.

He checked and saw that Kendall was speaking earnestly with Ann and gambled that she would be there a while and hurried toward the door.

Outside, the street was dead quiet. But down the block, he just caught a glimpse of someone rounding the corner.

He ran and turned the corner himself.

He came out on Royal Street, not far from Kendall's apartment. The whole block was houses. There were a half-dozen narrow alleys and twice as many doors.

He stayed where he was for a long time, watching the street. Waiting. Finally he admitted he had lost whoever he had seen and was probably being a damned fool, besides. Anyone could have walked down the street; there was nothing illegal in that. For all he knew, he might have been following an underage drinker who thought he was a cop.

But Kendall lived on the next block.

The breeze shifted. He heard laughter from Canal Street and hurried back, afraid he might have missed Kendall. He didn't want her walking home alone.

Back at the bar, Kendall had managed to extricate the girl from her friends. She was trying to be light and assertive at the same time.

The girl was giggling. "I met so many cute guys tonight. And lots of them asked to see me later."

"Did you tell them where you were staying?" Kendall asked. "Are you alone?"

"No, I'm sharing a room with my friend." Ann giggled again. "She went back early, but she'll leave if I need her to. We have an agreement when it comes to men, you know?"

Kendall sighed. One of the men from the group walked over from the bar.

"Annie? Anything wrong?"

He was older than the girl. Maybe thirty.

After Aidan returned, he had been keeping his distance, but he decided to move in. "How do you know Ann?" he asked.

"We work together," the man said.

"We're just worried," Aidan explained. "There's a guy going around hitting on women and robbing them. Ann fits the look of the girls he goes after." Not true, but it didn't matter. "We're just trying to make sure she's safe tonight."

The man frowned at Ann, then looked up at the two of them. "Don't worry. I'll keep an eye on her." He looked at Kendall. "I thought she said you were a psychic, so what are you doing acting like a cop?"

"I—"

"She's with me, and I'm a private investigator working the case," Aidan explained, and produced one of his business cards.

"I'm Joe Zimmer, and like I said, I'll have my eye on her all night."

Ann was pouting. Something flashed in her eyes.

She had made arrangements to meet someone, Aidan thought. But who?

Whoever had disappeared when he had looked toward the door?

He took a deep breath. At worst, the girl just wasn't going to get lucky tonight.

At best, her life had just been saved.

Aidan set an arm on Kendall's shoulders. "Well, have a great cruise. All of you. Good night."

He steered Kendall out of the bar.

In the street, she drew away and faced him. "Thank you," she said.

"Sure. Not a problem."

"Are you going to lay off Vinnie now?" she asked, but there was no real venom in her tone. She just sounded tired.

"I need Vinnie to show me where Jenny Trent was staying," he said.

"And if you're nice, Vinnie won't have a problem in the world with showing you," she said.

"Glad to hear it. And now it's late and time to go home."

"Okay. Thanks again. I, uh, just live a couple of blocks away."

"I know. I'll walk you."

"Please, you've walked around enough already on my behalf."

"You know I'm going to walk you home."

She actually offered him a weak smile. "Okay."

He was annoyed with himself when he realized he was expecting to feel that sensation at the back of his neck that warned him they were being followed again.

Simple instinct, he told himself.

But the feeling didn't come. If there had been a danger on the streets before, it was gone now.

When they arrived at her place, she opened the outer door, and he walked with her into the hallway.

She opened the door to her apartment, then leaned against the door frame and slipped off her sandals. Her smile was rueful as she said, "Thank you again. I know you think I'm crazy."

"You think I'm a jerk," he replied with a shrug.

"But you do come through in a crunch," she told him.

"And you may be a little insane, but you're also absolutely gorgeous."

He thought she might stiffen up again, retreat. Slam the door in his face.

But she lowered her head, her smile deepening. "And you're not bad-looking yourself—for a jerk," she told him, and her eyes met his again. "Look, I'm not making a pass or anything, but…would you mind looking around my place?"

"Are you nervous?" he asked her.

"Silly, huh?"

"No. And I don't mind at all."

He stepped past her, gave the parlor a quick glance, then stepped into the first bedroom, and then the second. He checked in closets, under the bed, and all around. He went through the kitchen, and the family room, and moved on to the French doors. They were locked. The drapes across the windows were drawn. Everything appeared to be just fine.

She was behind him, barefoot, rich dark hair with its glimmers of red and gold sweeping sleekly over her shoulders. Her eyes were expectant and focused on him.

"Looks like you're safe and sound," he said.

"I know it's ridiculous to feel worried. I've lived here so long, and I've never been uneasy about anything before," she told him.

"I didn't think you frightened easily. You stayed out at a lonely plantation with just an elderly dying woman, and you never ran, no matter what she thought she saw."

"I thought I was still sane myself then," she said softly.

He found himself walking across the room to her. He really meant just to give her comfort, even though he wasn't sure it was comfort she wanted.

He lifted her chin, the pad of his thumb moving gently across her cheek. "Hey, I'm sure you're sane."

She stared into his eyes. "I thought you just admitted that you think I'm crazy."

He shrugged. "Crazy beautiful."

He never meant to kiss her. He meant to keep a careful distance.

But he was there, and she was there, and suddenly kissing her was something he had to do or go completely mad. His lips met hers, and his free hand cupped her nape. It wasn't a comforting peck; it was a kiss that quickly intensified. She tasted of the sweet fruit nectar she'd been drinking, and her lips seemed to mold to his naturally, without thought. Her lips parted easily, and it quickly escalated into one of those deep, arousing kisses that sent lightning-swift desire down to his groin and through his limbs. A voice in his head shouted it was time to pull back, time to apologize, but his hand started moving through her hair and down her back. He drew her flush against him, and the intense flashes the kiss had ignited grew into a sweeping inferno of desire.

Crazy. This was crazy.

He felt her hands on him, on his shoulders, then streaking down his back, clutching his hips. When he drew his lips from hers and looked into her eyes, he was still expecting indignation, a protest, anger.

But her eyes were on his with an expression of glazed confusion, and she quickly told him, "I didn't…I didn't ask you to look through the house to…to…"

"I never thought you did," he assured her.

Then he kissed her again, and she kissed him back. Passionately, her tongue entering his mouth with sweet provocation, her body pressing against his again as if of its own accord, fitting against him as if she had been created only for that purpose. As their mouths connected with hot, wet urgency, he found his hand moving, covering her breast, and she pressed even more tightly against him. Something moved against his leg suddenly, and he jumped. She broke away from him, gasping.

"Jezebel!" she cried.

They both looked down, and the cat looked back and meowed. Then they looked at one another again, smiled and burst into laughter.

She was tousled and beautiful, and she whispered, "I'm still not sure I like you."

"Fair enough. Do you want me to go?"

She shook her head. "No."

So he went to her again and kissed her, gently this time. With her face cupped in his hands, he asked softly, "You're sure?"

She nodded. And when he kissed her next, they both went for each other's clothes. They shed their clothing across the hallway floor as she drew him backwards to her bedroom, where they fell naked onto the bed.

Somewhere, from a distant bar, the sound of music was carried to their ears. A drumbeat seemed to throb through ground and space. The room was lit only by the glow of the hall light, but even that was enough to catch the brilliance of her eyes and the luster of her hair, the satin of her flesh. He kissed her lips again and caught her eyes, then slowly pressed his mouth to her throat, between her breasts and upon each nipple. Her nails raked lightly down his back, teased his buttocks. He felt his erection hardening painfully, felt the mindlessness of need sweeping over him.

But he knew her name. Knew *her.*

It didn't matter.

He moved against her carefully. He made love to *her.* There had been other women, but he hadn't made love in a long time.

He kissed her flesh as if it were fragile, and when she pressed against him, he teased her with his teeth and tongue. He meant to create the same maddened desire in her, but he found he was savoring every torturous moment. Her breasts were firm and beautiful, he loved the feel of his face against her ribs and belly. The taste of her was intoxicating, the feel of her supple flesh writhing beneath him exquisite and damning. He moved against her, settling his body between her thighs, his fingers teasing the sensitive skin beneath her knees, her inner thighs, the heart of her sex, aware of the heat and energy of her every twist and curve, the supple sleekness of her limbs. When he thrust into her at last, she wrapped her wickedly long legs around him, and he felt as if he were gloved in velvet. They moved in a rhythm as old as time and uniquely new, exploring, gasping, their lips locking, their eyes meeting, and her fingers danced against him, her lips fell against his flesh, her nails raking his shoulders. He could still hear the distant music, the drumbeat. It was in his head, and then the surge was cresting and he knew nothing but the thrusting and the movement, the scent of her, and finally, the burst of climax that left him thrusting again and again, more slowly, yet fully, drawing out the end, finding a new release as she shuddered beneath him, the aftermath as sweetly warm and satisfying as everything that had come before. He rolled to her side, drawing her against him, suddenly feeling oddly vulnerable and not wanting to see whatever was in her eyes just then. He rested his chin on her head, stroking her hair, both of them breathing hard. He heard the hum of her air conditioner, the tick of a clock on the mantel, and felt the coolness of the sheets beneath them, damp now from their exertion.

She spoke first. "All right. I guess I like you," she said softly.

He laughed. "I *know* I like you," he told her.

Then she fell silent, but after a moment—and he could tell she found it hard to ask—she said, "Can you stay…the night?"

Was she afraid?

"I'm all right. Honestly," she said, as if reading his mind. And then she moved, rising on an elbow to look down into his eyes. "I'm not afraid."

Was she a mind reader?

"And I really didn't ask you in for…this." She gave him a little smile. Her hair was a complete mess, and her eyes had that brilliant green-gold quality that tugged at his heart.

He pulled her against him. "Too bad. I wouldn't have minded," he told her.

She didn't answer, just rested easily against him. They were silent, and it was okay.

In a while, they made love again. He didn't know who initiated it. Maybe they just moved together simultaneously. She was bolder this time, playing with his body in a way that all but turned his blood into liquid fire.

At length they slept.

He watched the house, anger sizzling inside him as if his insides were meat on a grill. His blood was boiling, charring his soul…and dripping into the fire.

He fought the anger.

Anger drove a man past control.

Anger made a man behave foolishly and rashly.

A genius did not give way to anger.

He should be grateful, even though they had snatched his prey right out of his grasp and the urge within him was growing to unbearable dimensions. They had done him a favor, he tried to tell himself. She had not been alone among strangers, as he had believed. She had been with a group of people she knew. People who would have reported her missing immediately.

It was good. It was all good.

But Flynn was still in with Kendall. His vision for the future. A painful vision now, for he ached to see those eyes looking into his own. Perhaps with laughter. Then excitement. He wasn't her lover, not yet. For now, he just watched. He could wait his turn.

But the agony came back.

Flynn was in there. Seeing those eyes, touching that sweet flesh, knowing her.

He turned and walked away.

But the hunger...

It was growing.

Brilliant men were in control. Brilliant men did not make mistakes....

But how had she known? How had Kendall Montgomery known to hunt down the girl, the little blonde who was so full of herself, so intent on having a high time? How had Kendall known to find her and insist that she stay with her group?

Tea and Tarot.

It couldn't be real, could it?

She knew. For the love of God, *she knew.*

To his amazement, he felt what a genius should never feel. Panic mingling with the unstoppable hunger.

Kendall awoke, immediately aware that he was lying next to her, that his leg was thrown over hers, that his arm was heavy across her abdomen. She opened her eyes and turned toward him, and discovered that he was already awake and watching her.

She couldn't remember the last time she had slept so deeply and so well. Or when she had last awakened in her bed with a man beside her.

Never, she realized. Never in this bed.

The great affair of her life so far had been Rob Thierry. He had left New Orleans to answer the call of the big city. To his credit, he had tried to get her to go. Maybe she should have. But she hadn't, and last she'd heard, he was working at a good job as a stage manager off Broadway. She wasn't still pining for him; she just hadn't found anyone else she wanted.

No, she'd had to wait around for a hard, embittered widower. A man as crazy in his own way as she was surely becoming herself.

But she was so glad he was there. His shoulders were revealed above the sheets, bronzed and broad, and his head looked so right against her pillow, his dark hair mussed and a hint of beard shadowing his jawline. And his eyes…

Those dark blue eyes, not icy now but still so unfathomable as he studied her.

He touched her face. "Kendall," he said, and it was as if her name had a deeper meaning.

She smiled slowly.

Then they heard a phone ringing. A cell phone, from out in the hall.

"Not mine," she told him.

"Mine."

He jumped out of bed. She couldn't help but notice that even in the full light of day, he had a gorgeous body. It was scarred in a few places, but muscled, firm and beautiful.

She followed him.

He had dug his cell phone out of the pocket of his pants and was frowning as he listened.

"I'll be right out," he said, and snapped the phone closed.

"What is it?" she asked.

"That was Zachary."

"What's wrong?"

"Apparently someone has been decorating the plantation for Halloween."

"Oh?"

"There are voodoo dolls on the front lawn."

"Voodoo dolls?"

"Three of them. With pins through them. And red slashes across their throats."

11

Miss Ady was ready when Kendall came for her. She was in a cotton dress and a little pillbox hat. She was wearing gloves, and carried a little flowered handbag.

She was bright and cheerful. "Rebecca wants you to know that she's mighty grateful you offered to take me in," Ady said. "Seems like it's been hard for them to take off time at the morgue lately. They're still catching up, even after all this time," she said seriously. "And there's new crimes, too. They blame it all on the city, but it's not just the city, you know, it's Orleans Parish, and that's a fact. Seems we get to see the best man can be, and the worst of it, too."

"I'm happy to take you. And I'll bet Mason is happy that I'm taking you, too. He gets to finish decorating the shop without me," Kendall assured her.

"Well, Rebecca went on in early, so she can take a break and pop over to the doctor's office. She went in at six this morning, so she can take her lunch break at ten."

"Wonderful. I'll get a chance to see her."

Ady went to a doctor in the CBD, or central business district, right over Canal Street from the Quarter. She'd been going to him for a long time. He had managed to stay in private practice, despite the medical trend to form huge partnerships. That meant survival for many physicians, Kendall knew, but she was glad for Miss Ady that Dr. Ling was on his own, so the elderly lady never ended up shuttled from partner to partner. Many of his patients were older, like Miss Ady, and he was always willing to listen to stories about little aches and pains that some other doctors might just put down to old age.

They had a wait of about twenty minutes. Dr. Ling tried not to overschedule, but he was always willing to spend a little extra time with any patient who needed it. While they waited, Kendall chatted with Miss Ady about the city, Halloween, the expected rise in tourism for the Halloween weekend, and Miss Ady's grandchildren. Anything and everything, so she didn't keep thinking about the night that had just passed, as if thinking too much would ruin it. And she wanted to hang on to the way she felt for as long as possible, because she felt wonderful. Excited. As if she'd discovered something new, which, in a way, she had.

So she didn't want to think about all that might be *wrong* with what she had done. He wasn't exactly the easiest going guy in the world. And he had a real bone to pick with Vinnie, for some reason, and she loved Vinnie. Friendships could be more valuable than any one-night stand. Except she was hoping against hope it would be more than just a one-night stand. No matter how he rankled her, she just wanted to be with the man. Big mistake. They had met the wrong way. No matter what he said, he still disdained her for being a so-called psychic. And she resented him for thinking ill of her and was totally indignant that he could think badly of

Vinnie. The rest of the world might suspect she was resentful of him for having inherited the Flynn plantation, while she honestly didn't resent him or his brothers at all. He'd left that morning in a mood of grim retrospection, almost as if they were strangers again. The way he'd looked at her, she wondered if he wouldn't have suspected *her* of planting the voodoo dolls if not for the fact that he'd been with her all night.

When she had needed him, though, he had come through.

"Girl, are you with me?" Ady asked her.

"What? Yes, of course, I'm sorry."

"I'm going in now. You wait out here for Rebecca."

"Don't you want me to go in with you?"

"No, I would appreciate it if you would just wait here for Rebecca. I've been taking good care of myself for years, and I'm no coward. I know how to give all the right answers and ask all the right questions," Ady informed her.

So Kendall was left with her own thoughts and worries once again. And she started to wonder if she hadn't ruined Ann's wild vacation, or if chasing down the young woman had even been the right thing to do.

Ady hadn't been gone long before Rebecca arrived. Kendall stood to give Rebecca a big hug as the other woman looked at her anxiously and asked, "How's Mama?"

"She just went in a couple of minutes ago."

Rebecca searched her eyes. "Did she pass out? Do something that worried you?"

Kendall shook her head. "No." She hesitated. "Rebecca, I'm sorry. I can't explain it. Something just made me think she should come in for an exam."

Rebecca might not have been sure Kendall's instincts

were correct, but she apparently believed her heart was in the right place. "Okay. We'll wait and see what's up."

"You can go on in with your mom, if you want," Kendall said.

"Lordy, no. She's got a bit of a crush on Dr. Ling, I think. Anyway, she taught us never to lie. Whatever is going on, she'll tell us both." They sat on the sofa together. Rebecca gave Kendall's knee a pat. "So how you doing, my friend?" she asked.

"Fine, thanks."

"You still missing Miss Amelia?"

"Well, I'll always miss her. We don't stop missing people."

"You should have gotten that plantation, not those wretched boys who came out of the blue!"

Kendall was surprised by her friend's vehemence. "What would I do with a plantation?" she asked.

"Sell it, of course."

Kendall laughed. "Actually, 'those wretched boys' are all right."

Rebecca grimaced. "Not according to Dr. Abel!"

Jon Abel was Rebecca's direct boss. There were a number of medical examiners for Orleans Parish, but Rebecca was one of Dr. Abel's lab assistants. As she looked at her friend, waiting for an explanation, Kendall suddenly remembered the man she had seen at the bar the other night, the one who had looked familiar to her, though she hadn't been able to place him at the time.

It had been Jon Abel.

"Why? What does Dr. Abel say?"

"He was so angry. Seems the Flynns came on like gangbusters, demanding that some old bones be given preferential treatment. Well, honey, he can be a pisser to work for at times, but I can't say I blame him this time around." Rebecca smiled then. "They sure are good-looking fellows, I'll grant 'em that," she said.

"You've met them?" Kendall asked curiously.

"I saw the oldest when he came into the lab. I didn't actually meet him, just saw him aggravating Dr. Abel. Which I don't like, 'cause then the doc gets all grouchy. I thought he'd be pitching a fit, wanting me to work harder and faster. But he just put those bones in a drawer—I think he got a kick out of that. And how that Flynn boy found a speck of blood in his graveyard is beyond me. He had his FBI friend bring that one in. It's probably too compromised to give us much. But Abel didn't even get on me over that. Said we should send it off to the folks up at the Smithsonian who do the work for Quantico, though I can't see anybody up there getting all excited about a drop of blood when nobody's even found a body."

"Wouldn't those bones be considered parts of bodies?" Kendall said.

Rebecca waved a hand in the air. "Honey, we got shootings to deal with. And drug O.D.s. Bones just aren't anything to get excited about."

"But…people have disappeared here!"

"Yeah. Lots of them. We'll never get the final toll."

Kendall was silent for a moment. If not for the fact that Jenny Trent was missing and she herself had had that strange experience with that tarot card, wouldn't she still believe the same?

"Rebecca, are you telling me that Abel isn't going to do anything about those bones Aidan Flynn found?"

"I didn't say that. I just said that he was shelving them until he finished with more important things." Rebecca stared at her curiously. "What's the matter with you, girl?"

Kendall shook her head. She honestly didn't know the answer to that question.

"Doc Abel seems to dislike the lot of them, though I haven't even seen the youngest one yet, but I saw the middle brother last night."

"Last night?"

Rebecca nodded. "I was at that place you like, the Hideaway, 'til all hours. Why do you think I look like something the cat dragged in this morning?" she asked.

"You look fine to me," Kendall said.

"Girlfriend, you are one fat liar. Anyway, they're saying there might be some big Halloween bash out at the plantation, can you imagine that?"

Kendall didn't have to form an answer, because Ady came out of the inner office just then, followed by Dr. Ling.

They both stood. Dr. Ling greeted them cordially, then said, "I've set Miss Ady up to have a biopsy. There's a tiny speck on her lungs."

"Oh, dear Lord!" Rebecca said, a hand over her heart.

"Now, now, I don't want you all getting excited. Miss Ady and I have talked this out, and she understands everything. I think we'll be nipping this right in the bud, and Miss Ady is going to be just fine. I'm proud of her for coming in. Most patients wait until they're really sick before doing anything, and that's when we're in trouble."

Rebecca had an arm around her mother. "You feeling okay, Mama?" she asked.

"Right as rain—now that I've seen Dr. Ling."

Kendall smiled. It was true. Miss Ady really liked Dr. Ling.

"I can take Mama on home," Rebecca told Kendall after they said their goodbyes to the doctor.

"You sure?" Kendall asked, smiling at Miss Ady. "I don't mind."

"No, you've been a godsend already, girl," Rebecca told her.

Ady took Kendall's hands and stood on tiptoe to plant a kiss on her cheek. "You got the sight, and you know that, Kendall," she whispered. "Most of us, we just play at it. But you've got it, the real gift. The sight." She drew away, still holding Kendall's hands. She winked and nodded, as if they shared a sacred and secret knowledge.

Kendall should have felt good, but instead she just felt cold. She was sorry to be right about Miss Ady, and she was terrified she might be right about others, too.

As she drove back to the French Quarter, she thought about Ann, and wondered if she would ever know if the girl had sailed away safely.

Jenny Trent had disappeared.

And the only other time she'd seen Death smile…

Had been with one of her closest friends. Sheila Anderson.

Aidan was hunched over the front lawn, not touching the little dolls as he stared at them. He had an empty feeling in the pit of his stomach because of what Jeremy had just told him. Jeremy had seen dolls just like them before.

At Kendall's shop.

"I thought I should get you out here before calling the cops," Zach said.

Aidan stood, looking at the house. Workmen were everywhere, and two electricians' vans and one from a plumbing company were parked nearby. A truck from Southern Plaster and Molding was just pulling up the drive.

"You think maybe some crazy electrician did this?" Jeremy asked, only half joking.

"No, this is someone local, someone who really is crazy," Aidan told him. "What fool thinks he can scare away the three of us with voodoo dolls?"

"Maybe a fool who wants to get his hands on this place. It's worth a lot of money, you know? The thing is, the house is actually in good shape, structurally," Zach said. Aidan stared at him. "Seriously. I have the engineer's report. The repairs are mostly superficial. Some work on the columns, updating the electric and plumbing. The place needs a lot of paint, some new woodwork. But the contractor has everyone moving already. We're in good shape. Maybe someone out there was hoping that the house would be in total decay and we'd just take a hike and leave it for him. But it's not—and *we're* not."

"We're not calling the cops, either," Aidan said.

"I guess they *would* just think we were being pains in the ass," Zach agreed.

"They're just voodoo dolls," Jeremy acknowledged.

"Pretty grisly voodoo dolls, though, don't you think?" Zach asked.

"I say we bag 'em and tag 'em," he suggested. "None of us has touched them, and at some point we may need to look at them for prints or trace evidence. If our prankster gets more serious."

Aidan wasn't sure this was just a prank, but he agreed with his brother in principle. And he refused to believe Kendall had had anything to do with this, even if Jeremy was right and these were the same dolls she carried in her store.

After all, he knew exactly where she had been all night.

They bagged the dolls. Then Zachary told Aidan, "I have some interesting information for you."

"Oh?"

"I did a little hacking. Come on and I'll show you."

Zachary had his laptop computer set up in the only place where there were no workmen: Amelia's bedroom.

This room, at least, had been kept up. It sported a huge sleigh bed in dark mahogany, with a dressing table, wardrobe and side tables to match. French doors led out to the balcony, and in front of them, in contrast to the dark wood, sat a freshly painted beige wicker table with chairs upholstered to match the drapes and comforter. The hardwood floors had been cleaned and buffed, and an Oriental rug with a floral motif covered the floor. There was nothing musty about the room, nothing that hinted of age or decay, or even that the longtime owner had died here.

Zachary had set up his computer on the dressing table.

Aidan and Jeremy pulled up the wicker chairs and sat on either side of Zach to see the screen. "I cross-referenced all kinds of things to come up with this list. It actually goes back about ten years, and then—with an interruption of pure confusion after Katrina—it looks as if it continues, and it's escalating."

Aidan read the chart his brother had pulled together. There were ten intriguing and never-solved missing persons cases in the area. The first went back a decade. The second, seven years. Then five years. Then there were two from the year before the storm. Then, since the storm, there had been five more, including Jenny Trent.

Each of the women who had come to the area never to be

seen again had been between the ages of twenty and thirty. Each had been starting out on a long vacation. They were all single. And in every case, the disappearance hadn't been reported until they'd been gone for several weeks, because they didn't live with anyone who would be concerned immediately. In two of the cases, they hadn't been reported missing until they had been gone several months.

"How the hell could that have been?" Aidan wondered aloud.

"Joan Crandall disappeared ten years ago. She left Chicago for Houston, and was supposedly driving to New Orleans from there. She had worked at a fast-food restaurant, and, I suppose, lots of people just walked off the job, so her boss just figured she'd decided to stay down here. The other was Kristin Ford. She disappeared five years ago, and she was driving here from Memphis, but she hadn't been there very long. She was working on again, off again as a stripper. She was only reported as missing when the neighbors noticed a terrible odor from her house. Apparently, a neighborhood cat had gotten in and died, and it was only when the authorities were called that she was reported missing at all. Her credit card was last used at a gas station just outside the Quarter. Her car was never found, she never wrote another check, and the trail just ended. In most of these cases, the investigators just reached a dead end, and since there was no one to push for action, they all ended up filed as cold cases."

"If these *are* all connected—and I think they are—then the killer's definitely escalating," Aidan said with a sinking feeling.

"Want me to get on this, contact the local authorities that took the missing persons reports?" Zach asked.

Aidan nodded, then looked at Jeremy. "Let's go see your guitar-playing buddy."

As they left, Aidan looked back at the house. A workman was replastering a column. A painter's van drew up and parked by the front steps.

The old place wasn't really such a white elephant after all. He could already envision how nice it was going to look with a coat of paint.

Jeremy caught him looking at the house. "Halloween party, you wait and see," he said.

"Maybe," Aidan agreed.

There was still something that seemed off about the house. It wasn't rot; it wasn't decay.

It was something else.

A hunch.

Damn, he hated hunches.

Vinnie was expecting them.

He lived in a large house down toward Rampart on Dauphine. It looked as if it needed paint even more than the plantation did, but inside, it was well-kept. He greeted them at the door, shirtless and holding a cup of coffee, and he invited them in politely enough.

"If you had called, I'd have been ready," he told Aidan with a slight scowl.

"Had a late night, huh?" Aidan asked.

Vinnie shrugged. "You were out just as late."

Had Vinnie been out even later, planting voodoo dolls on their lawn? Aidan wondered.

Aidan and Jeremy sat in the parlor and drank coffee while they waited for Vinnie to grab a shirt. The room held a grand piano covered with a quilt, a few guitars on stands, and bookshelves with dozens of music books and a few novels. It didn't look as if Vinnie was into the occult. His choice in reading, as evidenced by the one shelf that held commercial fiction, tended toward legal thrillers.

When he reappeared from his bedroom, he looked like any ordinary guy, in jeans and a T-shirt.

"Nice house," Aidan commented.

"It was my folks'. They moved to North Carolina, to a place in the mountains, to retire. I'm buying it from them, and since they bought it thirty years ago, the price isn't bad. I could never afford it otherwise."

"Do you ever take in boarders?" Aidan asked.

Vinnie shook his head. "I'm too hard to live with. Can't keep a girlfriend, either."

"I wouldn't think you'd have any problem meeting women," Aidan said.

"I don't. I'm just the kind for one-night stands," Vinnie told him. "Maybe I'll change one day, but right now, there are too many pretty women out there. And they all seem to like sleeping with musicians."

Aidan glanced at his brother, but Jeremy shrugged. "Don't look at me. I'm not a musician."

"Bullshit, man. You're one hell of a musician," Vinnie objected.

"I'm not a working musician."

"You should be," Vinnie told him. "But I guess you must be good at the investigation thing, too, huh?" He turned to Aidan. "You guys must do really well, to be putting that plantation back in order."

"We're good at our jobs," Aidan said evenly.

"Come on, we can walk over to where Jenny was staying," Vinnie suggested.

Jeremy glanced at his watch, then looked at his brother apologetically. "Can you two take it from here? I'm due to make a public service announcement at noon. We're giving away two tickets for the gala Saturday night."

"We're fine," Aidan said. "Aren't we, Vinnie?"

"Yeah, just like two old pals," Vinnie said dryly.

It was a three-block walk. They passed a man walking a dog and a woman getting out of a FedEx truck. Both of them knew Vinnie and seemed happy to see him.

There were no tourists in evidence, but then, this was a residential area of the Quarter. Some tourists probably took a walk around the area now and then, admiring the old houses with the pots of flowers on their porches, but it didn't offer the bars of Bourbon Street or the shops found on Royal or Decatur, so there was no draw to bring most people here.

"Why do you have it in for me?" Vinnie asked Aidan suddenly.

Aidan turned to look at Vinnie, surprised by the question. The guy seemed sincerely puzzled.

"The trail ends with you, that's all," Aidan said.

"The trail, as you say, ends at the place where I'm taking you now," Vinnie said firmly.

They came to a house that was only a little larger than Vinnie's. A nice-looking place with a big veranda sporting a traditional porch swing, a stone wall out front, and a sign that advertised La Fleur Bed and Breakfast.

Vinnie walked on ahead, trying the front door. It wasn't open, so he knocked.

A tiny woman with glasses and a gray bun at the back of her head opened the door. "Hello. Are you looking for a room?"

Aidan stepped ahead of Vinnie. "Hi, how are you? No, we're looking for some help, ma'am."

She arched a brow. "Well, I'm delighted to help you if I can."

Aidan thanked her, introduced himself and produced the picture of Jenny Trent. He explained that she'd been in the city three months earlier, that Vinnie had walked her to the bed-and-breakfast, and that she hadn't been seen since. But before he even finished, she was frowning and staring at him. "I wondered when someone would come," she said.

Kendall was nervous. She couldn't help worrying about Sheila.

She wandered aimlessly around the shop, brewed tea, sold some Halloween decorations, then found that she was scheduled for a reading. She looked at Mason. "Want to do this one?" she asked him.

"It's Gary, one of the guys from the Stakes. He asked for you."

Gary was a nice guy. He had glossy shoulder-length blond hair, the kind that made women jealous. He tried to talk her into singing with the band more often, but she begged off and gave him the cards, telling him to cut them, wary of what was going to happen. She laid out his spread. The cards looked like cards. She was so relieved that she talked with him for a long time, telling him honestly that the cards were just a way for him to look at his own life and know his own mind, and that his spread suggested he needed to work harder at pursuing his goal.

"How am I supposed to do that?" he asked. "We play almost

every night. And even when I'm not playing with the Stakes, I can usually find work on my own or with other groups. But it doesn't feel like I'm really going anywhere, you know?"

I don't know, she might have told him. You're looking at someone who caved early on and easily, afraid that her dreams would never earn a living.

"You keep your eyes open," she said instead, "and you listen for every opportunity. Take gigs that support a cause or could get you some good publicity. Maybe you need to *look* for opportunities, too, even create them. Don't just wait around for opportunity to find you."

"Yeah, you're right. You're good." He winked at her. "Better than any shrink I've ever seen—or bartender, for that matter."

"Yeah, well, thanks," she told him.

She looked at the cards. They were still just cards. She left the little inner room with him, they exchanged a few pleasantries, then he gave her a kiss on the cheek and left.

"You okay?" Mason asked her.

"Sure."

"The reading was fine?"

"Yeah. I spewed my usual uplifting bull."

"Alas, what an unbeliever."

"And you really believe?"

"I never mock what my heart tells me," he assured her. "I'm going to lunch, and it's going to be a long lunch, okay? There are more boxes to open in back, if you get bored."

She wasn't bored; she was restless. On the one hand, she couldn't stop thinking about the fact she was actually engaged in a sexual relationship with a man who was fascinating, compelling and unbelievable in bed. At the same time, she kept telling herself that no matter what she'd told him, she still wasn't sure she even liked him. But she did want to see him again. Talk with him, even argue with him. Definitely sleep with him. And maybe…more. That was the scary part.

She tried not to think about Aidan, but not thinking about Aidan made her more nervous. She wandered into her office and picked up the deck of tarot cards she always used for readings. Since she was alone, she brought them back out front with her. She shuffled them and turned them up, not in a spread, but one by one.

When she found the Death card, it just stared up at her. It was flat. It was inanimate. It was a card.

She wasn't doing a reading, though. Maybe she should read her own tarot spread.

No. No way.

But the thought of doing a reading made her even more anxious about Sheila Anderson.

She put through a call to the historical society where her friend worked, but Sheila's boss seemed surprised by her call. "You know she isn't due back until this weekend, right?" he asked her.

"Right. Thank you."

Frustrated but still uneasy, she hung up.

She carefully returned the deck to her reading room, went into the back, pulled out the boxes Mason had mentioned and opened the first to find a new shipment of voodoo dolls. She walked out front and looked up at the shelf. There had been ten dolls in their first order.

She remembered selling two right away, and she had sold another three earlier this week.

But now there were only two on the top shelf.

When had Mason sold the others? This morning? Or…

There was no way out of it. Three were missing. Exactly three. The same number that had been found in front of Flynn Plantation.

The woman who owned the bed-and-breakfast was named Lily Fleur. Her husband's name, she explained, as she cheerfully led them out to an old carriage house that was now her storeroom. He'd passed away a few years ago, and her daughter had moved to New York and her son to California. They were always urging her to move out to be with one of them, but this was her home, and she loved running a B and B.

"I called the police when she didn't return," she said now, "and they suggested I just hold on to her belongings, said she'd probably come back. I didn't hear from them again, and quite frankly, I put the things away and then kind of forgot about them. I should have been more persistent, I guess, but I wasn't. And I think I got her name wrong, anyway, because they didn't find any record of her. I'll show you where she signed in. It looks like she wrote Sherry Frend, not Jenny Trent. We talked a bit when she checked in, but she was only here for the night, and she paid me cash." She opened the door to let them in.

"It was just the one backpack, so I figured she'd left most of her luggage in her car, or that she knew how to travel light."

Aidan was glad she was so willing to turn the backpack over to him, rather than contacting the police again.

"Is Sherry all right?" the elderly woman asked. "Jenny, I mean."

"I'm afraid she's missing, Mrs. Fleur," Aidan told her.

"Missing?" The woman was clearly upset. "That's terrible!"

"She was trusting," Vinnie said suddenly. Aidan looked at the man. He looked genuinely worried, more subdued than Aidan had ever seen him, as if he'd finally realized that something might really have happened to the girl he had walked home that night three months ago.

"Let's see what she left," Aidan said.

"Oh," Mrs. Fleur said suddenly. "Should I be letting you do this?"

"I've been hired by her next of kin to try to find her," Aidan assured her.

"You'll take her backpack, then, right?" Mrs. Fleur asked, as if she had decided that she needed to back off from anything that might have belonged to the girl, as if that would distance her from anything bad that might have happened.

Aidan nodded. "Yes, I'll be taking it."

"I only saw her when she checked in, you know, and then before she went out for the night," Mrs. Fleur said nervously.

"So you don't know if she actually came in or not after Vinnie here walked her home?" Aidan asked.

"She made it to the porch. *I* know that," Vinnie said.

Lily Fleur shoved the backpack quickly into Aidan's arms. "I hope you find her."

She sounded sincere, but she was clearly dismissing them.

Aidan thanked her for her help. "Mrs. Fleur," he asked, "do you remember any commotion that night—late, after she would have gotten back to her room?"

"Good heavens, no. I run a quiet place."

"And you're sure that if anything was going on in a room here, you would hear it?"

"Of course! I'm old, not deaf," she said huffily, as she led them back through the house and down the hallway to the front door. Aidan picked up one of her cards as he passed the front desk, thanking her again and alerting her that he might need to call her again.

Distressed, she nearly pushed them out the door.

"We can check out the pack at my place," Vinnie suggested. "It's closer than your hotel."

He still seemed worried. As they walked, he met Aidan's eyes. "I don't know why you've decided you don't like me, but I swear to you, I've never hurt anyone in my life."

Aidan decided going to Vinnie's was a good idea. It would let him watch the other man's reaction to whatever they found.

When they dumped the backpack, they found several guidebooks, along with a hairbrush, ten pairs of skimpy underwear, several bras, a heavy sweatshirt, two pairs of jeans, a pair of shorts, and two knit dresses that would work for a casual occasion or a night out. Aidan noticed Vinnie staring at one of the dresses.

"What?" Aidan asked.

Vinnie looked at him. "She definitely went back to her room after I left her. She was wearing that dress when she came to the bar."

Aidan looked at Vinnie assessingly. "You said you two just flirted. She obviously liked you, and she let you walk her home. Why didn't you try to get her into bed?"

Vinnie flushed. "I didn't say I didn't try. I understand signals, and I respect the word 'no,' so I left her on the porch and went home. I swear."

"Did she seem anxious about anything?" Aidan asked.

Vinnie pursed his lips, thinking. "She did keep looking

at her watch. And she was excited, but she was one of those bubbly people, anyway, so I just assumed she was all excited about her trip."

Aidan picked up one of the guidebooks as Vinnie spoke. He leafed through it, and something fell out.

He picked it up.

"Well, now we know she never left the country," he said.

"Why? What is it?" Vinnie asked.

"Her passport."

12

Aidan started with Jonas Burningham.

Jonas was in his office, and he came right out when Aidan asked for him, ushering him back to his office quickly.

"I was going to call you," Jonas said.

"Oh? You have something, too?"

Jonas frowned. "Too? Why are you here?"

Aidan flung the backpack onto Jonas's shiny wooden desk. "The other day I went out to see Jenny Trent's cousin-in-law. And I traced her last charge to a bar—the same bar where we all seem to be hanging out these days, by the way. Our guitar-playing friend Vinnie walked her back to a B and B, where she'd paid cash for her room. She left this backpack there. Her passport is in it, by the way."

He had returned everything to the backpack. Except for the brush. He wasn't sure why, but something had just told him to hang on to it, even though it was the most reliable source of Jenny's DNA that they'd come up with.

Jonas stared blankly at the backpack for a moment, then turned to Aidan. "Oh."

"Why did you think I was here?"

"I thought maybe…nothing."

"Okay, yes. I heard Matty came looking for you, and that you were fooling around. That's your business. You're an idiot, but hey, you're a grown man."

"I love Matty," Jonas said guiltily.

"I told you, your marriage is your business. Now pay attention to me, damn it. This girl came to New Orleans and was most probably murdered here. Would you get on the stick?"

Jonas looked up at him. "If you think that she was murdered here," he said, "it's a matter for the local police."

Aidan leaned on the desk. "Jonas, in the first place, Hal Vincent refuses to pay any attention to me. And in the second place, if what Zach turned up is right, she's part of a serial case, and that puts it right smack under the Bureau's jurisdiction, so do you think you could help me out here?"

Jonas straightened. "Yes. All right. I'll give Hal a call. I'll get him moving. And I'll start looking into it, too." He reached for the backpack.

"I'll take it over. You just call and let him know that I'm coming. And do me another favor."

"Of course."

"Call that M.E. Jon Abel. If he doesn't want to work on this, tell him to hand those bones over to someone who isn't as famous but actually wants to work."

"Yeah, of course." He hesitated, then said, "Listen, Aidan, you're not going to say anything to Matty, are you?"

"What the hell would I say to her, Jonas? Confessing to your wife is *your* job."

Physical activity was always good, Kendall decided. By the time Mason returned from his extended lunch, she'd opened all the boxes, and finished restocking and redecorating the store. One customer had come in to have her tea leaves read and been so disappointed that Kendall was the only one in the store that Kendall had relented and done the reading at one of the little café tables in the main room.

The tea leaves had been tea leaves, and she'd felt ridiculously relieved. Still, the first thing she asked Mason when he walked in was what had happened to the dolls.

"What dolls?" he asked.

"The voodoo dolls. We're missing three of them," she told him.

"No, we're not."

"We are."

He looked at the shelf, then stared at her as if she were crazy.

"I just put those up there. There were only two left, and there should have been five."

"Oh, yeah. I sold three of them yesterday afternoon."

"To who?"

"Some woman in a scarf."

"What was her name?"

"I don't know," Mason said impatiently. "I don't give all our customers the third degree, you know. Neither do you!"

"Did she pay with a credit card?"

"No, she had cash." He paused, thinking for a moment. "She was really weird, come to think of it. Even for New Orleans. I thought she might be part of one of those silly vampire cults. She was wearing big dark glasses and a black cloak, with a big black scarf over her head. She had a wheezy voice, like she had a cold or something. I tried not to touch her, in case she was contagious." He shivered, grinned, and said, "I was afraid to let her touch the dolls, but she wanted three of them. I told her they were expensive, and she just produced a roll of cash, so I sold them to her. This is a business, after all. And you've got to admit, we've sold things to creepy people before."

Creepy people.

But could the dolls he had sold be the same dolls Zach had found? Wouldn't it be just great if Aidan decided she had arranged for someone—Vinnie, maybe—to turn the dolls into some kind of death caricatures and leave them on his lawn?

No. The Flynns were too smart for that, and Aidan knew her too well now to think something so stupid. Didn't he?

Yeah, he knew she believed the Death card had come to life.

"You know, I wondered if she had a skin disease or something," Mason said thoughtfully.

"Why?"

"She wore black gloves, too."

He looked at her, his frown deepening when he saw the worried look on her face. "Okay, so I sold the dolls to a weirdo. Big deal. What the hell is the matter with you?"

"The Flynns found three of these voodoo dolls on their front lawn this morning. I guess they were pretty messed up. Like three death warnings."

Mason laughed. "And you're *worried?*" he asked her.

"Well…"

"Only an idiot would think the Flynns could be scared off by *dolls.*"

That was true, she knew.

Still, the whole thing was unsettling. She decided she should call Aidan and let him know what had happened. She picked up the phone, then she set it back down.

She didn't have his number.

"What are you doing now?" Mason asked her.

"I was going to call Aidan, and tell him about the sale and your weird woman."

"Why didn't you?"

"I don't know his number."

"That's easily solved."

"How?"

"Call Vinnie, get Jeremy's number, and Jeremy will know Aidan's," Mason said. "Heck, I'll do it for you."

He picked up the phone, then looked at her thoughtfully when he finished dialing.

"What?"

"Do you think the woman who bought those dolls was wearing a costume?" he asked. She didn't get a chance to answer. "Hey, Vinnie, can you give me Jeremy Flynn's number?" After a moment, "Yeah, it's for Kendall. She wants to call Aidan."

She could hear Vinnie talking on the other end of the line, but she couldn't make out what he was saying. Finally Mason scratched a number on a piece of paper and hung up, grinning.

"Oh, God, what? Did Aidan give him a hard time?"

"No. He's all excited. He said he was helping investigate."

She arched a brow distrustfully. "Vinnie is *excited?*"

"Yup. He said he and Aidan are tracking down that girl, Jenny Trent, together."

"Where's Aidan now?"

"I don't know. Do you want me to call Vinnie back?"

"No." She took the phone from him and dialed the number he had gotten from Vinnie.

"Oh, that's Aidan's number, by the way, not Jeremy's. Sounds like those two are just like *this* now," he said, crossing two fingers.

Was Aidan playing Vinnie? she wondered. Lulling him into a false sense of security? Or had he decided her friend was innocent?

Aidan answered his phone immediately.

"Flynn."

"Aidan?"

"Kendall."

That was it. Just her name. But he had said it as if he enjoyed it.

"I'm calling about those dolls on your lawn, Aidan. I think they came from my shop. Mason told me that he sold three of them yesterday." She glanced at Mason. "To a—"

Mason grabbed the phone from her. "Hey, Aidan. It was some freaky woman dressed all in black. Looking back, I think someone was disguising her—or his—identity."

Mason listened and nodded, then hung up the phone.

Kendall stared at him. "Hey! I was talking."

"He's busy. Said he'll call back." Mason shrugged, then started wiping down the counter and straightening the napkins.

Kendall tried not to feel anxious.

And she tried even harder to convince herself that she didn't care one way or another what Aidan Flynn really thought of her.

Jonas called both Hal Vincent and Jon Abel, then rang Aidan to fill him in, so Aidan made his first stop the M.E.'s office. To his surprise, Jon Abel came out to see him right away. He wasn't exactly cordial, but he was at least polite. Aidan offered him the dress that Vinnie had identified as the one Jenny Trent had worn on what had possibly been her last night on earth. "You have bones—from two different women, you've told me—and you have the blood sample I brought you, and I believe your technicians might be able to pull skin cells from the lining of this dress, which belonged to a woman named Jenny Trent. I'm hoping that if you run DNA testing on all those items we'll be able to find out if one of those bones was hers."

"I can try," Abel told him, looking down at the dress. "I can try. The blood sample is extremely deteriorated. I don't know about the bones. And they *may* be able to find sloughed-off skin cells. I'll try. I can't promise you anything more than that."

"We have a girl who definitely disappeared from the French Quarter. She had family, and that family deserves our best," Aidan said.

"I told you, we'll do what we can," Abel told him.

Aidan didn't know why he didn't offer Abel the brush, or why he didn't intend to turn it over to Hal Vincent, either. If DNA couldn't be pulled from the bones or the blood, the DNA they could pull from any hairs in the brush wouldn't be much good anyway.

He thanked the M.E. and left.

At the police station, Hal Vincent came out to see him. It was hard to read what the man was thinking, but when he brought Aidan back to his office, Aidan gave him the backpack, complete with Jenny Trent's passport, and told him everything he'd discovered so far.

"I'll bring Vinnie down here and talk to him," Hal said.

Aidan thought for a moment, then surprised himself by saying, "I think Vinnie is telling the truth when he said he left her at her door. I don't think he did it."

"Yeah?" Hal asked, looking up at him.

"You learn to read a man," Aidan said.

Hal looked quickly down at the backpack. "Sure. Sometimes. If you know for a fact that this girl disappeared from here, I'll see to it that some of our best officers are assigned to the case."

Aidan leaned forward. "What about her car?"

"Her car?"

"It was found in a public lot," Aidan said.

Hal Vincent stroked his chin. "Was it? Well, I'll find out if it's still impounded or what." He looked at Aidan. "What's your stake in this?"

"I've been hired by the next of kin."

Hal sat back, a touch of resentment in his expression. "Oh, yeah? How did you manage that?"

"Easy. I asked a question." Aidan rose. "Thanks for your help."

"It's my job," the detective said, and there was a touch of steel in his tone. "Thanks for your help."

"Yeah, I'll be touching base," Aidan said pleasantly, then rose and left the office. He could feel Hal's eyes on him through the window as he exited the station.

It was close to six when the shop phone rang. Trying not to appear as anxious as she felt, Kendall moved to answer it, but Mason reached it before she did. There was pure mischief in his eyes as he answered it, talking pleasantly to whoever was on the other end.

She sighed in exasperation, and finally he handed the receiver to her.

"It's for you."

"Gee, thanks." She put the receiver to her ear and said, "Hello?"

"Hey, it's Aidan."

"Hey." She hesitated, then tried for a joking tone. "I hear you saw Vinnie and you didn't send him straight to jail."

"Yeah." He was quiet for a moment, then asked, "You all right?"

"Of course," she told him.

"I'm heading back out to the plantation. I've decided to sleep out there tonight."

"Oh. Well, I guess that's good. I mean, you'll be there if anyone tries to play another prank." At least it didn't sound like he thought she was guilty of anything.

He was silent for so long that she was beginning to think she'd lost the connection, but finally he spoke again, "Kendall, this might sound like a strange request, but…don't go out tonight, huh? Go home, lock yourself in and just take it easy. Don't go chasing around after any errant tourists, okay?" The last was said with an effort at lightness.

"Is something wrong?" she asked.

"Nothing new. But just stay home, will you?"

"All right," she agreed, wondering why he sounded so adamant about it. Was he worried about her for some reason? Or just afraid she'd hook up with some other guy? They weren't going steady or anything, and what kind of woman did he think she was, anyway?

But deep down she knew his caution had nothing to do with the fact he'd slept with her. Something was bothering him, and that bothered *her*. She didn't like this new feeling of nervousness. This was her city. She loved it. She hated having to feel afraid of it.

"Call me if…well, for any reason," he told her.

"I will," she said.

Then he spoke again, somewhat awkwardly. "You've heard about that charity thing Jeremy's been promoting at the aquarium Saturday night, right?"

"Of course."

"Would you mind going with me?"

She was surprised. Was he asking her on a *date?* Or did he just not want to show up solo?

Did it matter?

"Sure. I'd been thinking I should spring for a ticket. It's a good cause."

"I've got plenty of tickets. We bought about twenty, just to kick it off." He was quiet again for a long moment. "You can bring friends, if you want."

Okay, so it wasn't a date. Maybe he was hoping she'd bring Vinnie, so he could keep an eye on him.

Then again, on a Saturday night, Vinnie would be working.

Oh, hell, she couldn't read signals over the phone. And maybe there weren't even any signals to read.

"That sounds great. I'll let people know. I would have loved to bring my friend Sheila, but she isn't back from vacation yet." She winced inwardly. Sheila *was* out of town. She had to be.

"See if Mason wants to come. And if he can take the night off, ask Vinnie."

So he *did* want to keep an eye on Vinnie. "Okay," she said, feeling ridiculously disappointed.

"I'll talk to you soon, then," he said.

"Sure. Bye."

He didn't say goodbye, just hung up. She set the phone back into the cradle.

"Can we close up now?" Mason asked.

"Of course."

He walked over and set an arm around her shoulders. "Want to come out and play with me, little girl?"

"Are you heading out to the Hideaway again?" she asked.

He shrugged. "When you find a place you like, why change? Hell, I don't even have a cat to go home to."

"And you think you're going to find the love of your life in a bar?"

"Maybe not. But I'm easy. I'm happy with a halfway decent-looking girl who's just looking for some hot and heavy sex for the night," he teased.

"Gee, forgive me. I'll pass. I'm going to stop off on the way home and get something to eat, then enjoy some deliciously bad television and get some sleep."

They locked up and parted ways. She headed for home, and he went on toward Bourbon Street.

Aidan had packed his bags and checked out of his hotel, thinking he might as well start living at the property while it was under repair. At first he'd thought that they would be knocking down walls, and that there would be no water or electricity. But with nothing major going on structurally, there was no reason to go on paying for a hotel when he could stay in comfort in the master bedroom. There was no cable, so Zach was still going back to the city every night so he could continue his Web investigations, and Jeremy had also opted to keep on staying in town. But Aidan felt like something quieter, and he had a flashlight in case the electricity failed while the place was still being rewired, so what the hell.

He arrived when the sun was setting, and despite all the

wheelbarrows, cement bags and other paraphernalia left on the grounds, the house was beautiful on its little rise above the river. The dying sunlight hid the chipping paint, and the spots where the stucco and plaster had recently been repaired. She looked like the grand old dame that she was.

He parked in the graveled driveway and walked around the outside of the house. The workers were thorough; the windows and doors had all been locked at the end of the day.

He was about to take his key and open the front door when he looked across the grounds and through the trees to the burial ground.

With dusk at hand, there was something fascinating and forlorn about it. Rather than enter the house, he found himself walking toward the cemetery.

The family had planned it as a pleasant oasis. The trees were like a barrier—holding the living out or keeping the dead in—but it was the kind of barrier that defined the space attractively. As he entered the graveyard, though, he could sense that it was a place of loneliness and neglect. There were stones and slabs that were now illegible, and even many of the more recent aboveground tombs bore legends that had been erased by the wear and tear of time.

Tall grass, wildflowers and weeds grew at will, and the moss-draped trees added a bittersweet pathos to the scene. He judged the distance from the graveyard to the house, and from the graveyard to the outbuildings.

The river ran downhill from the rear of the house, past the parallel rows of trees that had once led to a magnificent rear entrance. At one time it might even have been considered the main entrance, since most visitors would have come from the river. The house sat well up on its little hill, and all the ground around it, including the cemetery, rolled toward the river.

It wasn't that unlikely that a storm could have moved earth, branches, refuse and even human bones from the graveyard toward the river—right past the slave quarters and other outbuildings.

Aidan sat on one of the aboveground tombs, surveying the realm of the dead. Looking around, he found himself studying the ground.

It just didn't look as if any of the graves here had been disturbed. Of course, maybe a grave had been disturbed during Katrina, and then new winds and rains had covered up what had been compromised before.

Still…

He looked toward the largest of the family vaults, then got up, strode over to it and walked in. He looked at the fresh engraving that identified the final resting place of Amelia Jeanine Flynn. He touched the stone. "You must have been quite a woman," he said. "If Kendall felt so devoted to you…well, I wish I could have known you."

He realized he'd spoken aloud and shook his head with amusement. At least he was alone in a family graveyard surrounded by fifteen mostly empty acres. There wasn't even a car passing by out on the road.

He went back outside and looked around the graveyard some more, trying to ascertain why something just didn't seem right. No matter how hard he looked, he didn't see anything out of the ordinary.

It was dark when he left the cemetery, swinging the gate closed behind him. It made no noise. Someone had oiled it, and not long ago, either. He turned to look back at the graves.

Darkness had fallen, and there was only enough moon-light to offer a trickle of illumination.

Still certain he was looking right at something and not seeing it, Aidan headed back for the house. He unlocked the door and went in, and turned on a few lights, then headed for the kitchen. He was pleasantly surprised to discover that one of his brothers had gone shopping. The refrigerator offered the basics: soda, water, beer, condiments, cheese and sandwich meat. There was bread on the counter. He made himself a sandwich, then went back out to the car and brought in his bags.

He spent part of the evening walking around the down-stairs, checking the windows, which were all secure and in good working order, as were the locks on the doors.

There were only two doors to the house itself, at the north and south ends, and both were solid.

Upstairs, he went through the same ritual, then he pulled out the charts Jeremy had printed off and read through them. He decided he would follow Jenny Trent's trail until he dis-covered the truth about her disappearance or came to a genuine dead end. And if that happened, he would hunt down someone who had known one of the other women who had apparently vanished off the face of the earth and start all over again until he figured out who was behind the deaths.

It was late. He set the Colt he was licensed to carry on one of the old mahogany tables near the bed, then stripped down to his jeans and lay down to sleep. Sleep wouldn't come, though, and he realized he was just lying there, lis-tening to the night.

It was impossible not to remember the previous night, which had been so close to perfection. Impossible not to remember the woman he had shared it with.

He'd been a fool to stay away tonight. It actually hurt to stay away. He didn't know what the hell it was about her, but he felt a burning need to be with her, to protect her.

He frowned as he lay there, wondering if he was going off the deep end.

Why had he been convinced that he needed to see her home last night? How he had *known* someone was there? Lurking. Watching from the street.

Was it the same person who had planned on meeting Ann?

The same person who had arranged a meeting with Jenny Trent?

Had they ruined the killer's plans for Ann and made him turn his attention to Kendall, even though she didn't fit the profile?

Or was he just creating demons in his own mind?

It was during that thought that he saw a strange light blink across the night sky outside his window.

Instantly tense, he rose, slipped his feet into the deck shoes he'd left by his bed and picked up the Colt.

He waited, and the flicker of light came again. It was coming from the rear, near the slave quarters.

Not the graveyard.

He hurried downstairs and slipped out the front door, then, his back against the house, moved carefully toward the back.

There it was. A small pool of light inside the farthest slave cottage.

Keeping to the shadows, he left the concealment of the house and made his way from shack to shack. Someone was inside the last one.

He carefully made his way closer, then paused and looked over his shoulder, trying to determine if the intruder had any accomplices. He heard something moving, but not from anywhere around him.

He moved toward the door of the building and held out his gun with both hands, finger on the trigger.

And then he kicked the door in.

13

For the first time ever, Kendall felt uncomfortable walking home.

The action was starting on Bourbon Street, but toward home, the streets seemed unbelievably still. It wasn't late, but for some reason, none of the other residents seemed to be out and about.

As she walked the last block, a streetlamp sputtered and died.

Then she thought she heard footsteps. Someone was following her but managed to disappear every time she turned around.

She felt a sense of growing fear, which she told herself was ridiculous. She had to get past this new edginess if she ever wanted to feel normal again.

A car went by. That should have made her feel better, but it didn't. She looked over as it passed and felt spooked, because it seemed to be moving in slow motion.

In fact it was, she realized, then told herself it was probably just someone looking for a certain address or maybe a parking space. She kept walking until she passed it, then got the uneasy sensation that it was following her.

She made an abrupt turn toward Bourbon Street. The car couldn't follow, because the street was one way against it.

She almost ran up the block to Bourbon. Even at this end of the street, there were a few bars. And luckily, there seemed to be a lot of drunks out as well.

A shill was handing out three-for-one flyers. A couple of men were standing in front of a strip joint, trying to lure in the unwary. A voluptuous woman in a skimpy outfit and badly fitting wig was hovering in a doorway behind them.

She turned down the next street, back toward Royal, thinking how ridiculous it was to think she was being followed. And anyway, even if she *had* been, she had shaken off whoever it was.

But as she headed toward home again from the opposite direction, she felt a growing sense of unease once more. She started walking faster.

As she neared her front door, someone suddenly rose from the front step. She let out a scream and turned to run.

"No! Jesus, Mary and Joseph! Don't hurt me!"

The frantic plea came from a man in threadbare jeans and a worn tweed jacket who was sitting on the floor, leaning against the wall of the shack, a small fire burning at his feet, a dirty newspaper in his hands, and a flashlight, a bag of chips and a can of beer at his side. He was fifty or sixty years old and had a full beard, but he looked clean enough, despite his shabby appearance.

And with Aidan leveling the Colt on him, he also looked terrified.

"Who the hell are you, and what are you doing here?" Aidan demanded.

"Please, for the love of God, put that gun down," the man begged.

Aidan took his finger off the trigger and lowered his two-handed grip. He didn't completely lower the gun or his guard, though. "Answer me," he snapped.

"Jimmy. I'm just Jimmy."

"What are you doing here, Just Jimmy? And get the hell up," Aidan commanded.

"Okay, okay, just don't hurt me." The man carefully put down his newspaper, then showed Aidan his empty hands as he got to his feet. "Please, mister, I don't do no one any harm."

Aidan quickly surveyed the little hut. Jimmy seemed to keep all his belongings in a shopping bag against the back wall.

Easy to pack. Easy to unpack.

"How long have you been living here?" Aidan demanded.

"Oh, I don't live here—"

"How the hell long?" Aidan repeated.

"About…six months," the man responded quickly. "Look, I work nights at the gas station down the road—'til three o'clock sometimes. I've been trying to save up for a place." The little man was speaking very fast. "I've got to get enough money for a car before I can find a real place to live. I never broke into anyplace else, honest. I've never set foot up in the big house. I just come here to sleep. To stay safe."

Harmless bum? Or homicidal maniac?

Jimmy was skinny as a rail. His eyes were huge in his face. He didn't look like he had the strength to kill a fly, much less kill and dismember a woman.

Aidan tucked the gun into his waistband. "You've been living here for six months?"

"I swear, I didn't hurt no one, and no one even knew I was here. Look, I'm a coward. I walk down the road fast as I can, come in here, then close the door and pray for morning."

"Why do you pray for morning?" Aidan asked.

The little man shook his head. "I don't look out the door. I don't see nothing."

"What are you going on about?" Aidan asked with exasperation.

"Please, I'll just get my bag and go."

Aidan didn't move from the doorway. "Not so fast."

The man started shaking. "Please don't get me arrested for trespassing. I'll lose my job. I need that job."

"I can't just let you walk away," Aidan said quietly.

"Why in God's name not?" the fellow pleaded.

"Because there was a human bone in your pile of trash the other day," Aidan told him.

Jimmy gasped; he looked as if he would fall flat with the slightest breeze. This man was no killer, Aidan thought.

"I swear to God, I ain't never hurt nobody in the whole of my life," Jimmy whispered. "I'm Jimmy Wilson. I work down at the gas station. You can tie me up to keep me here, then go down with me come tomorrow. They'll tell you. They'll tell you it's the truth. There might have been a chicken bone, mister. I try to remember to pick up the trash. Just sometimes, I'm so tired. It's a long walk both ways. There was nobody at all here for so long, and before that, just the old lady, and I never bothered her none, I swear it."

Aidan wasn't sure what to do with the man. He was pretty sure this pathetic wretch had never hurt anyone. But if he'd been living out here all that time, he might have seen something.

Amelia's lights already made sense. She had seen the flicker of the flashlight or a fire, just as he had done tonight.

"Please, just let me go. I swear, I won't come back here no more, just don't call the cops on me."

"Ex-con?" Aidan asked.

Jimmy stared at him. "Drugs. I was an addict. I stole stuff, but I never hurt no one. I got caught, I did my time and I'm clean. Beer, that's it. But if I get in trouble again…it'll kill me to go back. I've been clean, I swear it."

"Why did you say you come here, close the door and pray?" Aidan asked. "What are you hiding from?"

Jimmy stared back at him, looking as if Aidan had just asked him the most idiotic question in the world.

"Why, the ghosts, of course."

"Kendall, stop! It's me."

She was halfway down the block; she'd moved like lightning, glad she'd put on sneakers that morning. But she knew the voice.

She turned around and trotted back, her heart still beating like a drum. "Vinnie, what the hell's the matter with you? You just scared ten years off my life," she accused him.

He stared at her, perplexed. "I was just sitting on the step, waiting for you," he told her.

Maybe he *had* just been sitting on the porch. But he was wearing his long black cape, and he'd risen like a mountain of evil.

She shook her head, walking past him to the door. Her fingers trembled as she put her key in the outer lock. "You scared me," she said again.

"Well, I didn't mean to. And you've never jumped like a

scaredy-cat over the slightest little thing before. Sheesh, Kendall. What's the matter with you?"

She didn't reply to that. "What are you doing here? You're obviously supposed to be working."

"I'm on a half-hour break, and I've just wasted most of it sitting on your steps," he told her. "Thank God, it doesn't seem as if the neighbors heard you scream or the cops would probably be arresting me now."

"I doubt it. You know half the force, at least," she told him. "And it was stupid of you to come here in the first place. Why would you assume I'd be home?" She was opening the door to her apartment at that point, and then she stepped back, allowing him to step inside ahead of her. She realized that even though he had scared her to death, she was glad to see him.

"So why were you waiting for me?"

"Because I'm your friend."

She arched a skeptical brow to him. "All right, because I'm broke. I had to pay my bar tab."

"Oh, Vinnie…"

"Come on. You know I don't drink that much. I'm just a friendly guy, and I like to buy drinks for people. I'll pay you back. I get paid tomorrow. But I need a hamburger or something."

"You're kidding me," she said, staring at him.

"No, I'm not."

She walked back to the kitchen and opened her bag, found her wallet and gave him forty dollars. "You *are* going to pay me back, because you're no kid and you've got to learn how to budget."

"Okay, okay." He gave her a wink. "So guess what I did today? I helped your boyfriend on his latest case."

"My boyfriend?"

He grinned at her, leaning on the counter and helping himself to a banana from the fruit bowl.

"Aidan Flynn. I hear you two are getting along."

"I like the guy. So what? It doesn't make him my boyfriend." Not that she would mind if he were, she thought.

Vinnie shrugged. "He suspected me of being a psychotic murderer, but I set him straight."

"Walking around town looking like Dracula doesn't exactly help create a boy-next-door image," she told him, reaching into the refrigerator for a bottle of water. She tossed him one, too. He caught it deftly.

"Hey, haven't you heard? It's always the boy next door who turns out to be the bad guy."

"You'd better get back. Your break must be over soon."

"I have a few more minutes. Jeremy is sitting in again tonight. He's talking up his thing on Saturday night. I wish I hadn't blown all my cash so I could buy a ticket. Actually, what I really wish is that we'd auditioned to play that night. There's bound to be a ton of publicity."

"Well, if you didn't have to work, you could go."

"I'm in. But how? Is my fairy godmother going to turn me into a prince?"

"Aidan has a bunch of tickets, and he asked me to come and bring my friends. But how can you get off work? It's a Saturday night."

"This town is full of guitar players. I can find someone to fill in for me."

"Cool. You'd better get going, though, since you *are* working tonight."

He grinned. "You bet." He came around the counter and

gave her a kiss on the cheek. "Thanks for the money. I'll pay you back."

She nodded. "Don't worry about it. You fill in at the store on short notice often enough. I guess I kind of owe you."

"Yeah, you do, don't you? Just kidding, I'm going to repay you."

She walked him back down the hall and locked the door behind him. As soon as he was gone, the quiet seemed to envelop her. She hurried into her bedroom, and turned on the lights and the television.

She had time. What a great night to read. The diary was still in her bag.

First, though, she walked around the apartment and turned on all the lights, then turned on the television in the family room for good measure. She wanted noise, lots of it. And not music, either. Tonight she wanted to hear talking. Sitcoms. People laughing.

Even if they were only on a laugh track.

At last she slipped into a long cotton sleep tee, washed her face, brushed her teeth and crawled into bed.

Had it only been last night that she hadn't been alone in this same bed? It had been amazing, making love, sleeping as if she didn't have a care in the world. But that had been last night. Tonight her struggle was not to unnerve herself so badly that she couldn't sleep.

But opening the diary she had been longing to finish didn't help. It should have been fascinating. Fiona was writing about her love for Sloan Flynn and how he had never wanted to see a war between the states. Before it had started, he and his cousin Brendan had often talked about the possibility that, with their opposing views, they would end up on opposite sides. But they hadn't fought about their differences, only prayed war would never come. But it *had* come, and they had indeed ended up as enemies.

One entry was filled with excitement. Sloan had written to tell her that he was coming home, and that they could be married, but it would have to be secretly. With the Union forces encroaching, he didn't want to put her in a dangerous position. She could claim Brendan's protection, if it became necessary, as long as their marriage was secret.

In another entry she wrote about her wedding night, delicately, in terms that might be used by a proper young woman of the time who was madly in love with her husband.

Kendall found it all so sad, because she knew how it had ended. The war had come between the family in a way they had never expected. The cousins had killed one another, and Fiona had leapt to her death.

But to learn of the earlier events through Fiona's own words…

Kendall stopped reading, suddenly and inexplicably feeling frightened again. Refusing to be cowed, she got up and walked through her apartment, ready to meet the threat head-on, but except for Jezebel, the apartment was empty. When she returned to her bedroom, the cat went with her. It was as if Jezebel, too, needed company.

Kendall set the diary on her nightstand and cuddled the cat close to her as she started watching a romantic comedy.

That wasn't great, either. All she could think was that just last night…

More nights would come, she assured herself.

But tonight was going to be very long.

She turned to a cartoon station, but the subject was space

vampires, and she wasn't sure she wanted to deal with that right now, either. She finally found a channel that showed nothing but old sitcoms and closed her eyes at last.

Laughter should have filled her dreams.

It didn't.

At first she thought she was standing on a cliff in the dark. The moon was high in the sky, but the glow it cast down was eerie and filled with shadows. There was a storm brewing somewhere in the night.

She looked around and realized she wasn't really on a cliff. She was on a small hill, the small hill where the Flynn plantation house stood.

She could see the house, stark white against the darkness. Except for the windows. They looked like eyes staring out blankly at the world. It reminded her of one of the Halloween decorations at the store, and she thought that if she could only plug it in, the windows would fill with light, instead of staring at her with such dark emptiness.

She felt a breeze lift her hair and she looked up.

And there was the ghost.

Fiona MacFarlane Flynn, running across the upper-level wraparound balcony, her mouth open in a silent scream.

She was dressed all in white, her gown floating behind her as she ran in terror. Because she was being chased.

Kendall strained to see her face and then started and tried to escape the dream.

Because she knew that face. It was the face of the girl Aidan was searching for.

Jenny Trent.

Then the face morphed and was no longer Jenny's. It was

the face of Death as she knew it all too well from her tarot deck. And it was no longer screaming.

It was laughing, mouth open and eyes maniacal.

The storm swept around Kendall. She was shouting to the sky that the card didn't mean death but change, trying to be firm and unafraid. She was fighting the wind, because it was threatening to sweep her to the ground, and she was afraid that if she went down, she was never going to get up again.

It started to rain, and she lifted her hand to see that the drops were blood.

And then, she saw what was coming behind the ghost with the laughing face of Death.

Bones.

A tidal wave of bones.

And it was washing down over her, threatening to engulf her.

She woke up screaming and felt something sitting on her chest and staring at her with eyes that glowed in the night.

"What ghosts?" Aidan asked.

Jimmy's eyes widened in fear. "I hear them sometimes. From the old graveyard."

"Hear them doing what?"

"They laugh," Jimmy said. "And they whisper."

"What do they say?"

"Do you think I'm crazy? I don't go out and ask them what they're talking about. I close myself in here and I pray."

"Do they whisper after a few beers?" Aidan asked him.

Despite his situation, Jimmy drew himself up straight. "I get off work. I buy two cans of beer and something to eat. I walk here, close the door, eat my dinner and read my paper. I keep the door closed. I keep it closed when it rains, when it's windy and when the ghosts are out. I don't get drunk, I just ease down a bit. Then I sleep good. I think the ghosts know I'm here, but if I just stay in here and don't bother them, they won't bother me. They're not always out—not that I hear. Just sometimes."

Just sometimes when Jimmy had more than two beers?

"You were here last night, right?"

"Yes."

"Did you hear the ghosts?"

"No," Jimmy said. "Maybe they were out when I was sleeping, but I didn't hear them." He brightened, as if he was eager to please Aidan. "I did hear a car. Heard the engine, heard a door open and close."

Too bad Jimmy was too scared to look out his door, Aidan thought, or he might have gotten a good lead on who'd delivered those voodoo dolls.

"Stay here. Just stay here," he told Jimmy.

His eyes had adjusted to the dark, and he made his way easily to his car. He pulled his keys from his jeans pocket, and went into his trunk and found the sleeping bag he always kept there, just in case. He took it and a couple of bottles of water, then headed back to Jimmy with them. "Here, so you don't have to sleep on the ground," he told the man.

Jimmy stared at him with amazement. "You're going to let me stay here?" he asked warily.

"For now. I'm Aidan Flynn, and my brothers and I own this place now. We'll talk more come morning. I don't know what we'll do then, but we'll figure something out. For now, just go to sleep."

Jimmy was staring at Aidan as if he were going to cry.

Aidan left Jimmy and went back to the house. He'd left

the door open when he'd run out to catch the trespasser, so he locked it once he was inside, then started going through the house room by room.

It took a lot more time than going through Kendall's apartment. The house was huge, but at least there were wardrobes rather than closets, each one containing clothes that represented decades worth of history—and reeked of mothballs. The attic took him the longest. While he was up there, he found a rocking chair by a trunk and realized that not all that long ago, someone had come here, set a glass—which was still there—on the trunk and enjoyed some quiet moments, looking out the dormer window at the river.

Kendall?

He could almost breathe in her scent…

Maybe he was losing his mind. Maybe he should have stayed in town—with her. She had been so doubtful when he had left that morning, as if she was afraid he would hold her responsible for the voodoo dolls.

Should he? Admittedly, she couldn't have done it herself, but what about one of her friends?

No. He just couldn't imagine her doing anything like that.

And he couldn't forget her expression when she had seen the picture of Jenny Trent and learned that she was missing, or how frantic she had been to find Ann. No one who worried that much about people she hardly knew would ever pull a stunt like the one someone had pulled with the voodoo dolls.

As hard as it was to believe, as much as he had never thought he would be able to feel something for a woman again after Serena's death, she was slipping under his skin. He couldn't get her out of his mind, couldn't forget the feel of her skin, the look of her eyes, the tone of her voice. For so long he'd held back, feeling the guilt of living when Serena was dead. It wasn't fair that he was even alive, so how could he be allowed to find happiness again?

And, to be honest, he hadn't wanted to find it before he met Kendall.

He was still standing in the attic, he realized. Looking at a rocking chair, imagining her sitting in it, wondering what she had been thinking about as she stared out at the world.

Kendall had definitely taken root in his mind.

He wished that she were here with him.

But she wasn't. He had chosen to come out here—alone. Good thing, really. He'd found Jimmy and solved at least one mystery.

He forced himself to finish checking out the attic. He even looked in some of the trunks, where he was amazed to find Civil War weapons, old letters, clothing, boots, buckles… some things that probably even predated the Civil War. A trove of riches.

So why the hell hadn't Amelia left this place or at least some of these rarities to the young woman who had become like a daughter to her?

Maybe she hadn't known what she had.

He went back to bed at last, where he lay awake, pondering just what was making him feel so uneasy about this house. He should have been pleased at solving the riddle of Amelia's eerie lights, which had only been Jimmy, living there in the old slave quarters. But something was still bugging him.

Impatient with himself, he got desperate enough to try counting sheep, which failed when his sheep kept turning into voodoo dolls. He gave up and counted those instead, and at last, when the light was just starting to brush the horizon, he fell asleep.

He woke when he heard the first workman coming up the drive.

Kendall gasped, then realized she was staring straight into Jezebel's eyes.

She didn't know whether to scream or laugh. Then Jezebel meowed pathetically, and she managed to laugh.

Light was also peeking around her drapes, and she realized it was morning.

She cradled Jezebel to her. "What is it, cat? Am I scaring you? That's okay, I'm scaring myself. But things are going to get back to normal, I promise. Come on. I'm betting you want some breakfast."

She rose, fed the cat, put on the coffee and went to take a shower. The water was bracing, and she studiously concentrated on washing her hair, shaving her legs and scrubbing her face. A few minutes later, wrapped in a bathrobe, she went out to pour her coffee. Last night's dream seemed ridiculous in the light of morning.

Freud had said most dreams had sexual undertones. She thought about her nightmare, which had seemed so real— and yet on some level she had known all along that it was only a dream. Try as she might, she couldn't find anything sexual about it. It had been frightening, plain and simple, and she wasn't going to think about it anymore.

She decided to think about Aidan Flynn instead. She was torn. She wanted to dislike him, but she couldn't help it: for some reason, she respected him. It was like a love-hate thing. There had been times—admittedly mostly early on—when she had come pretty close to hating him. She hadn't known him long enough to love him, though. Had she? She did love sleeping with him, and a part of her admitted that she was terrified of getting too close to him, because he just might be the man she could fall in love with, and she probably *wasn't* a woman he could ever want to be with forever.

She poured herself another cup of coffee, then walked to the back of the apartment and pulled the drapes back from the French doors. It looked like a beautiful day—no threat of storms, much less a rain of blood—and she unlocked the door and stepped out into the courtyard.

Even though she had just showered, she found herself looking at her hand.

No blood.

Out in the courtyard, she sipped her coffee. None of her neighbors were in evidence, so she stood there in solitude and enjoyed the soft breeze. October was a beautiful month, she thought.

The courtyard still looked much as it had for almost two centuries; her house was one of the few that had survived the fire of 1788, which had destroyed most of the city. This neighborhood might be called the French Quarter, but most of the architecture for which the city was so famous, including the "cities of the dead," dated from the period when the area was under Spanish rule. Once, the narrow alley that ran behind the courtyard had been the main entrance. There was still a huge old gate there, which was used early every morning by the lawn maintenance company that kept up the courtyard.

Wicker tables and chairs were surrounded by flower beds and beautifully potted plants. The old carriage house stood to one side, and a high brick wall protected the tenants' privacy.

She wandered toward a chair and sat, taking a moment just to enjoy the beauty of a morning that reminded her why she loved this city that had always been her home and would never want to leave.

As she sat there, she noticed something lying near the French doors of her apartment, something she had missed when she first stepped outside.

Something…

She felt her fingers tense around her coffee mug.

She set it down and rose, walked back to her doors and bent down to see exactly what had caught her eye.

It was a doll.

A voodoo doll.

Not like the beautifully crafted ones she sold, but the kind for sale at any souvenir store, but with the addition of long hair made out of auburn yarn, and big green buttons for eyes.

When she instinctively went to pick it up, it fell apart, and she saw the deep slashes at the juncture of head and neck, the arms, legs and torso, where the pieces had been held together by mere threads.

The doll had been made to look like her. And it had been dismembered.

14

Saws were whining, and hammers were slamming.

One cup of coffee gave Aidan enough energy to get into the shower and out of the house. On the lawn, the contractor was meeting with the electricians, and he turned, pleased to see Aidan.

"Your brother wants the place by Halloween," the contractor told him cheerfully.

"And you can make that date and still do everything all right?" Aidan asked.

"I'll show you the plans."

He spent an hour going over blueprints and schedules, and had to admit that his brothers had managed to bring on an efficient captain who knew what he was doing.

The house should have been his biggest headache, Aidan thought. Instead, it was proving to be nothing at all.

Except for that feeling he couldn't shake...

There were ghosts in the cemetery, Jimmy had said. Aidan found himself walking in that direction again, almost as if drawn. It was just a graveyard, he told himself. He was probably only spooked because he had found dried blood on one of the tombstones. Even so, he promised himself to look around more thoroughly later in the day.

But first, he had things to do in the city. He got into his car and reached the end of the driveway just in time to see Zach coming toward him on the river road. He beeped and waved to tell his brother to pull over, then filled him in on the squatter who had been living in the old slave quarters.

"Did you throw him out or call the police?" Zach asked.

"Neither. I gave him my sleeping bag."

Zach grinned, called him a soft touch, then asked, "You're sure he's harmless?"

"Pretty sure. He works nights up at the gas station. I'm going to check into his story. If he was lying, I'll give him the boot, but if he was telling me the truth, I want him around a while longer."

"Really?" Zach asked, surprised. "You don't think he was fooling around with voodoo dolls to drive us off the place, huh?"

"That guy couldn't buy a two-dollar voodoo doll, much less a collectible," Aidan assured him. "I'll check him out, don't worry."

"But why do you want him around? Or is it just that you feel sorry for the guy?"

"I kinda do. If he's telling the truth, maybe we can find a few things for him to do around the place, even fix him up a bit. Mainly, he's been around. He was Amelia's 'ghostly presence.' On the other hand, *he* thinks there are ghosts in our graveyard, too. Who knows, maybe he does know something, even if he doesn't know he knows. Know what I mean?"

Zach nodded. "All right. Check him out. I'll keep Jeremy in the loop."

They said goodbye, and Aidan drove on.

His first stop was the gas station. He spoke to the manager

and found out that there was indeed a Jimmy Wilson who worked there nights. The manager looked at Aidan as if he wanted to say more, so Aidan waited.

"I guess I should tell you he's an ex-con, but I checked his record. He wasn't even arrested for breaking and entering, just petty theft. He was found with a woman's handbag in an alley up in Shreveport. He gave the bag right back. He was on drugs, but his stint in the slammer cleaned him up. Hey, someone has to give those guys a chance, and Jimmy was honest with me from the get-go, so I took him on. You didn't have any trouble with him or anything, did you?" he asked.

"No, no trouble," Aidan said, and thanked the man. "I was just making sure he really works here."

"He does. My hire, my mistake if anything goes wrong." The man looked at him worriedly.

"Everything's fine," Aidan reassured him. "I was thinking of giving him some odd jobs around the place, that's all."

"You're one of the Flynns, right?"

"Yes."

"I hear you plan on keeping the house, opening her up for special events, school groups, stuff like that."

"We're hoping to."

"That's great. Well, I hope it works out for you."

Aidan left, fairly certain from his conversation that at least some people didn't harbor any ill will toward them.

From the gas station, he intended to head in to see Lily Fleur. If he couldn't get her to give him the names and contact information for the other guests who had been there the same night as Jenny Trent, he would have to head over to see Hal Vincent and somehow cajole the policeman into helping him.

It was still early to go see the older woman, though, and somehow he found himself driving down Decatur to make the loop back onto Royal Street. When he did, his heart lodged in his throat.

There were two police cars drawn up in front of Kendall's building.

Aidan barged in. And "barged" was definitely the right word. The officer standing at the door never stood a chance of stopping him.

Kendall handed steaming mugs of coffee to Sam Stuart and Tim Yates, a couple of local cops she'd known forever. They had been just up the street when they'd gotten the call. She'd barely had time to get dressed before they arrived.

Another couple of officers had arrived in their wake, one stationing himself at the front door and the other going to look around the courtyard. Suddenly the one by the door was shouting, and she looked up to see Aidan racing toward her, the cop flying after him. The other three jumped forward to help their buddy.

She rushed forward, yelling, "It's all right! He's a friend!"

"What the hell happened?" Aidan demanded. "Are you all right?" He glared at all four cops, who stepped back warily.

"You sure he's all right?" the cop who'd run in from the courtyard asked.

"He's a friend, honestly," she said.

"And a P.I.," Aidan added.

The cops all returned to their original positions, and Sam and Tim, though they still looked stunned by Aidan's dramatic entrance, went back to drinking their coffee.

Kendall herself felt blindsided by Aidan's sudden appearance, yet inwardly warmed. Surely this meant that he actually cared, at least a little.

"Sam, Tim, this is Aidan Flynn. You know his brother Jeremy."

"Nice to meet you—I think," Tim said, reaching out a hand.

Aidan took it, still staring at Kendall. "Well? What the hell happened here?"

"Nothing, really," she said quickly.

"A prank. Has to be," Sam told him reassuringly.

"There was a voodoo doll at my back door," Kendall explained. "I just thought I should call someone."

"Was it like the ones at the house?"

"Someone left a voodoo doll out at the plantation?" Tim asked.

"*Three* of them," Kendall said. "Handmade ones. I rated the cheap kind," she told Aidan lightly.

"Where is it?" Aidan asked.

"We've bagged it, and we're taking it in," Sam explained. "I didn't hear anything about voodoo dolls out at the plantation."

"That's because I didn't call the police," Aidan said.

"Well, yeah, you should have," Sam said. "That's malicious mischief."

"And almost nothing can be done about it, right?" Aidan said.

"Well, once we find out who did it, you can get a restraining order against them," Tim said.

Was that a shade of self-importance in his voice? she wondered. She knew Tim liked to think of himself as a hero, but right now Aidan seemed to tower over him in every way. Tim was puffing up a bit, emphasizing the fact that he was a police officer, while Aidan just seemed to emit power without even trying.

Careful, she warned herself. She had to stop thinking of him as…so damned perfect.

"I'd like to see the doll," Aidan said.

"Sure," Sam said affably.

It was in an evidence bag, lying on the table. Aidan opened the bag and slid the doll onto the table without touching it, moving the pieces around with a pen so he could look at them more closely.

"Creepy, but probably nothing to worry about," Sam said. "It's coming around to Halloween. All of the crazies are out."

Aidan looked across the room at Kendall. "Isn't that gate locked at night?" he asked, indicating the courtyard with an inclination of his head.

She nodded.

"Officer Pratt is outside looking around now," Tim assured him.

Aidan didn't reply, just headed out the door himself.

"How well do you know that guy, Kendall?" Sam asked, sounding slightly worried.

She hadn't even known him a week, she realized, but somehow…

"I've gotten to know him pretty well because of the plantation and Amelia," she said simply. "If you'll excuse me…?" She smiled to take any sting out of the dismissal, then hurried out to the courtyard, where Aidan was talking to Officer Pratt.

"I don't know how the guy got in here, Kendall," Pratt said, seeing her. "Hey, you don't have any weirdos for neighbors, do you?"

Kendall laughed. "The Foys, on the other half of the ground floor, are raising two little kids and own a café up on Conti. Mrs. Larsen, above me, is seventy-seven. And the owners keep the fourth apartment for themselves for whenever they're down here from New York, which they're not at the moment."

"Well, we'll bring the doll in, and we'll send a car by a few times a night for the next few days. And we'll let you know if we find out anything about the doll."

The officers all left a few minutes later, Tim looking back at her as if he would have liked to hang around longer and offer a heroic shoulder.

He would forget her the minute a blonde walked by, Kendall knew.

When she closed the door behind them, she was surprised by Aidan's sudden fierce demand. "Why didn't you call *me?*"

"I—I didn't know if I should bother you about something so silly."

"Now the cops have the doll."

"And they'll use it to investigate."

"Kendall, to the cops this is a prank, but... Dolls at the plantation, a doll here. It means something."

She picked up her coffee cup, willing her hands not to tremble. On its own, the doll would have upset her, but it wouldn't actually have scared her. But combined with the dream she'd had...

"I'm sure it *does* mean something," she said. "Someone out there is upset with me because of my association with the Flynn plantation and mad that you *own* it, so they're taking advantage of this being New Orleans and trying to freak us out."

His expression was disbelieving as he stared at her, hands on his hips, his eyes like ice again.

"Aidan, please," she said weakly. "Let's not overreact."

"Overreact?" He stared at her grimly. "I've found bones—human bones, at least one of which may belong to a young woman who came here, then disappeared. And she's not the only one. My brother found records indicating that nine other young women have disappeared from New Orleans in similar circumstances. So forgive me if I *overreact* to what looks to me a hell of a lot like a subtle threat to back off—or else."

He turned away from her, paced, paused, then took a deep breath. "Kendall, I've studied serial killers. At any given moment, there are hundreds at large in the United States. Some killers want their victims found, but some don't. Think about it. How do you make sure you never get caught? Make sure the bodies you leave behind are never discovered. So those bones I found could be all that's left to find of those missing women."

"Aidan..." She lifted her hands in frustration. He had no proof of anything, including that something bad had happened to those women. He had to know himself that he was grasping at straws.

But was he? She had seen a skeleton on a piece of paper laugh at her.

And she had been afraid. So who was drawing unfounded conclusions now, huh?

"Want to stay out at the house with me?" he asked.

"What?"

He hesitated before repeating the question. Had he surprised himself by asking? she wondered.

"I've decided to stay out at the house from now on. Keep an eye out for whoever's causing trouble. Actually, I did make an interesting discovery last night."

"What?" she asked carefully.

"I met a man named Jimmy. A guy who's been staying in the old slave quarters."

"Someone's been living on the property?" she asked.

"For six months."

"Oh, God!" she exclaimed. She and Amelia *had* been in danger.

"He wouldn't have hurt you. He's just a down-and-out guy looking for a way to get back on his feet, so I told him he could stay. He's got himself a job at the gas station out there, and he's saving up for a car and a place to live."

"And you believe that?" she asked.

"I do."

She smiled.

"What?" he asked her.

She laughed. "I don't know. I guess I didn't expect you to be that trusting." She avoided adding, or generous to a stranger.

He looked back at her for a long moment, and shrugged. "Well, I did go by and check with his boss this morning. Jimmy thinks there are ghosts in the graveyard. He comes 'home,' closes the door and stays inside all night, hiding from them."

"A cemetery is a good place for ghosts to be," she said dryly.

"You haven't answered me," he said.

"I'm sorry?"

"About coming out to the house with me. There's no hurry or anything. I can meet you after work, bring you back here to pack some clothes."

It was rushing things. She shouldn't go.

She sure as hell didn't want to stay here another night, though. Not when someone who didn't belong there was playing around in her courtyard.

Lurking at her very door.

And leaving a sliced-to-pieces voodoo doll that resembled her.

The cops would be watching the house. But how well?

None of that mattered. She shouldn't go with him because she was afraid. She should go with him because she wanted to, because she wanted to be with him. Because she cared about him.

And she did.

"Yes, I'd like to go stay at the house with you," she told him.

He nodded. "Thanks," he said huskily. "I'm glad."

"We close up between five and six."

"Okay. Don't leave. I'll come meet you there."

"All right."

He was still standing there, staring at her.

"You ready to go to work?" he asked her.

She frowned and glanced at her watch. Amazingly, it was just after ten.

"Just about," she told him.

"I'll wait and drop you off."

It wasn't necessary. But she saw the way that he was standing and knew he was taking the voodoo doll very seriously. He was taking *everything* very seriously.

So what? Wasn't she?

She didn't want to be afraid, and she refused to be afraid to walk down Royal Street in broad daylight.

But she was getting to know him well, and she could tell he wasn't going to leave without her.

"Give me just a minute," she told him. "Help yourself to coffee," she added, as she went back into her bedroom to gather up a few things for the day.

Aidan heard Jeremy's latest radio interview just after dropping Kendall at her store. Jeremy announced that he was delighted to say that the benefit had sold out, but that the radio station had two tickets left to give away. Aidan hoped that if the benefit at the aquarium went well and they were able to pull off the Halloween gala at the house, Jeremy could lay to rest a few of the ghosts haunting him.

Ghosts.

They just kept popping up, Aidan thought, even in his own thoughts.

He found parking near Lily Fleur's B and B. She was smiling when she answered the door, but her smile faded as soon as she saw who was standing on her stoop.

"Good morning, Mr. Flynn."

She didn't step back. Obviously she didn't want to ask him in.

"Mrs. Fleur."

"Call me Lily." He had a feeling she was speaking by rote; she didn't really want him calling her Lily. She didn't want him talking to her at all. She wanted him to go away.

"Mrs. Fleur, I know what a good person you are," he told

her. "And I'm sorry to bother you, but I need to ask for your help, so I can try to figure out what happened to Jenny Trent."

"What can I do for you?"

Was it his imagination, or did she sound slightly less unhappy about his presence?

"I'd like to get a list of any other guests who were registered with you when Jenny was here," he told her.

"Hold on."

She didn't close the door on him, though she still didn't invite him in. When she came back a moment later, she had a neatly printed sheet of paper in her hand.

"This is what I have," she told him. "Copied straight out of the book."

"Did you know I'd come asking?"

"A police officer—a real policeman—came by and asked for the same thing." She looked a little prim, then added, "He also said that you were a legitimate investigator. I figured if he had asked for the list, you'd be around for it soon enough, too."

"Thanks. By the way, what was the officer's name?"

She waved a hand in the air. "Oh, it was Hal. I've known him for years."

"Hal Vincent."

"Of course. He's the best, you know."

Aidan smiled. "I'm sure he is," he told her, then thanked her again and walked away.

"You should let me give you a reading, Kendall," Mason said.

The store was finally quiet, and they were trying to clean up.

As she set a coffee cup in the dishwasher, she wondered if she should have told him that someone had left a voodoo doll by her back door. But the store had already been filled with customers when she'd arrived, and maybe because it was Friday, they had been rushed off their feet all day, so she'd never had a chance. In fact, they'd been so deluged with business that she'd had to call Vinnie and ask him to run over to the bakery and pick up some more pastries.

Vinnie had agreed cheerfully—maybe because he owed her forty bucks. Or maybe just because he was her friend. He'd even hung around helping for the rest of the afternoon.

"You're going to give Kendall a reading?" Vinnie asked Mason.

"You bet," Mason said.

"No readings," Kendall said. Was it because she didn't believe?

Or because she did?

Vinnie picked up one of the crystal balls off the shelf and stared into it. "I'll do the readings, thank you. I see someone tall, dark, handsome—and suspicious, even threatening. Someone who will be taking our princess to the ball. And guess what else I see? She's accompanied by the most striking footman ever. He's lean, he's mean, he's a walking sex machine. And his name is Vinnie."

"What the hell are you going on about?" Mason asked.

Vinnie set the ball down. "The charity thing at the aquarium tomorrow night. Hey, Kendall, I found someone to sit in for me, so I can go."

Mason quickly shot Kendall a hurt glare. "You're going,

and you asked Vinnie to go, and you didn't even mention it to me?"

"Mason, we didn't get a chance to say two words to each other today."

"You certainly said more than two words to me. You said, 'Mason, clear that table. Mason, they need coffee. Mason, take that reading and I'll handle the register.' You said, 'Mason, quick, brew another pot of pecan-cinnamon coffee.' You said—"

"All right, all right," Kendall said, laughing. "I get your drift. And don't look at me like a puppy I threw out in the rain. You're invited, too."

"I am?" he said, brightening immediately. "Cool. But it's a benefit. I think I'd feel...smarmy if I didn't pay. Wait, I get it. The Flynn brothers get freebies. They're smarmy, then."

"No, they bought the first twenty tickets or something like that," Kendall corrected him.

Mason looked at Vinnie. "She likes him, you know."

"Yeah. Go figure."

"You did call him tall, dark and handsome," Mason reminded Vinnie. "Though he was kind of a jerk to you."

"He was suspicious of me," Vinnie said. "But he isn't anymore. I don't think he is, anyway. Is he, Kendall?"

"I don't know. I think, when you're straight with him, he's straight with you."

"You *do* like him," Mason teased.

Kendall refused to take the bait. "And you'd better like him, too, since it's thanks to him you're both going.

"So should we meet at your place Saturday after work and all go together?" Vinnie asked.

She hesitated, not about to tell them that she was spending the night—maybe more than one night?—at the Flynn plantation. Not that it mattered, since she had to come in to open in the morning, then go home to change for the party. "Sure, we'll meet at my place. It starts at eight, and I'm sure Aidan will want to be there when it starts."

Kendall was just about to lock the door when Ady came in with Rebecca. Neither had an appointment for a reading, and Kendall thought at first that they had just stopped by to say hi, but then Rebecca said to Kendall, "Mama wanted a minute with you. Not a full reading or anything, just a minute alone."

Ady was looking at Kendall so anxiously that she agreed, leading the old woman back to her private reading room. Her tarot cards sat on the table, but she avoided looking at them.

"Miss Ady, you don't want a reading," she said, after the old woman was seated and she had taken her own chair on the opposite side of the table. "You just had one a few days ago."

Ady pursed her lips. "I had a dream," she said.

Kendall smiled. "We all have dreams. I just had a terrible nightmare myself. But that's all they are, just dreams, Miss Ady. Sometimes they have something to do with things that happened during the day, sometimes with things we're afraid of. Are you worried about what Dr. Ling told you?"

Ady waved a hand in the air. "I'm not worried about me at all, Kendall Montgomery. You've taken care of me, and I'm right grateful. It's you I'm worried about."

"Me?" Kendall said, surprised.

Ady leaned forward, her old face set with determination.

"Do you know why Amelia didn't leave that plantation to you?"

Kendall lifted her hands. "Because I couldn't afford to fix it up and keep it, for one. Plus I'm not a Flynn."

Ady sat back, shaking her head. "That ain't the reason, child. That ain't the reason at all. Amelia believed you could do anything."

"Miss Ady, tell me, please. What's wrong? I don't want you to be worried about me."

"I saw Amelia last night in my dream," Ady said.

"You were probably thinking about her."

"She wasn't in my mind one bit, I tell you. She came into my dream because she knew if she talked to me while I was awake, I'd just think I was turning into a crazy old woman."

"Tell me about the dream," Kendall said.

Ady leaned forward again, and her voice was agitated when she spoke. "She said that plantation's evil. Said it wasn't always, even though there were always ghosts. They were the ghosts of good people. But something had changed a while back, she said, and it only started making sense to her toward the end, when she was getting close to going over to the other side herself. She said it was like some kind of evil from the past was coming back. Said she heard crying, like somebody was scared of the way the place was changing, going bad. And she doesn't want that evil touching you, Kendall. That's why she came to me. She's afraid, and she wants me to warn you that something evil is out there, and that you have to be careful, because it's coming for you."

15

For a second Kendall just sat there, staring and feeling a chill creep up her neck. Then she took a deep breath and forced the feeling away as she realized what was going on here. Miss Ady was so sweet. Kendall had worried about her, so now Ady's subconscious had found a way to return the favor.

Kendall nodded gravely to her.

"Thank you for coming to tell me that, Miss Ady," she said.

"Amelia told me to warn you."

Dreams could seem so real. Kendall knew that all too well.

"You believe me now, Kendall, don't you?"

"Of course I believe you," Kendall said, and realized as she spoke the words that they were at least partly true. She *did* believe in the power of dreams to terrify.

Because what could it have been but a waking dream when she had seen the skeleton on a tarot card come to life and laugh?

She smiled gently and promised, "I'll be very careful." After what had happened this morning, it wasn't a promise she would mind keeping.

Ady's eyes remained grave, but she nodded and rose. "Well, that's it, girl. You just mind me and Amelia, you hear?"

"Of course."

Ady started out, and Kendall followed her. When they reached the front of the shop, she saw that Aidan had arrived, and everyone seemed to be getting along fine.

"We're fine to go now, Rebecca," Ady said.

Rebecca stood, and Aidan, Mason and Vinnie rose automatically.

Rebecca offered her hand to Aidan. "Mr. Flynn, it was a pleasure to meet you. Mason, Vinnie, you two behave." She walked over and gave Kendall a quick kiss on the cheek, whispering, "Sorry. Mama just had a bee in her bonnet, and I had to bring her to see you."

"I'm always happy to see you both," Kendall said, squeezing Rebecca's hand.

When she and her mother reached the door, Rebecca hesitated and looked back. "Mr. Flynn, if you repeat me on this, I'll call you a liar, but I have a suggestion for you. Find yourself a polite way of getting those bones back. You got to understand. The people where I work, they mean well, but this city's still got troubles, and they're busy dealing with that. I hear you got friends in high places. Use them."

She nodded firmly. Clearly she, too, had had her say.

Kendall cleared her throat as soon as the door shut behind the two women and looked at Aidan. "What was that all about?"

He was still staring thoughtfully after Rebecca as he answered her. "Vinnie asked me if I was getting anywhere searching for Jenny Trent. I mentioned that I thought the bones I'd left at the M.E.'s office might be connected. I guess she thought it over and decided to tell me what she thought before she left."

"What about the voodoo dolls?" Mason asked. "Do you think they're related to Jenny Trent? Or is someone just trying to drive you off the plantation so they can snap it up themselves?"

"Why leave a doll for Kendall, then?" Aidan asked him, watching carefully to see his response to the question. "She has nothing to do with the plantation anymore."

"Someone left you a voodoo doll?" Mason asked, turning to Kendall. "And you didn't tell me?"

"It just happened last night," she said. "And in case you didn't notice, we were busy all day, so I didn't get a chance to tell you. Anyway, it was no big deal."

"No big deal?" Mason repeated disbelievingly. "I can't believe—"

"Hey, I didn't know about it, either," Vinnie put in. "But if Kendall says it's no big deal, I believe her. Anyway, the way I see it, you're looking at two different things. One, some idiot thinks it will be all spooky or something to leave voodoo dolls lying around. Two, maybe the bones Aidan found came from some old grave or maybe they're recent, but either way, they still got him started looking for Jenny Trent, and that's a good thing, whether it has anything to do with the plantation where he found the one bone or not." He stood. "As for me, I've got to go to work."

"Vinnie, thanks so much for helping out today," Kendall told him.

"My pleasure. Mason, see you later?" Vinnie asked.

Mason shrugged. "I'll check my calendar. Hmm. Nope, no pressing engagements. Yeah, I'll see you in a bit. I'm going home for a shower first, though. I smell like a giant cinnamon scone."

Vinnie looked at Aidan. "Hey, man, if you ever think I can help you..."

"Thanks," Aidan told him.

Vinnie left, and Kendall turned to Mason. "You can go on home. Aidan can wait while I just give the place a once-over and lock up."

"All right." Mason started for the door, then turned back, "Aidan, by the way, I remembered something else kind of weird about that woman who bought the dolls."

"What?" Aidan asked.

"Those gloves she was wearing?" He grimaced. "I think maybe they were made of latex."

"Odd," Aidan said. "Thanks. That info might come in handy."

"Sure."

When Mason was gone, Aidan surprised Kendall by walking quickly over to the counter and asking, "Do you keep your sales slips organized by the week?"

"Yes. I do my banking Mondays. Usually. Right now I've got two weeks' worth of sales slips. I didn't make it in on Monday. Why?"

"I want to find the receipt for those voodoo dolls."

"Why? If the woman was wearing gloves, you won't get any fingerprints, and she paid cash, so there won't be anything to identify her. Or him."

"I just want to make sure there *is* a sales slip," he said.

She stared at him blankly for a minute, then realized that now he was suspecting *Mason* of being in on something.

"Come on, Aidan," she groaned. "There are tons of people in this city, and dozens of them are probably guilty of something. Why are you picking on my friends?"

He looked up at her. "Because Jenny Trent's trail put her here and then at the Hideaway. Two people—besides you, I might add—are generally both here and at the bar. Vinnie and Mason. Simple enough? Now, are you going to get me those sales records?"

"Yes," she snapped. *Jerk!* She'd been glad to see him— anxious to see him, even—and now he was turning into the high inquisitor again. "But you know, maybe you should be listening to what Vinnie said. Maybe those voodoo dolls don't have anything to do with Jenny Trent being missing. And while you're at it, maybe you should be listening to Rebecca, too. If you're so interested in finding out about those bones, you should just get them back and send them somewhere else."

He ignored everything she'd said and asked again, "Can I see those sales slips?"

She let out a snort of aggravation and went back to her reading room, which doubled as her office, annoyed to find herself trying to avoid looking at her tarot deck while she unlocked the bottom drawer of her desk to pull out the daily receipts.

She turned to bring them back out front, then saw that Aidan had followed her. He took the stack of receipts from her hands and sat down at her reading table. She stood in front of him, and her eyes fell on the deck of cards. They did nothing.

What the hell had she been expecting?

"Have you seen the sales slip?" he asked her, going through the receipts.

"No," she admitted. "I trust Mason."

He paused suddenly.

"That's it, right?" she demanded.

He placed the receipt in front of her. The computer had written, "Collectible voodoo doll, quantity, three." The price and the amount, a cash sale, were filled in after.

"See?" she asked quietly.

"Of course, Mason isn't stupid," he mused.

"Oh, will you stop!"

He looked up at her. She didn't know what he was thinking, because that crystal curtain had come down over his eyes.

"Yes, of course. Sorry."

He wasn't sorry at all. He simply knew nothing he could say to her would change her mind.

He rose. "Thanks. Anything I can do to help lock up?"

"No," she said stiffly. "Thank you." She locked the receipts back in her desk, then went to make sure the rear door was locked.

The thing to do, the *right* thing to do, was tell him that she had changed her mind about going to the plantation, that she was just going to go home and stay there for the night. She owed her friends a certain loyalty, after all.

But she didn't want to go home. And didn't she owe something to herself, as well? Admittedly, she didn't know Aidan Flynn well, but she wanted to know him better. Even if they constantly clashed.

They weren't in a relationship, of course. But they could be. And wasn't that part of a relationship? Making things work even when you disagreed or got angry?

Hold on, you are nowhere near to that point, she warned herself.

But no warning was going to help her now. Not even Miss Ady's insistence that there was evil at the plantation. Evil that was after her.

Now that voodoo doll... It had been left at her home. While she was sleeping. That was far creepier, when you thought about it. Of course, voodoo dolls had been left at the plantation, as well. But not when any of the brothers were staying there, which told her that whoever had done it was a coward, only willing to go after women and empty houses.

Aidan was waiting for her in the front of the shop, staring thoughtfully at a life-size skeleton dressed in a tux and hanging near the door.

He turned to her. "Ready?"

"Yes, thanks. I need to run by my place," she reminded him. "I have to grab some clothes and feed Jezebel."

"Of course."

He went in with her, and while she gathered a few things from her room, he offered to feed the cat. Jezebel, the little hussy, had liked him from the beginning. Kendall could hear the Persian purring from the bedroom.

When she came out to the kitchen, she saw that he had unlocked the rear door and stepped out back.

He saw her, waved, then walked over to the gate. It was big and heavy, and wide enough to allow a carriage to pass through. He scaled it without visible effort, putting himself on the outside, in the alley, then climbed back into the courtyard.

"Kendall," he called.

She walked out to the back, curious.

"It wasn't much of an effort to scale this," he told her. "The hinges make great footholds."

She saw exactly what he was saying. She doubted it was a feat an octogenarian could accomplish, but it wouldn't take a gymnast, either.

"This has to be how he, or she, got in," Aidan said.

"I imagine." She was silent a moment. "Should I ask the police to come back? See if they can get any prints or anything?"

"The cops around here don't get excited about bones," he said. "I don't think—no matter how much they like you—they're going to pull out all the stops to find some prankster." He looked at her and shrugged. "Besides, I doubt there'll be any fingerprints other than mine."

"Why not?"

"Because whoever bought those dolls was wearing gloves."

"But my voodoo doll was a cheapie. Your voodoo dolls were the expensive ones."

"You really think there are two people out there planting slashed-up voodoo dolls?"

"No," she admitted, then crossed her arms over her chest, feeling a little shiver. Night was just starting to fall. Suddenly she was glad she had decided to go with him.

She didn't want to be here alone when the darkness came.

The nighttime DJ at the radio station was a heavyset giant of a man named Al Fisher. He was a decent sort who loved music, loved people and had been the first one to contact Jeremy about doing PR. Tonight's call-in segment was going great, Jeremy thought, as he reminded listeners that they had an hour left to call in for a chance at winning the last available tickets.

Then he got a call from some guy with a voice like a Halloween bogeyman.

"Your first event is this thing at the aquarium, right?" the caller said.

"Yes," Jeremy said.

"They say you're planning a second event out at that plantation you inherited," the caller said in his raspy voice.

Jeremy hesitated. The idea of doing a gala out at the plantation hadn't been a secret, but neither was it common knowledge. He wondered how this guy had heard about it.

"Well?" the caller said.

"The idea has come up, yes."

"Well, get that idea right out of your head," the caller said, his raspy whisper taking on a menacing quality. "What you're doing is wrong. You may be a Flynn, but if you start bringing people out to that place, bad things are going to happen. Really bad things. The dead need to rest in peace. You need to get out of there or you're going to die."

"All right, great Halloween prank," Al put in, hitting the cut-off switch and disconnecting the caller.

The rest of the hour passed pleasantly, but in light of the voodoo dolls that had shown up on the lawn, Jeremy couldn't get the caller out of his mind. When they were finished, he took off the headphones and looked at Al. "You've got caller ID at the switchboard, don't you?"

"Sure."

"Find out who that was for me, will you?"

"Just some idiot," Al said dismissively.

"I'd still like to know."

"Gotcha."

Jeremy followed Al into the hallway, then waited while Al headed out to check the switchboard log. He came back frowning.

"Sorry, Jeremy. The call was made from one of those prepaid cell phones. No way of tracing it. None at all."

"Thanks," Jeremy told him. Aggravated, he left the station. He thought about calling his brothers, then decided it could wait. Maybe, come Monday, Aidan could ask his FBI buddy if there was any way to trace the signal. But he doubted it. As far as he knew, not even the FBI could trace a prepaid cell phone, especially if the caller had been smart enough to buy the thing with cash.

It was dark when they left the hubbub of the city. The highway offered lights and plenty of cars, but the river road was dark.

As they drove, Kendall asked Aidan about his day, determined not to let herself be bothered by his suspicions of her friends.

"It was good. I went back to the B and B where Jenny Trent stayed and got a list of the other guests that night. Three other rooms rented, two singles and a couple. The couple was from South Dakota—the guy asked his wife for his hearing aid while we were on the phone, so I didn't think he'd be helpful, but he was. The kid staying in the attic came back and passed out at one, didn't hear a thing and never saw Jenny Trent. There was a teacher from Detroit in the other room who had met Jenny and wanted to be helpful, but she didn't know anything and hadn't heard anything. The old guy, though. He got up in the middle of the night to go to the bathroom, which was off the hall, and saw Jenny. Said she was dressed up in black jeans and an inside-out T-shirt, and told him she was going out to meet some genius and get in on a great discovery."

"See!" Kendall said triumphantly. "Vinnie was telling the truth. He's as innocent as a snow-white lamb."

Aidan glanced her way. "'Innocent as a snow-white lamb' and 'Vinnie' don't really sound like they go together to me, but yeah, he's probably telling the truth."

"Probably?"

He grimaced. "How do we know Vinnie wasn't the genius who was going to let her in on a great discovery?"

"'Genius' and 'Vinnie' don't exactly go together, either."

"Come on, you've got to admit he's a genius with a guitar."

She was quiet for a minute. "Aidan, even if Jenny Trent was in my shop and at the bar, it doesn't mean that she didn't meet someone during the day, somewhere else, and make arrangements to meet him late that night."

"You're right."

He was staring straight ahead.

"Where do you go from here?" she asked. "It sounds as if you're at a dead end."

"When you hit a dead end, you just go back out to the street and find a new route," he told her, flashing a smile. "Thanks to your friend Rebecca, I'll go back and start over with Jonas, get him to put in a Federal request to have the bones and the blood and the dress analyzed, and get them up to either Quantico or D.C. I'll call on some old friends up there for help."

"But you still won't know what happened once Jenny left the B and B."

"I know."

"So?"

"We'll start researching the other victims."

"Other victims?"

He glanced her way. "There have been at least ten disap-

pearances just like Jenny's over the past decade, most of
them in the last few years. We'll look into them all, one by
one. I'm convinced that most of them, at least, are connected, so eventually we'll catch her killer."

"You act as if you know for certain that she's dead."

He didn't answer, but then, she thought, he didn't have
to. She felt as if she knew Jenny was dead, too.

They stopped at a restaurant for dinner on the way out to
the plantation, and to Kendall's surprise, Aidan seemed
ready—even eager—to talk about other things. Music,
books, even the weather. After they left the restaurant, Aidan
pulled into a gas station.

A small, skinny man came out to serve them.

"Hey, Jimmy," Flynn said.

"Mr. Flynn, miss," the man returned, tapping his base-
ball cap.

"Jimmy has been staying out back at the plantation,"
Aidan explained pleasantly.

"Oh," Kendall said, for lack of another response.

"Don't worry, I won't be bothering you none," Jimmy
said hurriedly. "I can leave if you need me to."

"You can stay out there, Jimmy. I talked to my brothers,
and they don't mind."

The man frowned uncertainly. "You're not…you're not
pulling my leg or nothing, are you, Mr. Flynn?"

"No. Maybe we can work out some kind of a deal. We'll
get you set up back there a little better, and you can keep an
eye on the place if we're not around."

The man's hands were shaking, and he looked too over-
come to speak, so he only nodded.

Jimmy filled up the tank, which hadn't been anywhere

near empty, Kendall noticed. Then Aidan paid him, and they drove off.

"Very generous," Kendall said.

"No. Selfish," he told her.

"How?"

"I like him being out there."

"Why? He'll never see anything going on. You said he just closes the door and hides in there all night. Frankly, it's a little creepy to know he was out there all that time, scaring Amelia with his light."

"He has to come and go, doesn't he?" Aidan said.

"So you think he's the one creating all the mystery at night?" Kendall said.

"He didn't plant the voodoo dolls," Aidan told her.

"Honestly, Aidan, I know this is what you do for a living, but don't you think people who do things like that—try that kind of scare tactic—are usually kind of frightened themselves? That they do things like that because they're too scared to face the person they're attacking."

"Usually," he agreed, his eyes on the road.

Usually.

She read the unspoken corollary. Usually—but not this time

She had been feeling more relaxed than she had all day; dinner had been easy, pleasant, natural.

But his comment had spooked her, and then, as they crested a slight rise, she saw the plantation.

It rose high and white in the moonlight, and there were lights on inside, so many that it should have looked warm and welcoming. But somehow, tonight, the place she had once loved looked like a cruel jack-o'-lantern.

Aidan parked in the drive, looking up. "I can't believe what they've accomplished since this morning," he said as he got out and reached into the back to take Kendall's bag, then started up the steps. She quickly followed him, unwilling to be alone outside.

It hadn't been that long ago that she had slept here most nights. After Amelia had died, she had been determined to leave everything as nice as she could. She had stripped off the old bedding, washed it and given it to the Salvation Army. She had purchased new sheets and new drapes, and she had scrubbed the bathroom and kitchen herself. She had never really known why, except that she didn't want anyone coming in and saying that the place smelled musty or like a nursing home—or like death.

Inside, the floors were covered with plaster dust and there were white handprints on the banister. She could see that one of the hallway walls was freshly plastered and painted, and she imagined that most of the plumbing pipes had gone in behind it.

"They *are* working hard," she said, as she looked around.

"Yeah, they're trying to finish and get out as soon as possible. My brother wants to do something here for Halloween. I can hardly believe it, but I think they'll be done in less than a week. They've got people coming in tomorrow and Sunday."

"Amazing. I love my landlords, but I can't get a drain unclogged for a week," Kendall told him.

He started up the stairs. "I was actually surprised to find that the bedroom was in such great shape. It was Amelia's room, right?" He stopped and looked back at her. "Your work, I take it?" he asked with a smile. "Why? Amelia had died."

"I just didn't want anyone coming in and thinking badly of her."

"Well, thanks. I had a comfortable sleep last night. *While I slept.*"

"I'm kind of glad of it now myself," she said lightly.

She followed him up, thinking that the house felt strangely chilly, as if it wasn't happy to have them there. She told herself not to be ridiculous, that it was a house, nothing more, and didn't have any feelings about anything. Once upon a time, she reminded herself, she had loved it—especially the attic, filled with all Amelia's family treasures.

Flynn family treasures, she corrected herself.

She wanted to ask him about the attic and whether they were tearing that apart, too. She felt indignant about the very possibility, then told herself again that it was no longer any business of hers and remained silent.

In the master bedroom, he set her bag down at the end of the bed. She saw that there were logs by the fire and more arranged on the hearth. She looked at him, and he shrugged a little sheepishly. "Zach has been spending most of the day out here, so when you agreed to come, I asked him to buy some logs and kindling."

"Nice," she said.

"There's all kinds of stuff in the kitchen, too," he said.

"Great."

"And I have one of those little DVD players and some movies."

"Do you really want to watch a movie?" she asked him softly.

He walked over to her, set his hands on her shoulders and met her eyes. "No."

Suddenly the house didn't feel menacing at all. She felt as if she were stronger than the entire world. And then even the world didn't matter, once he kissed her.

His kiss was seductive, electric. Their mouths were locked as their clothing was shed and he backed her toward the massive sleigh bed. He fell onto the mattress, bringing her down with him. His laugh was husky, exciting. His body molded to hers, and still she couldn't get enough of his mouth. She felt him moving, and every pulse and supple brush of his body seemed to fill her with a rising urgency. With some kind of shared inner instinct, they both knew that foreplay would have to wait for next time, and she clasped her thighs around his hips, spiraling into sensation as he thrust slowly into her, held for breathless seconds, then stroked in earnest. She clung to him, rising madly against him, aware that the mind was indeed a wicked tease, because on some level she'd done nothing all day but anticipate the sleek heat and energy of his body, done nothing else since the first time he'd touched her.

She was aware of the almost desperate sound of their breathing, the thunder of their hearts. She savored the damp, powerful feel of his body, the tautness of his abdomen and thighs, and the fact that he was in her, arousing parts of her she hadn't known existed. She knew the frantic fever of wanting more and more, the honeyed feel of rising and needing, and then the sweet explosion of a violent climax that left her shuddering against him as they both trembled and surged again and again, until the tidal wave receded and his erection became an intimate and gentle warmth.

He moved to lie beside her then, stroking her hair, and she curled against him, happy, for the moment, just to *be*.

She was still drowsy when he rolled over, reached into the nightstand near the side of the bed and produced a gun, which he set on top of the stand.

She rose on an elbow, looking at him.

"We're out in the middle of nowhere," he reminded her.

She nodded, suddenly uneasy again.

But not nearly as uneasy as she would have been at home, she admitted. Or anywhere without him.

Would any broad-shouldered, powerful man have done? she asked herself mockingly.

But the answer was an honest *no*.

"All you all right?" he asked her.

"Sometime," she said, "you need to teach me how to shoot that thing."

"It's pretty easy. You aim, hold your arms steady and squeeze the trigger. But we can practice anytime you want."

He decided to run downstairs for drinks; Kendall opted to take a shower. While she was drying off, she heard noises below and ventured out in her towel to the top of the stairway. She listened, and realized that he was checking the locks on the windows and doors.

A few minutes later he was back, bearing a thermos of cocoa, cups and a bottle of brandy. She laughed, and applauded his arrangements.

They poured themselves hot chocolate with brandy, lay in bed and talked about the things they could do for the Halloween party. Then they made love again, indulging in long, slow kisses that tasted like chocolate. And they were kisses that traveled. Her shoulders, his ribs. She was fascinated with every inch of him, and she noticed details. Like the three scars on his back, the swirl of hair just below his beltline, the fact that his second toe was longer than his first. Then she concentrated on the area most crucial for lovemaking, covering his body with the length of hers. Later, when she could have sworn he was dozing, she felt a quickening along her skin as his lips teased along her spine, and fingers ran over her hip and down the length of her thigh. They made love again, and again; it was demanding and passionate, the climax rich with energy and wonder. At last they fell asleep in one another's arms, her last thought that she was so happily sated and exhausted that she would certainly sleep like the dead.

And she *was* sleeping deeply when she was startled awake, by...what? A whisper? A voice? A touch? She didn't know.

But she was wide awake. And Aidan wasn't with her.

16

He was walking through a deep fog, as gray and opaque as a shroud.

He could hear a distant and mournful tolling, like a call for the dead.

And then they came.

An army of them. They walked past him, their skin as gray as the mist. Their eyes were black, hollow and deeply shadowed. They marched in rows, as if they had been summoned to some great meeting, and at first he thought that they didn't see him as they passed.

And then he realized that, from the dark pits of their eye sockets, they were watching him.

Then he saw her.

She was still distant, but a light radiated from her. She was clad in a flowing white gown, and alone among the hordes of the dead, she was beautiful.

She was trying to speak to him, and he tried to hear.

He was no longer just standing there, letting the dead march by. He was walking, trying to make his way to her. She needed to tell him something, and he needed to hear it.

But the fog was like soup; walking through it was like wading through a swamp. He strained…and then he stopped.

The dead were no longer walking past him, with him.

They were strewn in front of him, like dolls. Dolls torn apart by a maniacal child, a head tossed one way, an arm, another. But the detached heads had eyes, and the eyes were looking up at him, beseeching him.

Their lips were moving in silent prayer.

He had to pass them to get to the woman in white, but he knew that he couldn't, and that she couldn't reach him, because those hands would reach for him, clutch at him, trip him....

Go to her. Help her.

He heard the words as clear as day. Though he couldn't see her, he could feel the old woman behind him, trying to push him through the fog and past those poor dismembered dead.

She is the one with the strength, the old woman said, panting as she pushed him.

He turned to look at her.

"Amelia?" he asked, somehow knowing it was true.

The rest is legend, this is real, Amelia said. *You're a Flynn. Can't you feel it? I felt it, when it changed. He came back evil, as evil as the one before him. And of everything that is bad, he is the worst.*

"Aidan!"

He heard his name, felt someone shaking him.

He woke up—and found himself standing, stark naked, on the stairway landing. Kendall, her face lined with concern, was holding his arm, shaking him awake.

What the hell?

"Aidan, thank God! You were sleepwalking, and I couldn't wake you," Kendall said.

"I don't sleepwalk," he told her.

She stepped back, looking at him with a grin that indicated where he was standing and how he was dressed—or rather, *un*dressed. She had thrown on his shirt, and he wasn't at all sure why, given that he was a confident man, but he felt vulnerable and embarrassed.

"Wow. I guess I *was* sleepwalking," he said, and offered her an awkward grin. "Thank heaven we don't have kids, or that we weren't spending the night with the relatives, huh?"

She nodded. She looked almost scared. Oh, God, a perfect night, and now this.

He took her by the shoulders. "Kendall, I'm so sorry I scared you. I swear, I've never done this before."

She flushed slightly. "I'm not frightened. I was worried when I couldn't waken you, but I'm not scared." She was silent for a moment. "You were dreaming, I think," she told him.

"Oh?" He gave her a half smile. "Tell me about it. But let's go back upstairs first."

When they reached the upstairs bedroom, Aidan realized the first pale streaks of dawn were just beginning to break in the east. He kept trying to shake the feeling of vulnerability; it was a new sensation, and one he didn't like. And he didn't want to talk about his dream yet, he realized; he wasn't ready.

"Hey, I'm just going to pop into the shower," he told Kendall, who was still watching him with concern. "I'm sorry, I'm being rude. Do you mind if I go first?"

"You're more than welcome to the first shower. I'll run down and put some coffee on," she said.

She seemed to understand that he needed to regroup, he thought, and found himself feeling closer to her than ever, even as he stepped away.

He turned the showerhead on full blast. He tried to shake the feeling that something about the dream had been real.

"Where the hell is Freud when you need him?" he asked himself aloud.

Kendall was perplexed. It wasn't just that Aidan had been in the midst of a nightmare; everyone dreamed, and some dreams were bound to be bad.

But his eyes had been open. He had spoken Amelia's name.

She'd been awakened by...something to discover that he'd gotten out of bed and was standing in the middle of the room. When she had touched his arm, he had shaken her off and started walking toward the door. She'd followed and seen him start down the stairs. She had called his name. She had touched him. Finally she had all but shouted in his ear, and had grabbed his arm and shaken it as hard as she could. Only then had he turned to her. Blinked. Awakened.

She measured coffee into the pot, knowing that Aidan's dream wouldn't have bothered her so much if Ady hadn't come to her and warned her about her own dream. There was evil in this house. Ady had said so, had said that *Amelia* had said so, that the evil hadn't always been there but now it was.

And that it was coming for her.

Rubbish. The house was just a house, and she and Aidan were the only ones there.

She still found herself thinking about Miss Ady's words, though.

No one had died at the plantation in years. Amelia's parents had both died in the hospital. No one had been buried here since then, until Amelia. So whose ghost was supposed to be the newly arrived evil entity? It just didn't make sense.

She wished Sheila were home. Sheila knew all about the house, but she wasn't due home until sometime this weekend. But maybe, with or without Sheila, she should head over to the historical society where her friend worked and see what she could discover on her own.

Was she actually admitting that there might be ghosts in the house? she asked herself.

The coffee was ready, so Kendall thoughtfully poured herself a cup and turned.

A man was standing there. Tall, lean, wearing a flannel shirt, breeches and suspenders, a worn straw hat on his head. His eyes were a sad and watery green, and his skin was the color of café au lait. And she was absolutely certain she had seen him before.

At the bar, though he dressed differently there.

But he was the same man.

He was staring at her, but she wasn't afraid, because the sadness in his eyes took away any thought of fear.

She tried to speak, but before she could make a sound, she blinked—and he was gone.

Her hand was shaking so hard that she had to set her cup down. She looked all around the kitchen, then ran to the back door, which was still securely locked. She turned and rushed around the lower level of the house, checking every window. Then she hurried to the front door. As she neared it, she backed away in horror. The door was opening.

By the time he had finished with his shower, Aidan had reconciled everything in his mind. He knew from Kendall that Amelia had been a kind and caring woman. He knew what she looked like, because there was a picture of her in the family gallery in the formal dining room. So the dream made total sense. He was certain that Jenny Trent—and probably at least some of the others—had been murdered in this vicinity. And though all he'd found so far were the two thighbones from two different women, he was willing to bet that those bodies had been disposed of here at the plantation or nearby. And what he needed was to find the rest of her body. His dream had been a subconscious push to do just that.

He stepped out of the shower, vigorously towel-dried his hair, then got dressed. He planned to drive Kendall into town to open her shop for the day, then come back and explore the family plot more thoroughly. If he'd found one bone, the rest of the woman had to be somewhere. He made a mental checklist of the facts he considered certain: there was a killer on the loose, a clever killer who targeted women who were heading off on long trips. How did he do it? Most people were friendly, and those who frequented Bourbon Street tended to have a few too many drinks, which made them more talkative, helping the killer to figure out who fit his profile. It was likely, but not certain, that the killer haunted the Hideaway, the bar where Vinnie played, though it was possible he made the rounds of the Bourbon Street hangouts. Maybe the "evil" Amelia had been afraid of before she died had started with the killer disposing of his victims here, but did he lure them here first, then kill them, or kill them elsewhere and then bring the bodies here after?

He had just pulled on a clean pair of jeans when he heard his cell phone ringing from the pocket of the pair he had worn the day before. He extracted it and answered.

"Flynn."

"Aidan?" a tentative female voice asked.

"Yes, sorry, Aidan Flynn. Who is this?"

"It's Matty, Aidan. Jonas's wife."

"Matty, hi. What can I do for you?"

"Aidan, would you consider meeting me for a quick lunch or even just a coffee today?" she asked. "I'm sorry, I shouldn't be asking. I know you must be busy, and I'm going to see you at the charity party tonight anyway, it's just that… No, never mind. I'm sorry. I shouldn't be calling you."

He winced, remembering that Jeremy had told him that Jonas had been flirting at the bar, unaware that his wife was in the room.

"It's all right, Matty." He hesitated and glanced at his watch. He could take Kendall to work and meet Matty for half an hour, and still get back here with plenty of time to look around before he had to shower and dress for tonight.

"Matty, can I meet you just after ten?" he asked.

"Yes. Aidan, you won't tell Jonas, will you?" she asked anxiously.

"No, Matty, not if you don't want me to."

They made plans, then hung up. Jonas was an idiot, Aidan thought, wondering what the hell he was going to say to Matty.

As he slipped into his shirt, he found himself wondering if Jonas was something worse than just an idiot.

Much worse.

Kendall backed away from door, almost screaming, and then it registered in her mind that she had heard a key turning in the lock.

She stopped herself from running and stood dead still, her eyes wide.

Sunlight poured in, and for a moment, all she saw was a tall silhouette in the doorway.

"Hey there!"

It was Zachary Flynn, she realized, and he seemed as surprised to see her as she was to see him.

"Hey," she returned. It was definitely an awkward moment, but she wasn't as frazzled as she might have been even an hour ago. After all, he wasn't a total stranger who appeared out of thin air and disappeared in the blink of an eye.

A stranger, who looked at her with such sad eyes, and who hung out at the Hideaway at night.

Zachary seemed to take her presence in stride. "So where's Aidan?" he asked cheerfully.

"He's upstairs," she said.

He nodded. "Mmm. I smell coffee."

"In the kitchen," she said.

Aidan made his appearance just then; she heard his footsteps on the stairway and felt him come up behind her. "Hey, Zach."

"I'll just run up and shower and get ready. Saturday is one of our busy days," she said. No point in pretending she'd just dropped by. Given her current apparel, it was more than obvious that she had slept here....

"Excuse me," she mumbled, and fled.

When she came back down a little while later, she found the brothers in the kitchen, talking.

"It's a ridiculous threat," Aidan was saying.

"What's a ridiculous threat?" she asked, going for a second cup of coffee.

"Jeremy got a caller last night who knew we were thinking of having another benefit out here, which is kind of strange because we haven't really talked about it. Not that it was a secret. I mean, we've all mentioned it to someone. But the guy had a really creepy voice and said we were all going to die if we brought people out here for a party."

"Maybe it was our guy with the voodoo-doll fetish," Zach said.

"Maybe," Aidan agreed.

"Wouldn't that make him…kind of a nutcase?" Kendall asked.

"Oh, yeah," Aidan agreed. "And it just means we'll work all the harder to have this place ready for Halloween."

"So you're into the idea now, too?" Zach asked.

Aidan grinned. "Nothing like telling me I *can't* do something to make me want to do it." He took a long swallow and finished his coffee. "Listen, Zach. I'll be back in a few hours. I just have to take Kendall in and meet someone for coffee. While I'm out, will you ask the contractor to talk to the electrician about getting some wiring into that far back shack?" He paused. "And if our tenant is still out there, would you let him know? I told him yesterday that he could stay, that we'd work something out."

"I'll take a walk back there, see if I find him," Zach assured him.

"And if you have a chance, go through the rest of those files you pulled off the computer. See who you can call to get any information about the other women who've disappeared. See if they actually made it here to New Orleans."

"Will do," Zach said.

As they left, the drive was beginning to fill up with the various subcontractors' vehicles.

Kendall looked back at the house as they drove away. It was gleaming white and beautiful in the sun. And it was just a house.

A house where she had seen a mysterious man in the kitchen.

"Are you all right?" Aidan asked, looking at her.

"Fine," she told him quickly.

They were both silent for a moment.

"Are *you* all right?" she asked him then.

"Fine," he said.

"You never told me about your nightmare."

He shrugged. "I swear, I've never sleepwalked before. And the dream was...bizarre. I guess I've been getting obsessed with this case. I dreamed that Amelia was telling me that I had to help...someone."

"Really?" Kendall asked. *Just like Miss Ady.*

But neither of them had dreamed of a sad man with skin the color of café au lait.

The same man who went to the bar. If he was a ghost...

She almost asked Aidan if he had ever noticed the man, but she bit her lip and kept silent. This was getting crazy, though. He was having dreams, and she was seeing ghosts.

Matty Burningham was already at the coffeehouse when he arrived. She told him she'd waited to order, and he decided to go ahead and have an omelet with her.

She was nervous, talking about the dress she'd bought for the gala, asking him about the house. At last he set his hand over hers and stopped her. "Matty, what's up with you? Why did you want to see me?"

For a moment he thought she was going to cry, and he really hoped she wouldn't, because he wasn't much good with tears.

"It's Jonas, of course."

"Matty, I wouldn't worry about anything. He loves you."

"You think?" she asked a little bitterly. She looked at him squarely. "Aidan, is he cheating on me?"

"Matty, I haven't seen an awful lot of Jonas lately, you know."

"But you know him. You did work together once."

"Matty, I'm sure he loves you," Aidan said.

"I did everything for him," she said. "Boobs, face—and it wasn't as if I were wrinkled like a prune or anything."

"Matty, you're beautiful now, and you were beautiful before. It's all a matter of how you feel about yourself."

"That's just it. I didn't care. I did it for him, and it doesn't seem as if... He doesn't seem interested in *me* anymore. It's as if... I don't know. It's as if he's bored."

"Matty, I'm sure things will work out. Have you tried talking to him?"

"Yeah, he acts as if there's nothing wrong."

"Maybe there isn't."

"Oh, Aidan. You're just being sweet."

"Matty, we can all be flirts."

She stared at him, shaking her head. "Not you," she said softly. "When Serena was alive, you never... I'm sorry. It's just that you never acted like...you even noticed any woman but her."

He didn't even know what to say to that. It was true, though.

"Aidan, there have been nights when he hasn't come home."

"What has he said to you?"

"That he was working."

"Maybe he *was* working."

"Right. At a bar."

"Matty, honest to God, sometimes you do start working at a bar. Surveillance. And you have to act like you're there for the good times and the show."

"Talk to him, will you?" she asked.

"Matty, this has to be between the two of you."

"If he's cheating on me, yes. If he's already called a divorce lawyer, I want to know."

"I'll talk to him and see if I can get him to talk to you. How's that?"

"Thanks, Aidan. Only, please, don't tell him that I called you. He'll be furious."

"I won't say anything, Matty," he promised. "I'll be subtle."

"He likes that place where Vinnie plays. He says he goes for the music. That it's some of the best in the city."

"I suppose it depends on what you like, but I can tell you this," Aidan told her gently. "He really might be going for the music. Both my brothers—who know their stuff—agree that the Stakes are really good. So he's not lying to you about that."

Matty shivered suddenly. "I don't know. Sometimes the place gives me the creeps."

"Really? Why?"

"I've been in there with him a few times, you know, and I always feel like someone is watching me."

"Well, I told you. You're a beautiful woman. I'm sure lots of men watch you."

She didn't blush, smile or even thank him. "No, it's not

like that. Not even like…well, a drunken leer. I just feel like there's someone who skulks in there and pictures all the women with their clothes off or something…. Oh, I don't know. It's just not a nice feeling."

She gave herself a little shake and met his eyes again. "Anyway, thanks, Aidan. And I'm sorry about Serena, you know. So sorry. Isn't life ironic? Here are Jonas and me, and it's not looking so good for us. There were you and Serena, and everything about the two of you was perfect, and so life took a brutal swing at you." She gasped then, as if she'd just realized she might be trespassing on territory that was too private. "Oh, that was a horrible thing to say, Aidan. I'm so sorry."

"It's all right."

She brightened. "Three years…and here you are, in New Orleans. I hope you find someone new, Aidan. The right person. She'll be very lucky."

"Thank you, Matty. And listen, things will work out."

He wanted to leave it at that, but he couldn't. "Matty, how long has this been going on? I mean, Jonas not coming home at night?"

"The first time was about three months ago. The last time? Let me think. Week before last. Oh, Aidan…"

"Matty, don't worry. I'll talk to him."

When he left her, he thought she was happier. He wasn't.

He was suddenly wondering just how his old friend *was* spending those nights out.

Saturday brought a continual flow of people in and out of the shop. Luckily Vinnie had come in and stayed to help.

Kendall had decided that she wasn't going to do any

readings that day. She told Mason from the start that she wouldn't; any walk-ins who demanded her services specifically would just have to make an appointment for the next week. She was looking forward to the party that night, even though she wondered if she was becoming too dependent on Aidan's company.

And she was already in a slightly weird place. Had she imagined the man in the kitchen? She must have, because she had checked the entire downstairs and there had been no one there.

She didn't believe in ghosts, she told herself. She *didn't*.

At two, when it trickled down to empty for a few minutes, she noticed Mason and Vinnie standing side by side and staring at her, grinning.

"Hey. Where did you go last night?" Mason asked her.

"Go?" she said.

"I went by your place to see if you felt like going out. You weren't home. Your car was there, but you weren't. Or at least, you didn't answer when I rang your bell." He moved closer, winking confidentially. "Were you sleeping? Or were you out?"

"She was out, all right," Vinnie teased.

"Out at the plantation," Mason said knowingly. They looked like a pair of boys hiding behind the bleachers and telling exaggerated tales of their dates.

"Yes, I was out at the plantation," she said, staring back at them.

"Well, that was no fun. She gave in too easily," Mason said.

Vinnie shrugged. "I thought we'd get her to blush, at least."

"Hey, did you hear about the guy who threatened the Flynns on the radio last night?" Mason asked her.

"Yes, Zach came in and mentioned something about it," she said.

"They're not scared, right? Anything else weird happening out there?" Vinnie asked.

She shook her head. "Nothing last night," she said casually.

This morning, though, she added silently, I thought I saw a ghost.

"You know, that story about the cousins is supposed to be true," Mason said. "So somewhere along the line, you should be hearing the neighing of horses and the clash of sabers or something."

"The Flynn cousins shot each other," Vinnie said. "No sabers."

"Hey, Vinnie," Kendall said. "Is there anything in that story about a man of mixed blood?"

"Oh, no, she's being haunted by the ghost of the caretaker!" Vinnie exclaimed with a laugh.

"I'm not being haunted by any ghost. I was just trying to remember the whole story. I remember the part about the Union soldiers attacking Fiona, and that's why she jumped off the balcony."

"Fiona, huh?" Mason teased.

"That was her name, I'm pretty sure," Kendall said. She didn't know why, but she didn't want to admit, even to the two of them, that she had borrowed the old diary from the attic.

"Well, as a matter of fact," Vinnie said, "the caretaker's name was Henry. And he *was* a man of mixed blood. When everyone wound up dead, the soldiers who had been there ran back into the city. Henry had been with the family for years, but he was a free man. And he rescued the baby—

Fiona and Sloan's baby—who was the ancestor of Amelia. And the Flynn brothers, too, of course."

All this talk of history made Kendall think about Sheila again. Shelia and the laughing card. Death.

Sheila was dead, she suddenly thought with complete certainty.

No! Sheila was on vacation; she would be back this weekend.

The bell above the door tinkled. "Customers," she said firmly, forcing herself away from the scary direction her thoughts had taken.

The graveyard was a mess.

Aidan, dirty, sweaty and frustrated, sat on one of the low sarcophagi and stared around.

He'd dug some pretty deep holes.

He'd found four old graves in which the old wooden coffins had completely decayed and only skeletons remained.

He was certain that the work crew, glancing over now and then from the house, must think they were employed by a complete lunatic.

He was searching for a needle in a haystack, he knew. All the skeletons he had uncovered so far had been intact.

He had refilled the graves, and in doing so, he had discovered that many of the graves had shifted. Even if there were a plan for the graveyard, something that didn't seem to exist, it would be no help in showing him where all the bodies were. Trying to discover if the thighbone had indeed come from an old skeleton didn't seem like a logical plan.

But even as he sat there, he kept thinking that there was *something* he should be discovering here.

Jimmy had said that the ghosts came out in the cemetery.

He had found what he was certain was dried blood on a gravestone.

There was something here.

What was the connection between the plantation, Kendall's shop, the bar where Vinnie played and a girl who had disappeared?

Maybe there was *no* connection. Or not a meaningful one, anyway. Sure, Vinnie had walked Jenny back to where she had been staying. But another guest had verified the fact that she had changed clothes and gone out again to meet someone.

He thought about what he knew about people, what he had seen and learned over the years. He didn't believe that Vinnie would have been quite so forthcoming if he were guilty.

Not to mention that he didn't even know if the ten missing women whose cases Zachary had found were related.

What did he really have so far?

Two human bones—that might or might not be recent. The knowledge that at least one young woman had disappeared from New Orleans without a trace.

A pattern of disappearances *most probably* from the same area, a pattern that had been escalating in the last few years.

And a nightmare in which a sea of dismembered corpses clutched at him and a woman in white begged for help.

He still felt the answer or at least a crucial clue lay buried somewhere in this graveyard, but it was getting late, and he had to give it up for the day.

As he walked back into the house, covered with dirt, even Zachary looked at him strangely.

"Don't ask," he told his brother.

"I won't. I'm heading into the city now to get ready for Jeremy's deal tonight."

"I'll see you there," Aidan told him.

Upstairs, he showered again and dressed for the night. He walked back down to the formal dining room and looked at the family paintings and photos on the wall. Amelia had been captured in her mature years; she was a handsome woman still, slim, with a brilliant smile and a face lined with experience.

"I would deeply appreciate if you wouldn't haunt my dreams," he told the woman in the painting.

She continued to smile back at him, unperturbed.

It was nothing but a picture. A picture that had somehow haunted his sleep. Just his subconscious, he told himself. And yet he couldn't escape the thought that the house—or at least the ghosts of the past that haunted it—was urging him to solve the mystery.

He began to study the paintings of the long-ago Flynns, pausing at one of a beautiful woman in a white gown with tiny roses embroidered on it. The little plaque at the bottom identified her as Fiona MacFarlane Flynn but "Flynn" had been etched on in a different and more primitive hand. Curious.

He remembered seeing the woman's elaborate tomb in the graveyard, but the inscription there said only Fiona MacFarlane. He recalled that she was the one who had died jumping off the balcony. For some reason, he touched the painting, and as he stared at it, he had the odd sense that someone was standing behind him.

As he swung around swiftly, his peripheral vision seemed to catch a shadow just disappearing into the kitchen.

He followed, determined to find out if someone else was in the house.

The kitchen was empty.

It must have been a workman.

But the back door was locked, and the remaining workmen were all outside, packing up their tools for the night.

Obviously, he told himself, he hadn't actually seen anyone, and no one had been standing behind him.

And if there were shadows in this house and they were human—and those voodoo dolls had definitely been left by human hands—they were in trouble. Because he was going to be wearing the Colt on his person at all times from now on.

17

The aquarium was done up in black and orange, since it was October and Halloween was coming, but none of the decorations were scary. The pumpkins all wore happy grins, and the only witches present were good witches, dressed in bright colors with cute hats. They were played by volunteers from the local colleges, and they were serving punch and special snacks for the kids. Since children were welcome guests tonight, there were many in attendance.

The city was represented by employees from every department. The band the radio station had brought in was good, though, in Kendall's opinion, not nearly as good as the Stakes, and Vinnie agreed.

They were standing by a tank displaying hundreds of tiny octopi. Vinnie was mournfully watching the band, while Mason was watching a pretty young blonde. Kendall was watching Aidan, who was deep in conversation with a man with slicked-back dark hair and his Kewpie-doll companion. Frowning, she tried to place the man, who looked naggingly familiar.

As she stood there, Kendall felt a nudge and heard someone say, "Hey there, girl."

She turned. It was Rebecca. "Hey, yourself."

Heather Graham

"We dress up pretty good, huh?" Rebecca said.

"I didn't know you were coming," Kendall said with pleasure.

"Honey, I'm not sure all these people would be thrilled to know that half the morgue is here," Rebecca told her, grinning.

"Is Miss Ady here, too?" Kendall asked.

"No, this is too much bash—and too many young children running around—for my mama these days. No, I'm here as a supportive civil servant. And what are you three doing, moping around here like a trio of logs? Let's get on that floor and dance."

"Why, Rebecca, what an idea," Mason said approvingly. "Think you can dance me over to that blonde?"

"I'll do my best," she promised.

"I guess that leaves you and me," Vinnie said to Kendall.

"Oh, cheer up, we're good together," Kendall said, and laughed. "Remember Miss Louisa's Cotillion for Young Southern Citizens?"

"I do," he said, groaning.

They headed for the floor, and she realized she enjoyed dancing with Vinnie. Before the number ended, though, Aidan cut in.

"Having fun?" he asked her.

"Yes. Well, except for when Vinnie is whining about the band."

Aidan laughed. "The Stakes *are* better."

"It seems like a huge success."

"It is. Jeremy is thrilled."

"That's who it is!" Kendall said suddenly, noticing the dark-haired man over Aidan's shoulder and finally placing him.

"Who *who* is?" Aidan asked her.

"Dr. Abel. He looks terrific in a tux. I've only ever seen him with his hair wild, his glasses halfway down his nose and wearing a lab coat. I've met him a few times, but I've never seen him cleaned up. He's not half so creepy like this."

Aidan grinned. "Maybe not so creepy, but he's still a jerk. Doesn't matter. Thanks to Rebecca, I've got Jonas stepping in to tell him that the Feds are taking over. The bones are going to some experts up in the D.C. area. I'm going to pick them up on Monday and oversee the transfer myself, along with a dried blood scraping and a dress that I hope will produce some skin flakes."

Before she could reply, Rebecca was cutting in on her. "Excuse me, there's a fox-trot coming up, and this man looks like a fox to me."

"Please, enjoy," Kendall said with a laugh.

She danced with Mason. Then, to her surprise, when Mason finally got a chance to dance with his blonde, she found herself on the floor alone, facing Dr. Jon Abel, who had apparently just lost his partner, too.

"Miss Montgomery, right?" he said.

"Yes. Hello, Dr. Abel."

He offered her a hand. "Would you like to dance?"

"Thank you," she said.

"Nice affair, isn't it?" he asked cheerfully. "I'm glad to see people out in force for the benefit of New Orleans."

"How are things? Is the crime rate still high?"

"We're not the worst in the country, but a lot of the parish is still struggling." He smiled. "I'll let you in on a secret."

"Oh?"

"You came with Aidan Flynn, right?"

"Yes."

"Well, I know he's frustrated that I haven't gotten some results for him yet. And I'm sure he thinks I'll be angry about turning the work over to the Federal lab. Here's the secret. I'm not angry at all. I'm relieved. We're still too busy with the present."

She nodded. "I guess that makes sense."

She'd already noticed that he was a smooth dancer, and now she was pleased to discover that he was also a pleasant man. Rebecca had said a few times that he could be fierce, but that probably just came with the territory.

"This is a lovely party, don't you think? I hear they're going to announce another one tonight, something out at that place they inherited," he said.

"Oh?"

"You don't know?"

"I'd heard they were talking about it."

"It should be good, casual instead of formal like tonight. Don't tell Aidan I applaud his family's efforts, though. It's better if he keeps thinking I'm an old grouch."

"My lips are sealed," she assured him.

The music stopped, and it looked to Kendall as if there were going to be some announcements. Sure enough, the mayor got up on the stage, thanking everyone for making the city great again. Then he turned the mike over to Al Fisher, the DJ emceeing the event, who in turn gave it over to Jeremy.

Jeremy promised to keep his remarks brief, saying he didn't want to stop the evening with a speech. He talked a little about Children's House, then said, "I know this is short notice, folks, and it will be first come, first served, but I want to announce a benefit bash out at the Flynn plantation on the thirty-first. We're calling it our Haunted Holiday Happening, and we're hoping to raise a lot more money while everyone has a lot more fun."

The DJ came back then to talk about how, where and when people could buy tickets, and while he was talking, Vinnie reappeared at Kendall's side.

"They have to hire us this time, Kendall. You've got pull. Tell them they've got to hire the Stakes."

"Vinnie, I can suggest it," she said. "You know Jeremy pretty well. Why don't you talk to him about it?"

"Yeah, but I think your boy calls the shots where that house is concerned."

"That's not true at all. And who knows? The radio station hired this group, maybe they're in charge for the next party, too."

"Just ask Aidan, would you?"

"Ask Aidan what?"

He was back at her side. She glanced up at him and felt very warm all of a sudden. The room was full of beautiful people tonight, but Aidan wore his tux exceptionally well. His hair was so dark and his eyes so deep a blue, and his broad shoulders, tapering hips and sheer height gave him a James Bond quality. And once, she realized, he really had been a G-man, even if not a British one.

"Vinnie wants me to ask you if the Stakes can play at the Halloween benefit," she said. "He thinks they should."

"So do I," Aidan said.

Vinnie stared at him. "Really?"

"Yeah. I'll ask Jeremy what he has in mind. It's his decision. Kendall, care to dance?"

"You've made his day," she said as she swept out on the floor with Aidan.

She wanted to ask if he'd totally cleared Vinnie of suspicion, but she decided not to. They seemed to be getting along, and she wanted to keep it that way. After all, maybe he just wanted to keep a close eye on Vinnie.

He could dance so well that at first she didn't realize he had maneuvered them into a spot where he could watch Mason, who was dancing with the blonde again.

"Are you always like this?" she asked him.

"Like what?"

"Conducting surveillance?"

He had the grace to grimace. "Not always. I won't be later, I promise."

"Later?"

"Aren't you coming back out to the plantation with me? Tomorrow is Sunday, and Mason said you decided to close tomorrow so you could both take a break after the gala. I admit, workmen will be clomping around the house, but..." His brows knit into a frown as his words trailed away. "I didn't scare you off, did I? I mean, I suppose it's rather bizarre when your first night in a man's house ends with him sleepwalking."

"No. And yes, but we have to go to my place first. I need some things—and the poor cat. She looked at me today as if I were a traitor."

"She can come, too."

"Too many workmen. She'll have to learn that cats are supposed to be independent."

Soon after, while Aidan was talking to Jon Abel—a conversation that looked pleasant, at least from a distance—

Kendall found herself standing with Hal Vincent and a few of the other police officers she'd known forever. Hal rolled his eyes when the upcoming event at the Flynn plantation came up. "They're going to have to hire some outside security. That place is dark as hell, and you're sure to have a few idiots who think it would be fun to go play in the grave-yard or get lost in the woods down by the river." He shook his head. "I don't know. This went well, but I think they're pushing it, having something out at that old place."

"But the plantation is a piece of history, and it's for a good cause," Kendall objected.

"People are people. There are idiots in every crowd. Haven't you ever seen any of those teen slasher movies? The kids keep going back out to the woods to fool around, even knowing there's a killer on the loose. And when you watch those movies, you think nobody is that stupid. Sad thing is, people actually are," Hal said. "And that place? It's haunted," he assured her in a dead-serious tone.

"This from a jaded homicide detective?"

"I may mess with the living, but I don't go up against ghosts," Hal told her. "Hey, my mama taught me there are some things best left alone, and that includes ghosts."

"I'm sure they'll arrange for good security."

"They'll be paying for it, too," Hal said grimly.

As they were speaking, Jonas and his wife approached them.

"Miss Montgomery," Jonas said, and introduced himself, "you may not remember me, but we've crossed paths a few times. I'd like you to meet my wife, Matty."

Matty looked as if she'd probably paid for her plastic surgeon's newest Mercedes, but her smile, as she took

Kendall's hand, was warm and genuine. "I've read about you," she said.

"You've read about me?"

"In the 'Neighbors' section of the paper," Matty explained. "After Amelia died. There was a real nice article in there about the way she'd helped you when you'd been orphaned and then opening your shop, and how you returned that favor, caring for her. It was a nice write-up. Anyway, when I read it, I felt kind of like I knew you. I lost my folks when I was young, too."

"I'm sorry. It's nice to meet you. And I'll have to look up that article. I never saw it."

"Are you really a psychic?" Matty asked.

Kendall hesitated. "I really know how to read a tarot deck," she said.

"Great. I've been wanting to check out your shop. I'll come by next week." She smiled.

Eventually the party wound down, and Kendall left with Vinnie, Mason and the three Flynn brothers. It was late, but Café du Monde stayed open to all hours, so they headed in that direction for coffee and beignets. When Kendall and Aidan got up to leave, she asked Mason about his blonde. "Did you get her name and number?"

He grinned. "You bet. I'll be seeing her again."

It had been a long day. Kendall was still keyed up when they finally returned to the plantation after a stop at her place to pick up clothes and spend a few minutes with Jezebel. Once again the windows were shining from within, and she could see that a light had been rigged back by the old slave quarters, too. But it was just a house, she told herself. Just a house.

It was welcoming, beautiful. And besides, Aidan was wearing his gun. She knew because she had felt the bulge beneath his jacket.

Inside the front door, Aidan paused and kissed her. "You need anything?" he asked her.

She smiled. *Just you* was on the tip of her tongue, but she didn't say it.

"Have you got any water in the fridge?" she asked.

"Should have," he said. They walked through the dining room to reach the kitchen, and she was surprised when Aidan slowed to look at the family portraits as they passed. He stopped by the portrait of Fiona MacFarlane Flynn.

"You know, she's got a beautiful tomb in the graveyard, but she was buried as Fiona MacFarlane."

"Her marriage was a secret, because of the war. Her husband, who owned this place, was fighting for the South, but with the Union closing in, he probably thought she'd be in more danger here if they arrived and thought she was married to a Confederate soldier," Kendall told him. "I guess that was the reason, anyway."

"I think we should have her name corrected, don't you?" Aidan asked.

Kendall was surprised. He had never seemed like the sentimental type, especially not over something that had occurred over a century and a half ago.

"That would be a nice touch," she agreed.

They grabbed a couple of bottles of water, then moved casually and sedately enough up the stairs, but once inside the master bedroom, they were in one another's arms in seconds. Their relationship was still so new that just touching him intimately was absolutely fascinating. Feeling his lips on her naked flesh was like lightning striking. She wondered if she would ever tire of him, and she thought it just wasn't possible. Nor would she grow weary of the sound of his voice, the look in his eyes, the ripple of his laughter. He made love aggressively at first, then with an almost awed tenderness, but every climax was equally cataclysmic.

She would never tire of lying beside him, or of the sense of being one with him. And sleep… Even sleep was better in his arms. Deep, complete.

Until the dream came.

They had been looking at Fiona's portrait earlier. That explained the first vision that played out in her dreams. She was just there, watching, as if she were a fly on the wall, a pair of eyes in the breeze. She heard the pounding of a horse's hooves, and then there were shouts and men in Union officers' uniforms, while only one man—a man who looked so much like Aidan—was decked out in butternut and gray, his cavalry insignia threadbare and worn. It was his horse she had heard, as he galloped to reach the house. And there, on the upper balcony, was a beautiful woman in white. Fiona.

There was someone else, too. Someone behind Fiona.

And then she heard a whisper.

I knew I was going to die. I had to die, because I suspected what was going on. I was out in the graveyard. He had brought women there before. It was where he used and discarded them…. Can you hear me? I couldn't stop it then, and now it's happening again. Someone has to stop it now. Can you hear me? Oh, please, can you hear me?

She heard gunshots, exploding loudly all around her.

What happened next was like a dream within a dream.

Fiona, beautiful in white, came running across the balcony, and then…she fell, tumbling in slow motion, almost as if she were flying.

There was a silent scream.

Can you hear me?

The scene faded, changed.

And the man was there.

The man with skin the color of café au lait and the sad eyes. And he was bent down over the woman, weeping.

From the house came the sound of a baby, crying.

The scene began to shift, and she thought she was about to wake up. She willed herself to wake up, because even in her sleep, she could remember that she had the diary and knew that it was important to read it. So important.

She didn't wake up, though. Instead, she was walking, moving furtively, keeping her flashlight aimed low. She was looking for someone. She didn't know who, but she was excited. Excited because of the note. It had to be from a co-worker. Someone who wanted her to be in on the solution of a historical mystery, someone who had slipped onto the property and had uncovered evidence from the past. She thought she knew who it was.

And he liked her. She almost giggled at the thought.

She heard a name called in the night. Kendall tried to listen harder, because she knew the name, but it wasn't hers.

"Come on. Hurry up."

The voice was coming from the cemetery.

Then the part of her that was still Kendall, even in the dream, knew. She knew that if she went, she would die. A thick gray mist began to swirl around her, and there were bones, bodies, faces, all beginning to emerge from the earth, warning her to stay away, and yet the woman she was in the dream didn't seem to see them.

She urged the woman she had become to stop, but it was no use.

She was going to die.

She couldn't stop her body, so she had to wake up. It was the only way to live.

"Kendall!"

She heard her own name clearly, felt strong arms around her. She blinked, and then she was wide awake and held tightly in Aidan's arms. He was staring down at her with concern and tenderness mingled in his eyes.

Nightmares.

Were they doomed to be plagued by them here?

He had shaken off the dream quickly. She still felt as if gray mist was clinging to her, as if she had to figure out the meaning, the message, of the dream. Would he still look at her with such tenderness if he knew she was on the verge of total insanity, thinking she could enter the past, enter into someone else's body, in a dream?

"Sorry. I guess it was my turn for a nightmare," she told him, and forced a smile. She reached up and touched his hair. "I'm sorry I woke you."

"It's fine. But what was it? What were you dreaming?" She didn't have a chance to answer. He winced as they heard a truck honking as it lumbered into the yard. "Workmen," he said.

She looked at him and smiled—more genuinely this time. "Then I suggest you take the first shower."

"Do you remember your dream?" he asked her, clearly not entirely reassured that she was okay.

"No," she lied.

He studied her face with concern for another moment, then kissed her and rose, heading for the bathroom. When she heard the water running, she was tempted to race in and join him. Maybe that would wash away the remnants of the dream, still clinging to her like a miasma of fear.

Her foot itched, and she reached down to scratch it. Her fingers touched something gritty, and she looked down.

Her feet were dirty, as if she had been running around barefoot on raw earth.

In a cemetery?

Without further thought, she ran in and joined Aidan in the shower. He might have been surprised, but he certainly didn't protest. She slipped into his arms and let the water beat down on them. When he held her, she could forget the dreams in the magic of reality.

It was good just to stand in the hot shower, wet flesh sliding against wet flesh, knowing nothing but the sheer physical pleasure of making love.

Eventually they had to get out. He got dressed in jeans and a T-shirt, and headed downstairs to meet the workmen, while she dried her hair.

As soon as he was gone, she reached into her bag and found the diary she had stuffed in it when she packed.

She could tell by the aroma wafting up the stairs that he had made coffee. She went downstairs, poured herself a cup, then headed up to the attic and the rocker where she had liked to sit and read when Amelia was alive.

Jeremy and Zach arrived just minutes after the workmen. Aidan met them downstairs, and they looked over the contractor's schedule again. The electricity would be off all day Monday, as would the water. By the end of the week, though, except for a bit of detail work, the house would be done according to the work plan. A new kitchen, something they would want eventually, would take another week, at least, at a later date, since all the appliances, counters and cabinets would have to be special-ordered. And a cleaning crew had been scheduled to come in and spiff up the stables, which were being called into use for the party.

Just as they finished speaking, a car came up the drive. Aidan, shielding his eyes from the sun, saw that Vinnie was driving, accompanied by another member of the band and Mason.

"Good, you're all here," Vinnie said, hopping out of the car. Mason followed, looking up at the house, and the other guy—Gary, Aidan thought—came last.

"What are you three doing out so early?" Aidan asked, walking over to them.

"We're not trying to be pains in the ass," Gary said quickly, shaking Aidan's hand and grinning at Jeremy and Zach. "We just want the gig."

"The gig?" Zach asked.

"Playing for the benefit," Gary said.

Vinnie's face had gone a slightly mottled shade of red, but he spoke quickly. "I asked Aidan about it last night. He said it was your call, Jeremy."

"And I said they should come ask you right off," Mason said with a shrug. "Strike while an iron is hot, you know?"

Jeremy looked at his two brothers. "Why not?"

"Best band on Bourbon Street," Zach agreed.

Vinnie just stared at them. "That easy?"

"Yeah, that easy," Jeremy said.

"Cool," Vinnie breathed.

"Told you," Mason told him, setting his arms around his friends' shoulders.

"Yeah, you told us," Gary agreed. He looked around. "Where do you think you'll want us to set up? You guys going to have a haunted graveyard or anything like that?"

"No," Aidan said sharply. Maybe too sharply. "We'll limit events to the stables, maybe the downstairs of the house. But since there hasn't been a horse around in years, the stables will be the best place."

"Great," Vinnie said, then pumped their hands one by one. "It'll be great. You have to sit in with us, Jeremy. And the publicity we'll get from this, well, it's priceless. Thank you."

Aidan couldn't help it. He still felt a slight reservation. Had he been right to erase Vinnie from his mental suspect list? Even though Vinnie hadn't lied about taking Jenny back to her B and B, what was to say that he wasn't the person she'd gone out to meet later?

Then there was Mason. Always at the store, always at the bar. And now studying the house as if he'd never seen it before. Aiden *knew* he'd been out there, so why stare at it now…unless he was looking for something that might give him away?

"The place looks great," Mason told them.

"First time you're seeing it?" Zach asked.

"Oh, hell, no," Mason said, laughing. "Vinnie and I both used to come out here with Kendall. You know, when she was staying with Amelia."

"Right," Aidan said.

At that moment Kendall suddenly came tearing out of the house, brandishing a book. "I've figured it out!" she cried.

They all turned to stare at her.

"Hey, guys. Hi. What are you doing here?" she asked, her glance moving from Vinnie to Mason to Gary.

Vinnie picked her up and spun her around. "It's official! We got the gig!"

"Super!" she said, as he set her down.

Aidan watched the two of them. They were close. Brother and sister close. Was it possible that Vinnie could be a sadistic killer and Kendall truly have no idea?

"What was that you were saying when you ran out here?" Aidan asked her.

She looked at him, then Jeremy and Zach. "I found out the truth about Sloan and Brendan," she said, smiling again.

"Are you talking about that old story again?" Vinnie asked.

She nodded, obviously feeling triumphant. "They didn't kill each other. Not the way we always heard it."

"Kendall, stop. You're about to ruin the one good ghost story that goes with this place," Vinnie objected.

"No, actually, it makes it an even sadder ghost story." She lifted the book she'd been holding. "This starts out as Fiona's diary, and it's charming. She talks about her secret wedding to Sloan. Brendan was there, so he knew they were married. Then Sloan rode off to fight again. Almost a year later, Sloan went AWOL when he was on a mission close to home. Meantime, a couple of Union soldiers came out from the city. But here's the thing—they weren't just a couple of greedy bastards, out to see what they could steal. One of them was a killer. He used his position with the military to "interrogate" women, and then he killed them. He'd been using this property to kill them and hide their bodies for a while. Fiona heard something one night, so she slipped out to see what was going on and saw him leaving, and that was when she looked around and saw what he'd done. What he'd been doing for a while. But he saw her, and after that, she was afraid every day. She wrote everything down in her diary, but she knew no Union officer was going to listen to her, so she was waiting for Brendan to get back, so she could tell him and *he* could report what was going on. But he didn't come back in time. The killer, a man named Victor Grebbe, didn't come just to harass her and to steal from her, but to kill her. She knew when she saw him ride up that she was going to die, so she gave the diary to Henry, the caretaker, who had stayed on to help her. She didn't want him to die, too, so she told him to take the diary and the baby Sloan never even got to see and hide.

"Grebbe found her, then, and Sloan rode up just in time to see her die when Grebbe chased her onto the balcony and she threw herself off to get away from him. He shot and wounded Grebbe, and then Brendan showed up. He didn't recognize Sloan, probably thought he was a deserter from the Confederate army, attacking a Union officer. So they did shoot each other, but they never intended to. And they weren't fighting over Fiona."

"How on earth can you know all that from *Fiona's* diary?" Aidan asked. "She was dead once she went off the balcony."

Kendall opened the book to a page near the end. "See where the writing changes? This was written by Henry, the free black man who had stayed on the property to be with Fiona. When it was all over, he finished the story just before he took the baby—Sloan and Fiona's baby—with him to hide out until the war was over. The baby was named Declan Flynn, and when he was about ten, Henry brought him back to New Orleans, where he put in a claim for the property, and somehow, they won it back."

"Cool," Mason said.

"Wow, that will really help you publicize the event," Vinnie said.

"I'm not so sure we need that much publicity," Jeremy said. "We have to limit attendance to a couple hundred people, and I think we can guarantee that many tickets already. Then again, this is a matter of history, so it's important for people to know the truth, and good publicity can't hurt, right?"

"Well, I think it's wonderful to know that the cousins never meant to kill one another, war or no war—publicity or no publicity," Kendall said. "And at least Brendan managed to shoot Grebbe before he died." She smiled grimly. "Anyway, if you'll excuse me, I want to go back and read this over again." She turned to her friends. "Congrats, guys. And hey, Gary, here's your new beginning." She waved and went running happily back toward the house.

Aidan caught Vinnie and Mason looking at him speculatively after she left.

The house was full of workmen, but that didn't bother Kendall.

She didn't want to stay in the house. She wanted to head out to the cemetery, but she didn't want to be seen. She didn't want anyone stopping her, and she didn't want to have to explain why she was sure there was some kind of a clue out in the cemetery. And she certainly didn't want to try explaining to Aidan that she was convinced Fiona was trying to communicate with her in dreams, much less that she had seen Henry—several times.

The workers didn't pay any attention to her as she passed, which made it easy enough to slip out, skirt around the stables and head through the trees to the burial ground.

She'd been in the cemetery before, including for Amelia's service, but today she was looking at tombs she had never really paid much attention to before. She bypassed the stones she had read a dozen times and skipped the family mausoleum. She forced her way through the overgrowth and took a closer look at some of the in-ground graves, especially those whose stones had been broken by the growing roots of large trees.

The cemetery looked strange. It had been dug up in places, and then dirt had been packed in little mounds over the graves again.

Aidan? It must have been Aidan or one of his brothers; she couldn't imagine that he would have let anyone else dig up what was now his family cemetery.

She went from grave to grave, glad of the breeze coming up from the river, and even glad that she could hear the noise of hammers and saws, along with the shouts of the workmen.

She headed for the tomb that held Fiona MacFarlane Flynn.

And then she saw, just steps away, a sarcophagus she had never paid much attention to before; the etching in the stone was old, and time and lichen had obscured it.

Heedless of her fingernails, she worked at the old writing until it was finally legible, though still difficult to read. The burial had taken place in 1887. The inscription read Henry LeBlanc, and below that, "Savior of this House."

She hesitated, sitting on the grave. The wind picked up suddenly, but she wasn't afraid. "Either I've lost my mind, or you're haunting this house, this city, and you know there's a man here killing people again," she said softly. "You wanted everyone to know the truth back then—that's why you finished Fiona's diary—and you want us to know the truth now, too, don't you? Well, we *do* know the truth now, Henry. We know there's a man killing women, and we'll catch him. I promise."

She stood up, surprised that she didn't feel the ease and relief she had expected. The air turned cold, as if warning her that nothing at all had been solved.

Then it hit her. A bone-chilling fear, like the fear she had felt in her dream. There was something bad here, something evil.

She spun around, as if convinced an evil entity was there at that very moment, watching her every move.

Waiting. Crouched and ready to spring.

"Kendall?"

She jumped and spun around. Aidan was walking toward her. The chill, and the feeling of being watched, faded away.

He was staring at her strangely, but she forced a smile, her heart still thundering.

"I wanted to find Henry's grave, and I did," she told him.

He nodded, reaching out to her.

She took his hand and asked, "Aidan, were you in here, digging up graves?"

"Yes."

"Why?"

"Looking for bones."

"Aidan, it's a graveyard. Of course there are bones."

He looked at her and smiled as he brushed her hair back

from her forehead. "Actually, I was looking for disturbed bones, or a suspicious lack of bones."

"Oh."

He paused, staring around the cemetery. She realized that she must have looked around exactly the same way before, as if sure there were something there, something that just couldn't be found.

"Let's go. Everybody wants to go get some lunch. Hungry?" he asked her.

"Sure."

They walked away holding hands, but when she looked back, a cloud had darkened the sun, casting the graveyard in shadow.

And in that shadow, she could have sworn she saw Henry. But he wasn't standing by his own grave, nor by Fiona's. He was standing in front of the Flynn family tomb and pointing to the door.

Then the clouds shifted, and he was gone.

18

The rest of Sunday proved to be uneventful.

They all went to lunch at an old house that had been turned into a restaurant, and as Aidan sat there, feeling warm and comfortable, he thought how nice it would be if only he could trust his own house.

It was a ridiculous thought, and it had come to him unbidden. He dismissed it quickly and turned his mind back to the conversation. With Vinnie and Mason there, it was his chance to see a whole different side of Kendall.

"I still think it's a shame Kendall didn't stick to her original plan," Vinnie said.

"Plan?" Aidan asked her.

She flushed slightly. "I wanted to found a local theater. A place for adults and kids to take classes and perform, where new plays and new actors could all get a chance together, and people could learn stagecraft, set design…" She shrugged. "I never really fleshed it out."

"It was still a great dream," Vinnie said.

She shrugged. "We needed a venue. I had lots of friends who would have worked for nothing to get it off the ground, but the rents everywhere were astronomical. So…when the shop came up, I figured I could make it work. End of story."

"Maybe not," Jeremy said. "Maybe you could supervise the decorations and activities for the Halloween bash."

"I'd love to do it," she said. "And I can do great things with no budget, so you can put all the money you make into Children's House."

"Great. That's settled, then," Jeremy said.

"I can tell you one good way to get people excited," she said. "Hire some of the mule carriages from the city. I have friends who will do it for practically nothing, given the publicity they'll get. People can park in that open area to the left of the house, then take a carriage ride back to the stables. I know some good catering places that will be happy to handle the food for cost. And I'm assuming you'll let someone do tours of the main house. People would pay extra for that, you know."

They were all staring at her blankly.

"Wow. Good thing she's on the team," Zach said.

She smiled. "I'm just happy to help. Amelia would have loved it."

It should be fun, she thought. *Would* be fun. Except...

Except that the house was haunted. She was sure of it.

She didn't understand why she still felt so spooked. They had found out the truth about the Civil War Flynns, and soon the record would be corrected and everyone would know that the cousins hadn't killed each other out of malice or because of some romantic rivalry. Surely that would please the ghosts, right? But Henry was afraid of something in the present, not the past. He'd pointed to the family tomb and looked at her as if she should understand what he was getting at.

A chill swept up her spine, even as she sat there smiling at the others.

Okay, so Henry was out to help her.

Then what the hell did the dreams mean?

And why had her feet been dirty?

She refused to think about it and ruin the day.

That night, as soon as she fell asleep, Kendall found herself in the cemetery again. Henry was standing by the family tomb again, and though he was speaking this time, she couldn't understand him. Suddenly a look of horror crossed his worn features, and he pointed behind her.

She could feel cold breath on her neck. Someone coming after her.

She struggled to wake up, and this time, she managed it, and without screaming out or awakening Aidan. He was asleep at her side, the rise and fall of his chest even and rhythmic. She curled closer to him and hoped that she would fall asleep again, this time without being plagued by dreams.

She lay awake for a while, wondering what to do. Should she tell Aidan that Henry's ghost was trying to keep watch at the Hideaway, and that he also seemed to be warning her about a killer in the cemetery? Aidan was already digging up the cemetery, anyway. What would he do if she flat-out told him that ghosts were speaking to her?

Ruby Beaudreaux was at reception when Aidan stopped by the medical examiner's office to pick up the bones and other potential evidence. Abel had been pleasant about the idea of him coming by to pick everything up, but he was suspicious that trouble might still be in the offing.

"I'll go tell Dr. Abel that you're here," she told him.

As he waited in the outer room, he was startled when Rebecca came out.

"Rebecca, hi, how are you?"

"In a mess this morning, I'm afraid."

"Why? What happened?"

"Besides a hit-and-run on Rampart and a dead woman in a house waiting to be demolished?" she asked wearily. "Abel is on the warpath. Someone snuck in here last night and went through our bones."

"Your bones?"

"We have drawers of them, actually. We use them for comparisons, showing juries at trial…all kinds of things. Anyway, things back there are a mess, bones everywhere, nothing labeled. I have to get back in there before I wind up in trouble—I'm on skull collection. Call me later if you think I can help you."

"Thank you, Rebecca," he told her.

Had someone broken in just to steal the bones he had discovered? Or had the break-in occurred for some other reason entirely? His money was on the former.

Jon Abel, his hair once again in a state of disarray from his fingers continually running through it, made his appearance just seconds after Rebecca left. "I'm sorry, Flynn, but it's going to take me some time to find your bones or even figure out if I still have them."

"Was there evidence tampering of any other kind?" Aidan asked.

"Oh, yeah. Mrs. Eames was switched with Mr. Nelson down in the morgue, some of the desks were rifled, and bullets taken from six victims found in the last twelve months have disappeared." Abel stared at him, shaking his head. "Flynn, trust me, this has nothing to do with your case. Now, if you'll excuse me, I need to get back in and go back to assessing the damage."

"Hang on. Even if the bones are gone, what about the blood scraping and the dress? I'd still like to get them up to Washington."

Abel stiffened irritably. "All right. Wait."

He returned with a brown bag and a small box. "Your blood is on a slide in the box, and the dress is just as you gave it to me. Is that all?"

"Yeah, thanks. Hope you get everything straightened out soon."

Aidan left the coroner's office and headed straight out to the police station to see Hal Vincent, who wasn't at his desk. Aidan decided to wait.

An hour later, Hal came in. When he saw Aidan, he held back a groan, then told him to follow him on back to his office. Hal took his chair and watched Aidan through weary eyes. "You want to know about the break-in at the morgue, I take it?"

Aidan nodded.

"All right. Someone dismantled the alarm—which anybody with a decent knowledge of wiring could do, because it's a pretty basic model."

"Did the security cameras catch anything?"

"Shadows. We're trying to enhance the images now, but so far, it looks like two people walked up to the rear door at two different times."

"Could it be a college prank? Abel said a couple of bodies were switched."

"I don't think so."

"Why?"

"In my opinion? It was made to *look* like a prank to camouflage what was really going on. My guess is it's tied to the missing ballistic evidence and someone's trying to keep one of those cases from going to trial. That's all I know right now, Flynn. If I get anything else, I'll let you know."

"One more thing. Did you bring the FBI in on this?"

"We were the ones who went over the place, dusting for fingerprints, looking for evidence. But I informed the FBI, yes."

"Thanks." Aidan left the cop then and headed straight for Jonas's office. Jonas wasn't in, so again he waited.

When Jonas arrived, he, too, seemed to hold back a groan. "Aidan, I'm sorry you didn't get your bones back. Bad timing."

"I want to know what you think about the break-in."

"Not too much. It's a local matter."

Aidan nodded. "I'd like to use your mailing facilities. I still have a blood sample and a dress I'd like analyzed." He didn't mention that he had tucked the hairbrush in the box, too.

"And what are you going to compare them to?" Jonas asked.

"I'd like to know if the dried blood goes with Jenny Trent, the woman who wore the dress."

"You're talking a long time, Aidan. I doubt if they can get anything."

"That's okay. I have a friend at Quantico who won't mind trying."

"I'll take you down to the mail room myself," Jonas told him.

After the package was duly sent off overnight to Aidan's friend, Robert Birch, Jonas led the way back to his office.

He seemed in no hurry to get rid of Aidan. "So you're seeing the Montgomery girl, huh?" he asked.

Aidan nodded.

"She's a pretty girl. Mysterious."

"Mysterious?"

"Claims she can read the future, doesn't she? I'd call that mysterious."

"Do you believe in any of that?" Aidan asked him.

"Do you?"

"How's Matty?" Aidan asked, changing the subject. "She's worried about you. Worried about the two of you."

Jonas flushed. "That's none of your business, Aidan."

"No, it's not, but if you want out of your marriage, you ought to just tell her."

"I said it's none of your business."

"Yeah, well, we used to be friends."

Jonas looked up at him. "We still are, aren't we?"

"Talk to your wife, Jonas," Aidan said. He turned to leave, then swung back and asked, "Where's Jenny Trent's car?"

"I don't know, it's been a long time. Still in impound, maybe."

"Find out, would you? I'd like to take another look at it, and I'm tired of waiting for Hal Vincent's men to get to it."

Monday morning was busy at the shop, but Vinnie came in to help, which made everything easier. Kendall had a friend at the paper, Jean Avery, and she called her, telling her about the diary she had found in the attic, and the new twist in the sad legend of Flynn Plantation. Jean promised to run a small piece the next day, and a larger human interest story on the weekend.

"Think you can get me the okay to go out there and take a few pictures?" Jean asked. "I've heard about the Halloween party, and this could get them some good PR for it, though I gather it's almost sold out already."

"A haunted plantation for Halloween. What could be better?" Kendall asked, and it was true. A lot of people who didn't attend might send in checks anyway. You couldn't give to a cause you knew nothing about.

"I'm sure I can arrange a photo op."

Vinnie was passing by just then and elbowed her, giving her a meaningful look.

"The Stakes are going to be playing that night," Kendall added. "Maybe we could get them together ahead of time to pose by the old barn or something." She was sure Vinnie genuinely cared about the charity, but she was equally sure his biggest interest was in getting publicity for the Stakes.

"Sounds fun. I'll get back to you." Jean paused and cleared her throat, then said, "I hear you've been seeing one of the new owners. Just can't get that plantation out of your blood, huh?"

Kendall was left speechless for a moment. She forced a light tone when she replied. "I guess that's it. Thanks, Jean, we'll talk soon."

She hung up. "Why does everyone think I was expecting to get that plantation?" she asked Vinnie with aggravation.

"Gee, let's see. You were everything to Amelia, you took care of her, and no one knew any heirs existed. How's that?" Vinnie suggested.

"Look, there's a customer, Vinnie. Go help her."

Behind the counter, Kendall took out the sketchbook she'd been filling with designs for the decorations. She'd started out with a basic sketch of the interior of the barn, then added in the stage and even made notes about wiring, then begun to plan what decorations would go where. At around five-thirty, the phone rang, and she picked it up absently.

"Kendall, it's Joe Ballentine. Sheila's boss. At the Society, you know."

"Hi, Joe," Kendall said, her heart sinking. All day she'd hoped to hear from Sheila, too afraid to make the call herself. If Joe was calling, it couldn't be good.

"I'm just wondering if you've heard from Sheila. She didn't come back to work this morning, and she's not answering her phone. She might have taken a few more days or been delayed, but I have to admit I'm worried."

Kendall felt as if someone had just tied a rock around her heart and dropped it.

She suddenly knew that no one would ever hear from Sheila again.

"Kendall?"

"I haven't heard from her, Joe, but I have the key to her house. I'll run out there and see if maybe she did get home and is just sleeping through the phone."

She hung up, set her sketchbook under the counter and brought out her handbag. "Vinnie, Mason, close up for me?"

"Where are you going?" Mason asked.

"Home to get my car, then out to Sheila's."

"I can run to Sheila's if you want," Mason offered.

"Just lock up for me."

It was close to six, Kendall realized, as she hurried out the door.

The minute it closed behind her, she felt...eyes on her.

She tried to tell herself that she was being silly, that no

ne was watching her. She tried even harder to convince
erself that Sheila wasn't dead.

But she was. Sheila was dead, just like Jenny Trent and,
f Aidan was right, at least nine others.

A fall evening, almost six, growing dark. There were
eople still on the streets, and plenty of businesses were still
pen or just closing up.

But among all those people, someone was watching her.
he knew it.

Kendall started to run. She made it to her house and down
he alley where she parked her car. She looked around as she
pened the door and slipped into the driver's seat. *No one.*
he slammed the door and locked it, looking around again.
here was still no one near her. She revved the engine and
ased out onto the street, convinced all the while that some-
ne was watching what she was doing.

Jeremy had come to stay out at the plantation, on call with
he workmen, that day, while Zach had stayed in the city to
ake advantage of the high-speed Internet connection while
e chased down more leads via his computer. Aidan had
sked him to look at everyone who had entered their sphere
f friends and acquaintances since they had returned, be-
ause he was beginning to think that the voodoo dolls had
ot been a prank, but a warning, though he had no guaran-
ee that whoever was sending the message was someone
hey knew personally.

He was certain the disappearances had something to do
vith Flynn Plantation. He just didn't know what. Someone
vanted to stop a large group of people from coming to the
ouse, and that someone also wanted them out. And the

only explanation was that there was something on Flynn lan●
the killer didn't want them to find.

Because someone was using the plantation—*his* planta●
tion—for murder.

Zach called Aidan late in the afternoon and read off a lis●
of all the police officers who had been with the force in on●
way or another for a decade.

That list included Hal Vincent.

Zach had confirmed that the medical examiner's offic●
had been contacted regarding each disappearance and give●
descriptions of the women, so their bodies could be identi●
fied if they were brought in. The office of coroner was a●
elected one, but most of the people who'd been workin●
there ten years ago were still there, including Jon Abel, wh●
had, interestingly, written a book on cases he'd solved usin●
forensic identification when there were only skeletal remain●
with which to work.

Vinnie and all the rest of the Stakes had grown up in Ne●
Orleans, as had Kendall.

Mason had been a frequent visitor from D.C., until he ha●
moved down permanently five years ago. "By the way, lik●
Kendall, he has a degree in psychology."

"But he wasn't here ten years ago."

"I didn't say that," Zach corrected. "I just said he didn'●
live here. I made a thorough check. And guess where Maso●
Adler was when our first girl disappeared?"

"Where?"

"Spring break, New Orleans. And I have another one fo●
you that you may not have known."

"Shoot."

"Your friend Jonas was assigned here then, too."

"That has to be wrong. I was with Jonas at Quantico ten years ago."

"That was actually his second time around for the FBI. He worked for the field office here in a civilian capacity. Then he decided to make a career of it, and that's when he wound up in Quantico with you."

If it hadn't been for that piece of information, he probably would have begged off when Matty called, crying, and asked him to meet her again, but knowing what he did, he decided that meeting her might turn up some valuable information.

He headed to the same café, checking the time as he entered. After five. He didn't have long. He didn't know why, but he didn't want Kendall leaving the shop and going home alone.

The minute he sat down across from Matty, she handed him a plastic bag.

"I found this in Jonas's car," she told him.

He took the bag and looked inside.

It was a woman's wallet.

According to the ID, it belonged to a woman—Sheila Anderson. A pretty blonde smiled up at him from her driver's license photo.

He stared at Matty.

"I found it under the passenger seat," she told him. "I think he must be having an affair with her."

He rose, suddenly anxious. "I'll look into this, Matty, I promise." He found himself hesitating. "Don't throw your marriage in the garbage just yet, okay?"

She tried to smile. "I won't. I just…help me, Aidan. Please."

* * *

Sheila lived in a more residential section, just inside the boundaries of Orleans Parish. She rented a big old Victorian that had been built in the late 1800s and was now on the historic register. It sat apart from its neighbors, with a good thirty yards on each side, and the rear of the property was filled with huge trees and overgrown brush, because Sheila didn't believe in gardening down nature.

Her car was in the driveway, but that was no surprise; Sheila would have taken a cab to the airport rather than pay to park there for an extended period.

"Sheila?"

Kendall banged on the door. Nothing. She tried to peek in the windows, but only a few lights had been left on and the curtains were down, so she couldn't see anything.

Kendall dug into the bottom of her bag for the ring of keys she didn't use on a daily basis, because her key to Sheila's house would be on it, along with one to Vinnie's, one to Mason's and extra set for the shop.

She slid the key into the lock and turned. The door opened to silence and gloom.

She stepped into the vestibule and set her purse down on the table. The house seemed very dark, so she closed and locked the door behind her, then fumbled around for lights. "Sheila?"

Kendall turned on every light as she went through the house, which was clean and neat, everything in its place, until at last, dreading what she might find, she walked up the stairs to the second floor.

There were three bedrooms. One was Sheila's home office and guest room, one was her storage room and one was where she slept.

Kendall noticed that in contrast to the neatness of the rest of the house, a casual cotton dress was lying on the bed, and a pair of shoes sat on the floor next to it.

As if they had been set out for her to change into quickly.

Kendall looked anxiously around the room. There was no luggage, which meant Sheila had probably left the house with it. But why had she left the outfit on the bed? Had she decided on different clothes at the last minute and not had time to put these away before her taxi arrived?

Leaving the lights on for reassurance, Kendall hurried back downstairs and into the kitchen, where Sheila tacked up notes on a bulletin board. There was a number for the hotel where she'd planned on staying in Caracas. Kendall reached for the phone and dialed it.

A man answered, speaking Spanish. Kendall fought for a few of the right words to be polite, then asked if anyone there spoke English. The man switched languages immediately. As they spoke, Kendall felt her heart sink. Sheila Anderson had been a no-show. She had never checked in. And the man was sorry to say that her credit card had been charged for the first night. They had a cancellation policy.

As she slowly set the phone back on the receiver, Kendall turned back to the board, where Sheila had tacked a message to herself: *Call Mason.*

There was nothing weird about that, she told herself. Sheila had had a bit of a crush on Mason for a long time, and she was pretty sure that Mason, for all his flirty ways, harbored a soft spot for Sheila, too.

But now Sheila was gone.

Sheila was dead. She knew it.

As she stared at the board, the house was suddenly pitched into darkness.

The door to the shop was locked. Aidan could see Vinnie sweeping up and Mason zeroing out the cash register.

He banged on the door.

Vinnie looked up, grinned and walked over to let him in.

"Hey, Aidan, guess what? Kendall called a friend at the paper. She's going to do a piece on the benefit. The band would be thrilled to come and pose—"

"Where's Kendall?" Aidan demanded.

"She left. Someone called her, and then she just told us to clean up, she was going over to Sheila's."

"Sheila's?"

"A friend of hers, hot little blonde," Mason told him.

"You let her go off alone?" Aidan asked angrily.

They looked at each other. "Um, yeah," Vinnie said. "She *is* an adult."

Aidan was being unreasonable, and he knew it. "Where does Sheila live?"

"I'll write it down for you," Vinnie offered, and hurried to get a pen.

Kendall let out a cry of alarm, then stood dead still and listened. Nothing.

She wished she had thought to bring a flashlight.

Too late.

Trying to retain a calm center, she made her way out of the kitchen, feeling her way along the hallway wall. Her heart was thundering. All she wanted was to get the hell out of the darkness of the house and into the nice reassuring darkness of the yard. She inched forward, bit by bit.

She thought she heard something from the back of the house and paused to listen. It was a creaking noise. *So what?* she asked herself.

Old houses creaked.

But there was a feeling in the air. She couldn't see anything, couldn't smell anything in the air, and yet…

She knew.

Someone was in the house with her.

She gave up all thought of keeping quiet and, guided by the glow of the streetlights coming in through the front windows, ran for the front door. She fumbled with the bolt, certain that any second someone would come flying down the hallway and slam into her, pinning her against the door.

She wrenched it open and went flying outside just as a car came jerking into the drive.

Aidan's car.

She raced toward the driver's side. He stepped out before she got there, and she threw herself into his arms.

"Sheila is dead," she told him. "I know it. And someone is in her house."

19

Aidan didn't want to leave Kendall alone, and he didn't want to take her inside with him, but speed was going to be of the essence. And even if he'd had time to call for backup, he didn't know who to trust anymore. The police? The FBI? There was nothing for it. She was going to have to come with him.

He ran for the house, telling Kendall to stick close behind him. The front door was gaping open. He pulled out his laser light with his left hand and his Colt with his right, then stepped inside, tense and wary.

He felt for the light switch and flipped it. Nothing.

He walked down the hallway, feeling her right behind him, doing exactly as she had been told. The laser illuminated the kitchen. Empty.

Dining room, empty.

He didn't need to go any farther. He could see the back door, open to the darkness of the night.

"Call the police," he told Kendall, handing her his cell. They would get whatever patrol car was in the area, but that would be fine.

He heard her punch in 911, then give the address, adding that they didn't need an ambulance.

He stepped out into the backyard and knew that unless he had an army with him, he wasn't going to find anyone, so he opted for standing on the back step, Kendall right behind him, and shining the light around, rather than going farther and risking trampling a clue.

He ran the light over the trees and bushes, but saw nothing. He aimed it upward toward the electric poles, tracking the beam along the line until he saw the wire leading to the house, which had been neatly severed.

"Someone was here, right?" she whispered.

"Yes, definitely."

They went back inside, and he started looking around the downstairs more carefully. He saw the note on the kitchen bulletin board and couldn't stop suspicion from niggling in his brain.

But Mason couldn't have cut the electric wire, because there was no way he could have gotten out here quickly enough, arriving ahead of Aidan himself.

A patrol car arrived a few minutes later, the officers polite and competent, accepting his ID and listening as Kendall explained that Sheila Anderson was her friend, that she hadn't returned to work that morning as scheduled, so Sheila's boss had called to ask her if she knew anything. She was calm when she explained that she had a key to the house, and that she had called the hotel where Sheila had planned to stay, and that she had never shown up.

Then Jeremy arrived, alerted by one of his friends on the force, and Aidan left Kendall with one officer as he and his brother went off with the other to survey the property. He had just noted a broken branch on an oak when Jeremy called out, "Footprint."

All three men hunkered down for a closer look. "Strange footprint," Aidan pointed out.

It was a blurred print in the shape of a human foot, but there was no heel mark and no tread pattern.

It could just have been the way the dirt had taken the print, Aidan thought, or the intruder might have wrapped plastic over his shoes to keep from picking up any trace evidence on them.

Aidan left the other two to check it out and headed back to the house, and then, when it was clear no one was there, out the front door. He was surprised—and suspicious—to see that Hal Vincent had shown up. Kendall was seated on the hood of one of the police cars, and Hal was speaking with her, gently, concerned.

"Hal," Aidan said, nodding in greeting. "I'm surprised to see you out at night for a simple break-in."

"I was just heading home when I heard the call on the radio," Hal explained. "And since I wasn't that far away..." He stared at Aidan—for once not as if he considered him nothing but a pain in the ass.

"There's a crime scene unit on the way," he said, glancing over at Kendall. "But there's no reason to panic yet. Maybe Sheila's plane was delayed."

"She never checked into her hotel," Kendall said flatly.

"Maybe she decided to switch to a different hotel," Hal said.

"Sheila is dead," Kendall said.

Hal looked at Aidan again. Aidan was certain that Hal agreed; he just didn't want to make Kendall feel any worse.

"Now don't you fret, we'll look into this." Hal looked meaningfully at Aidan again. "We'll really look into this."

"We've got a footprint out back," Aidan said. "I think

whoever was here had some kind of plastic covering on their feet. Like a doctor or a CSU technician might use. Or just a baggy or some plastic wrap. I'm willing to bet they were also smart enough not to leave any fingerprints. Your CSU guys aren't going to find anything."

Hal set a hand gently on Kendall's shoulder.

Aidan wanted to knock it away, surprising himself with the strength of his reaction.

"We'll start a trace on Sheila's credit cards right away," Hal promised. "Right now, let's get a look in her car."

One of the patrolmen went into his own vehicle for a window jimmy. In a minute, Sheila's car was open.

It was as clean as her house.

They popped the trunk. That was empty, too.

"CSU will look at the car, too," Hal promised her.

Finally Kendall was allowed to leave.

"Come on, let's get you out to the plantation," Aidan said.

"My car is here."

"I'll follow you."

"I have to go home and feed Jezebel," she said, her voice lifeless.

"Aidan, you take her. Zach can drive me out here tomorrow to pick up your car, Kendall," Jeremy offered.

Aidan nodded his thanks to his brother but said, "Jeremy, you take Kendall home, and stay with her until I get there."

Jeremy looked at him curiously but didn't ask any questions.

"Sure. Come on, Kendall. We'll take your car and leave mine, okay?"

Aidan watched them go. A minute later, as he got into his own car, he knew that Hal Vincent was studying him as he left.

* * *

Jezebel was all over Kendall the minute she stepped into her apartment. Jeremy entered quietly along with her and casually made an inspection of the place, checking the back doors.

"No one's been here," she told him. "But thank you."

He nodded, offering her a wry smile. "Habit, I guess. Way of life, maybe."

"What can I get you?"

"Don't worry about me."

"I'm having a large glass of wine," she told him.

"I'll have a beer."

She fed the cat, got the drinks, then sat with him in the family room, the drapes pulled over the French doors to close out the darkness. Once she had loved her courtyard. She wouldn't have thought a thing in the world of sitting out there at night. Now, the darkness seemed ominous and she had no desire to leave the safety of her four walls.

The phone rang, and she nearly jumped a mile. Jeremy answered it.

He spoke for a few minutes, then handed the receiver to her.

"It's Mason. He's at the Hideaway and Vinnie is playing, but he says they've left you a dozen messages, wanting to know if you're all right."

She handed the phone right back to him. She didn't want to talk to Mason or anyone else. "Explain what happened, will you, please?"

When Jeremy finally hung up and took a seat by her side again, he said, "He sounded pretty shaken up. He just kept repeating her name, like he couldn't believe it." He was silent for a moment, then said, "Kendall, she could be all right."

"She could be. But she isn't." She hesitated for a long time before speaking again. "I think I saw her being lured to her death," she said.

He stared at her, his eyes betraying nothing.

"Oh?"

"I think I saw it in a dream."

Matty opened the door before Aidan could knock on it.

"Aidan, hey." She sounded surprised. Maybe even disappointed.

"Hey, Matty."

"Did you…do you…?" She didn't seem to know what she wanted to ask.

"Is Jonas home?"

Just as he spoke, he heard the sound of a car in the drive. He turned around. Jonas parked and got out of his car. Aidan noted that his suit was crisp and perfectly clean, but he looked anxious.

"Matty, do you mind?" Aidan asked. "I need to speak with Jonas for a few minutes about a case."

"Of course." She looked at her husband suspiciously as he came up the walk, but she didn't protest as he kissed her cheek.

"Can I get you two anything? Iced tea, something stronger?" Matty asked.

"Nothing, thanks, Matty," Aidan said.

"We can talk in the den," Jonas said. He didn't seem surprised that Aidan was there.

Once the door was closed, Aidan didn't hesitate. He took the wallet out of his vest pocket and tossed it to Jonas.

Jonas caught it, looked at it and flushed. He sat behind the desk and sighed. "All right, what did Matty do, hire you?

My own friend. I should have gotten that thing right back to Sheila, but we'd just broken it off a couple of days before I found it in the car. I swear to you, Aidan, we had broken it off. It was just…stupid. On both our parts. I tried to give her the wallet back before she left. I drove out to her place to give it to her. Her car was there, but she didn't open the door, so I just figured she'd gone out with someone. I guess she got everything replaced before she left the country, because I never heard from her about it. Maybe she didn't even realize she'd left it in my car. But that was it, Aidan. Oh, I flirt in bars. Hell, everyone flirts in bars. But Sheila was the only one it went any further with, and we broke it off. You can ask *her.* She'll tell you that every word I've said is true."

"No one will be asking Sheila anything," Aidan said. "Sheila is dead."

He watched his friend's face. Jonas was capable of subterfuge on the job. But now his cheeks drained of color and his gasp sounded real. "What?"

"All right, I don't know for a fact that she's dead. But she's missing. She didn't check into her hotel, and she hasn't returned to work."

Jonas actually looked as if he were going to cry. He shook his head. "She…she extended her vacation. She chose another hotel."

"Sure. Those are possibilities. But I think she's dead, just like Jenny Trent, and I don't know how many others. At least nine." He leaned over the desk. "There's a serial killer on the loose, Jonas. An organized killer who plans his every move with exceptional care."

Jonas stared back at him. "We have no *bodies.*"

"We have bones—or had them, anyway. The bones I

found. Jonas, I'm going to let you explain it all to Matty. And tomorrow you're going to give that wallet to the police and explain everything to them."

Jonas still looked drained. "I'm going to lose my wife and maybe my job," he said.

"Jonas, you won't lose your job because of an affair, but if you withhold evidence, you might. And if you want to save your marriage, you'll do what's right."

They were in there, in the apartment. So very close, yet so very far away.

He'd almost made a mistake tonight, so he'd let it go, let *her* go.

He'd already made one foolish mistake with Sheila. Silly little Sheila, so full of herself and such a flirt—except with him. He'd had to really work at it to get her out there, though his ruse had worked in the end. Still, it had been wrong, not something a genius should have to do.

But so what? They would look for Sheila, but they wouldn't find her.

And even if they eventually did, what could they prove? Nothing.

He felt so restless, though, watching the house now, and he knew that he had to calm down, because anxiety led to mistakes.

Kendall would be a mistake; people would miss her.

But he had no choice, because she was already a mistake, one that had to be rectified. She heard things, knew things. She could read the future.

No, that was impossible. Even so, she was dangerous and he was going to have to take the risk and get rid of her.

She wasn't alone, though. Not tonight. He would have to be extremely smart to deal with her. Which should be easy, of course, since he was a genius. He had to bide his time, but not too much time. He kept hearing about her, about her abilities, and he couldn't give her a chance to use them.

There was nothing he could do tonight, though, and just standing there, even in the shadows, was dangerous. If he was seen, how would he explain himself?

They would never catch him here, though, and even if they did, he would come up with an answer. Tonight, though...

He wouldn't be able to touch her tonight.

Soon, he promised himself. Very soon.

She had to die.

Before she saw.

"I know you think I'm crazy," Kendall told Jeremy.

His eyes skidded away from hers, but he wasn't about to tell her that she was letting her imagination run away with her. Not after what she'd been through tonight.

"Kendall, I don't think that at all. I think you're bright and charming and extremely talented, and the best thing that's happened to my brother since...in years. But, let's face it, there are already a lot of odd things going on, and then tonight..."

"Jeremy, I think my mistake has been rationalizing everything." She hesitated. "I think we're not seeing the things we should be seeing, so the ghosts—or just our subconscious, speaking to us in our dreams, if you'd rather look at it that way—are trying to help. The thing is...who knows what a ghost really is? A memory? Energy? Energy doesn't die, the scientists say. Maybe ghosts come to us when we're sleeping, because in sleep we're more open, more receptive." She stopped short of telling him that her experiences with ghosts weren't limited to her dreams. She knew now that the ghost of Henry LeBlanc was haunting the property and the bar. He'd been a good man. He'd saved what was left of the family, and if he was here now, it wasn't to hurt anyone. It was to help.

Maybe when he came to the Hideaway he was trying to warn possible victims. Henry knew that a killer—an evil man just like Victor Grebbe—was at work, and he wanted to stop him.

There was a knock at the door. Jeremy rose quickly and she knew that he was armed, just as his brother was these days. She followed him down the hall, too nervous to stay by herself at the back of the house.

"Kendall? Jeremy?"

It was Aidan's voice.

Jeremy unlocked the door and let his brother in.

"Everything all right?" Aidan asked.

"Fine," Jeremy told him. "Now that you're here, I'm going to get going. I'll stay out at the plantation tonight, just to keep an eye on things."

"Thanks, Jeremy," Aidan said.

Kendall gave Jeremy a quick hug. "Yes, thanks. I'm sorry you got stuck babysitting me. I'm not usually such a weenie."

"Hey, strange times call for…careful action," Jeremy said a little lamely. "Talk to you tomorrow," he told his brother.

The minute Jeremy was gone, Kendall found herself shivering suddenly.

"What is it?" Aidan asked, locking the door.

"Paranoia setting in," she said. There had been someone

in Sheila's house. That was a fact, and she'd been right to be afraid. There was *not* someone in her courtyard, trying to spy on her through the drapes. Being afraid now was paranoia.

"Come here," he said gently, folding her into his arms.

"Is it wrong of me to be glad you carry a gun?" she told him.

"Of course not." He lifted her chin. "Are you all right?"

"She's dead, Aidan. I know it."

He didn't try to contradict her; he just held her.

She let herself cry for her friend. Other people might say she was being ridiculous, giving up hope so quickly. But she knew Sheila was dead, and now all she could do was make sure Sheila's killer was caught.

God help her, she wasn't going to be afraid to face the unknown. She was going to accept all the help she could get from the living or the dead to bring the killer to justice.

For Kendall, the next day seemed to last forever. Mason was as upset as she was. All morning, he kept suggesting that Sheila must have gotten tired of the academic life, that she had decided to go wild and crazy, and have fun. She had met some people and gone with them for a frolic in the islands.

"The police are investigating," she assured him.

Vinnie was depressed, too. "It's hard to think about having a party," he told her.

The one bright spot in the day was Jean's article on the plantation. Not only did she set the record straight about the cousins, she implied that the local historical society was likely to look into Victor Grebbe's life and he might at least be condemned by history, since it was far too late to see that he paid appropriately for his crimes during his lifetime. The article ended on a whimsical note, saying that the cousins' ghosts, now exonerated of any malicious intent, should be resting far more peacefully.

Ady came in just after lunch. Kendall was afraid to read for her, but she had promised herself that she was going to try to read every sign. But Miss Ady shook her head when Kendall led her into the back room and asked what kind of tea she wanted for her reading. "I'm just here to say thank-you. The doctor called me about the scan. He says they're going to give me a little shot of radiation, and some chemo. He says we caught the cancer before it could spread."

"I'm so thankful, Miss Ady," Kendall said, taking the older woman's hand.

"I heard about all the commotion last night," Miss Ady said. Her old eyes were kind and filled with empathy. "That pretty little friend of yours, that girl Sheila. They say she's missing now. And that someone might have been in that house when you were there. Oh, Kendall, I told you to be careful."

"Miss Ady, I was careful," she assured the older woman. "How did you know Sheila's missing? There wasn't anything in the paper."

Miss Ady sniffed. "Rebecca heard about it at work, and she told me. The cops asked them to be on the lookout for a Jane Doe that might be your friend."

Cold chills ran through Kendall's veins, but she already knew the truth. Whether they found her or not, Sheila was dead.

She knew because she had been walking in her friend's footsteps in a dream.

"Amelia came to me again, last night," Miss Ady said gravely.

"Oh?"

"She said she's very worried about you."

"Please, if you're ever able to answer her, tell her that I'm fine."

"Pull out a card," Miss Ady said, indicating the tarot deck on the table.

"What?" Kendall asked her.

"Shuffle your cards. Pull one out."

"Oh, Miss Ady, that's just silly."

"Please. Humor an old lady."

Kendall sighed. She didn't want to do it, but she didn't see any way out of it. She shuffled the cards, then shuffled them again. And then again. Finally she knew she couldn't procrastinate anymore and she pulled out a card.

Death. But at least it wasn't laughing. It was just there.

"It just means a new beginning, Miss Ady," she said, though she wasn't sure who she was really trying to reassure.

"And if we're believers in a higher spirit, isn't that what death is?" Ady asked her.

Kendall forced herself to smile. "Maybe it just means I've closed the door on being such a loner, and now I'm going to continue on a new path with Aidan Flynn. Maybe Amelia left me something far better than a plantation, maybe she knew somehow that Aidan and I would hit it off."

She had expected Miss Ady to smile, but the older woman didn't, only continued to study Kendall with grave eyes.

"Don't you go anywhere alone, you hear me? And don't you go off in the dark, neither. You make sure you stay around that Flynn boy of yours all the time, you understand?"

"Okay, Miss Ady, I will," Kendall promised her.

Aidan's first stop was the police department.

Hal was in and saw him right away.

"Did you ever get anything more on the break-in at the morgue?" Aidan asked.

"Yeah, we got a delivery man. He left a box of chemicals."

"That's it?"

"And we got a shadow. I can show it to you, if you like."

"There's a movie I'd love to see," Aidan told him.

Hal made a call, and they walked down to the computer lab, where the tech played the security tape, which he'd refined as much as was technically possible. Just as Hal had said, they saw a delivery man at the back. He rang the bell, and then, when no one answered, looked around, set down the box, hunched his shoulders and hurried back to his vehicle.

The tech fast-forwarded through what seemed like hours of nothing. Then, as Hal had said, they saw a shadow walking up to the back door. It was human, but there was no way to tell if it was a man or a woman. The face was completely obscured, and the person seemed to be wearing a hooded black cloak.

"As you can see, it looks as if the grim reaper paid a visit to the morgue," Hal said dryly.

Aidan thanked him for showing him the tape, then asked if there was anything new on Sheila Anderson.

"She never got on her plane," he told Aidan. "We're running a trace on her cards, but I'm not counting on anything to turn up. Meanwhile, we've got crews going over her car, her house, her yard. All we have so far is that the electric cable was cut by a sharp instrument. Oh, and Jonas was in here this morning. He delivered the girl's wallet. Told me they'd been having an affair, and that she'd left it in his car."

"And what's your gut feeling about that?"

"My feeling? Well, you're friends with the guy, so I'll be polite. I think he's a cocky SOB with a wife who's sweet as molasses, and he's been a real jackass, playing around on her. But do I think he's a murderer? That he did the girl in? No."

"Thanks," Aidan told him. "If I hear anything, I'll get with you. So you got nothing off the car?"

"Can't say nothing. She was driving on some rough terrain, not her usual ride into work and back. But I can't say exactly what it means. We've got gravel roads over half the state."

"Thanks," Aidan said again.

He knew one place where they had a gravel road. The driveway to his house.

After saying goodbye to Hal, Aidan planned to drive straight out to the plantation, but a call from Matty as he was walking out to his car detoured him.

He agreed to meet her at a café right across from the station, since they were both already in the area. When she saw him, she walked up to him and gave him a hug and a kiss on the cheek. There were tears in her eyes.

"Thank you, Aidan."

Oh, God, had she taken his time just to say thanks? Not that he didn't appreciate her feeling that she wanted to say something, but a few simple words on the phone would have done just as well. Still, what was she thanking him for? He'd proven that her husband was a cheat.

"Matty. You're welcome. But…"

She sat. "Oh, I know he's been a bastard. But, Aidan, last

night, he asked me for help. He *cried,* Aidan. I've never seen him do that. He said he was sorry he'd gotten messed up with that girl, and that he knows he acts like a fool sometimes. But he said he was scared. Like the years were passing. And he hasn't always gotten the promotions he wanted, and he just needed to know that someone else found him exciting. I guess that's why most guys cheat, huh? I told him I wished he had just squandered our savings on a Porsche. But he's scared now, really scared. He says that the girl he was seeing is missing, and that he had been out to her place. He swore to me that he'd never hurt anyone, and I believe him, Aidan. He may be in trouble, but he needs me now, and I'm going to stand by him."

"Good for you, Matty," Aidan said, then couldn't help himself and glanced at his watch.

"I know you're busy, Aidan, you don't have to stay. I just wanted to ask you a favor."

"What?"

"I need you to be his friend, too, Aidan. He thinks the world of you, always has, you know. He looks up to you. You—you just quit the Bureau. You walked away and made a success of your life. You never cared what anyone thought of you, just went out and did what you felt like doing."

"Matty, I lost my wife. I had to change my life."

She waved a manicured hand in the air. "I understand. Still, it would mean a lot if…"

"I'll be his friend, Matty," Aidan promised. *As long as he doesn't turn out to be a psychotic killer,* he added silently. After all, who made a better criminal than a cop, someone who knew how to avoid leaving evidence behind?

They said goodbye after that, and he drove out to the plantation. He could hear the workmen banging away, and he waved to the contractor when he saw the man standing on the porch, talking to a painter.

He didn't stop, though, but headed straight out to the graveyard.

He sat on the grave of Henry LeBlanc and studied the whole place. He could still see the mounds where he had recovered the old graves.

A cemetery. Where better to hide a body?

Would his brothers think he was crazy if he wanted to dig up the entire graveyard?

The cost might be astronomical. Could he even do it without a court order?

And what if he found nothing?

A weeping cherub nearby gave him no answer.

He stood and walked over to the family vault, pushed open the iron door and went in.

The cross on the small altar at the far end was catching the sun's falling rays and reflecting them into the vault like prisms of gentle pastel color. The place felt peaceful. He ran his hands over the two marble tombs in the center. They were completely sealed.

He checked the seals on the tombs that lined the walls.

Nothing appeared to be cracked or open in any way.

Once again feeling that he was missing something, he left the family mausoleum and headed back toward the house.

As he walked, he looked up, and there, on the balcony, was a woman. A woman in a white gown billowing in the breeze, the same breeze that played with her deep red hair. She was pointing, and she seemed to be weeping with infinite sadness, just like the marble cherub in the graveyard.

He turned in the direction she was pointing, back to the graveyard, yet nothing had changed.

He looked back toward the balcony, but the woman was gone.

"If a man is going to see ghosts," he said aloud, "then hell, they at least ought to stick around."

What the hell? He walked back to the cemetery and stopped at the tomb that bore the name Fiona MacFarlane.

He ran his hands over every possible crack in the tomb, but the only damage he could find had been done by time, not man.

Swearing again, he started back for the house. He pulled out his phone and was about to call Kendall when he heard footsteps coming up behind him and spun around.

Jimmy Wilson was walking toward him along the trail to the slave quarters. He saw Aidan and waved, a huge grin on his face.

"Mr. Flynn, thank you. The electricity works great. And those fellows, they fixed me up with running water, too. I swear, Mr. Flynn, I'll get you paid back."

"Don't you worry about it, Jimmy. Hey, aren't you supposed to be at work?"

Jimmy shook his head. "Night off," he said. "I thought I'd stack some of them lumber scraps them fellows left lying around. Thought that would be helpful."

"Thanks, Jimmy. Hey, listen for cars coming up the drive, will you?"

"Yes, sir, I sure will. And you need to think of more work for me to do, Mr. Flynn."

"I will, Jimmy."

"Your brother says I can help you fix her up for the party."

"Sounds like a plan," Aidan said, then waved and kept going toward the house. Just then his cell rang.

"Flynn," he responded automatically.

"You know, you really have to start saying *which* Flynn," Kendall teased.

"I'm on my way in to get you."

"It's all right. I packed up some things that will be great for the benefit and I'm bringing them out," she told him. "And I thought we'd cook there, if that's okay."

She sounded good, he thought. Strong.

"Can't wait," he said. "See you soon."

"You bet."

A little while later, Aidan was inventorying the refrigerator when his cell rang again.

"Flynn."

"Aidan?"

"Yes?"

"It's Robert. Robert Birch. At Quantico."

"Robert! Hey."

"So things are wild down there, huh?"

"I don't know about wild, but we do have a serial killer on our hands." He filled Robert in on some of what had happened.

"Odd, huh?" Robert said.

"What's that?"

"Two thighbones—two dead women—and they appear on the same day. Almost as if someone wanted you in on it, huh?"

"Don't put too much stock in that, since it looks like the bones are gone."

"That's odd, too, don't you think? Who breaks into a morgue?" Robert asked him.

"At least the police are finally paying attention," Aidan

told him. "So, did you get my package? I don't suppose you have anything for me?"

"I do."

"You're kidding. Hell, I thought I'd have to wait."

"I'm not kidding. You asked, I served. The boss still mourns the fact that you left the Bureau. He told me to give you priority."

"So what did you get?"

"I wasn't able to get anything viable from the dress, but I got DNA off the brush, and I was able to do something with your blood."

"And?"

"Not the same person. In fact, not a person at all."

"What is it, then?"

"Blood from a rodent. A rat, to be precise."

20

A rat? He had discovered rat blood?

"If you find me anything else, I'll be happy to get right on it," Robert offered.

"Thanks." Aidan couldn't help being disappointed, though he was glad that he'd held back the brush he had discovered in Jenny Trent's backpack until he was able to send it up to Quantico. At least it hadn't been at the morgue, waiting to be stolen.

He heard a car in the driveway—Kendall—and, the phone still held to his ear, walked out to the porch and waved to her. She gestured, and he saw that she had a number of large boxes in the car.

"Robert, thanks, and just so you know, you may be hearing from me, because I'm not turning over anything to the locals anymore."

"No?"

"Just to be on the safe side," Aidan said. "Thanks, I'll talk to you soon."

He hung up and headed out to the car.

"I packed up some of my favorite pieces," she said, after giving him a quick hug. "I want them here for the benefit."

"Great. Can't wait to see what you've brought."

As he stood there with her, Jimmy came around the side of the house. "Sorry," he said to Aidan. "You said to listen for cars. I was just doing that."

"Thanks, Jimmy."

"Evening, miss," he said to Kendall. He looked back at Aidan hesitantly. "Want some help with the boxes? I'm stronger than I look."

"Be my guest," Kendall said.

"Where do you want them?" Jimmy asked.

"Let's take them back to the kitchen," Kendall said, then glanced from Aidan to Jimmy. "We're going to cook some dinner. Would you like to join us?"

"Oh, I don't want to intrude, miss."

"You won't be intruding. I'm asking you."

Jimmy looked at Aidan for approval, and smiled broadly when Aidan nodded.

As they started carrying things—including several bags of groceries—into the house, Aidan thought that, even though Kendall was acting as if she were all right, he didn't think she was. They hadn't found the body, but she was sure one of her friends had been killed, and that wasn't the kind of thing you got over in a night.

As Jimmy and Aidan kept bringing in boxes, Kendall started dinner, something she called quickie jambalaya.

At one point Aidan paused by the stove, worried. "You left the shop and went to the grocery store alone? Was that wise?"

She shook her head. "Actually, there's a grocery store right down the street from the shop, and I didn't go alone. Mason and Vinnie were with me. I promise you, I'm not taking any chances."

Once the rest of the groceries were brought in, she started making a salad, and let Jimmy and Aidan open the boxes and check out the decorations.

The skinny ex-con was like a little kid. He pulled out the dancing skeletons, screeching black cats and singing skulls with great delight.

"Very interesting. Maybe we should just keep them up all year," Aidan said.

When dinner was ready, Kendall served it at the kitchen table. Afterwards, Jimmy insisted on helping her with the dishes, and then, just as firmly, told them that he was going back to his little outbuilding. "I want to get in before the ghosts come out," he said.

Aidan wondered how Kendall would react to that. She just smiled. "Jimmy, if we've got ghosts, they're good ghosts."

"If you say so, Miss Montgomery." He shook his head. "You two stay safe in here, too. Just keep everything closed up and pretend like there's nothing going on, and you'll be okay."

Aidan didn't argue with Jimmy; in fact, he locked the back door as soon as the other man had gone. When he got back to the kitchen, Kendall was wiping down the counter. He went over and swept her into his arms.

She looked up at him. "It's really nice, what you're doing for Jimmy."

He shrugged. "It's a big place, and he's not doing anyone any harm."

"Well, I still think it's really nice. Ready to head upstairs?"

He had thought that she was still fragile and was prepared to treat her that way. When they got into bed, she turned to him. He thought she wanted to be held, but she wanted more.

She was aggressive; she was passionate. He matched her urgency with his own, and wondered if they weren't both as fevered as they were because the act of intimacy between a man and a woman was such a strong assertion of life. They clung to each other, drowsed, made love again.

And slept at last.

Kendall was dreaming, and once again she knew it.

But this time she entered into the dream with determination. She intended to see this through.

At first all she saw was the mist. Then she heard shouting, and as the mist began to dissipate, she saw fields that were torn and trampled, and soldiers everywhere. Horses screamed as they died in the pursuit of war, just like their masters. One man kept reappearing, a rider who looked so much like Aidan and yet was clearly someone else, someone she had never met.

She saw the house.

Saw the woman.

And she saw the man who did not deserve to wear the uniform of any army. The man who used his uniform as a free pass to play out his fantasies of sickness and cruelty.

"If you touch me, they'll all know," the woman warned him. "Your friend…will see, and he'll tell."

The man laughed. "When I attack you, my friend will join in," he promised. His eyes narrowed. "When I kill you," he said softly, "he'll just walk away."

In her dream, Kendall felt Fiona's terrible fear for the baby, the son who was her life.

And then she ran, knowing he would follow.

The dream shifted, as if it were a movie, and Kendall saw Sloan Flynn.

She saw him riding toward the house, then walking through the mist to the front steps, where he stood, smiling, his arms open in welcome.

Then the woman was there, in a gorgeous white gown with tiny roses on it. She ran to him and was enveloped in his arms. A second man appeared, his uniform the deep blue of the Union army. Brendan Flynn. He walked over to the couple and was welcomed into the circle of their embrace.

She heard a baby crying, and the mist darkened and swirled, then lightened as the scene changed again to reveal Henry, holding the baby. He was looking at Kendall as if he knew that she could see him.

She called out softly to him, *Help me.*

Strangely, she could have sworn that she heard Amelia answer. *They're trying to, dear. Listen. You must listen.*

Then the fog darkened again, and this time she was running through it, no longer only Kendall but also Sheila, and she realized the ghosts were trying to show her what had happened to Sheila.

There were graves all around her. She tried to wend her way between them, one step ahead of the evil darkness coming up behind her. And then she left the graves behind and reached the water, but it was clogged with bones and limbs and skulls staring at her from their sightless, empty eye pits, and somehow she knew that one of them was the woman she had met in her shop. Jenny Trent.

Too much. It was too much.

Henry was ahead of her, telling her to keep running. He was reaching out for her. She touched his fingers...

And woke with a start.

Aidan was at her side, holding her hand.

"Another nightmare?" he asked, frowning. "I can't keep bringing you out here. It's making everything worse for you."

She stared back at him and shook her head, realizing suddenly that she was drenched with sweat. "I'm not leaving."

"I can throw you out, you know."

"But you won't. Because I'll just come back."

He pulled her close to him and kissed the top of her head. "We'll talk about it in the morning."

"Aidan," she said, "there's something in the cemetery. I...know it. The...the ghosts are telling me so."

She was certain he was going to mock her, but he didn't. Instead, he pulled her to him and said, "We'll figure it out, and we'll make it stop. I promise."

They fell asleep in each other's arms, and this time it was Aidan's turn to dream, but his was oddly comforting.

He'd seen the woman in the white gown again. It was as if he'd simply opened his eyes to find her there. She'd touched his cheek, and though she was beautiful and young, there had been nothing sexual in her touch, only tenderness. And then she'd whispered, *You have to help. It's happening again. He's like the one who came before.*

Who is he?

A killer. A man of pure evil. You have to stop him.

I'm trying. But how? And what does he have to do with the plantation?

History repeats itself. Amelia saw the lights.

Then he had roused, the dream still clear in his mind. It was just his subconscious trying to help him sort out what was bothering him, he told himself.

Amelia saw the lights.

Was his subconscious trying to tell him that Amelia's lights had been more than just Jimmy's flashlight?

He followed her into town. He even parked and walked her into the shop, then stayed to have coffee with Mason and Vinnie, who had opened for her.

"Anything on Sheila?" Mason asked him anxiously.

Aidan hesitated before answering. "Nothing. I'm sorry."

When Aidan left, he gave Kendall a kiss on the cheek and assured her that he would see her later. As he walked to his car, he was surprised to hear someone call his name.

It was Rebecca. She was wearing a scarf over her head, a trench coat and sunglasses, and she was carrying a large shopping bag.

"Rebecca, hello," he said, arching a brow. "Are you incognito?"

"I don't want anyone to see me giving you these. Just take the bag," she told him.

"What?"

"Take the bag."

"What is it?"

"Your bones," she told him.

Kendall skipped lunch and ran down to the florist's shop. She selected a number of arrangements and had the delivery boy take them to her car. On the street, she paused, feeling the air, looking around.

She didn't feel *it*. The sensation of being watched. Was she safe by day? she wondered.

She decided not to do any readings that afternoon. When she got back to the shop, she put her tarot deck in a desk drawer and closed it firmly.

Mason seemed to do too much thinking when he wasn't busy, so she did her best to keep him occupied. At one point, she asked him to go to her apartment and retrieve Jezebel, who was going to come and live in the shop for a while, because Kendall had decided that she wasn't leaving the Flynn plantation for home again until she had figured out what was going on. Despite her earlier good intentions, she was afraid to let the dream go any further, so maybe she had to start exploring while she was awake.

Later in the afternoon, when the store was quiet, she turned to Mason. "Can you watch the place alone for a while?"

"Alone? What am I?" Vinnie asked. "Chopped liver?"

"Actually, you're coming with me," she told him.

"Oh?"

"You're going to help me bring flowers out to the graveyard."

As they walked out to her car, she looked up at the sky, wondering what was going on with the weather. It was October, but the sky looked like winter. There were dark clouds forming overhead, and it seemed much too chilly for autumn in New Orleans. Something hinted at a thick gray fog, and dampness hung ripe and heavy in the air.

As they drove, Vinnie said, "I don't believe it. We've got a ground fog rising."

He was right, she realized. Mist hung low to the ground, swirling ominously.

A mist very like what she kept seeing in her dreams.

* * *

Aidan couldn't quite figure out how it had happened, but somehow Rebecca ended up in his car after she'd delivered the bones, so he took her with him to the FBI to send them off to Robert Birch, and then on to the historical society.

Sheila's boss was a decent guy. He told Aidan that the police had been in to look through Sheila's desk, and had taken her calendar and most of her files, but he was welcome to search for himself, in case he could come up with anything.

It was Rebecca who noticed the Post-it stuck in the closure of a drawer.

"'Before plane, meet Papa,'" Aidan read. "Papa. Her father?"

Rebecca shook her head. "Her mama and daddy were never married. I don't think she ever knew her father."

"Papa. Someone older, maybe?" Aidan mused. He rose swiftly. "Come on, let's go."

"Where are we going now?"

"Police station."

"Honey, you're on your own," Rebecca said, looking at her watch. "I got to pick my mama up from the doctor's now."

"I'll drop you at your car."

She studied him just before she got out of his car to get into hers. "You really do care for our girl, don't you? Mama approves of you, you know."

"I'm glad. Thank you, Rebecca."

Aidan headed to the police station. Hal was in his office, a stack of papers in front of him.

"Sit down, join me. I'm going through Sheila's files."

There was a box of disposable gloves on Hal's desk, the

kind cops had to wear when handling evidence, but they made Aidan remember that whoever had bought the voodoo dolls had been wearing black latex gloves.

He drew up a chair next to Hal's, they both put on gloves, and together they started going through Sheila's files in search of something—anything—that might give them a clue as to who had killed her. After a while, Hal excused himself to go get coffee.

He'd been gone a few minutes when Aidan got the creeping feeling at the back of his neck that he was being watched.

He looked up to see…

The woman in white.

Her face was tense with anxiety, and she was beckoning to him.

He stood up, not daring to blink, and started toward the door—and she faded into nothing just as Hal walked back into the office.

"What's the matter with you, Flynn? You look like you've seen a ghost."

"I have to go," Aidan said.

"What?"

"I've got to get out to the house."

Without another word, he hurried out to his car.

When Kendall and Vinnie arrived at the house, she thought it had never looked more beautiful than it did now, rising mysteriously from the mist. The last coat of paint was complete, and the columns were strong and white and tall.

"Isn't Aidan meeting us here?" Vinnie asked, sounding nervous.

"No."

"Maybe you should call him."

She hesitated. Aidan was going to be angry. She hadn't meant to come out here in the dark without him, but it had still been daylight when she had hatched her plan. Even now, it was only the fog that was making it so dark, wasn't it? Then she looked at the clock and realized it was after five. He would be getting to the store soon, and he wasn't going to be happy when he didn't find here there.

"You call him, Vinnie. Tell him to come straight out here when he's done with whatever he's doing. I'm sorry. I'm going to make you really late for work, but you can take my car."

"It's okay. The world won't end."

She got out of the car and took the first wreath, the one she had gotten for Henry.

"Give Aidan a call, then grab those flowers over there. They're for Amelia."

Kendall started walking toward the cemetery. She looked up and saw that the clouds were darkening and massing overhead. She almost turned back. But it wasn't the ghosts she was afraid of.

The cemetery had never appeared more ethereal. The fog curled around weeping cherubs and praying angels. It cast pale gray shadows upon ancient stone monuments, and snaked through the pathways between the sarcophagi. Now and then it seemed to be gently hiding a broken stone, as if shielding the dead from the intrusion of the living.

She quickened her pace, watching as the gray mist parted for her footsteps, and headed for Henry's grave, where she tenderly placed the flowers. "You were a good man, Henry. Thank you. If it weren't for you, I wouldn't have Aidan. And

I'm listening to you. I know you're watching for the killer, that you're trying to warn people at the bar."

She touched the stone, said a little prayer and looked up.

Henry was there.

He was tall, his features bearing the hallmark of both sorrow and strength. His eyes were dark and knowing, caring. Suddenly he started gesturing wildly.

She frowned. "They're flowers, Henry. A thank-you," she said.

He was trying to shout, but his voice was just a whisper that mixed with the gray swirl of the fog.

Get out. Hurry.

She turned around, the hair rising at her nape. Someone was there. It was Vinnie, she decided, Vinnie being a jerk. He was wearing his stage costume, the hood of his cape pulled up to hide his face, and he was carrying a plastic Halloween knife that must have fallen out of one of the boxes she'd brought out last night. He wasn't slashing it up and down, though, like a maddened movie monster. He was carrying it low and stalking her.

He moved slowly through the fog, as if this were a dream. He was being a showman, as always. But the dark and the mist were far too real, and she felt anger and fear mingling inside her.

"Vinnie, quit it!" she yelled, furious.

He was still coming for her, slowly, and she took a step backward and tripped over something, almost falling.

She looked down, trying to see what she had stumbled over, but the mist was heavy now, dark gray, making it hard to see. Whatever it was, it had been softer than a headstone or a tree root.

She peered through the mist, and there, beneath a weeping cherub and an angel with its face turned desperately up to the dark heavens, lay Vinnie, draped over a broken tombstone, like a piece of funerary statuary.

Like the weeping cherub.

And the praying angel.

Blood was trickling down his forehead.

She looked back at the figure coming for her, more quickly now. Weaving between the tombs. Past the statues of saints and angels and cherubs.

She started to run, but he was almost on her as she ran, blinded by the mist and the deepening darkness.

He reached for her, and she screamed, feeling the strands of hair ripping from her head as she somehow managed to escape. With no idea where to turn, she raced into the Flynn mausoleum and tried to slam and bolt the heavy iron door. It was almost closed, and she desperately threw her weight against it.

And then she realized she wasn't alone.

Henry was with her. Henry, futilely attempting to throw his ghostly weight into the fray. She drew strength from him, but a crack remained, and her pursuer shoved a hand through and sprayed something at her. She staggered back and fell, the world spinning, no matter how hard she fought against the sensation.

Without her weight to hold it shut, the door opened, and Kendall backed away in terror, stumbling toward the altar, because there was nowhere else to go. Henry was gesturing frantically for her to keep away from the altar, but she had no choice, so she kept backing away, fighting the darkness that threatened to overwhelm her, as the hooded figure with the knife loomed ever closer.

She circled the marble altar, fighting desperately to stay conscious, to stay on her feet.

Her pursuer reached her, and she knew she was about to be stabbed.

But she wasn't.

She was pushed.

And then she knew why Henry had tried to warn her away.

The floor behind her gave way with a loud scraping sound, and suddenly she was falling...

Falling, and landing hard in the sodden secret crypt that lay below the mausoleum. There was just enough light filtering down that she could make out the tombs, some single, some stacked, and some deep within the earth, just rotting coffins.

There was water on the floor, inches deep and seeming to flow around her.

Her eyes adjusted until she could see clearly, and a terrified scream escaped her lips as Sheila's rotting, bloated head bobbed by in front of her.

The killer jumped down beside her then, and the soft laughter she heard was all too real.

As was the figure so very close to her now, wielding its deadly knife.

Aidan tried Kendall's cell. No answer.

He tried the store, and Mason picked up. "Mason, it's Aidan. I have to talk to Kendall right away."

"She's not here—try her cell."

"I just did. She didn't answer."

"Try Vinnie. He's with her."

"With her where?"

"They were taking some stuff out to the plantation."

"Shit!"

Aidan didn't say goodbye. He sped past a Mazda on the highway as he dialed Vinnie's number. No answer.

He hesitated briefly, praying that his instincts were right, and called Hal. Hal couldn't be out at the plantation, because Aidan had just left him in his office.

It took him long seconds to be put through.

"Flynn, you're really starting to get on my nerves," Hal said.

"Hal, get some patrol cars out to my place now. *Please*."

"What the hell is going on?"

I don't know. But something is. A ghost just told me so.

"Just get them out there. There's an intruder on the grounds, and I can't find Kendall."

"All right, all right," Hal said, and hung up, but Aidan knew the man would do as he said.

He sped down the road to the house and jerked to a stop in the driveway, right behind Kendall's car. She wasn't in it, and neither was Vinnie.

He raced into the cemetery, pulling out his laser light. The fog was so thick that he couldn't even see the low-lying markers.

"Kendall!" he shouted her name, then paused to listen for a response. That was when he heard a groan and, with renewed hope, tracked his light around the cemetery.

A cherub seemed to stare back at him, mournful and weeping. A trick of the light.

An angel looked despairingly toward heaven as Aidan searched desperately through the dense fog. Suddenly he spotted a black mass lying on one of the graves. He squatted down and touched it, and it groaned again.

Vinnie.

"Vinnie, what's going on?" he demanded frantically. "Where's Kendall?"

But Vinnie's eyes didn't open. There was a huge gash on his head, trickling blood.

Aidan stood, pulling out his phone again. He dialed 911 and asked for an ambulance, trying to maintain enough calm to explain the situation while searching frantically for any sign of Kendall.

The cemetery was empty.

"Mr. Flynn?"

The tentative, terrified voice was real. He trained his light in the direction of the voice and saw Jimmy, shaking like a tree in winter, standing there.

"It's the ghosts, Mr. Flynn. It's the bad ghosts!"

"Where are they, Jimmy? Help me. Where are they?"

Jimmy pointed, but it was unnecessary.

Because *she* was back. The woman in white. And she was standing by the family mausoleum, beckoning to him. But she wasn't alone. Two men stood with her, one in a uniform of butternut and gray, one in deep blue, and all three of them were urging him to hurry.

He hurried.

Kendall staggered to her feet, facing the monster with the knife. She wasn't going to die without a fight, but how did you fight a huge knife?

"I have you at last."

The voice was familiar. Friendly.

"I've wanted you for so long."

"Great," she said, fighting the tremors in her voice. "Why didn't you tell me?"

"I've been trying to tell you for some time, but I kept my distance. I thought that you'd be the biggest mistake. You have such passion, but sometimes great passion must be denied. On the other hand, genius must be rewarded."

"You killed Sheila," she said.

"Obviously."

That voice... She knew it.

"You must understand. I'm considered a genius in my field...and my field has helped me so much. I know what they look for, when they find the dead. And I know that if they don't find the dead, they don't find what they should be looking for. And where better to keep the dead than where the dead should lie?"

"Jon Abel," she said flatly.

"Of course." He pulled off the hood. He looked just as he always did, and that was almost more frightening than anything else. He shook his head. "I guess I've gotten...hungrier lately. So many only come to me when they're broken, old, mutilated. There's something beautiful about death, you know. Especially death just as it happens. And the pressure of my job..."

"You've been killing for a long time," she told him.

He scowled at her. "I was not so hungry then, as I said. But...when I discovered that there was actually a crypt below the family vault, it was suddenly so easy. Meant to be, you might say. Of course, I didn't figure on the river and the water level—stupid, you say? Not really. In all this time, only two bones have ever washed out, and if it weren't for your lover, no one would ever have known. And you know, the women I've...shall I say *loved?* Have actually been better off. Their lives were small, unimportant. They're not the kind of women anyone would miss."

"Sheila is missed," she snapped.

"Well, yes, but Sheila...she was necessary. She was too interested in this place, in its history. I couldn't take the chance that she would find out about this little...retreat of mine. There was a casket of remains, a soldier from that unfortunate business between North and South. The body was quite rotted, of course, but he'd kept a diary, which was very nicely preserved in a piece of oilcloth. He was quite an interesting man. He and I had quite a lot in common. Not only that, in his journal he talked about the way he disposed of corpses out here. It made things so much easier for me. And so—"

"And so Amelia saw lights," she said.

He smiled. Just as Jon Abel always smiled. He still hadn't changed.

The only thing that had changed was that now she knew, knew exactly what kind of monster he was. Knew that he could kill and, if his victims ever *did* turn up, fill in false reports.

He could stage a break-in at the coroner's office.

"Okay, I'm sorry," she said softly, "this will probably sound like an in—a ridiculous question to you, but *why?*"

"Because of the *hunger,*" he said, as if she should understand perfectly. "And I'm a genius, but you already know that. Not every man can be allowed to indulge the hunger, of course, but as a genius, I deserve to have what I want. And because so much of what I see in my work is so ugly, that's why...lately...I've been hungrier. And that's why I need the pretty ones, alive and afraid.... I'm tender with them at first, of course," he said, walking toward her. But the knife was still down. He wasn't going to strike, not just yet.

If only she could find something to use as a weapon.

He paused in front of her. "You see?" he said softly, indicating the body parts floating around her. "Death can be so ugly. But not at first. It takes the terror in a woman's eyes and replaces it with peace, the peace that comes with death. And it's beautiful, so beautiful. Until the rot comes. And there is no one who can stop the rot."

From the corner of her eye, she saw an arm bone. Her heart quivered in her chest. It was still wearing the remnants of a black fleece sweatshirt.

He was close now, so close. He reached out, and she felt him touch her face. "You're such a pretty one."

Now or never.

She reached down for the bone and brought it up as hard as she could, striking him a tremendous blow across the face. He shouted hoarsely and recoiled, so she lifted her weapon to strike again. But he came back at her quickly, catching her arm with a surprising strength. He slammed her against the wall and held her there, but somehow she managed to retain her hold on her weapon.

"You don't understand!" he told her angrily.

"I do," she told him quickly. "You're the one who doesn't understand. The body rots, but the soul doesn't."

"What?" he demanded.

"I knew about you. The ghosts told me."

He hesitated, stunned by her words.

"That soldier, Victor Grebbe. He killed women here. The ghosts knew it, and they knew it was happening again. But they don't intend to let you get away with it. So if I were you,

I'd get out of here now. I'd run away. You can hide. You can disappear. You're a genius, remember? You deserve to live. But you need to get out—now—if you want to escape the ghosts."

"The ghosts?" he said coldly.

"They're here now," she told him.

"You're insane, do you know that?" His hand was twitching.

The hand with the knife.

She couldn't break his hold on her, but Henry... Henry was beside her, struggling to break that hold for her.

Jon Abel frowned, as if he sensed something touching him, and his grip eased, just the tiniest bit.

It was enough.

She struck him as hard as she could with the bone, this time aiming for his knife arm. She was rewarded by hearing the knife clatter against the stone wall of the crypt and then fall, with a splash, into the water rushing around her ankles.

It wasn't just that they were below sea level here, she realized. It was the river. It was close.

Somewhere here, there had to be a connection to the river.

She held on tight to her weapon, knowing he would come after her again as she forged through a sea of dismembered corpses, trying to find a way out. Henry was at her side, urging her on. Giving her strength.

But she didn't get far. She felt fingers twine into her hair, and she was jerked back. Struggling, they sank down to their knees together in the fetid water.

Somehow he'd found the knife.

And he brought it to her throat.

* * *

Aidan followed the ghost into the tomb, his light darting swiftly around. There was no one there. Except the woman in white, beckoning him on as she backed toward the altar.

And disappeared.

All of a sudden he *felt* his ancestors, Brendan and Sloan Flynn, at his side, urging him forward.

He raced around the altar and saw the false floor, the opening to whatever lay below.

Without hesitating, he jumped down into the darkness, his feet splashing hard, putrid water rising up to meet him. He staggered with the force of his landing, and fell, the Colt flying out of his hand.

"Aidan!" Kendall screamed.

"Stay back!" It was a man's voice, hoarse, almost inhuman. Jon Abel.

And he had a knife at Kendall's throat.

"Kill him, Aidan," Kendall said softly. "Or he'll kill us both."

He looked at her as reassuringly as he could, then turned his implacable gaze on her captor. "Abel, you haven't got a prayer of getting out of here alive, you know."

"Back off! I'll kill her right now," Abel said, his voice growing shrill.

"Don't be a fool, Abel. Even with a knife, you're no match for me. You—"

He broke off then. A thick mist was rising from the water. Rising, and taking shape.

The woman in white, Fiona, was to his left, Sloan standing to the other side of her. Brendan flanked him on the right.

But they weren't alone.

The mist was alive.

"They're here, Jon," Aidan said very softly. "All the women you've murdered. They're here now, with us. And they're going to kill you."

"You're crazy!"

"No, I'm not. Just look, and you'll see them."

At last, Abel looked.

Kendall felt his hold on her loosen. She met Aidan's eyes, and he nodded grimly. She kicked Abel as hard as she could, and it was enough to buy Aidan the split second he needed. As Abel screamed in pain, Aidan rushed him, pushing Kendall out of the way.

The two men plunged into the water together, struggling desperately for control of the knife.

Straining, Aidan gripped Abel's wrist, wrestling for the blade, and as he fought, the faces in the mist came closer. Ghostly hands reached out, and Abel began to scream and scream.

Aidan would never know the truth.

Had he meant to disarm the man, or kill him?

It didn't matter.

The knife was pulled from Abel's hold by ghostly hands and plunged into his heart.

Blood stained the water as the faces faded back into the silver fog.

"Please," Kendall whispered to Aidan as she threw her arms around him. "Please, we have to get out of here."

"God, yes!"

He turned, and for one moment they were still there, Fiona and the men who, one way or another, had died to protect her.

Then they were gone.

Aidan felt Kendall shivering, trembling, as he led her back toward the glow from above that showed where the drop into the crypt from the mausoleum lay. He pushed her up and through, then vaulted out behind her. Together, they staggered out of the mausoleum and then paused.

An array of people stood before them. Soldiers and businessmen, women in beautiful frocks. In the front of the group stood one man in blue and another in gray, and Henry was with them.

Fiona stepped forward, carrying a rose, which she set before them with a smile.

And then the entire crowd faded away.

The sound of sirens suddenly shattered the night. In moments there were police everywhere, followed shortly by Hal, and Jeremy and Zach. At some point Vinnie woke up, much to Kendall's relief.

The night was mass confusion, but one fact was clear.

The reign of terror had ended.

The bones and bodies would be retrieved, and the dead would be buried.

The ghosts could rest in peace at last.

Epilogue

Kendall was dressed in something black and gray and ragged. Her hair was streaming down her back, and, despite her makeup-induced ghostly pallor, she was stunning as she stepped on stage to duet with Vinnie. Together, they brought down the house on song after song.

The decorations were as macabre as the costumes, and the costumes were both varied and elaborate. Skeletons danced with Indian princesses, and there were at least three mummies, two wolfmen and a horde of Draculas. There were beautiful fairies, giant trees with gruesome faces and more.

The Haunted Holiday Happening was in full swing.

Admittedly, it was a full year later than planned, but no one was complaining.

It was also serving as an excellent way to introduce The Barn, as the new community theater was going to be known.

In the past, a killer had gotten away with murder here—until he had been killed himself during the commission of his last crime.

What psychosis had come upon Victor Grebbe, it was far too late to know, but contemporary doctors would have a field day studying the mind of Jon Abel, a brilliant man with a fine career who had been cursed with a criminal hunger.

The last number ended, and Kendall stepped off the stage with Vinnie, who was walking on air, now that Zach had offered to produce the Stakes's first CD.

"Hey, I'd like my wife back now," Aidan called to Vinnie.

"I'm returning her safe and sound."

Drawing Kendall to him for the slow dance that was just beginning, Aidan looked around the room. Jonas was there with Matty, and they were happy. She had been right; by forgiving her husband and standing by him, she had saved him.

Miss Ady, with a clean bill of health, was sitting on a bale of hay and tapping her toes. She smiled and accepted when Jimmy walked up and asked her to dance.

Both his brothers were deep in conversation with attractive women.

In short, everything was good.

And, most importantly, Kendall was in his arms.

"Can we slip out for a minute?" she asked him, her eyes dazzling.

"Out?"

"Please?"

He arched a brow but followed willingly as she led him into the cemetery.

"This is going to seem odd, I know," she told him.

"Oh?"

"I have something to tell you. And I thought… I thought they should know, too."

They.

He didn't ask her who she meant.

"We're having a little Flynn," she said in a rush, her eyes on his anxiously.

He picked her up and swung her around, then set her down carefully.

They were standing at Henry's grave, and now she placed a hand on it and said, "He saved the Flynn baby all those years ago, and he helped reveal the real story. And then, if he hadn't saved me, well, helped save me—"

They seldom spoke of that night. There was no need. They both knew what had happened, so what did it matter if the rest of the world knew, too?

"You were right to come out here," he said. "Henry *should* know. And Fiona and Sloan and Brendan, too." He smiled. "Nothing could make me happier," he told her, and pressed a tender kiss on her lips. "Except maybe ditching the last few minutes of the bash?"

"Hey, it's your brother's party, anyway," she said.

"We'll tell them tomorrow," he said.

He carried her past the barn full of revelers and up to the house, which was haunted by only the best kind of spirits.

And soon it would also be haunted by the sound of little feet.

Neither of them had all the answers, but they did have one another.

And that was more than enough.

* * * * *

*Turn the page for
an exciting excerpt from
Jeremy Flynn's story,
DEADLY HARVEST,
available in
November
from
MIRA Books*

Rowenna saw scarecrows.

They stood above the cornfields, propped on their wooden crosses, their faces blank and terrifying.

The cornstalks grew high, marching toward the horizon in their neat rows, seeming to stretch on forever.

And then, like sentinels, rising in a line and towering over the tall stalks that bent and waved in the cool breeze, there were the scarecrows.

The cornfields had always entranced her, along with the spectacular color palette of fall.

So it was only natural that when she dreamed, she dreamed of those fields, of running through them as the child she had once been. She ran and ran, and then she drew near the scarecrow.

Fingers of dread reached for her heart as she waited for it to see her, because she knew it would.

She didn't want to go closer.

But she had to.

The scarecrow raised its head, and a scream froze in her throat. The eye sockets were empty, the head a skull covered in rotting, blackened flesh, and somehow she knew it could see her, though nothing remained of what had once been its eyes.

What was left of the mouth was open, as if in a final scream. A ragged coat hung from the rotting body, the white gleam of bone showing through, dried blood staining fabric and bone alike. And as she stood there, her scream still trapped inside, the skull began to turn toward her, as if whatever evil consciousness still lived within it was drawn to her.

A crow landed on the gruesome figure's shoulder and plucked at the putrid flesh hanging from one cheek.

The skull began to laugh, as the wind rose and the sky was suddenly filled with the fluttering of brilliant fall leaves. And all the while, those eye sockets stared at her, and then red tears suddenly spilled from them, down the ravaged cheeks, as if the rotting corpse was locked in the field for all time, weeping blood.

Then the fingers of bone and rot began to twitch, reaching out for her, as a chant from her childhood echoed on the air.

Don't fear the Reaper,
Just the Harvest Man.
When he steals a soul
It's a keeper, so
Don't fear the Reaper
Fear the Harvest Man
For when he steals a woman's soul
She'll go to hell or deeper....

Rowenna Cavanaugh jerked up to a sitting position in bed, gasping, startled—and scared.

She took a deep breath and reached for calm. What a nightmare. She was surprisingly shaken by it, and she couldn't allow herself to be.

She had to wake up—had to get out of bed before she fell into another dream that was as bad or even worse.

She was living in the real world, the world of today. She had to pull herself together—and somehow manage another day with Mr. Jeremy Flynn.

MIRA®

The chilling
Flynn Brothers trilogy
from bestselling author

HEATHER GRAHAM

SAVE $1.⁰⁰

DEADLY NIGHT
DEADLY HARVEST
DEADLY GIFT

Coming October 2008.

SAVE $1.⁰⁰ on the purchase price of one
book in the Flynn Brothers trilogy
by Heather Graham.

Offer valid from September 30, 2008, to December 31, 2008.
Redeemable at participating retail outlets. Limit one coupon per purchase.
Valid in the U.S. and Canada only.

52608517

5 65373 00076 2   (8100) 0 11566

n o c t u r n e™

NEW YORK TIMES BESTSELLING AUTHOR

SHARON SALA

JANIS REAMES HUDSON
DEBRA COWAN

AFTERSHOCK

Three women are brought to the brink of death…
only to discover the aftershock of their trauma has
left them with unexpected and unwelcome gifts of
paranormal powers. Now each woman must learn to
accept her newfound abilities while fighting for life,
love and second chances….

Available October wherever books are sold.

REQUEST YOUR FREE BOOKS!

2 FREE NOVELS
FROM THE ROMANCE/SUSPENSE
COLLECTION PLUS 2 FREE GIFTS!

YES! Please send me 2 FREE novels from the Romance/Suspense Collection and my 2 FREE gifts (gifts are worth about $10). After receiving them, if I don't wish to receive any more books, I can return the shipping statement marked "cancel." If I don't cancel, I will receive 4 brand-new novels every month and be billed just $5.49 per book in the U.S. or $5.99 per book in Canada, plus 25¢ shipping and handling per book plus applicable taxes, if any*. That's a savings of at least 20% off the cover price! I understand that accepting the 2 free books and gifts places me under no obligation to buy anything. I can always return a shipment and cancel at any time. Even if I never buy another book from the Reader Service, the two free books and gifts are mine to keep forever.

185 MDN EF5Y 385 MDN EF6C

Name _____ (PLEASE PRINT) _____

Address _____ Apt. # _____

City _____ State/Prov. _____ Zip/Postal Code _____

Signature (if under 18, a parent or guardian must sign)

Mail to **The Reader Service:**
IN U.S.A.: P.O. Box 1867, Buffalo, NY 14240-1867
IN CANADA: P.O. Box 609, Fort Erie, Ontario L2A 5X3

Not valid to current subscribers to the Romance Collection,
the Suspense Collection or the Romance/Suspense Collection.

Want to try two free books from another line?
Call 1-800-873-8635 or visit www.morefreebooks.com.

* Terms and prices subject to change without notice. N.Y. residents add applicable sales tax. Canadian residents will be charged applicable provincial taxes and GST. Offer not valid in Quebec. This offer is limited to one order per household. All orders subject to approval. Credit or debit balances in a customer's account(s) may be offset by any other outstanding balance owed by or to the customer. Please allow 4 to 6 weeks for delivery. Offer available while quantities last.

Your Privacy: Harlequin is committed to protecting your privacy. Our Privacy Policy is available online at www.eHarlequin.com or upon request from the Reader Service. From time to time we make our lists of customers available to reputable third parties who may have a product or service of interest to you. If you would prefer we not share your name and address, please check here. ☐

BOB08R

HEATHER GRAHAM

32520	THE DEAD ROOM	___ $7.99 U.S.	___ $9.50 CAN.
32486	BLOOD RED	___ $7.99 U.S.	___ $9.50 CAN.
32465	THE SÉANCE	___ $7.99 U.S.	___ $9.50 CAN.
32424	THE ISLAND	___ $7.99 U.S.	___ $9.50 CAN.
32343	KISS OF DARKNESS	___ $7.99 U.S.	___ $9.50 CAN.
32277	KILLING KELLY	___ $7.99 U.S.	___ $9.50 CAN.
32218	GHOST WALK	___ $7.50 U.S.	___ $8.99 CAN.
32134	NIGHT OF THE BLACKBIRD	___ $6.50 U.S.	___ $7.99 CAN.
32133	NEVER SLEEP WITH STRANGERS	___ $6.50 U.S.	___ $7.99 CAN.
32132	IF LOOKS COULD KILL	___ $6.50 U.S.	___ $7.99 CAN.
32074	THE PRESENCE	___ $6.99 U.S.	___ $8.50 CAN.
32010	PICTURE ME DEAD	___ $6.99 U.S.	___ $8.50 CAN.
66665	HURRICANE BAY	___ $6.99 U.S.	___ $8.50 CAN.
32131	EYES OF FIRE	___ $6.50 U.S.	___ $7.99 CAN.
32321	THE VISION	___ $7.99 U.S.	___ $9.50 CAN.

(limited quantities available)

TOTAL AMOUNT	$ _____
POSTAGE & HANDLING	$ _____
($1.00 FOR 1 BOOK, 50¢ for each additional)	
APPLICABLE TAXES*	$ _____
TOTAL PAYABLE	$ _____

(check or money order—please do not send cash)

To order, complete this form and send it, along with a check or money order for the total above, payable to MIRA Books, to: **In the U.S.:** 3010 Walden Avenue, P.O. Box 9077, Buffalo, NY 14269-9077; **In Canada:** P.O. Box 636, Fort Erie, Ontario, L2A 5X3.

Name: _____

Address: _____ City: _____

State/Prov.: _____ Zip/Postal Code: _____

Account Number (if applicable): _____

075 CSAS

*New York residents remit applicable sales taxes.
*Canadian residents remit applicable GST and provincial taxes.

MIRA®

www.MIRABooks.com

MHG1008BL